WINGS OF FIRE

THE BRIGHTEST NIGHT

THE GRAPHIC NOVEL

For Wyatt — talented artist, expert
Minecrafter, and hilarious friend
—T.T.S.

For Tui, Barry, Rachel, and Maarta — I'm
incredibly honored to be a part of this team!
—M.H.

Story and text copyright © 2021 by Tui T. Sutherland
Adaptation by Barry Deutsch and Rachel Swirsky
Map and border design © 2012 by Mike Schley
Art by Mike Holmes © 2021 by Scholastic Inc.

Library of Congress Control Number Available

ISBN 978-1-338-73086-9 (hardcover)
ISBN 978-1-338-73085-2 (paperback)

10 9 8 7 6 5 4 3 2 1   21 22 23 24 25

Printed in China   62
First edition, December 2021
Edited by Amanda Maciel
Coloring by Maarta Laiho
Lettering by E.K. Weaver
Creative Director: Phil Falco
Publisher: David Saylor

WINGS OF FIRE

THE BRIGHTEST NIGHT
THE GRAPHIC NOVEL

BY TUI T. SUTHERLAND

ADAPTED BY BARRY DEUTSCH
AND RACHEL SWIRSKY

ART BY MIKE HOLMES
COLOR BY MAARTA LAIHO

graphix
AN IMPRINT OF
SCHOLASTIC

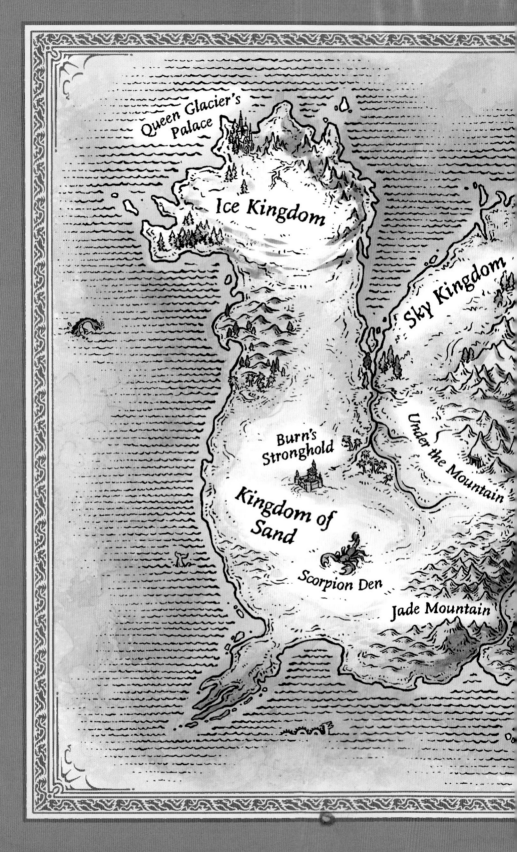

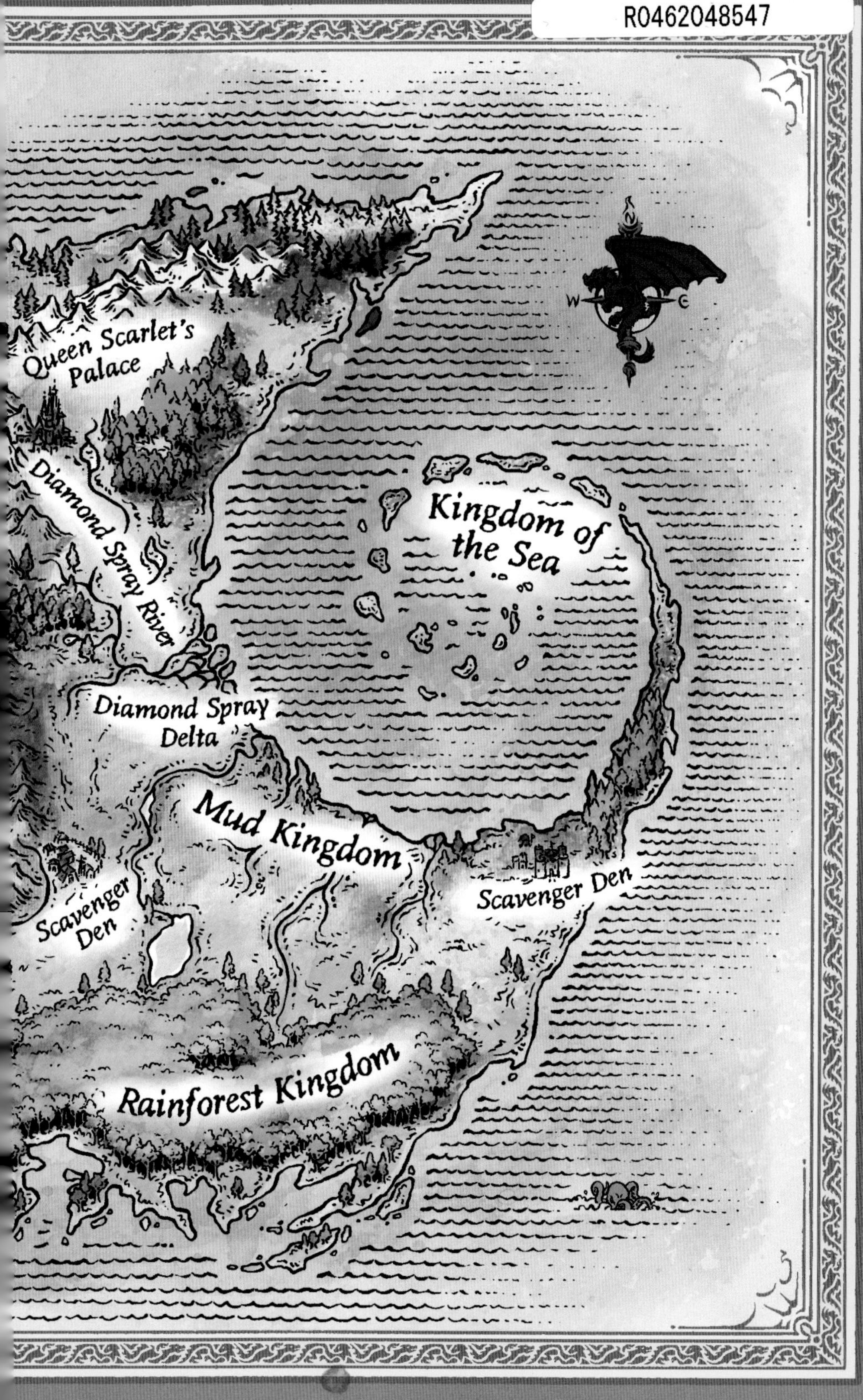
Queen Scarlet's Palace
Diamond Spray River
Kingdom of the Sea
Diamond Spray Delta
Mud Kingdom
Scavenger Den
Scavenger Den
Rainforest Kingdom

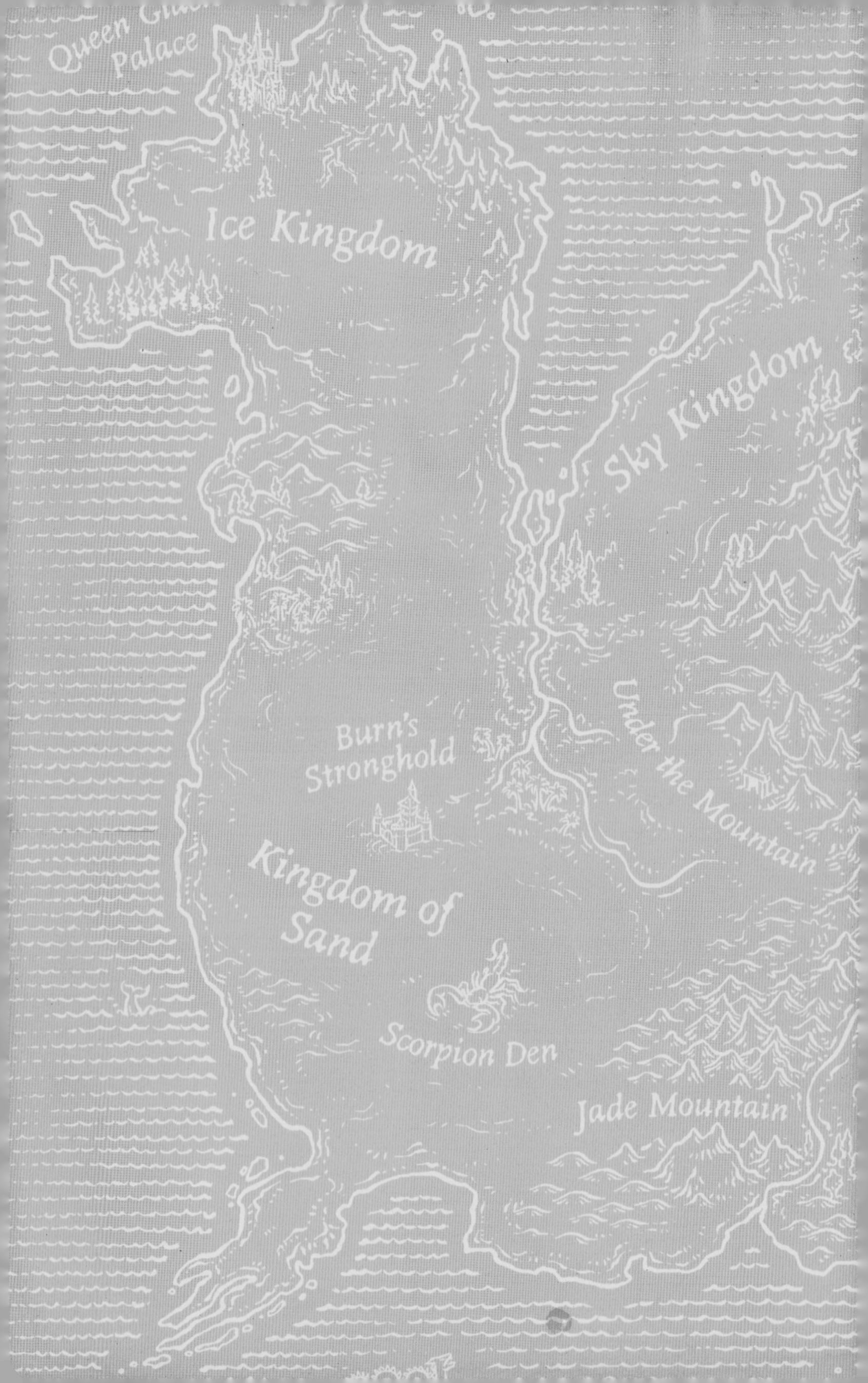

Queen Glacier's Palace

Ice Kingdom

Sky Kingdom

Burn's Stronghold

Under the Mountain

Kingdom of Sand

Scorpion Den

Jade Mountain

THE BRIGHTEST NIGHT

THE DRAGONET
PROPHECY

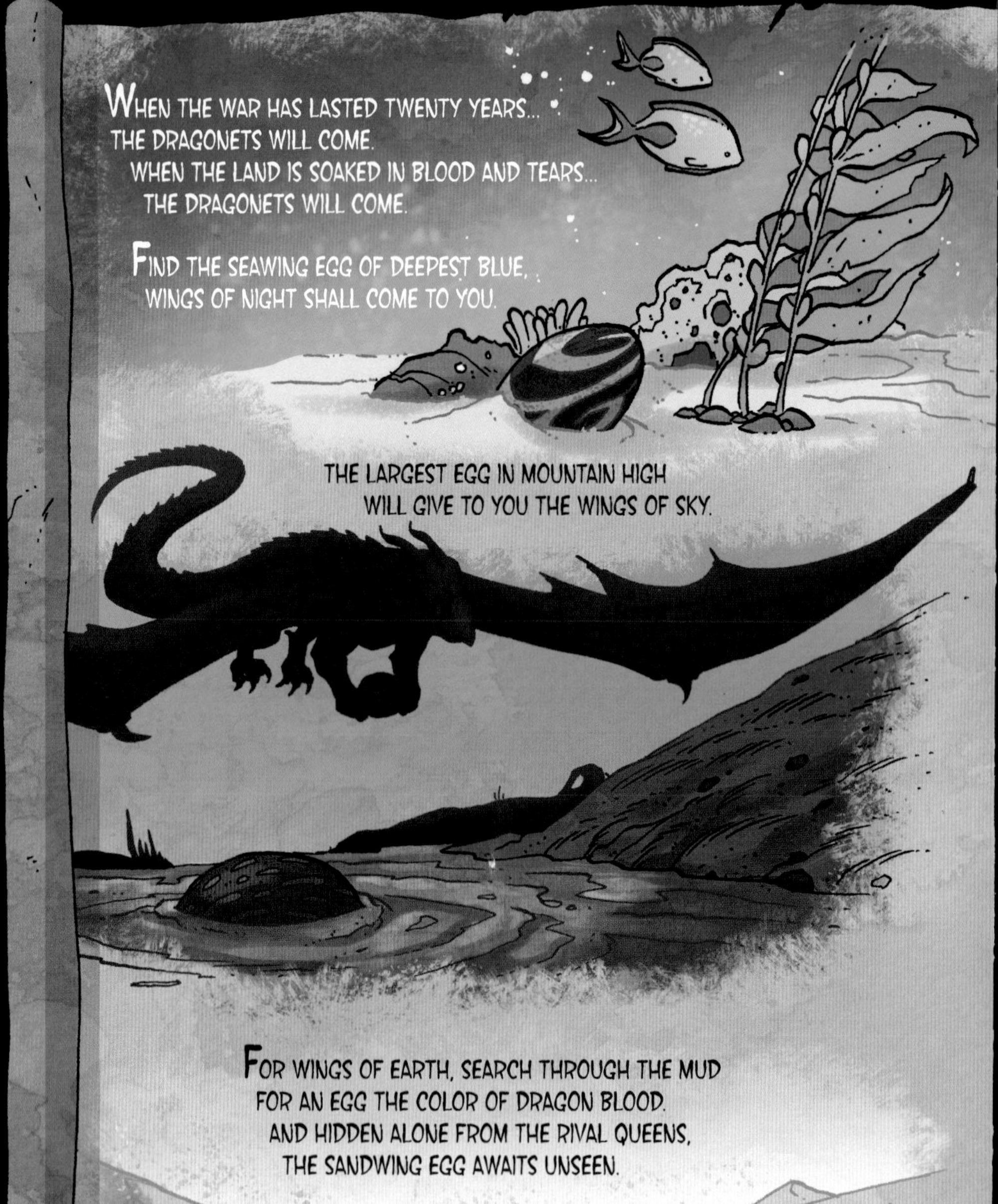
WHEN THE WAR HAS LASTED TWENTY YEARS...
THE DRAGONETS WILL COME.
WHEN THE LAND IS SOAKED IN BLOOD AND TEARS...
THE DRAGONETS WILL COME.
FIND THE SEAWING EGG OF DEEPEST BLUE,
WINGS OF NIGHT SHALL COME TO YOU.
THE LARGEST EGG IN MOUNTAIN HIGH
WILL GIVE TO YOU THE WINGS OF SKY.
FOR WINGS OF EARTH, SEARCH THROUGH THE MUD
FOR AN EGG THE COLOR OF DRAGON BLOOD.
AND HIDDEN ALONE FROM THE RIVAL QUEENS,
THE SANDWING EGG AWAITS UNSEEN.

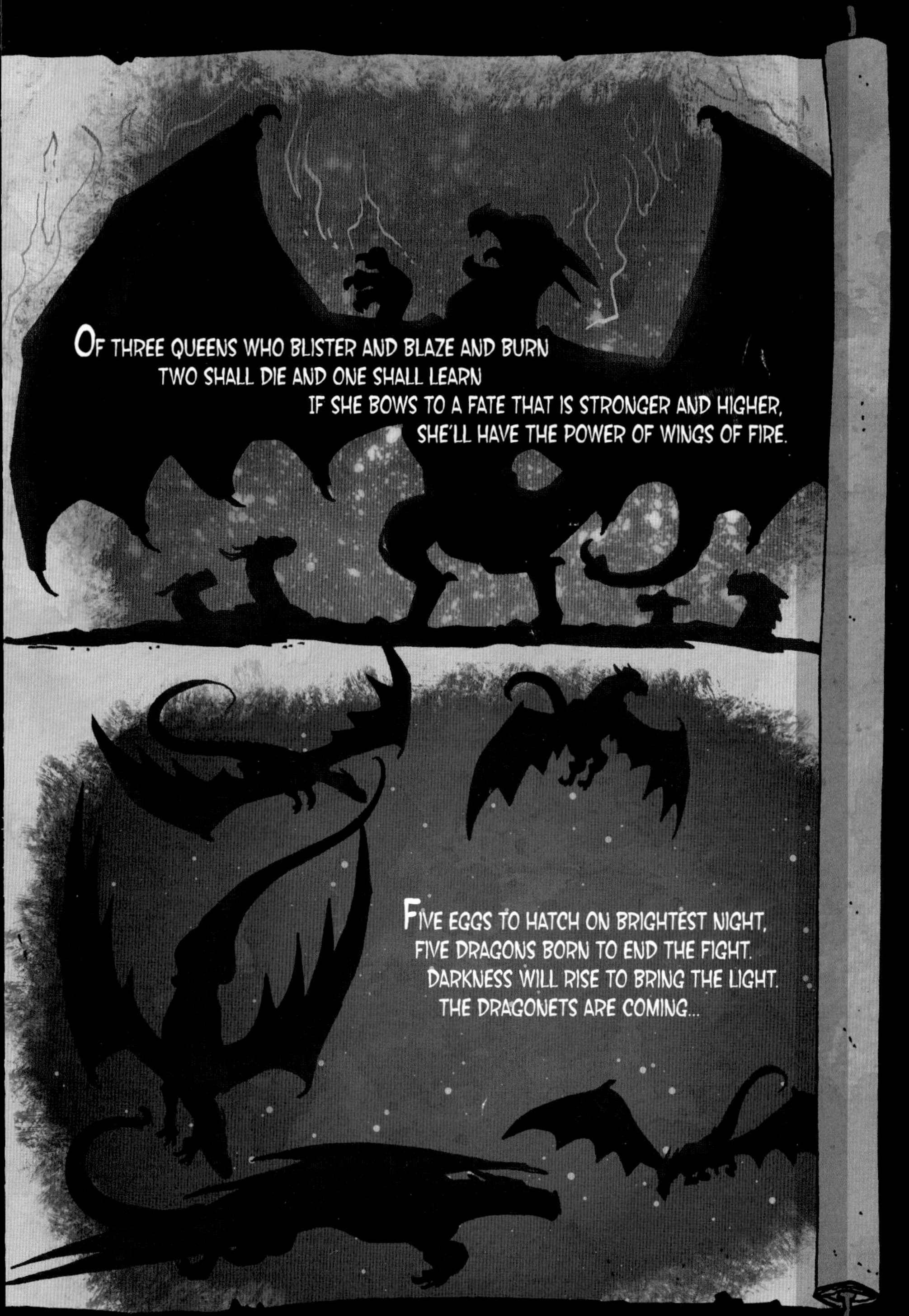
Of three queens who blister and blaze and burn
two shall die and one shall learn
if she bows to a fate that is stronger and higher,
she'll have the power of wings of fire.
Five eggs to hatch on brightest night,
five dragons born to end the fight.
Darkness will rise to bring the light.
The dragonets are coming...

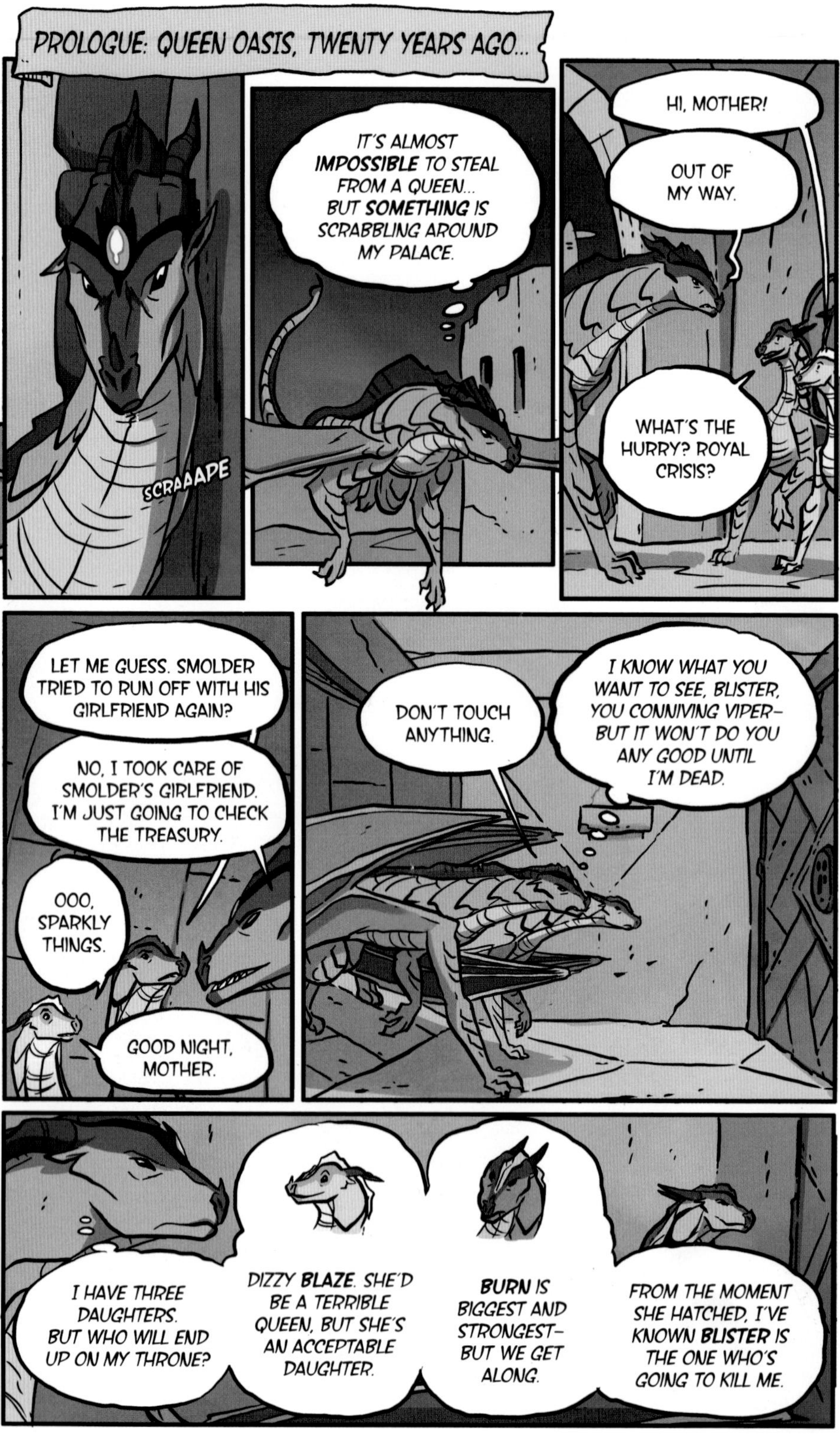
PROLOGUE: QUEEN OASIS, TWENTY YEARS AGO...
SCRAAAPE
IT'S ALMOST IMPOSSIBLE TO STEAL FROM A QUEEN... BUT SOMETHING IS SCRABBLING AROUND MY PALACE.
HI, MOTHER!
OUT OF MY WAY.
WHAT'S THE HURRY? ROYAL CRISIS?
LET ME GUESS. SMOLDER TRIED TO RUN OFF WITH HIS GIRLFRIEND AGAIN?
NO, I TOOK CARE OF SMOLDER'S GIRLFRIEND. I'M JUST GOING TO CHECK THE TREASURY.
OOO, SPARKLY THINGS.
GOOD NIGHT, MOTHER.
DON'T TOUCH ANYTHING.
I KNOW WHAT YOU WANT TO SEE, BLISTER, YOU CONNIVING VIPER– BUT IT WON'T DO YOU ANY GOOD UNTIL I'M DEAD.
I HAVE THREE DAUGHTERS. BUT WHO WILL END UP ON MY THRONE?
DIZZY BLAZE. SHE'D BE A TERRIBLE QUEEN, BUT SHE'S AN ACCEPTABLE DAUGHTER.
BURN IS BIGGEST AND STRONGEST– BUT WE GET ALONG.
FROM THE MOMENT SHE HATCHED, I'VE KNOWN BLISTER IS THE ONE WHO'S GOING TO KILL ME.

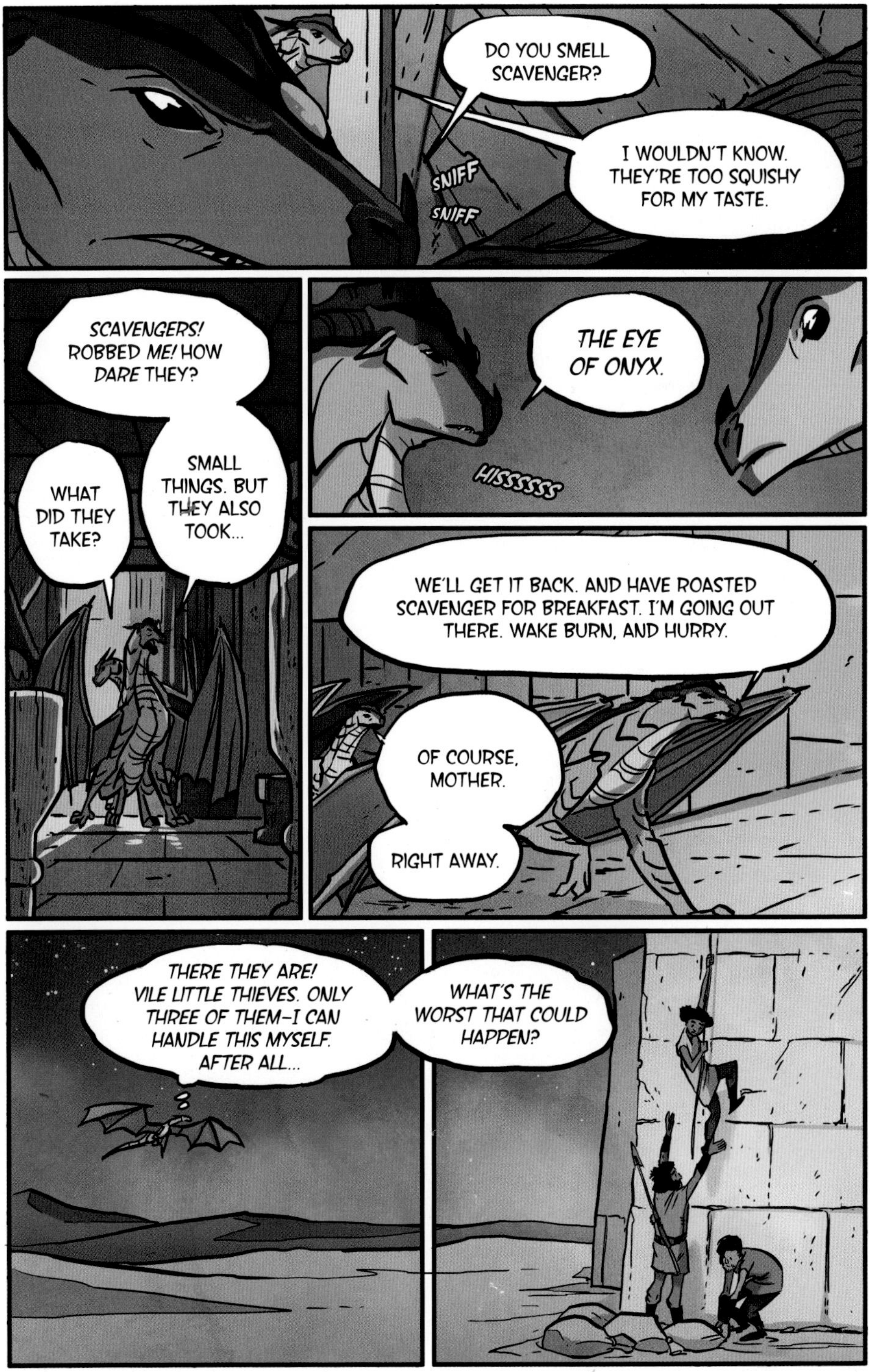
DO YOU SMELL SCAVENGER?
SNIFF
SNIFF
I WOULDN'T KNOW. THEY'RE TOO SQUISHY FOR MY TASTE.
SCAVENGERS! ROBBED ME! HOW DARE THEY?
WHAT DID THEY TAKE?
SMALL THINGS. BUT THEY ALSO TOOK...
THE EYE OF ONYX.
HISSSSSS
WE'LL GET IT BACK. AND HAVE ROASTED SCAVENGER FOR BREAKFAST. I'M GOING OUT THERE. WAKE BURN, AND HURRY.
OF COURSE, MOTHER.
RIGHT AWAY.
THERE THEY ARE! VILE LITTLE THIEVES. ONLY THREE OF THEM—I CAN HANDLE THIS MYSELF. AFTER ALL...
WHAT'S THE WORST THAT COULD HAPPEN?

PART ONE: THE SHIFTING SANDS

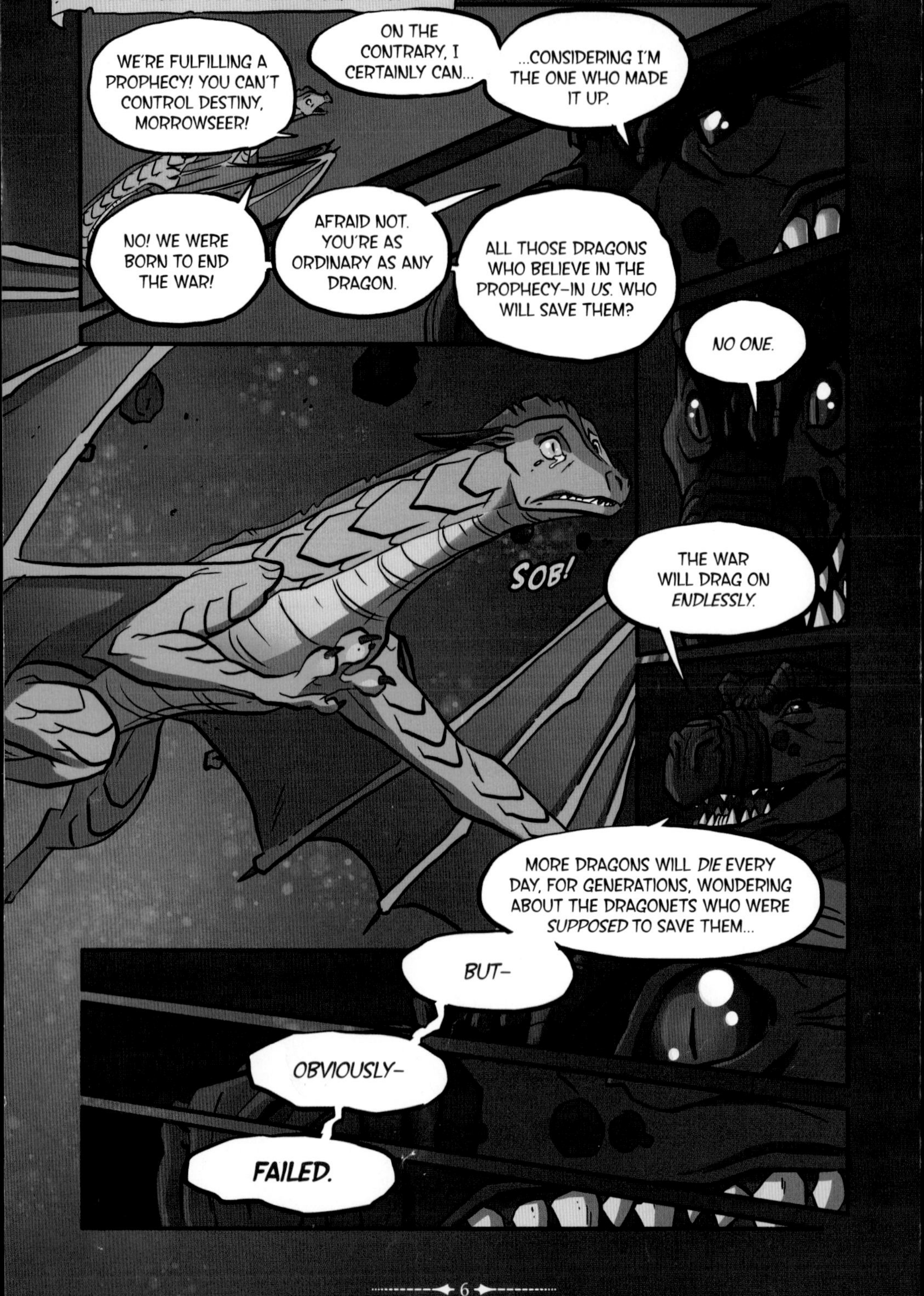
WE'RE FULFILLING A PROPHECY! YOU CAN'T CONTROL DESTINY, MORROWSEER!
ON THE CONTRARY, I CERTAINLY CAN...
...CONSIDERING I'M THE ONE WHO MADE IT UP.
NO! WE WERE BORN TO END THE WAR!
AFRAID NOT. YOU'RE AS ORDINARY AS ANY DRAGON.
ALL THOSE DRAGONS WHO BELIEVE IN THE PROPHECY—IN *US*. WHO WILL SAVE THEM?
NO ONE.
SOB!
THE WAR WILL DRAG ON *ENDLESSLY.*
MORE DRAGONS WILL *DIE* EVERY DAY, FOR GENERATIONS, WONDERING ABOUT THE DRAGONETS WHO WERE *SUPPOSED* TO SAVE THEM...
BUT—
OBVIOUSLY—
FAILED.

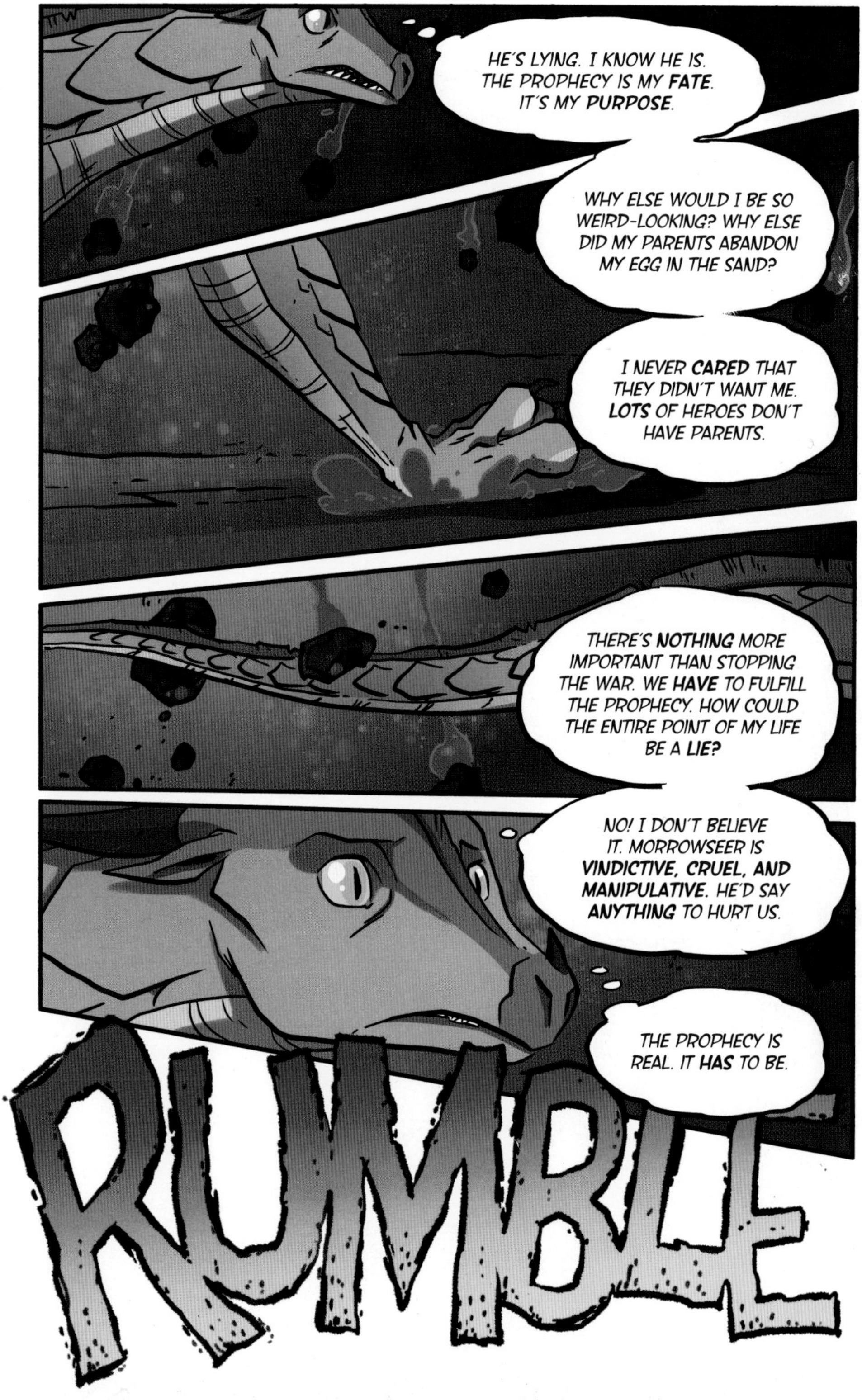
HE'S LYING. I KNOW HE IS. THE PROPHECY IS MY **FATE**. IT'S MY **PURPOSE**.
WHY ELSE WOULD I BE SO WEIRD-LOOKING? WHY ELSE DID MY PARENTS ABANDON MY EGG IN THE SAND?
I NEVER **CARED** THAT THEY DIDN'T WANT ME. **LOTS** OF HEROES DON'T HAVE PARENTS.
THERE'S **NOTHING** MORE IMPORTANT THAN STOPPING THE WAR. WE **HAVE** TO FULFILL THE PROPHECY. HOW COULD THE ENTIRE POINT OF MY LIFE BE A **LIE?**
NO! I DON'T BELIEVE IT. MORROWSEER IS **VINDICTIVE, CRUEL, AND MANIPULATIVE.** HE'D SAY **ANYTHING** TO HURT US.
THE PROPHECY IS REAL. IT **HAS** TO BE.
RUMBLE

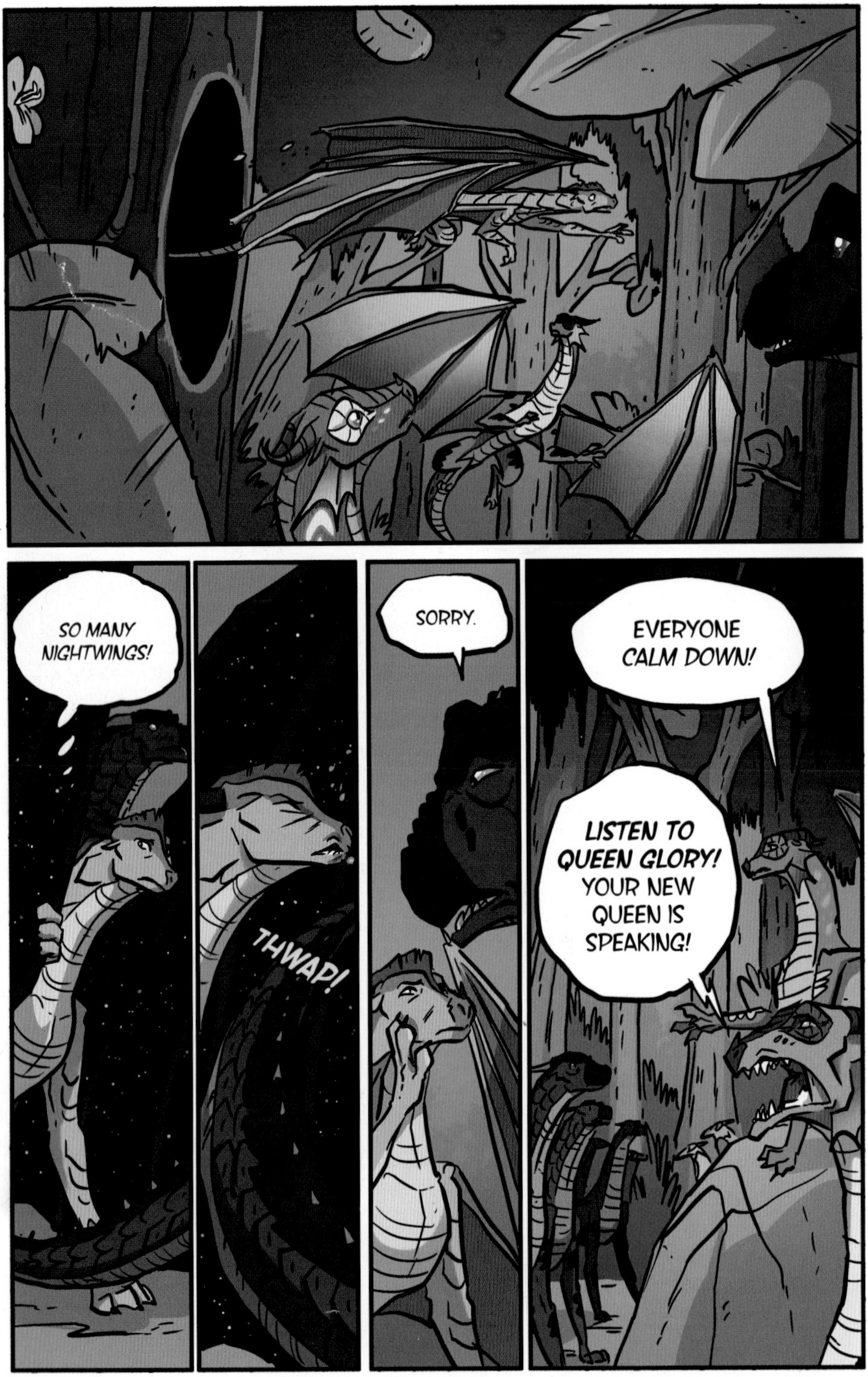
SO MANY NIGHTWINGS!
THWAP!
SORRY.
EVERYONE CALM DOWN!
LISTEN TO QUEEN GLORY! YOUR NEW QUEEN IS SPEAKING!

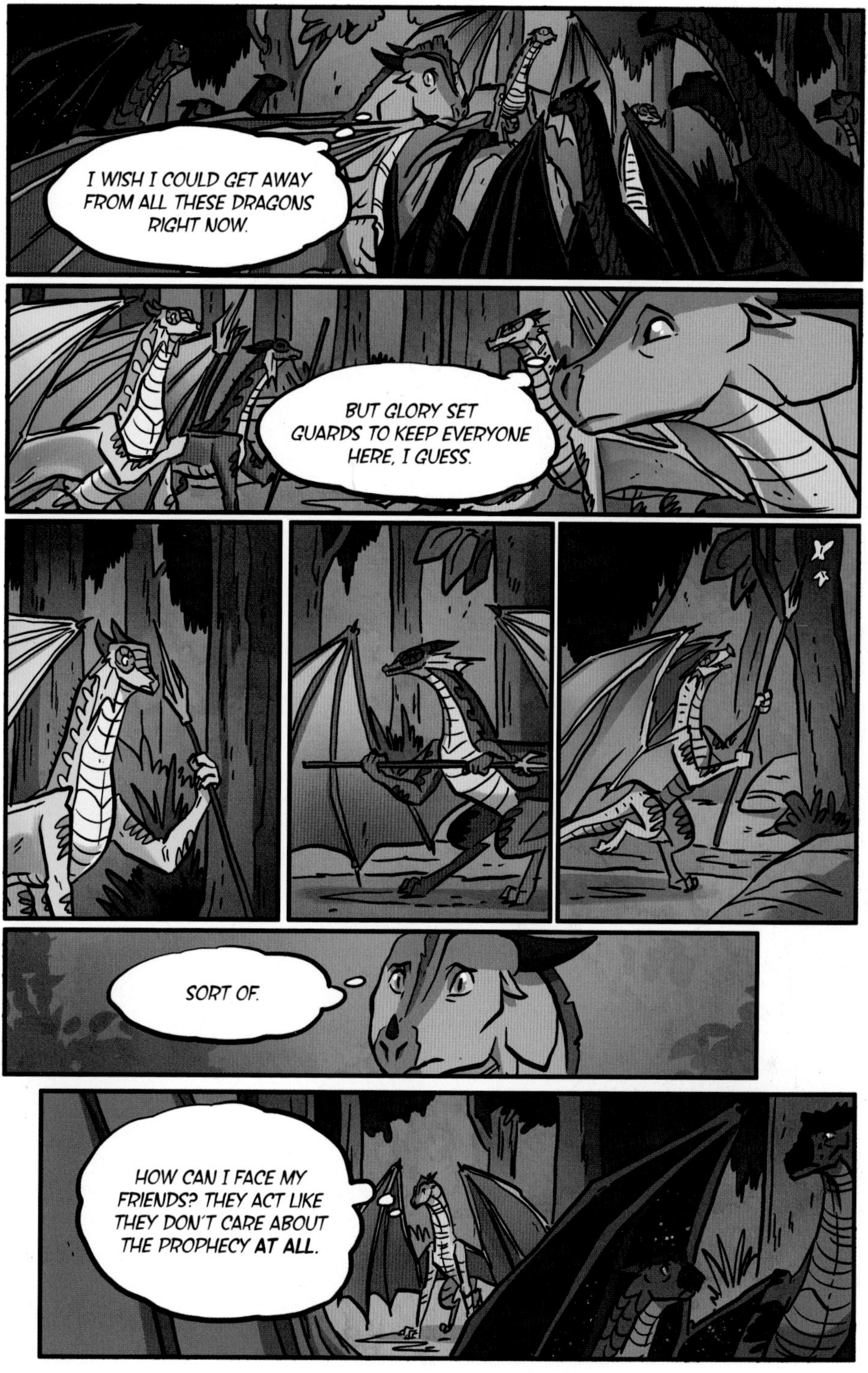
I WISH I COULD GET AWAY FROM ALL THESE DRAGONS RIGHT NOW.
BUT GLORY SET GUARDS TO KEEP EVERYONE HERE, I GUESS.
SORT OF.
HOW CAN I FACE MY FRIENDS? THEY ACT LIKE THEY DON'T CARE ABOUT THE PROPHECY **AT ALL.**

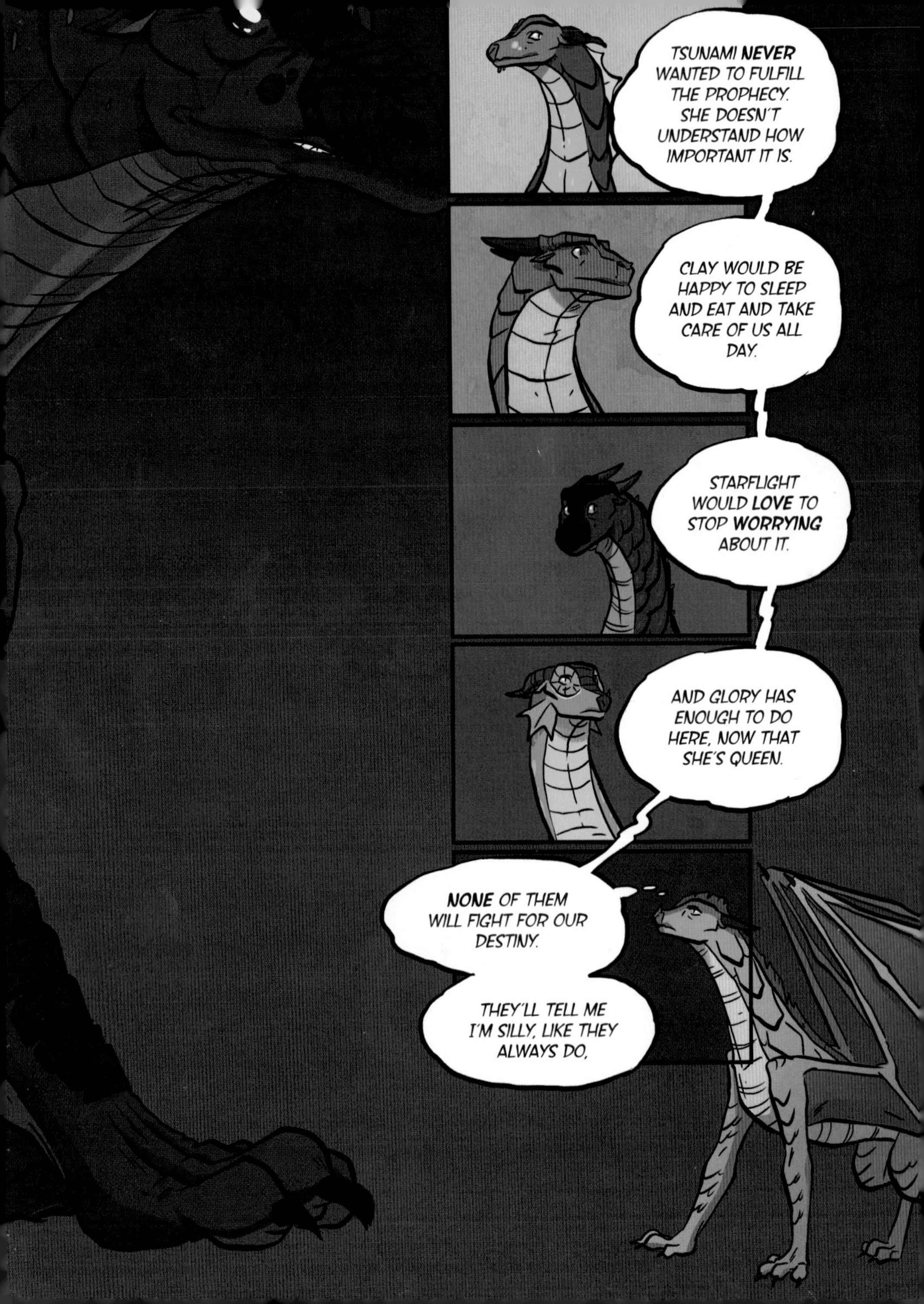
TSUNAMI **NEVER** WANTED TO FULFILL THE PROPHECY. SHE DOESN'T UNDERSTAND HOW IMPORTANT IT IS.
CLAY WOULD BE HAPPY TO SLEEP AND EAT AND TAKE CARE OF US ALL DAY.
STARFLIGHT WOULD **LOVE** TO STOP **WORRYING** ABOUT IT.
AND GLORY HAS ENOUGH TO DO HERE, NOW THAT SHE'S QUEEN.
NONE OF THEM WILL FIGHT FOR OUR DESTINY.
THEY'LL TELL ME I'M SILLY, LIKE THEY ALWAYS DO,

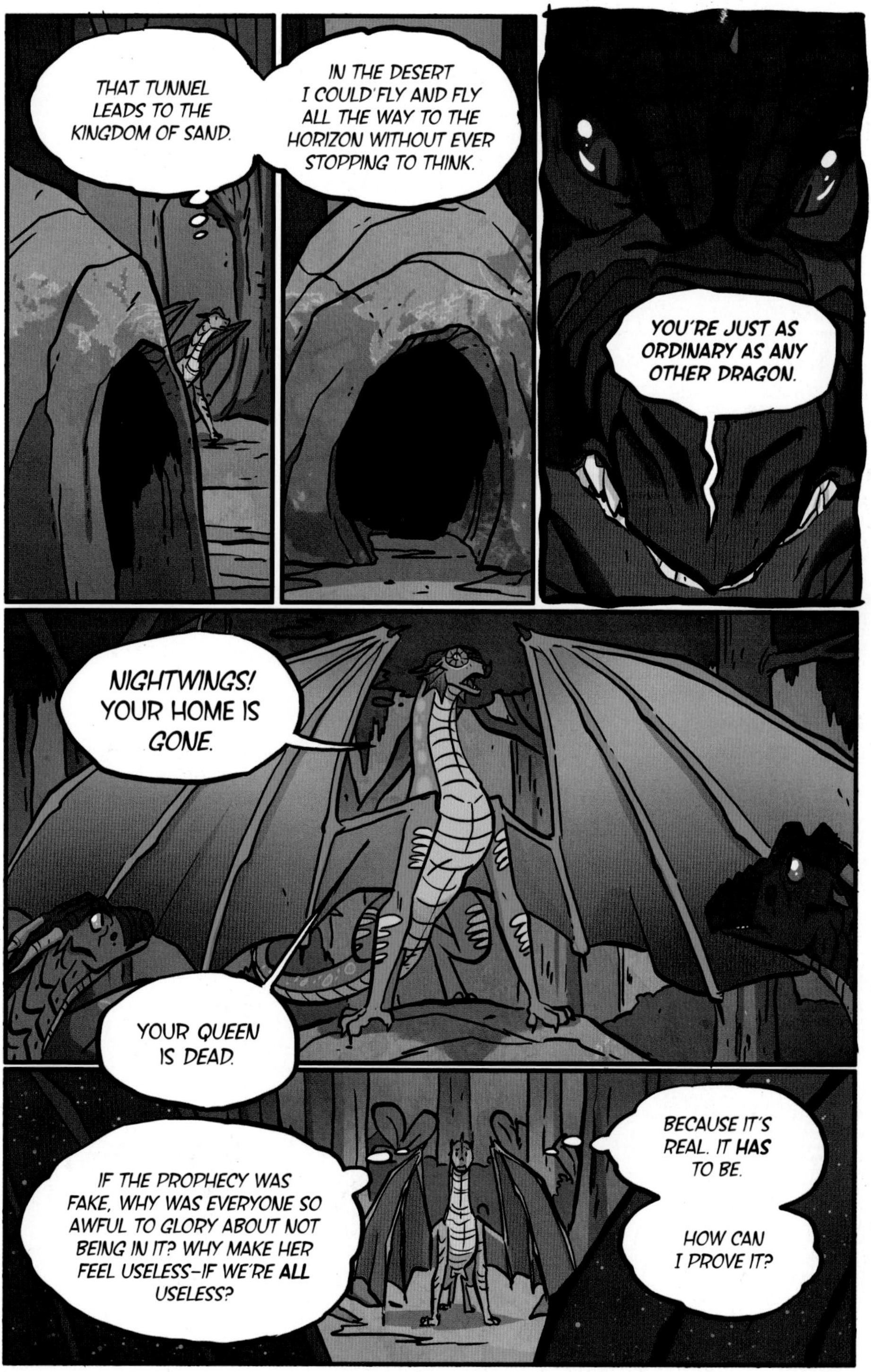

THAT TUNNEL LEADS TO THE KINGDOM OF SAND.
IN THE DESERT I COULD FLY AND FLY ALL THE WAY TO THE HORIZON WITHOUT EVER STOPPING TO THINK.
YOU'RE JUST AS ORDINARY AS ANY OTHER DRAGON.
NIGHTWINGS! YOUR HOME IS GONE.
YOUR QUEEN IS DEAD.
IF THE PROPHECY WAS FAKE, WHY WAS EVERYONE SO AWFUL TO GLORY ABOUT NOT BEING IN IT? WHY MAKE HER FEEL USELESS—IF WE'RE ALL USELESS?
BECAUSE IT'S REAL. IT HAS TO BE.
HOW CAN I PROVE IT?

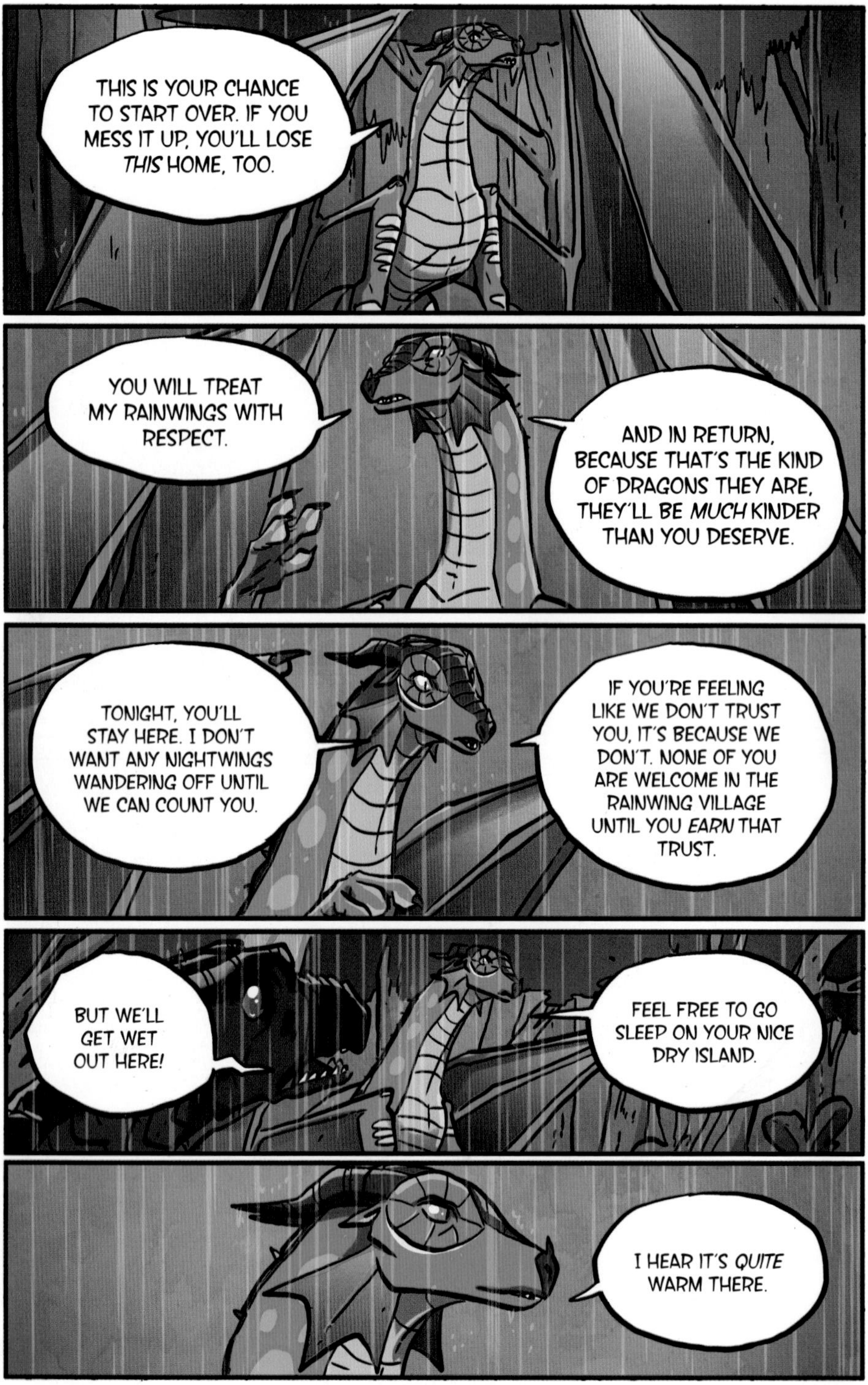
THIS IS YOUR CHANCE TO START OVER. IF YOU MESS IT UP, YOU'LL LOSE *THIS* HOME, TOO.
YOU WILL TREAT MY RAINWINGS WITH RESPECT.
AND IN RETURN, BECAUSE THAT'S THE KIND OF DRAGONS THEY ARE, THEY'LL BE *MUCH* KINDER THAN YOU DESERVE.
TONIGHT, YOU'LL STAY HERE. I DON'T WANT ANY NIGHTWINGS WANDERING OFF UNTIL WE CAN COUNT YOU.
IF YOU'RE FEELING LIKE WE DON'T TRUST YOU, IT'S BECAUSE WE DON'T. NONE OF YOU ARE WELCOME IN THE RAINWING VILLAGE UNTIL YOU *EARN* THAT TRUST.
BUT WE'LL GET WET OUT HERE!
FEEL FREE TO GO SLEEP ON YOUR NICE DRY ISLAND.
I HEAR IT'S *QUITE* WARM THERE.

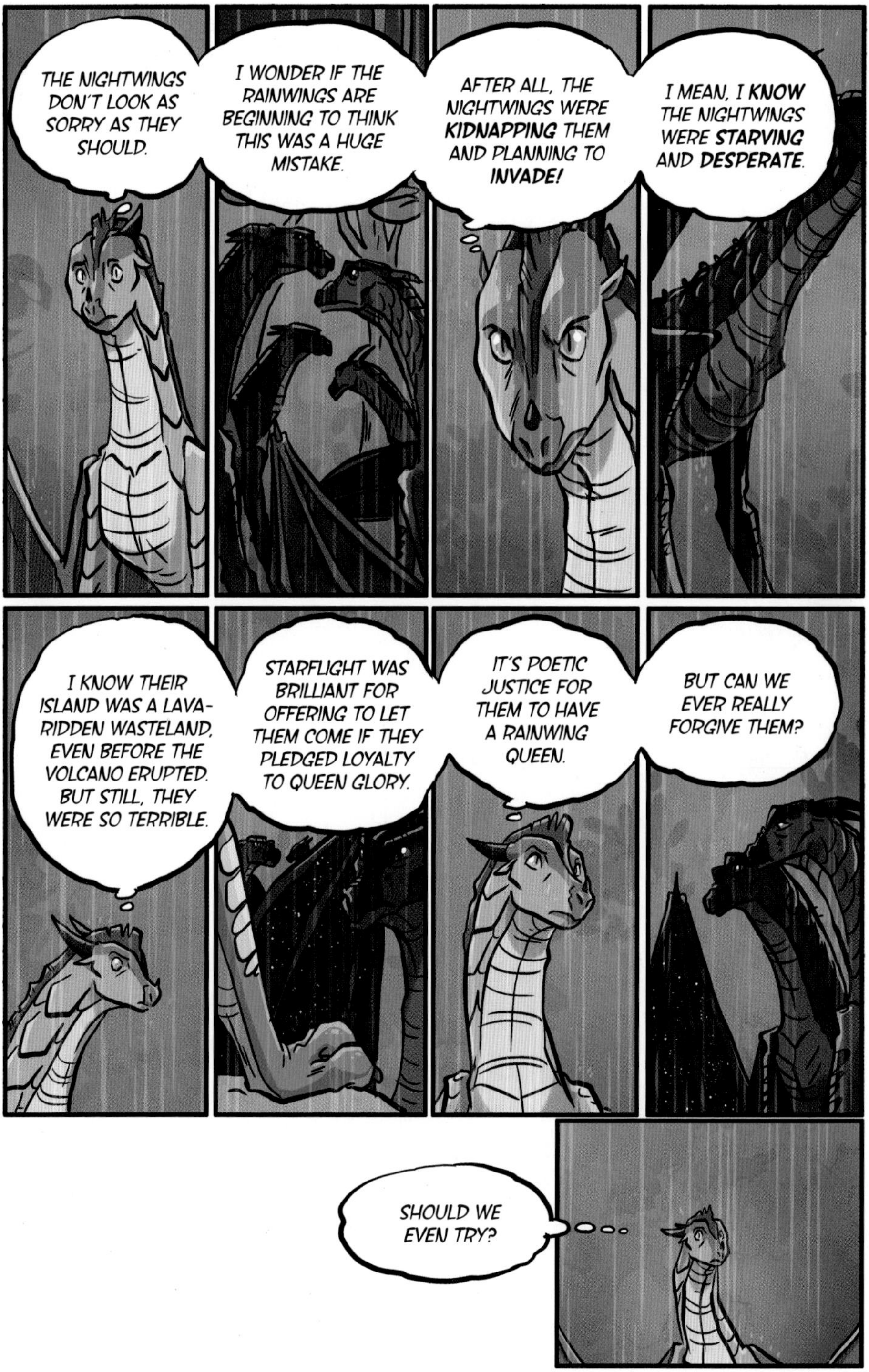
THE NIGHTWINGS DON'T LOOK AS SORRY AS THEY SHOULD.
I WONDER IF THE RAINWINGS ARE BEGINNING TO THINK THIS WAS A HUGE MISTAKE.
AFTER ALL, THE NIGHTWINGS WERE KIDNAPPING THEM AND PLANNING TO INVADE!
I MEAN, I KNOW THE NIGHTWINGS WERE STARVING AND DESPERATE.
I KNOW THEIR ISLAND WAS A LAVA-RIDDEN WASTELAND, EVEN BEFORE THE VOLCANO ERUPTED. BUT STILL, THEY WERE SO TERRIBLE.
STARFLIGHT WAS BRILLIANT FOR OFFERING TO LET THEM COME IF THEY PLEDGED LOYALTY TO QUEEN GLORY.
IT'S POETIC JUSTICE FOR THEM TO HAVE A RAINWING QUEEN.
BUT CAN WE EVER REALLY FORGIVE THEM?
SHOULD WE EVEN TRY?

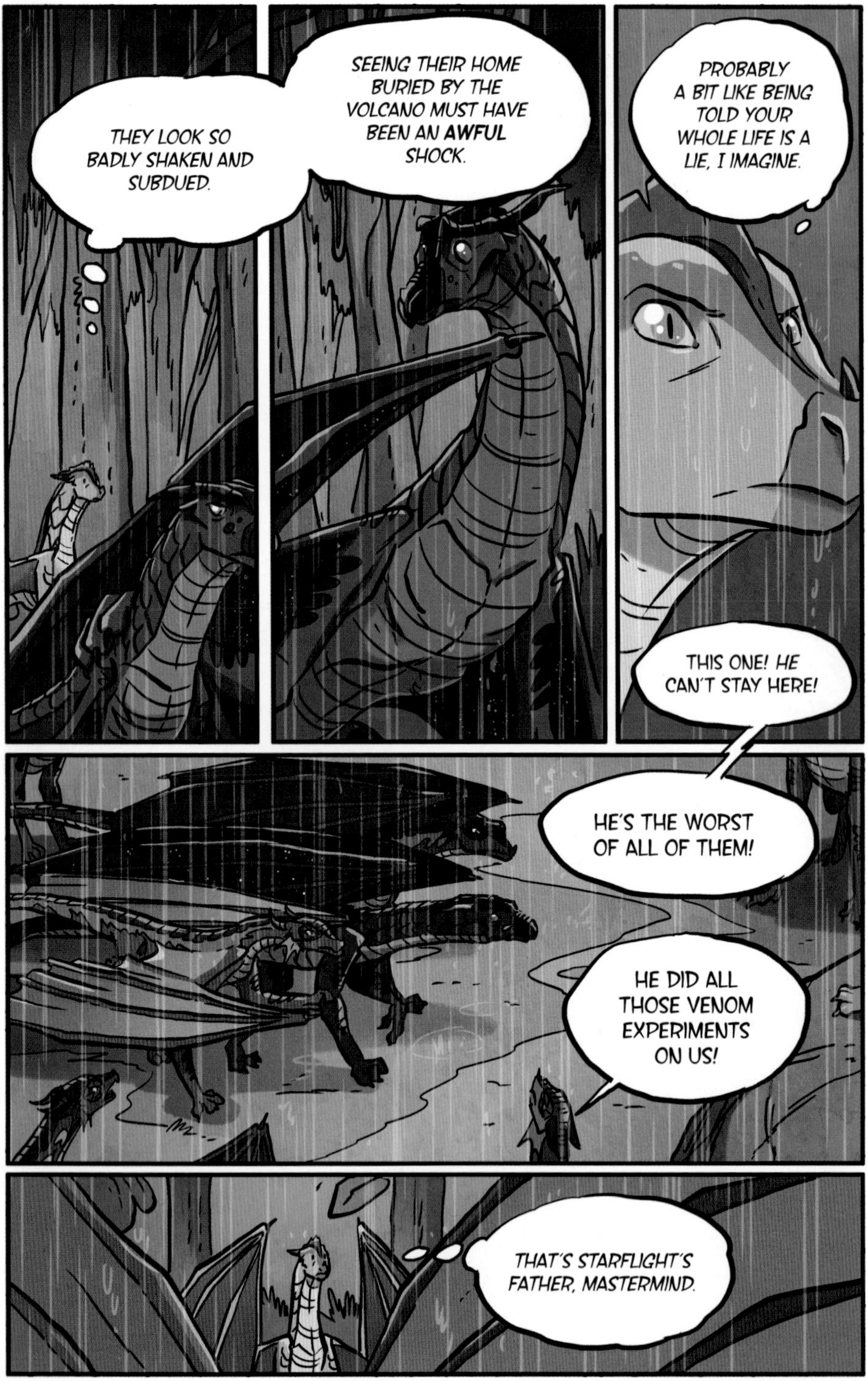
THEY LOOK SO BADLY SHAKEN AND SUBDUED.
SEEING THEIR HOME BURIED BY THE VOLCANO MUST HAVE BEEN AN **AWFUL** SHOCK.
PROBABLY A BIT LIKE BEING TOLD YOUR WHOLE LIFE IS A LIE, I IMAGINE.
THIS ONE! HE CAN'T STAY HERE!
HE'S THE WORST OF ALL OF THEM!
HE DID ALL THOSE VENOM EXPERIMENTS ON US!
THAT'S STARFLIGHT'S FATHER, MASTERMIND.

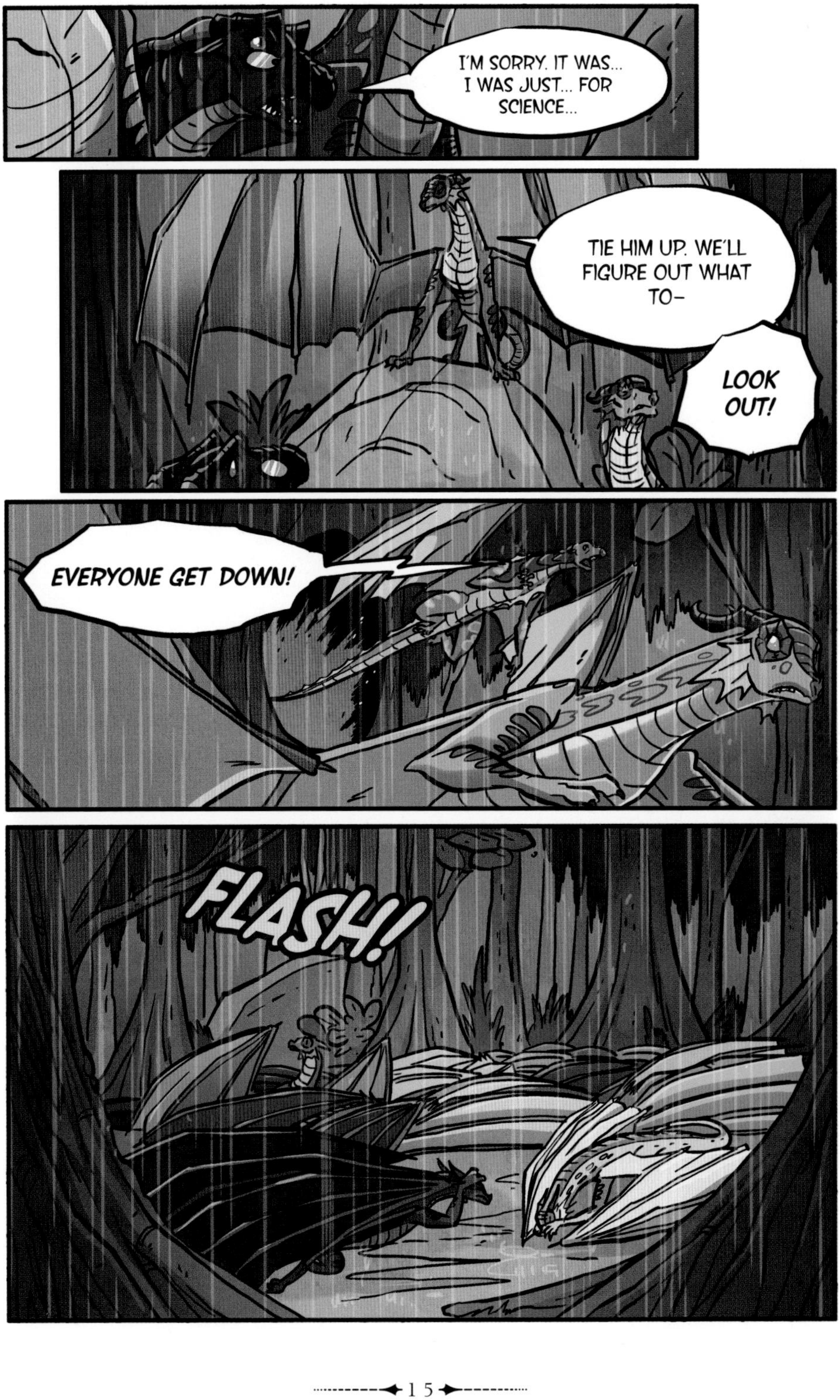
I'M SORRY. IT WAS... I WAS JUST... FOR SCIENCE...
TIE HIM UP. WE'LL FIGURE OUT WHAT TO–
LOOK OUT!
EVERYONE GET DOWN!
FLASH!

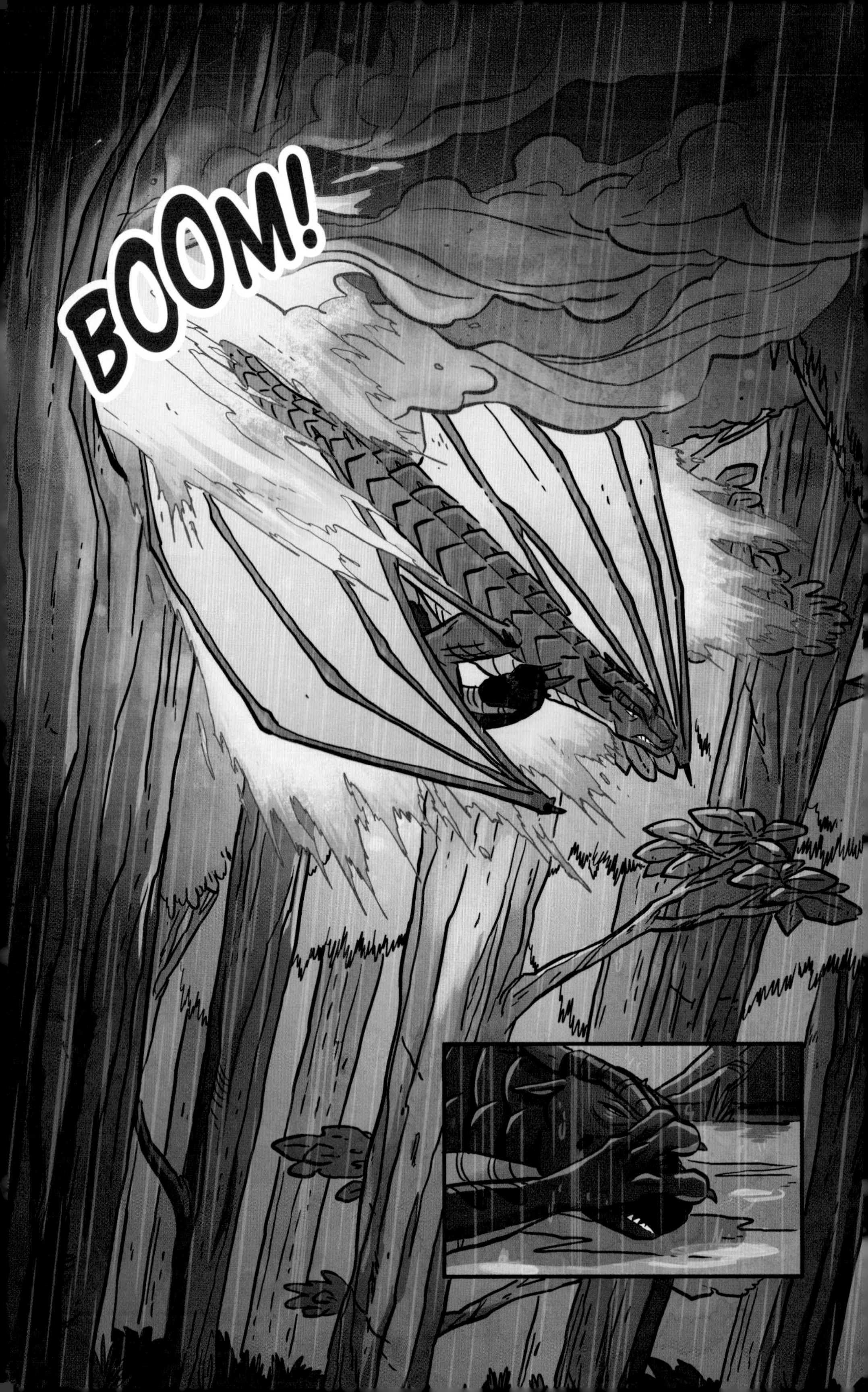
BOOM!

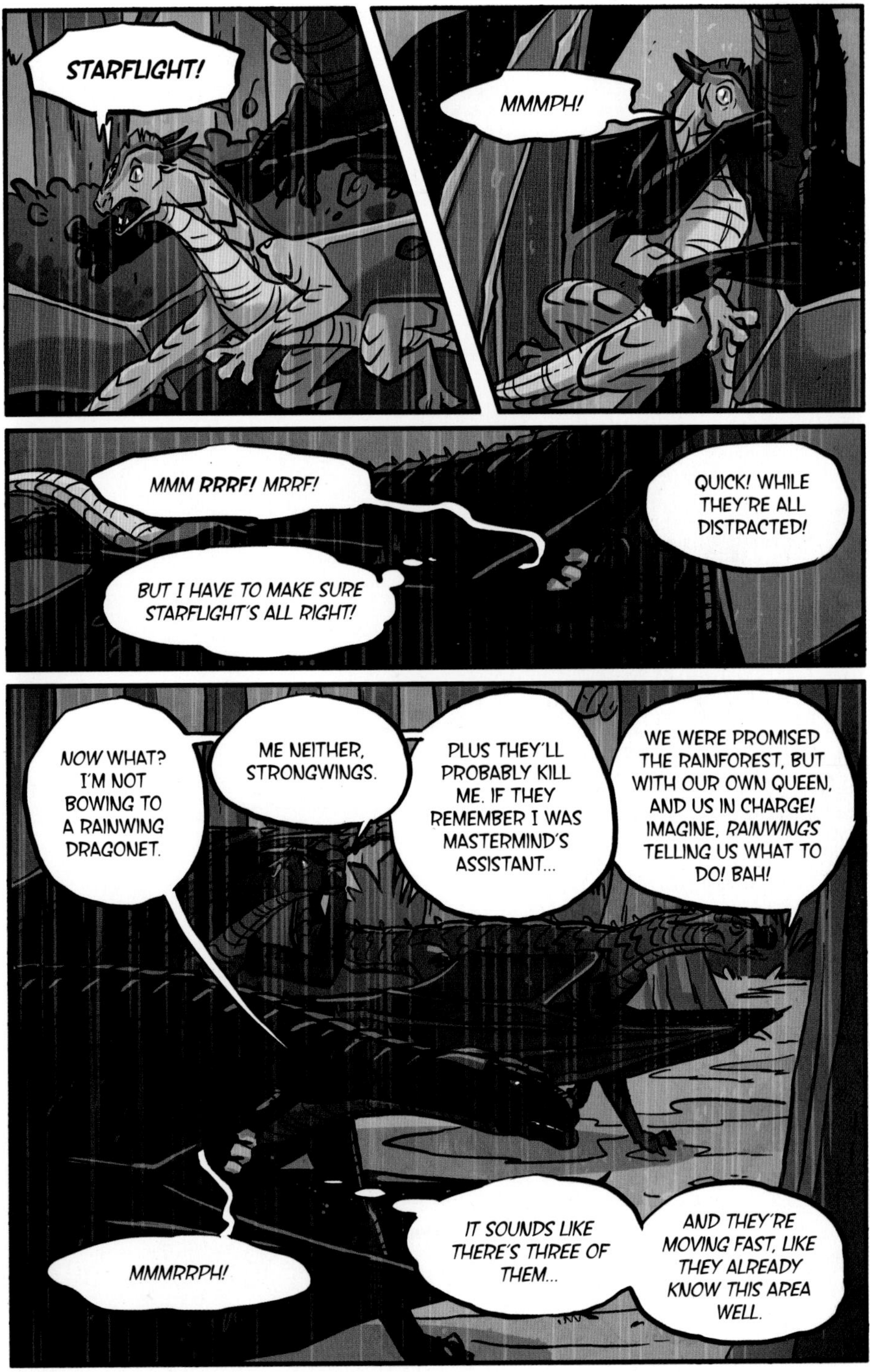
STARFLIGHT!
MMMPH!
MMM RRRF! MRRF!
QUICK! WHILE THEY'RE ALL DISTRACTED!
BUT I HAVE TO MAKE SURE STARFLIGHT'S ALL RIGHT!
NOW WHAT? I'M NOT BOWING TO A RAINWING DRAGONET.
ME NEITHER, STRONGWINGS.
PLUS THEY'LL PROBABLY KILL ME. IF THEY REMEMBER I WAS MASTERMIND'S ASSISTANT...
WE WERE PROMISED THE RAINFOREST, BUT WITH OUR OWN QUEEN, AND US IN CHARGE! IMAGINE, RAINWINGS TELLING US WHAT TO DO! BAH!
MMMRRPH!
IT SOUNDS LIKE THERE'S THREE OF THEM...
AND THEY'RE MOVING FAST, LIKE THEY ALREADY KNOW THIS AREA WELL.

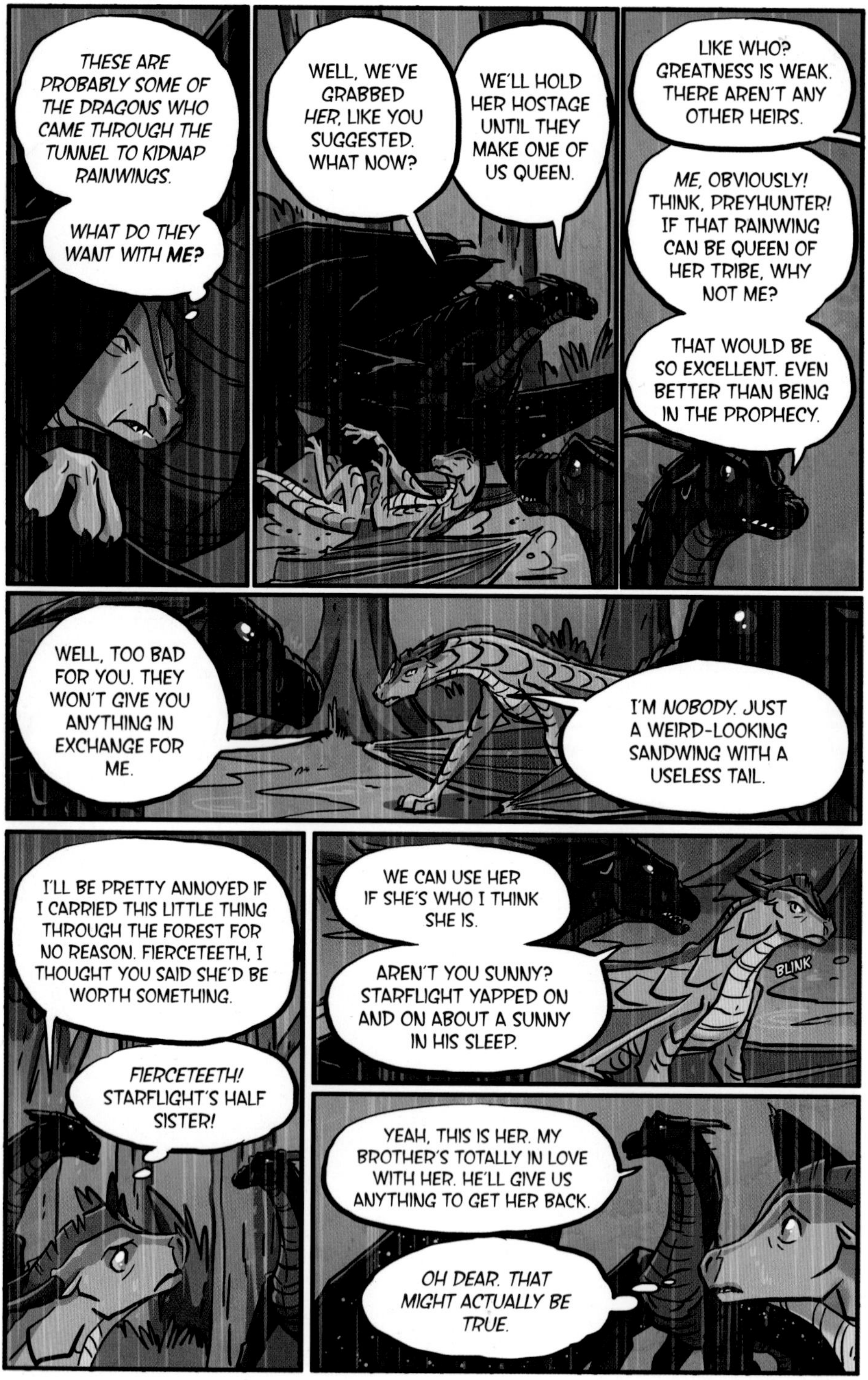
THESE ARE PROBABLY SOME OF THE DRAGONS WHO CAME THROUGH THE TUNNEL TO KIDNAP RAINWINGS.
WHAT DO THEY WANT WITH ME?
WELL, WE'VE GRABBED HER, LIKE YOU SUGGESTED. WHAT NOW?
WE'LL HOLD HER HOSTAGE UNTIL THEY MAKE ONE OF US QUEEN.
LIKE WHO? GREATNESS IS WEAK. THERE AREN'T ANY OTHER HEIRS.
ME, OBVIOUSLY! THINK, PREYHUNTER! IF THAT RAINWING CAN BE QUEEN OF HER TRIBE, WHY NOT ME?
THAT WOULD BE SO EXCELLENT. EVEN BETTER THAN BEING IN THE PROPHECY.
WELL, TOO BAD FOR YOU. THEY WON'T GIVE YOU ANYTHING IN EXCHANGE FOR ME.
I'M NOBODY. JUST A WEIRD-LOOKING SANDWING WITH A USELESS TAIL.
I'LL BE PRETTY ANNOYED IF I CARRIED THIS LITTLE THING THROUGH THE FOREST FOR NO REASON. FIERCETEETH, I THOUGHT YOU SAID SHE'D BE WORTH SOMETHING.
FIERCETEETH! STARFLIGHT'S HALF SISTER!
WE CAN USE HER IF SHE'S WHO I THINK SHE IS.
AREN'T YOU SUNNY? STARFLIGHT YAPPED ON AND ON ABOUT A SUNNY IN HIS SLEEP.
BLINK
YEAH, THIS IS HER. MY BROTHER'S TOTALLY IN LOVE WITH HER. HE'LL GIVE US ANYTHING TO GET HER BACK.
OH DEAR. THAT MIGHT ACTUALLY BE TRUE.

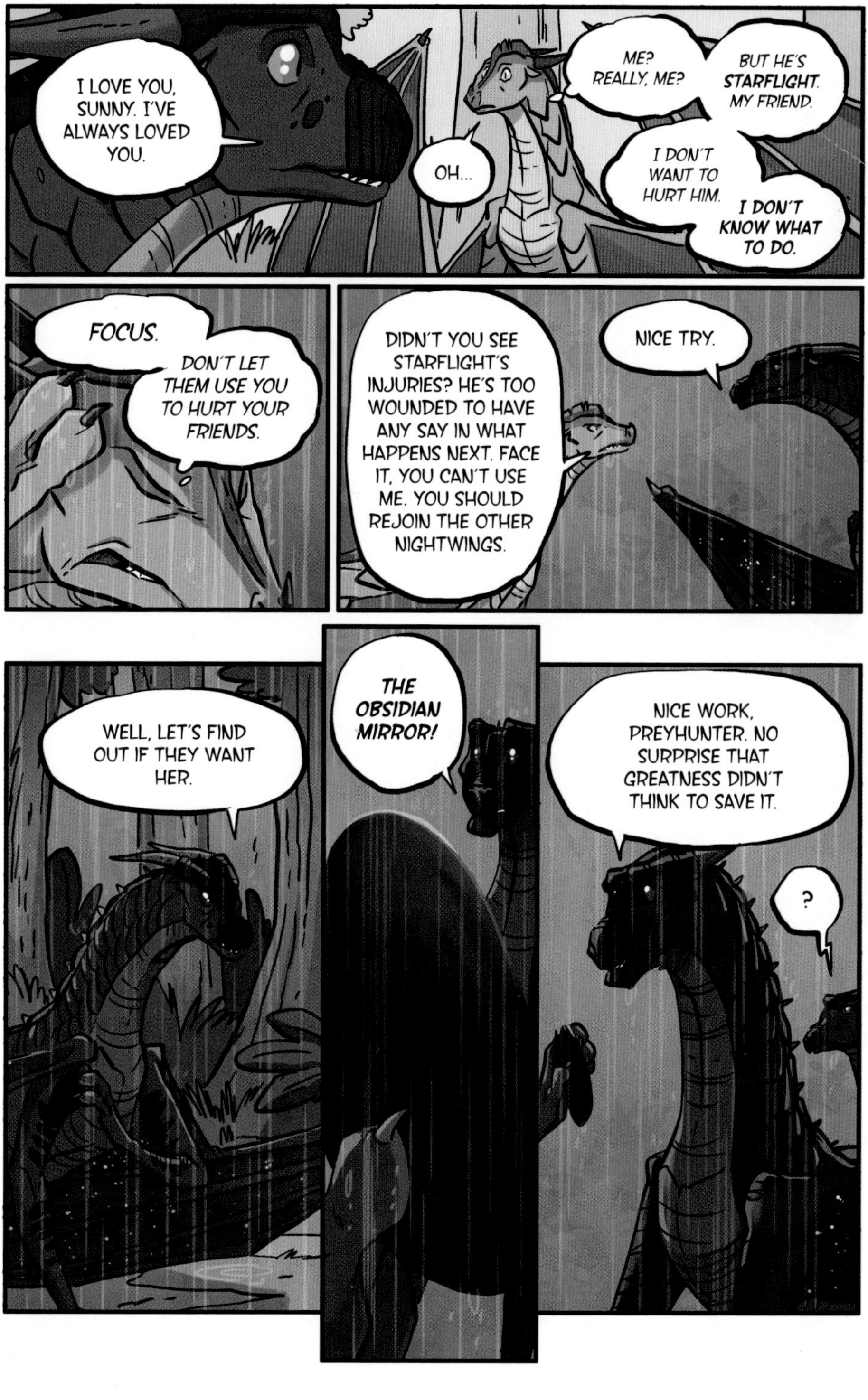
I LOVE YOU, SUNNY. I'VE ALWAYS LOVED YOU.
OH...
ME? REALLY, ME?
BUT HE'S STARFLIGHT. MY FRIEND.
I DON'T WANT TO HURT HIM.
I DON'T KNOW WHAT TO DO.
FOCUS.
DON'T LET THEM USE YOU TO HURT YOUR FRIENDS.
DIDN'T YOU SEE STARFLIGHT'S INJURIES? HE'S TOO WOUNDED TO HAVE ANY SAY IN WHAT HAPPENS NEXT. FACE IT, YOU CAN'T USE ME. YOU SHOULD REJOIN THE OTHER NIGHTWINGS.
NICE TRY.
WELL, LET'S FIND OUT IF THEY WANT HER.
THE OBSIDIAN MIRROR!
NICE WORK, PREYHUNTER. NO SURPRISE THAT GREATNESS DIDN'T THINK TO SAVE IT.
?

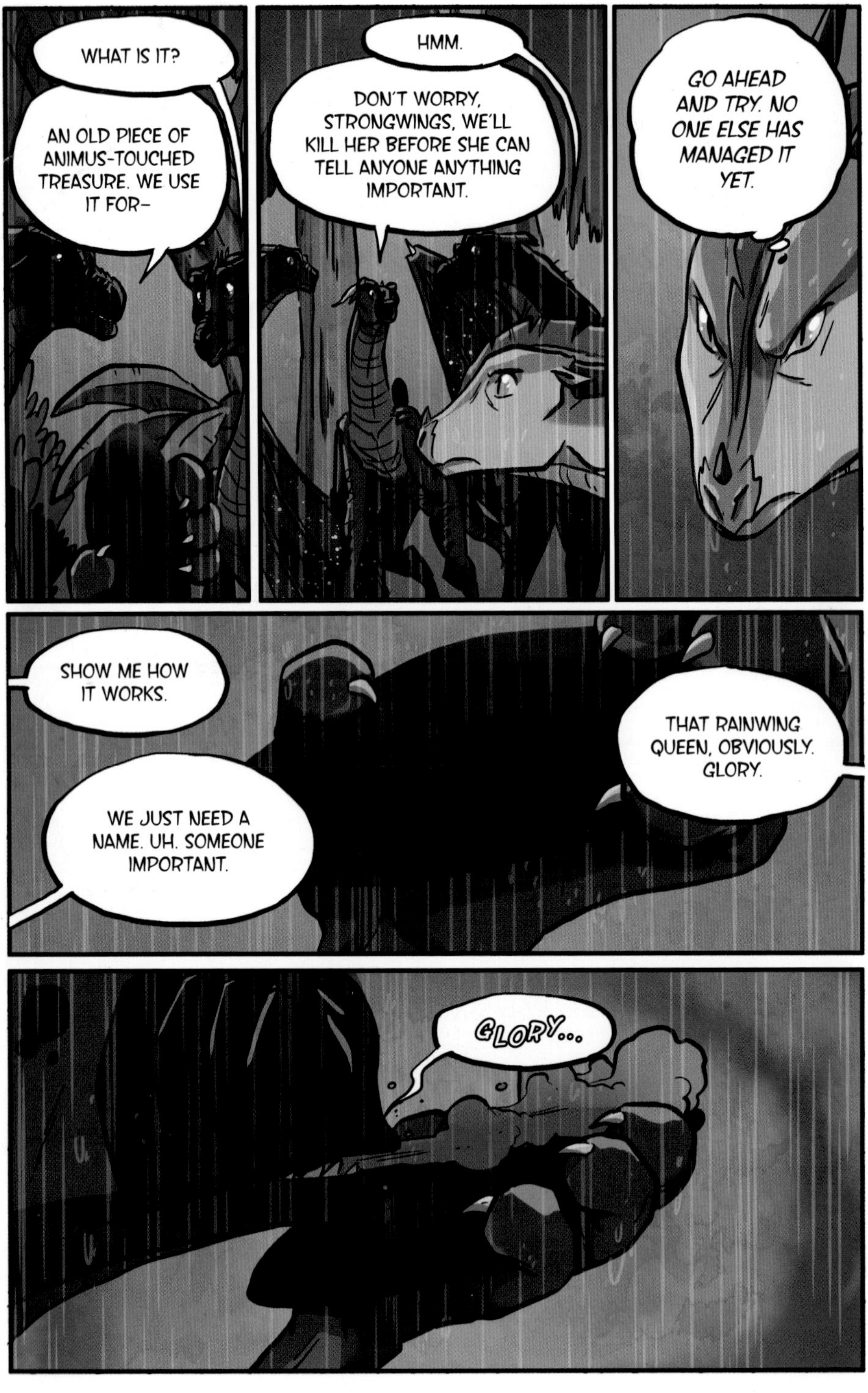
WHAT IS IT?
AN OLD PIECE OF ANIMUS-TOUCHED TREASURE. WE USE IT FOR–
HMM.
DON'T WORRY, STRONGWINGS, WE'LL KILL HER BEFORE SHE CAN TELL ANYONE ANYTHING IMPORTANT.
GO AHEAD AND TRY. NO ONE ELSE HAS MANAGED IT YET.
SHOW ME HOW IT WORKS.
WE JUST NEED A NAME. UH. SOMEONE IMPORTANT.
THAT RAINWING QUEEN, OBVIOUSLY. GLORY.
GLORY...

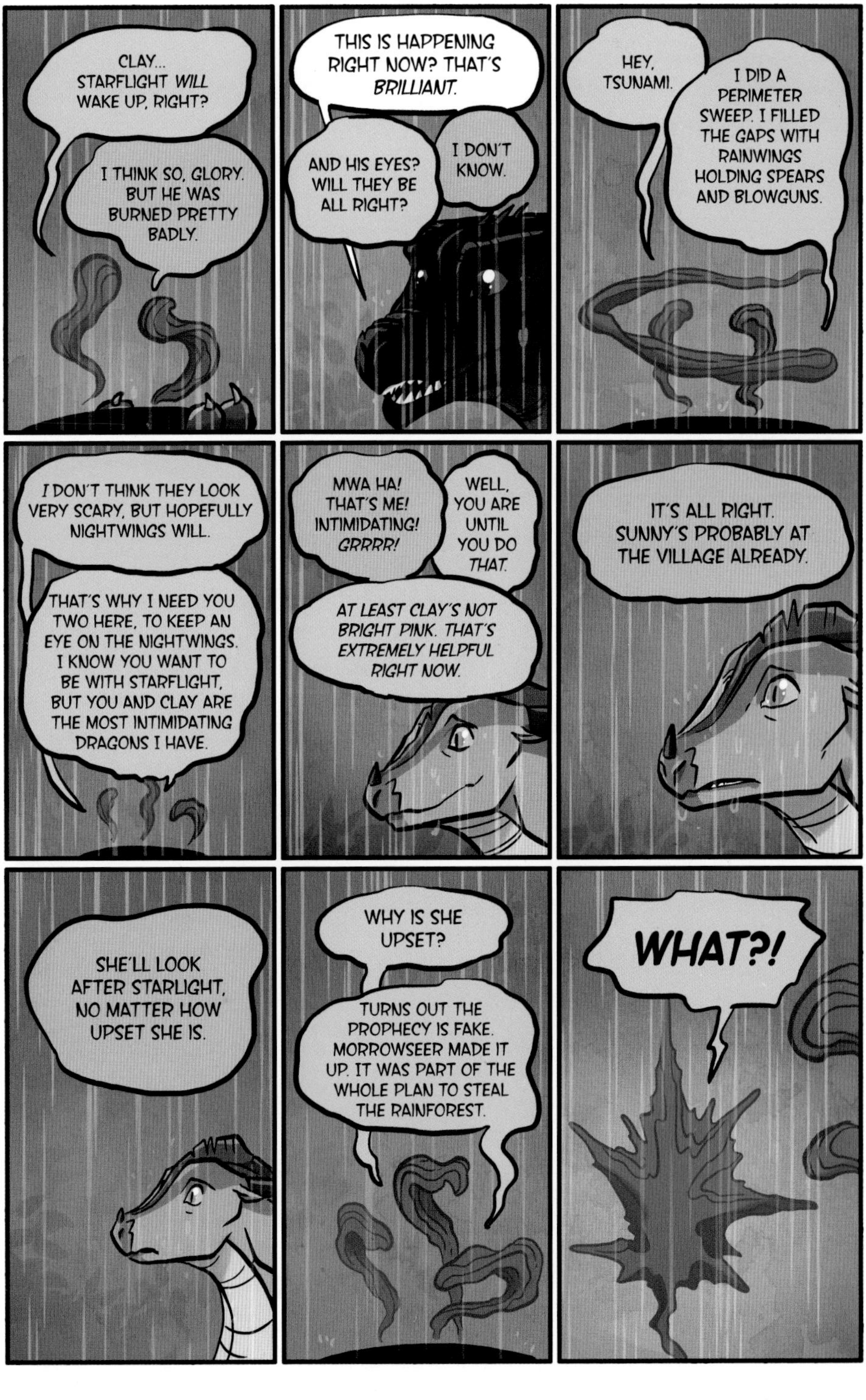

CLAY... STARFLIGHT *WILL* WAKE UP, RIGHT?
I THINK SO, GLORY. BUT HE WAS BURNED PRETTY BADLY.
THIS IS HAPPENING RIGHT NOW? THAT'S *BRILLIANT.*
AND HIS EYES? WILL THEY BE ALL RIGHT?
I DON'T KNOW.
HEY, TSUNAMI.
I DID A PERIMETER SWEEP. I FILLED THE GAPS WITH RAINWINGS HOLDING SPEARS AND BLOWGUNS.
I DON'T THINK THEY LOOK VERY SCARY, BUT HOPEFULLY NIGHTWINGS WILL.
THAT'S WHY I NEED YOU TWO HERE, TO KEEP AN EYE ON THE NIGHTWINGS. I KNOW YOU WANT TO BE WITH STARFLIGHT, BUT YOU AND CLAY ARE THE MOST INTIMIDATING DRAGONS I HAVE.
MWA HA! THAT'S ME! INTIMIDATING! *GRRRR!*
WELL, YOU ARE UNTIL YOU DO *THAT.*
AT LEAST CLAY'S NOT BRIGHT PINK. THAT'S EXTREMELY HELPFUL RIGHT NOW.
IT'S ALL RIGHT. SUNNY'S PROBABLY AT THE VILLAGE ALREADY.
SHE'LL LOOK AFTER STARLIGHT, NO MATTER HOW UPSET SHE IS.
WHY IS SHE UPSET?
TURNS OUT THE PROPHECY IS FAKE. MORROWSEER MADE IT UP. IT WAS PART OF THE WHOLE PLAN TO STEAL THE RAINFOREST.
WHAT?!

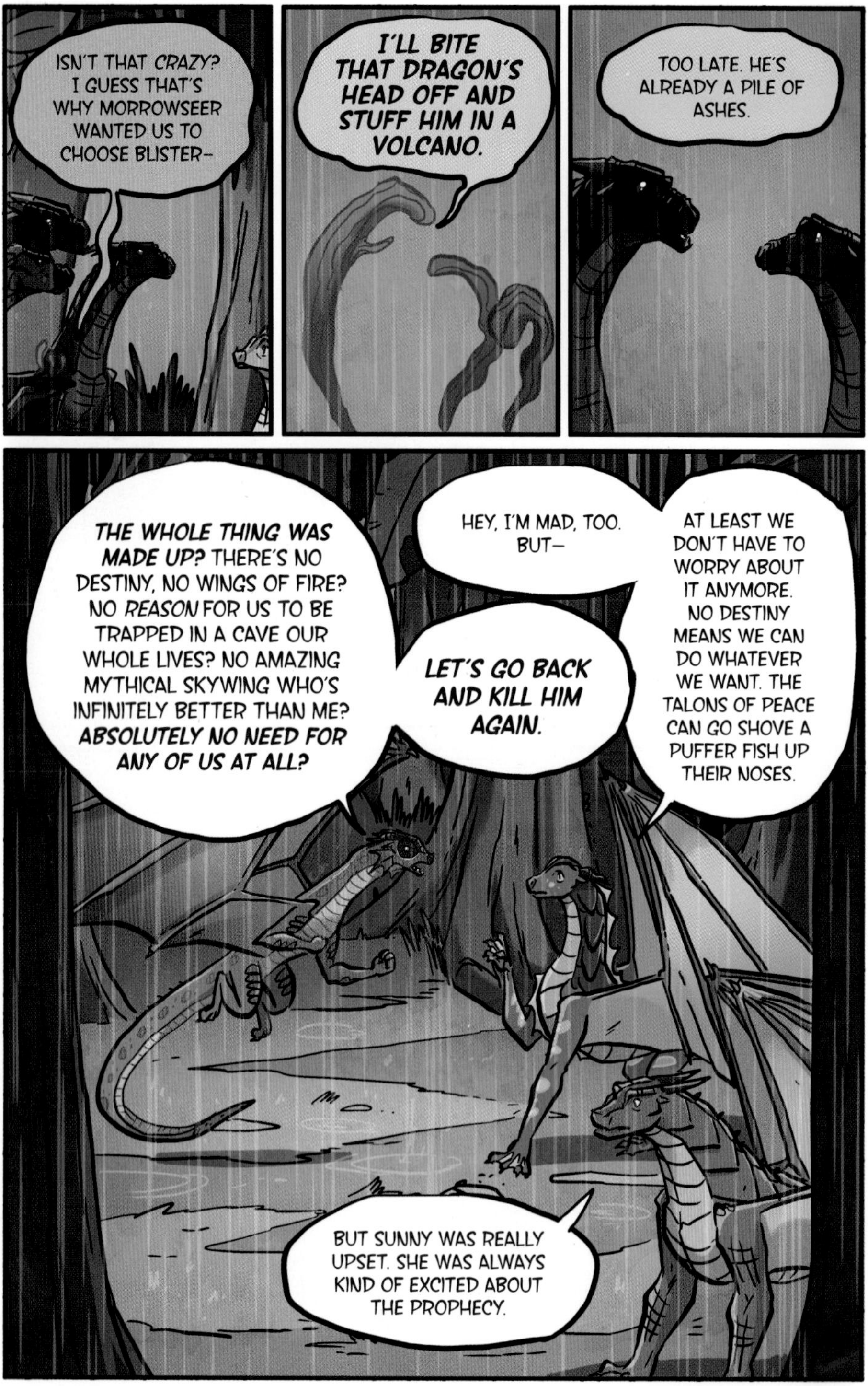
ISN'T THAT CRAZY? I GUESS THAT'S WHY MORROWSEER WANTED US TO CHOOSE BLISTER—
I'LL BITE THAT DRAGON'S HEAD OFF AND STUFF HIM IN A VOLCANO.
TOO LATE. HE'S ALREADY A PILE OF ASHES.
THE WHOLE THING WAS MADE UP? THERE'S NO DESTINY, NO WINGS OF FIRE? NO REASON FOR US TO BE TRAPPED IN A CAVE OUR WHOLE LIVES? NO AMAZING MYTHICAL SKYWING WHO'S INFINITELY BETTER THAN ME? ABSOLUTELY NO NEED FOR ANY OF US AT ALL?
LET'S GO BACK AND KILL HIM AGAIN.
HEY, I'M MAD, TOO. BUT—
AT LEAST WE DON'T HAVE TO WORRY ABOUT IT ANYMORE. NO DESTINY MEANS WE CAN DO WHATEVER WE WANT. THE TALONS OF PEACE CAN GO SHOVE A PUFFER FISH UP THEIR NOSES.
BUT SUNNY WAS REALLY UPSET. SHE WAS ALWAYS KIND OF EXCITED ABOUT THE PROPHECY.

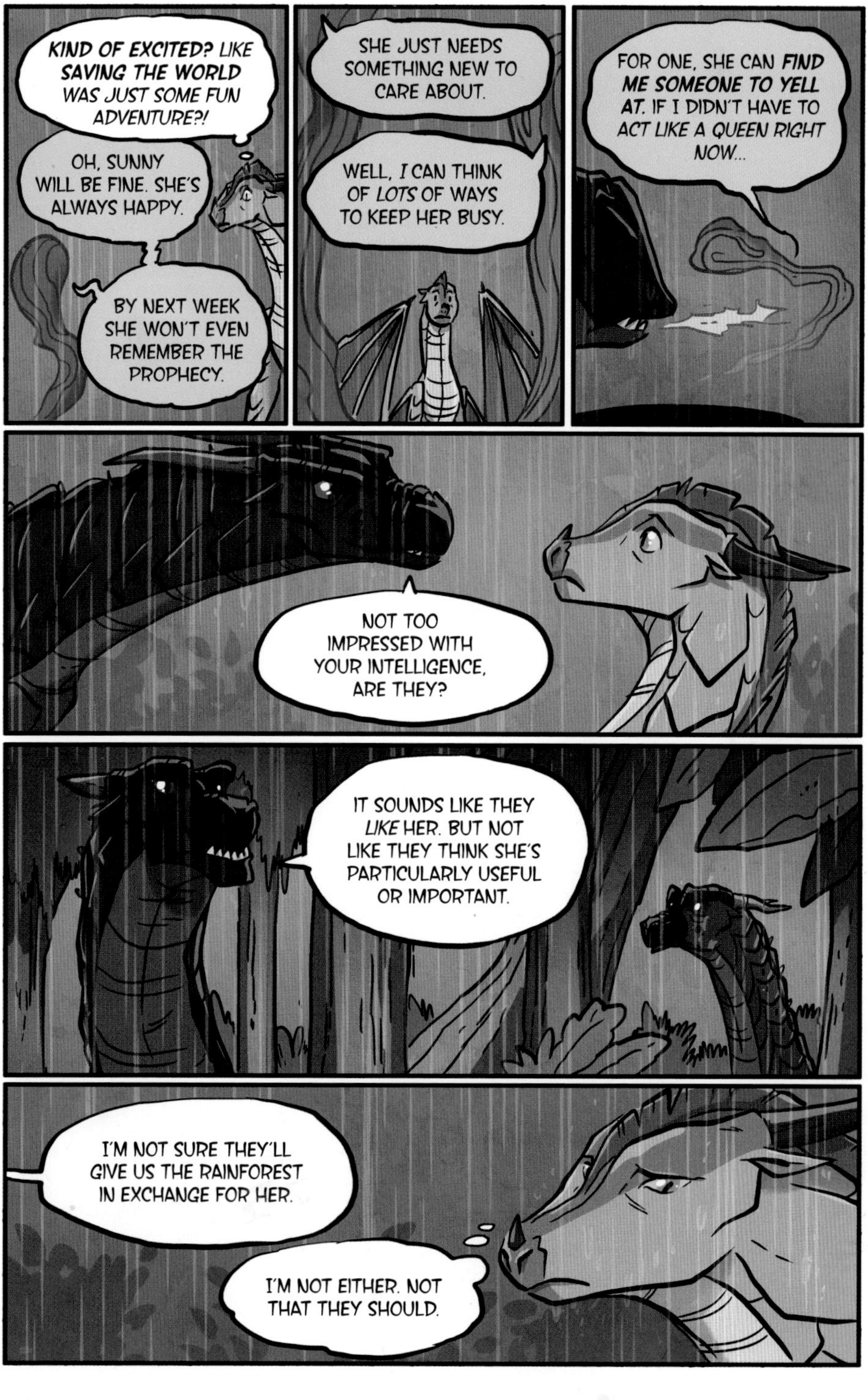
KIND OF EXCITED? LIKE SAVING THE WORLD WAS JUST SOME FUN ADVENTURE?!
OH, SUNNY WILL BE FINE. SHE'S ALWAYS HAPPY.
BY NEXT WEEK SHE WON'T EVEN REMEMBER THE PROPHECY.
SHE JUST NEEDS SOMETHING NEW TO CARE ABOUT.
WELL, I CAN THINK OF LOTS OF WAYS TO KEEP HER BUSY.
FOR ONE, SHE CAN FIND ME SOMEONE TO YELL AT. IF I DIDN'T HAVE TO ACT LIKE A QUEEN RIGHT NOW...
NOT TOO IMPRESSED WITH YOUR INTELLIGENCE, ARE THEY?
IT SOUNDS LIKE THEY LIKE HER. BUT NOT LIKE THEY THINK SHE'S PARTICULARLY USEFUL OR IMPORTANT.
I'M NOT SURE THEY'LL GIVE US THE RAINFOREST IN EXCHANGE FOR HER.
I'M NOT EITHER. NOT THAT THEY SHOULD.

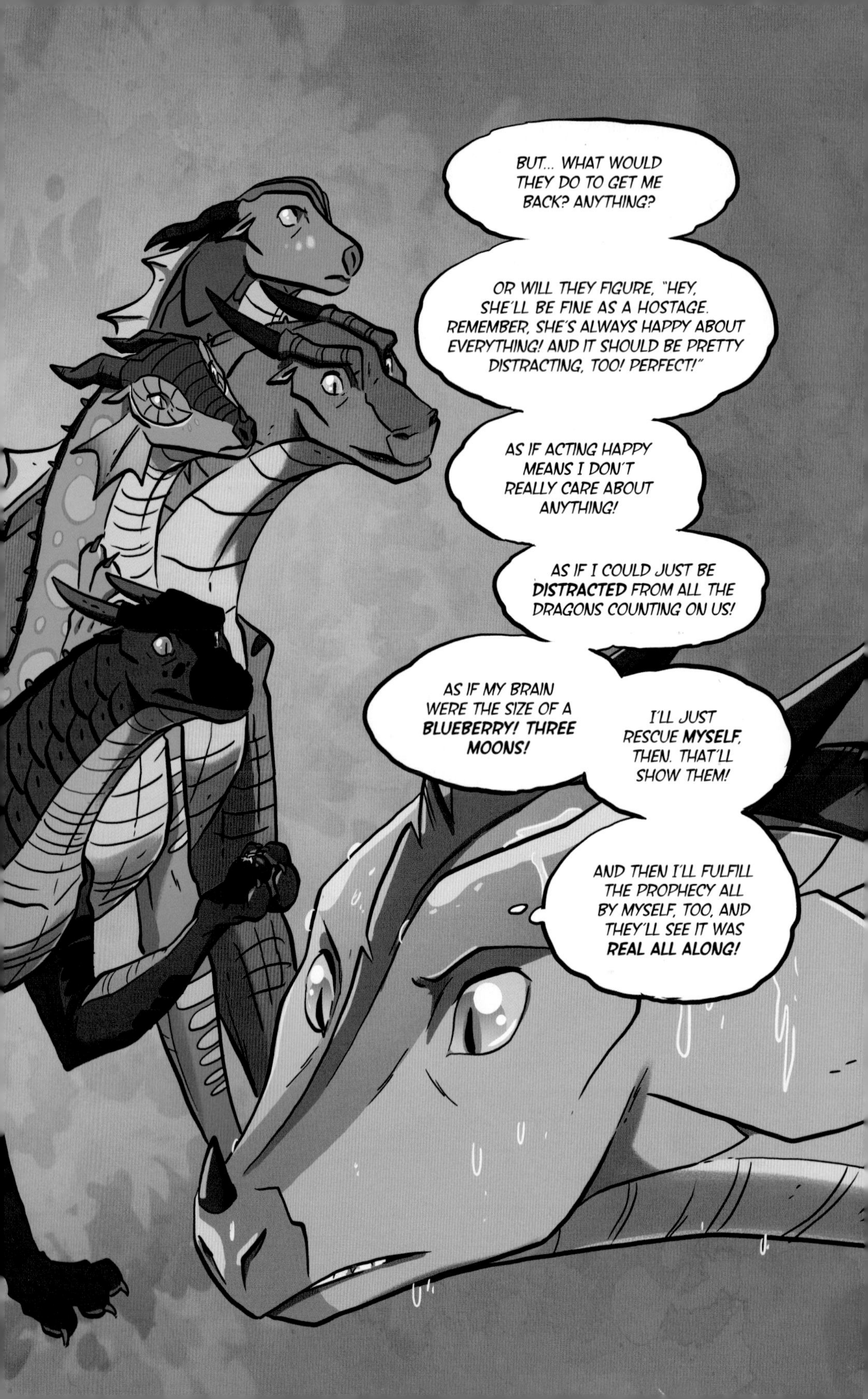
BUT... WHAT WOULD THEY DO TO GET ME BACK? ANYTHING?
OR WILL THEY FIGURE, "HEY, SHE'LL BE FINE AS A HOSTAGE. REMEMBER, SHE'S ALWAYS HAPPY ABOUT EVERYTHING! AND IT SHOULD BE PRETTY DISTRACTING, TOO! PERFECT!"
AS IF ACTING HAPPY MEANS I DON'T REALLY CARE ABOUT ANYTHING!
AS IF I COULD JUST BE **DISTRACTED** FROM ALL THE DRAGONS COUNTING ON US!
AS IF MY BRAIN WERE THE SIZE OF A **BLUEBERRY! THREE MOONS!**
I'LL JUST RESCUE **MYSELF**, THEN. THAT'LL SHOW THEM!
AND THEN I'LL FULFILL THE PROPHECY ALL BY MYSELF, TOO, AND THEY'LL SEE IT WAS **REAL ALL ALONG!**

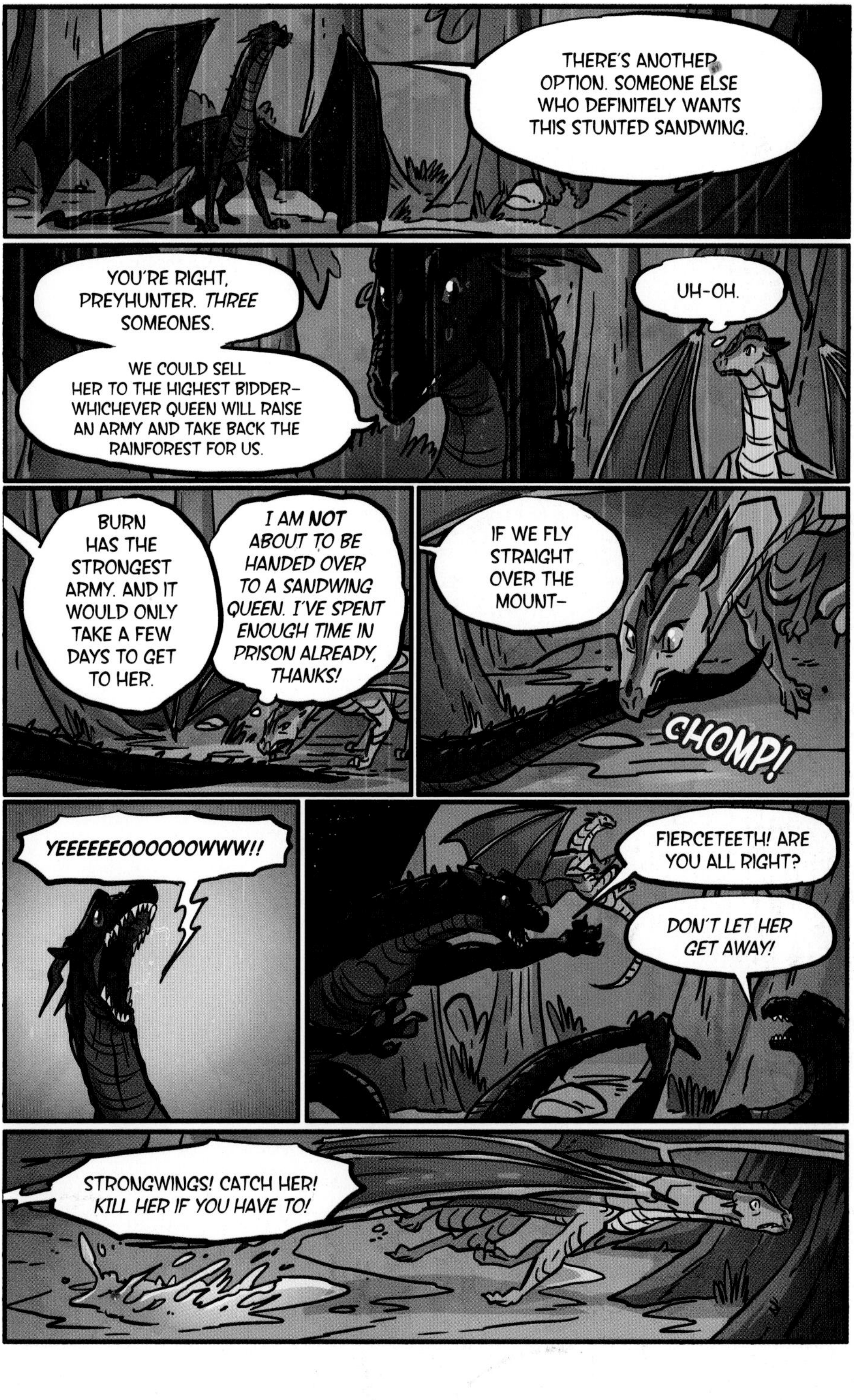
THERE'S ANOTHER OPTION. SOMEONE ELSE WHO DEFINITELY WANTS THIS STUNTED SANDWING.
YOU'RE RIGHT, PREYHUNTER. *THREE* SOMEONES.
WE COULD SELL HER TO THE HIGHEST BIDDER— WHICHEVER QUEEN WILL RAISE AN ARMY AND TAKE BACK THE RAINFOREST FOR US.
UH-OH.
BURN HAS THE STRONGEST ARMY. AND IT WOULD ONLY TAKE A FEW DAYS TO GET TO HER.
I AM **NOT** *ABOUT TO BE HANDED OVER TO A SANDWING QUEEN. I'VE SPENT ENOUGH TIME IN PRISON ALREADY, THANKS!*
IF WE FLY STRAIGHT OVER THE MOUNT—
CHOMP!
YEEEEEEOOOOOOWWW!!
FIERCETEETH! ARE YOU ALL RIGHT?
DON'T LET HER GET AWAY!
STRONGWINGS! CATCH HER! *KILL HER IF YOU HAVE TO!*

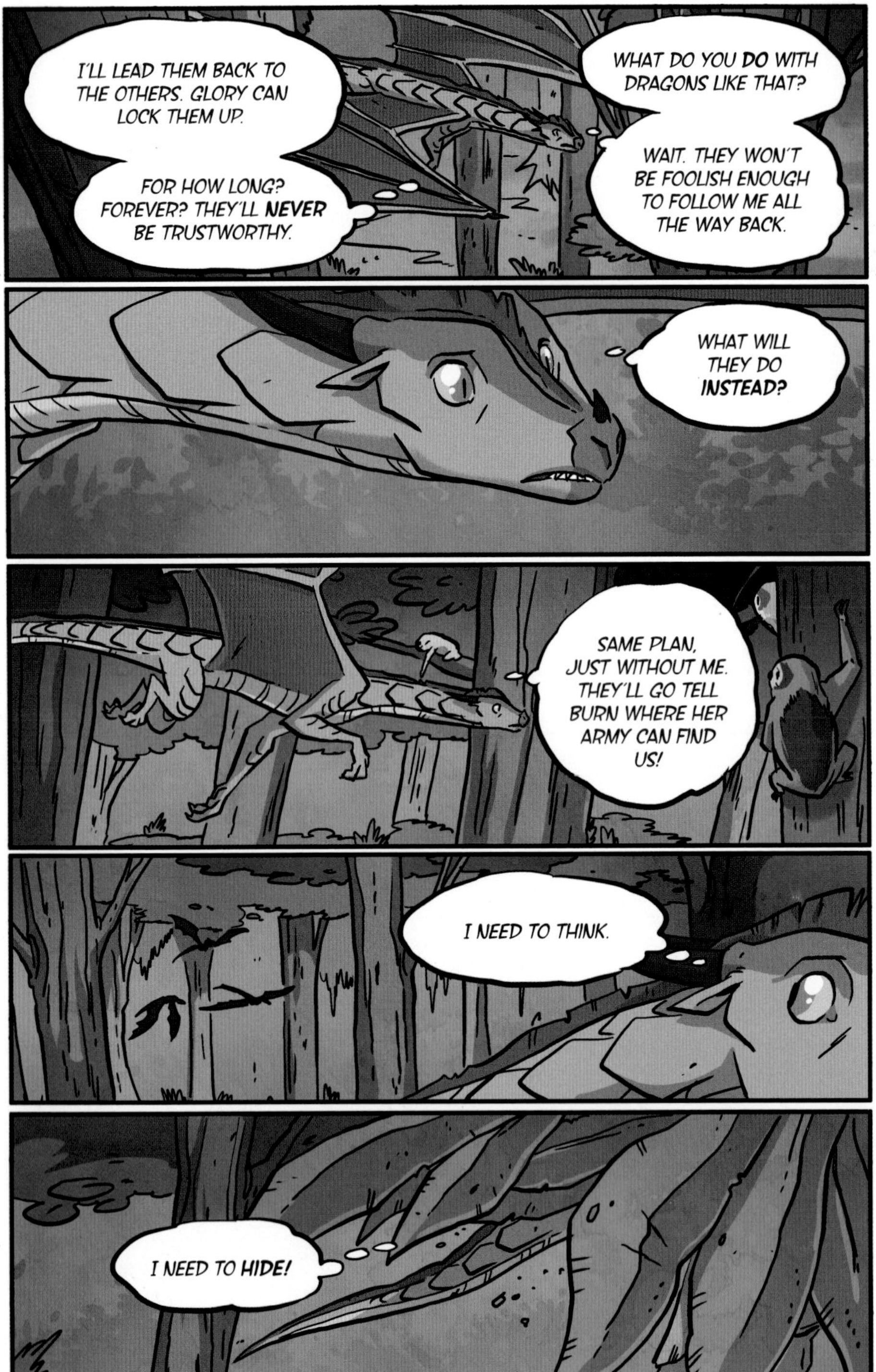
I'LL LEAD THEM BACK TO THE OTHERS. GLORY CAN LOCK THEM UP.
FOR HOW LONG? FOREVER? THEY'LL **NEVER** BE TRUSTWORTHY.
WHAT DO YOU **DO** WITH DRAGONS LIKE THAT?
WAIT. THEY WON'T BE FOOLISH ENOUGH TO FOLLOW ME ALL THE WAY BACK.
WHAT WILL THEY DO **INSTEAD?**
SAME PLAN, JUST WITHOUT ME. THEY'LL GO TELL BURN WHERE HER ARMY CAN FIND US!
I NEED TO THINK.
I NEED TO **HIDE!**

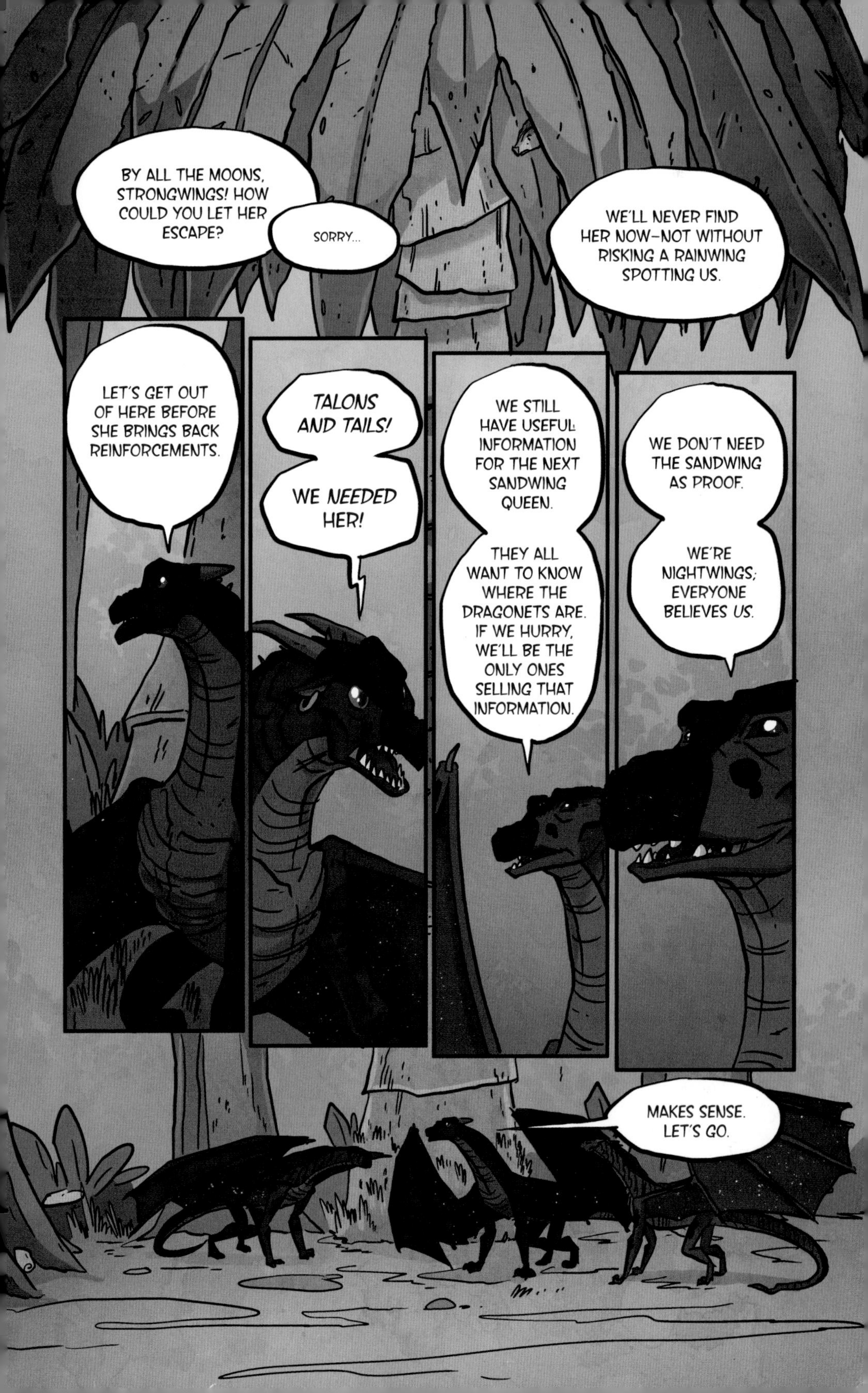
BY ALL THE MOONS, STRONGWINGS! HOW COULD YOU LET HER ESCAPE?
SORRY...
WE'LL NEVER FIND HER NOW—NOT WITHOUT RISKING A RAINWING SPOTTING US.
LET'S GET OUT OF HERE BEFORE SHE BRINGS BACK REINFORCEMENTS.
TALONS AND TAILS!
WE NEEDED HER!
WE STILL HAVE USEFUL INFORMATION FOR THE NEXT SANDWING QUEEN.
THEY ALL WANT TO KNOW WHERE THE DRAGONETS ARE. IF WE HURRY, WE'LL BE THE ONLY ONES SELLING THAT INFORMATION.
WE DON'T NEED THE SANDWING AS PROOF.
WE'RE NIGHTWINGS; EVERYONE BELIEVES US.
MAKES SENSE. LET'S GO.

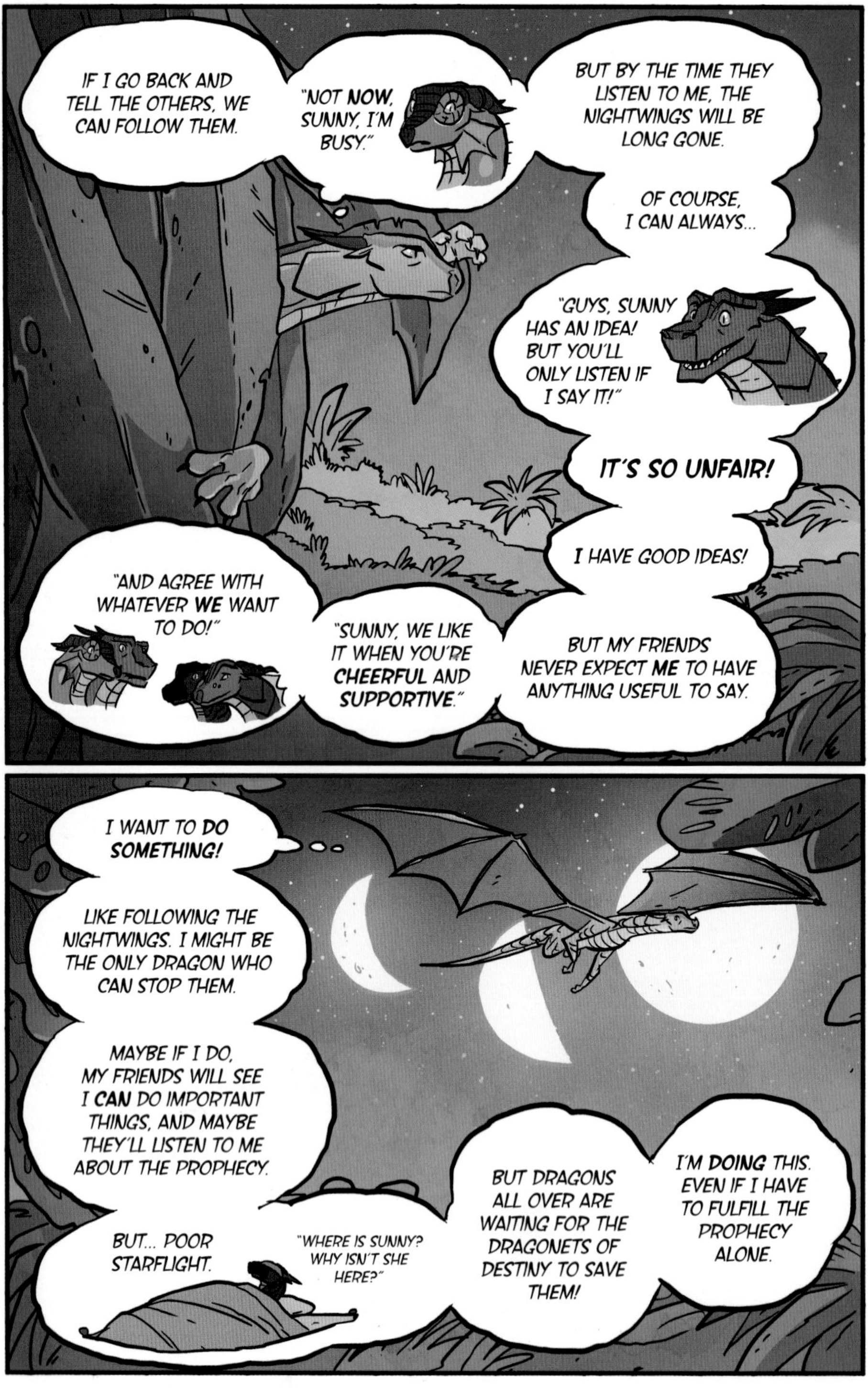
IF I GO BACK AND TELL THE OTHERS, WE CAN FOLLOW THEM.
"NOT NOW, SUNNY, I'M BUSY."
BUT BY THE TIME THEY LISTEN TO ME, THE NIGHTWINGS WILL BE LONG GONE.
OF COURSE, I CAN ALWAYS...
"GUYS, SUNNY HAS AN IDEA! BUT YOU'LL ONLY LISTEN IF I SAY IT!"
IT'S SO UNFAIR!
I HAVE GOOD IDEAS!
BUT MY FRIENDS NEVER EXPECT ME TO HAVE ANYTHING USEFUL TO SAY.
"SUNNY, WE LIKE IT WHEN YOU'RE CHEERFUL AND SUPPORTIVE."
"AND AGREE WITH WHATEVER WE WANT TO DO!"
I WANT TO DO SOMETHING!
LIKE FOLLOWING THE NIGHTWINGS. I MIGHT BE THE ONLY DRAGON WHO CAN STOP THEM.
MAYBE IF I DO, MY FRIENDS WILL SEE I CAN DO IMPORTANT THINGS, AND MAYBE THEY'LL LISTEN TO ME ABOUT THE PROPHECY.
BUT... POOR STARFLIGHT.
"WHERE IS SUNNY? WHY ISN'T SHE HERE?"
BUT DRAGONS ALL OVER ARE WAITING FOR THE DRAGONETS OF DESTINY TO SAVE THEM!
I'M DOING THIS. EVEN IF I HAVE TO FULFILL THE PROPHECY ALONE.

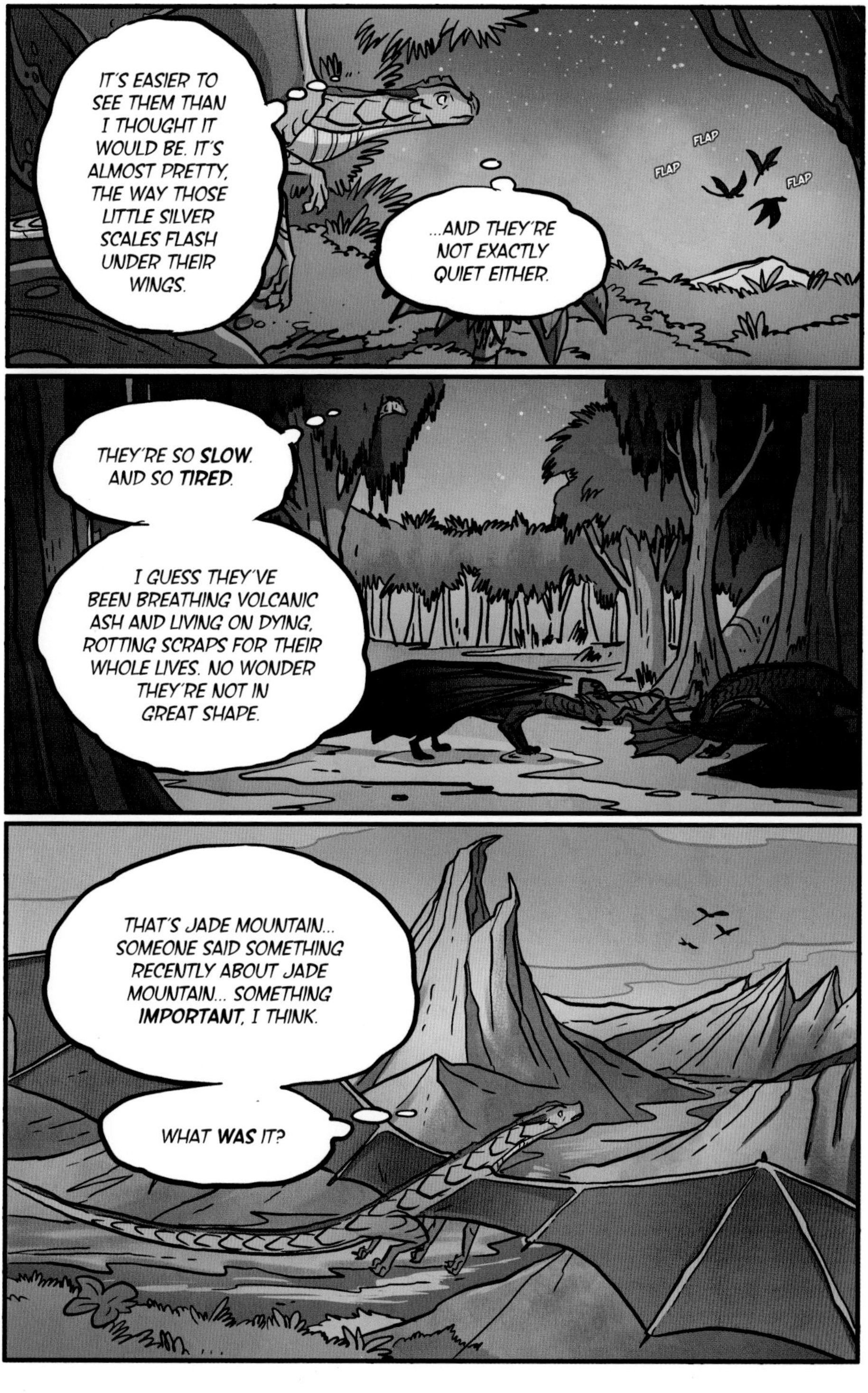
IT'S EASIER TO SEE THEM THAN I THOUGHT IT WOULD BE. IT'S ALMOST PRETTY, THE WAY THOSE LITTLE SILVER SCALES FLASH UNDER THEIR WINGS.
FLAP
FLAP
FLAP
...AND THEY'RE NOT EXACTLY QUIET EITHER.
THEY'RE SO **SLOW**. AND SO **TIRED**.
I GUESS THEY'VE BEEN BREATHING VOLCANIC ASH AND LIVING ON DYING, ROTTING SCRAPS FOR THEIR WHOLE LIVES. NO WONDER THEY'RE NOT IN GREAT SHAPE.
THAT'S JADE MOUNTAIN... SOMEONE SAID SOMETHING RECENTLY ABOUT JADE MOUNTAIN... SOMETHING **IMPORTANT**, I THINK.
WHAT **WAS** IT?

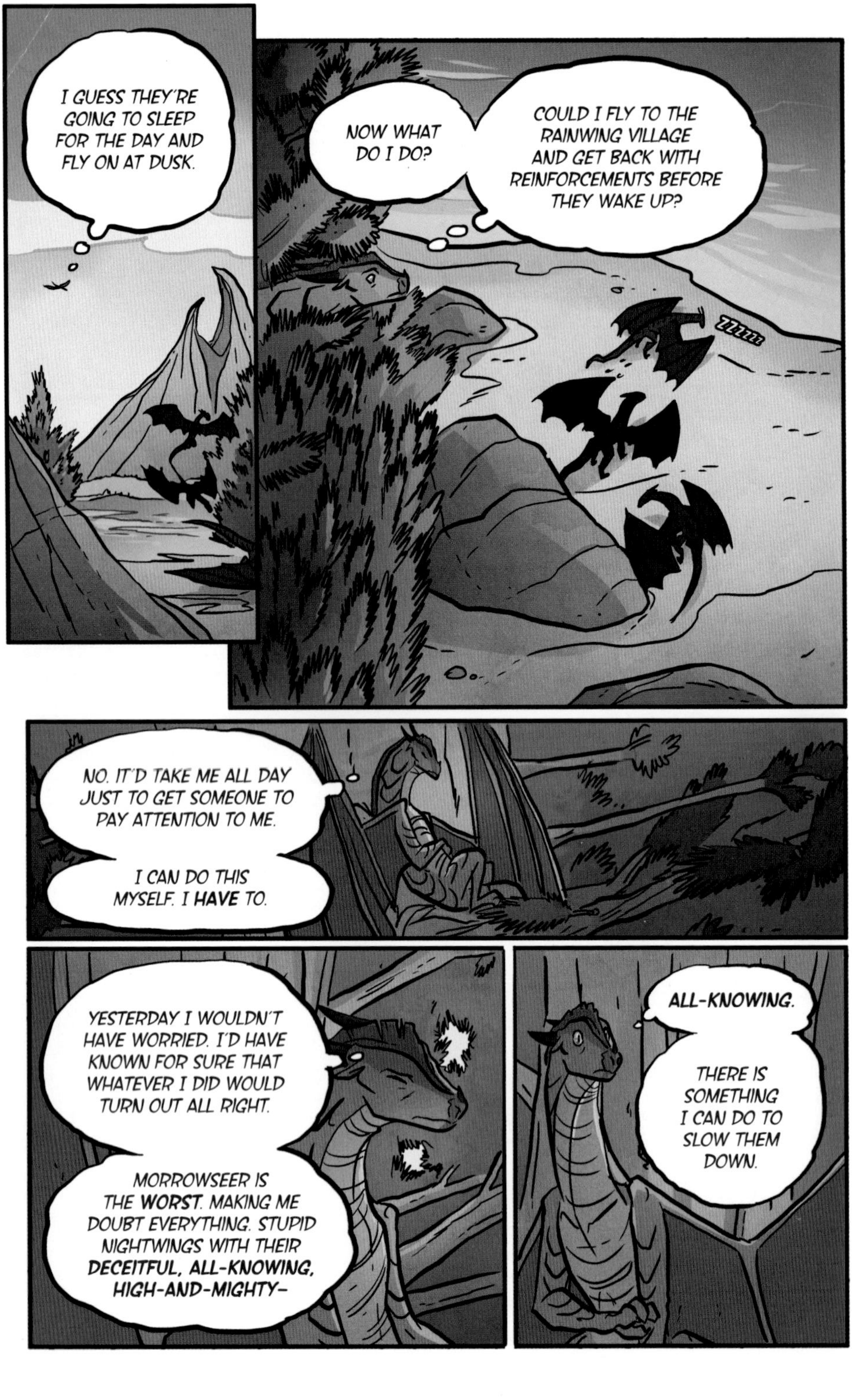
I GUESS THEY'RE GOING TO SLEEP FOR THE DAY AND FLY ON AT DUSK.
NOW WHAT DO I DO?
COULD I FLY TO THE RAINWING VILLAGE AND GET BACK WITH REINFORCEMENTS BEFORE THEY WAKE UP?
ZZZZZ
NO. IT'D TAKE ME ALL DAY JUST TO GET SOMEONE TO PAY ATTENTION TO ME.
I CAN DO THIS MYSELF. I **HAVE** TO.
YESTERDAY I WOULDN'T HAVE WORRIED. I'D HAVE KNOWN FOR SURE THAT WHATEVER I DID WOULD TURN OUT ALL RIGHT.
MORROWSEER IS THE **WORST**. MAKING ME DOUBT EVERYTHING. STUPID NIGHTWINGS WITH THEIR **DECEITFUL, ALL-KNOWING, HIGH-AND-MIGHTY–**
ALL-KNOWING.
THERE IS SOMETHING I CAN DO TO SLOW THEM DOWN.

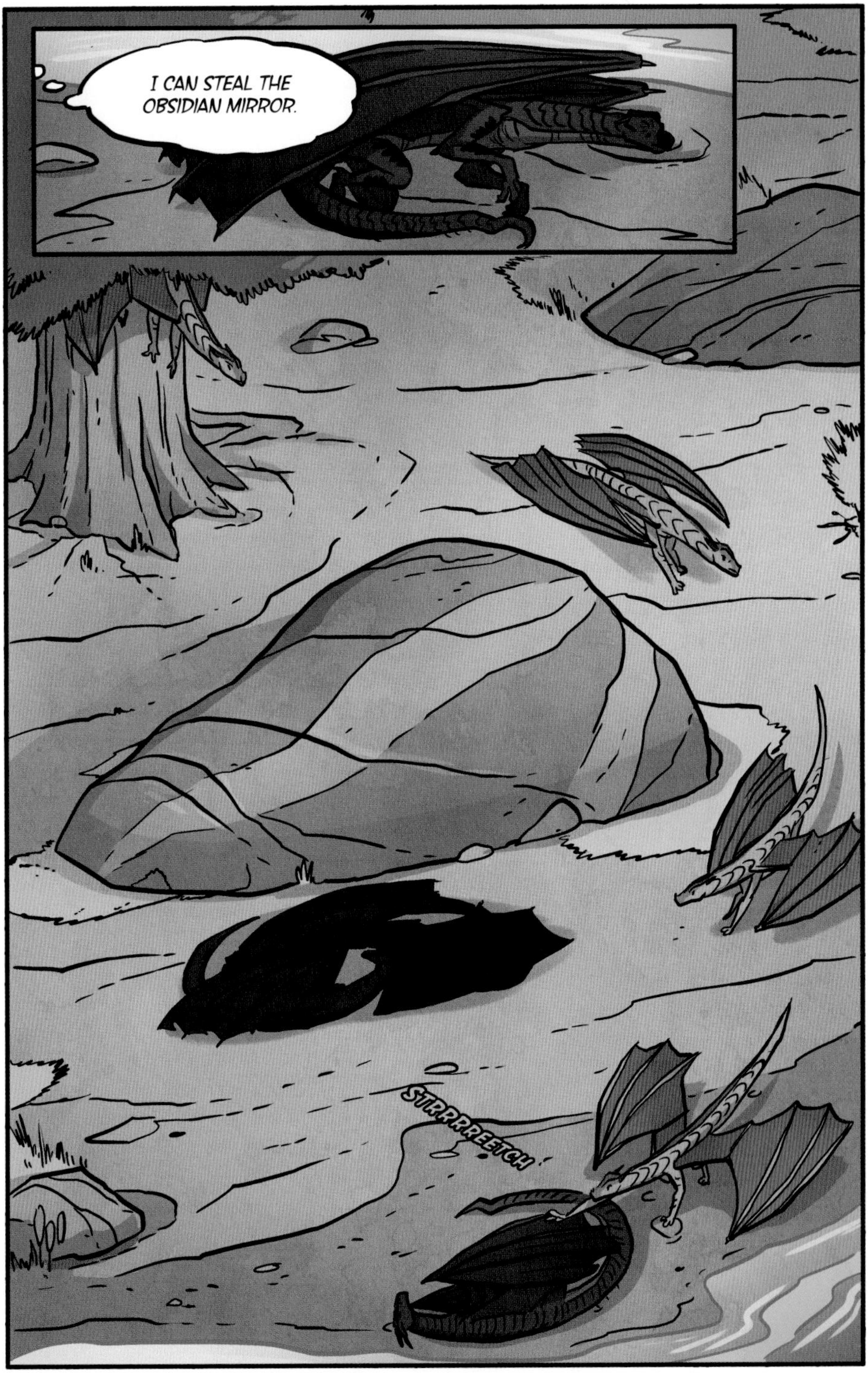
I CAN STEAL THE OBSIDIAN MIRROR.
STRRRREETCH

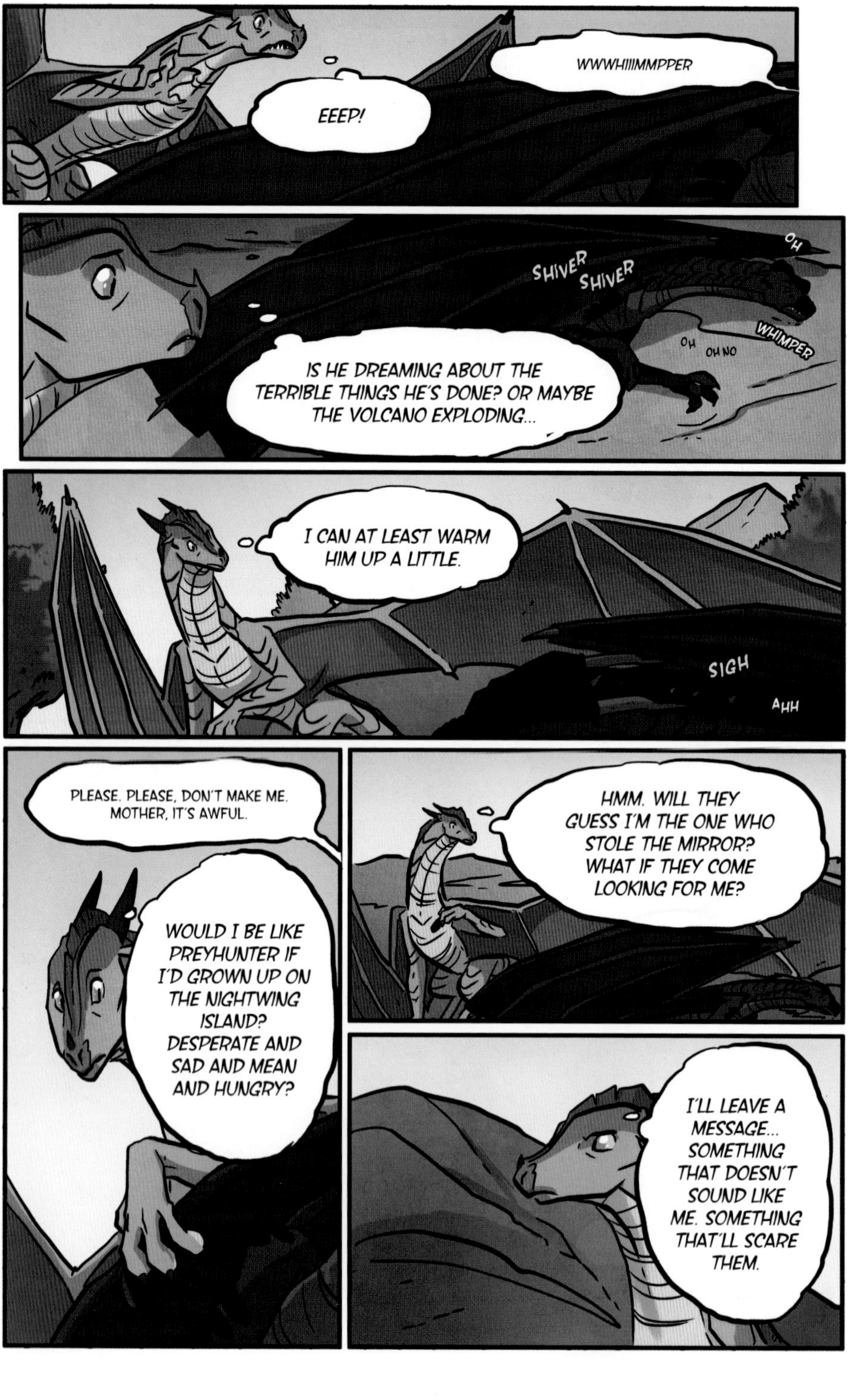
EEEP!
WWWHIIIMMPPER
IS HE DREAMING ABOUT THE TERRIBLE THINGS HE'S DONE? OR MAYBE THE VOLCANO EXPLODING...
SHIVER SHIVER
OH
WHIMPER
OH OH NO
I CAN AT LEAST WARM HIM UP A LITTLE.
SIGH
AHH
PLEASE. PLEASE, DON'T MAKE ME. MOTHER, IT'S AWFUL.
WOULD I BE LIKE PREYHUNTER IF I'D GROWN UP ON THE NIGHTWING ISLAND? DESPERATE AND SAD AND MEAN AND HUNGRY?
HMM. WILL THEY GUESS I'M THE ONE WHO STOLE THE MIRROR? WHAT IF THEY COME LOOKING FOR ME?
I'LL LEAVE A MESSAGE... SOMETHING THAT DOESN'T SOUND LIKE ME. SOMETHING THAT'LL SCARE THEM.

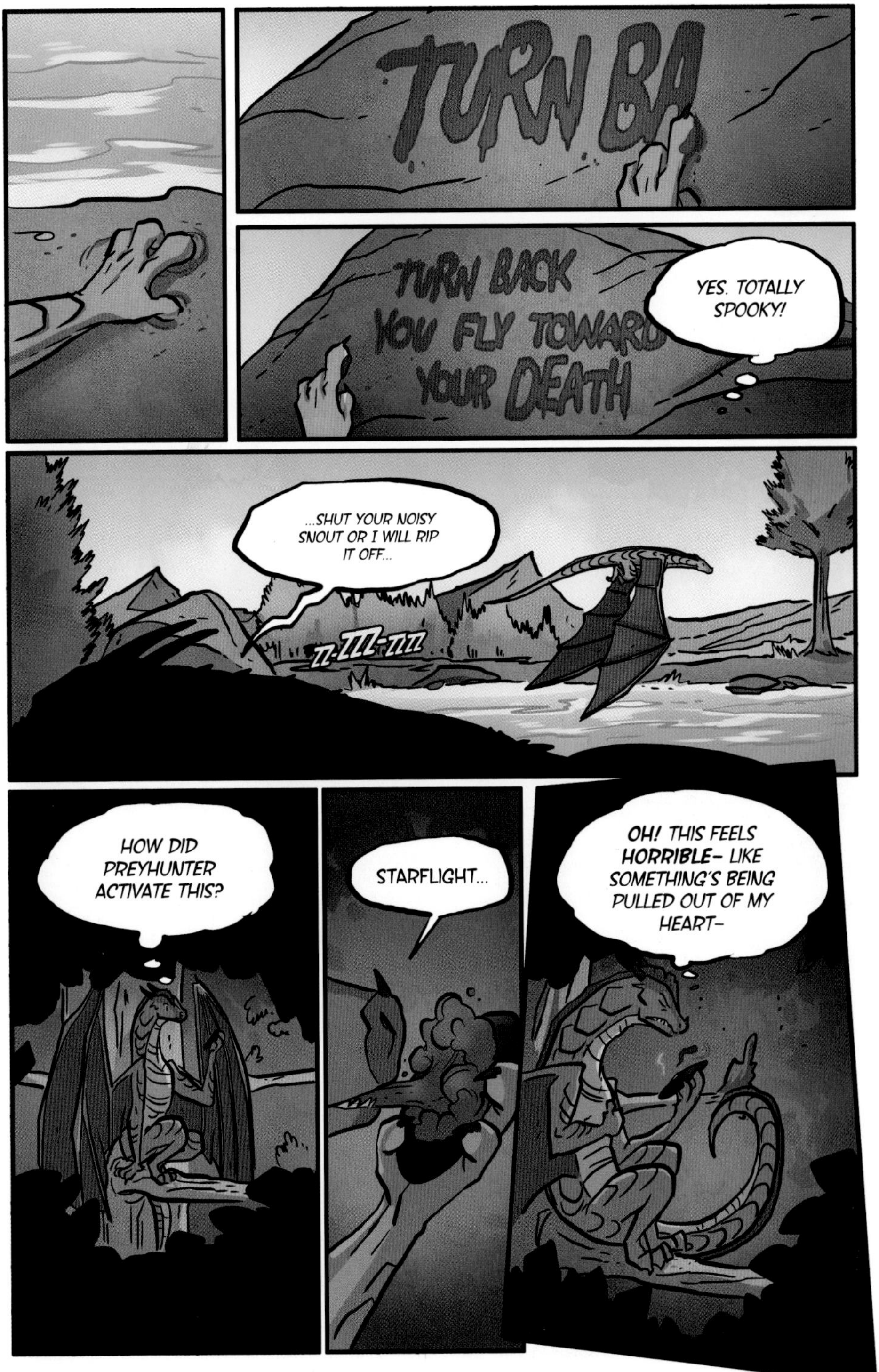
TURN BA
TURN BACK
YOU FLY TOWARD
YOUR DEATH
YES. TOTALLY SPOOKY!
...SHUT YOUR NOISY SNOUT OR I WILL RIP IT OFF...
ZZ-ZZZ-ZZZ
HOW DID PREYHUNTER ACTIVATE THIS?
STARFLIGHT...
OH! THIS FEELS HORRIBLE- LIKE SOMETHING'S BEING PULLED OUT OF MY HEART-

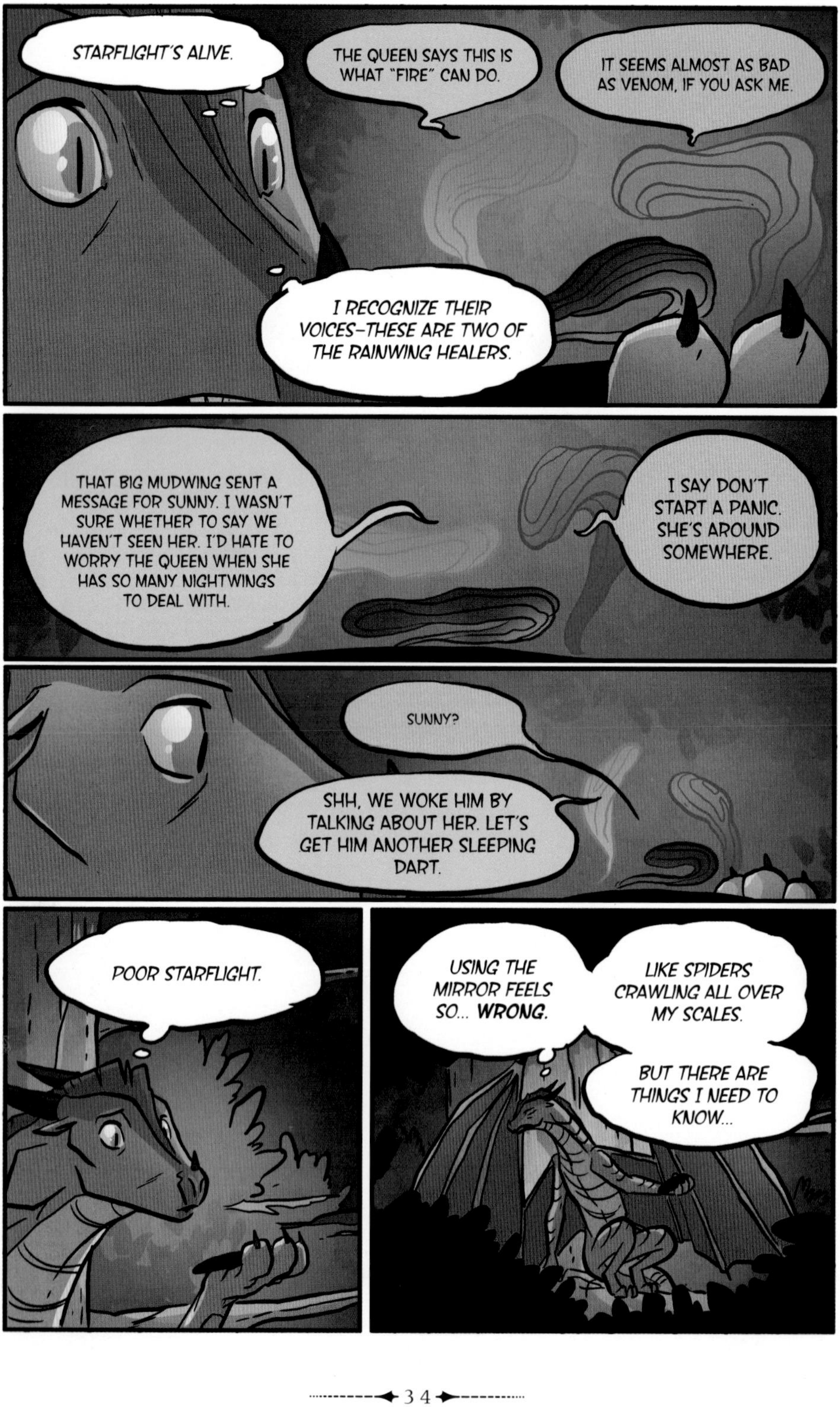
STARFLIGHT'S ALIVE.
THE QUEEN SAYS THIS IS WHAT "FIRE" CAN DO.
IT SEEMS ALMOST AS BAD AS VENOM, IF YOU ASK ME.
I RECOGNIZE THEIR VOICES–THESE ARE TWO OF THE RAINWING HEALERS.
THAT BIG MUDWING SENT A MESSAGE FOR SUNNY. I WASN'T SURE WHETHER TO SAY WE HAVEN'T SEEN HER. I'D HATE TO WORRY THE QUEEN WHEN SHE HAS SO MANY NIGHTWINGS TO DEAL WITH.
I SAY DON'T START A PANIC. SHE'S AROUND SOMEWHERE.
SUNNY?
SHH, WE WOKE HIM BY TALKING ABOUT HER. LET'S GET HIM ANOTHER SLEEPING DART.
POOR STARFLIGHT.
USING THE MIRROR FEELS SO... WRONG.
LIKE SPIDERS CRAWLING ALL OVER MY SCALES.
BUT THERE ARE THINGS I NEED TO KNOW...

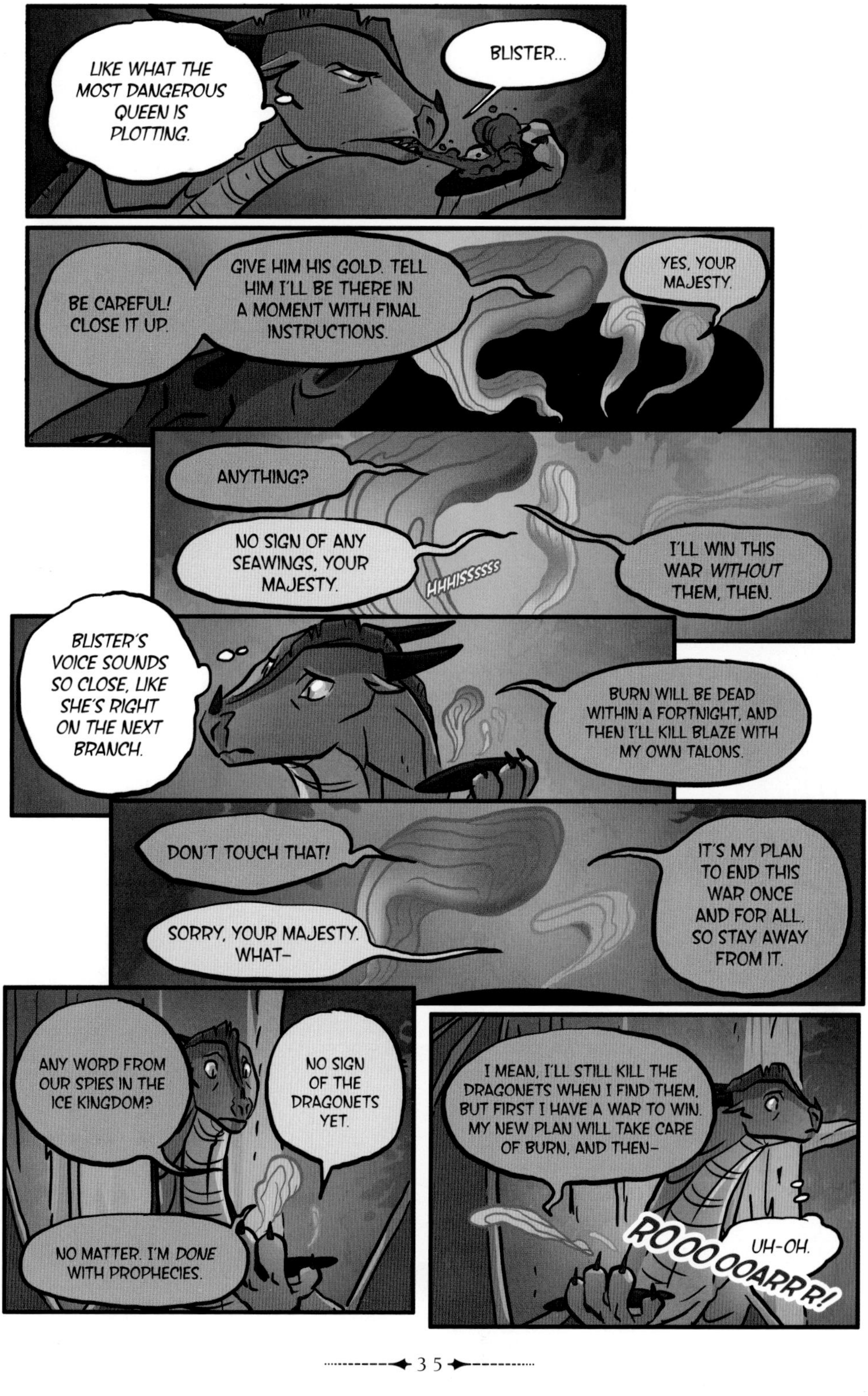
LIKE WHAT THE MOST DANGEROUS QUEEN IS PLOTTING.
BLISTER...
BE CAREFUL! CLOSE IT UP.
GIVE HIM HIS GOLD. TELL HIM I'LL BE THERE IN A MOMENT WITH FINAL INSTRUCTIONS.
YES, YOUR MAJESTY.
ANYTHING?
NO SIGN OF ANY SEAWINGS, YOUR MAJESTY.
HHHISSSSSS
I'LL WIN THIS WAR *WITHOUT* THEM, THEN.
BLISTER'S VOICE SOUNDS SO CLOSE, LIKE SHE'S RIGHT ON THE NEXT BRANCH.
BURN WILL BE DEAD WITHIN A FORTNIGHT, AND THEN I'LL KILL BLAZE WITH MY OWN TALONS.
DON'T TOUCH THAT!
SORRY, YOUR MAJESTY. WHAT–
IT'S MY PLAN TO END THIS WAR ONCE AND FOR ALL. SO STAY AWAY FROM IT.
ANY WORD FROM OUR SPIES IN THE ICE KINGDOM?
NO SIGN OF THE DRAGONETS YET.
NO MATTER. I'M *DONE* WITH PROPHECIES.
I MEAN, I'LL STILL KILL THE DRAGONETS WHEN I FIND THEM, BUT FIRST I HAVE A WAR TO WIN. MY NEW PLAN WILL TAKE CARE OF BURN, AND THEN–
ROOOOOARRRR!
UH-OH.

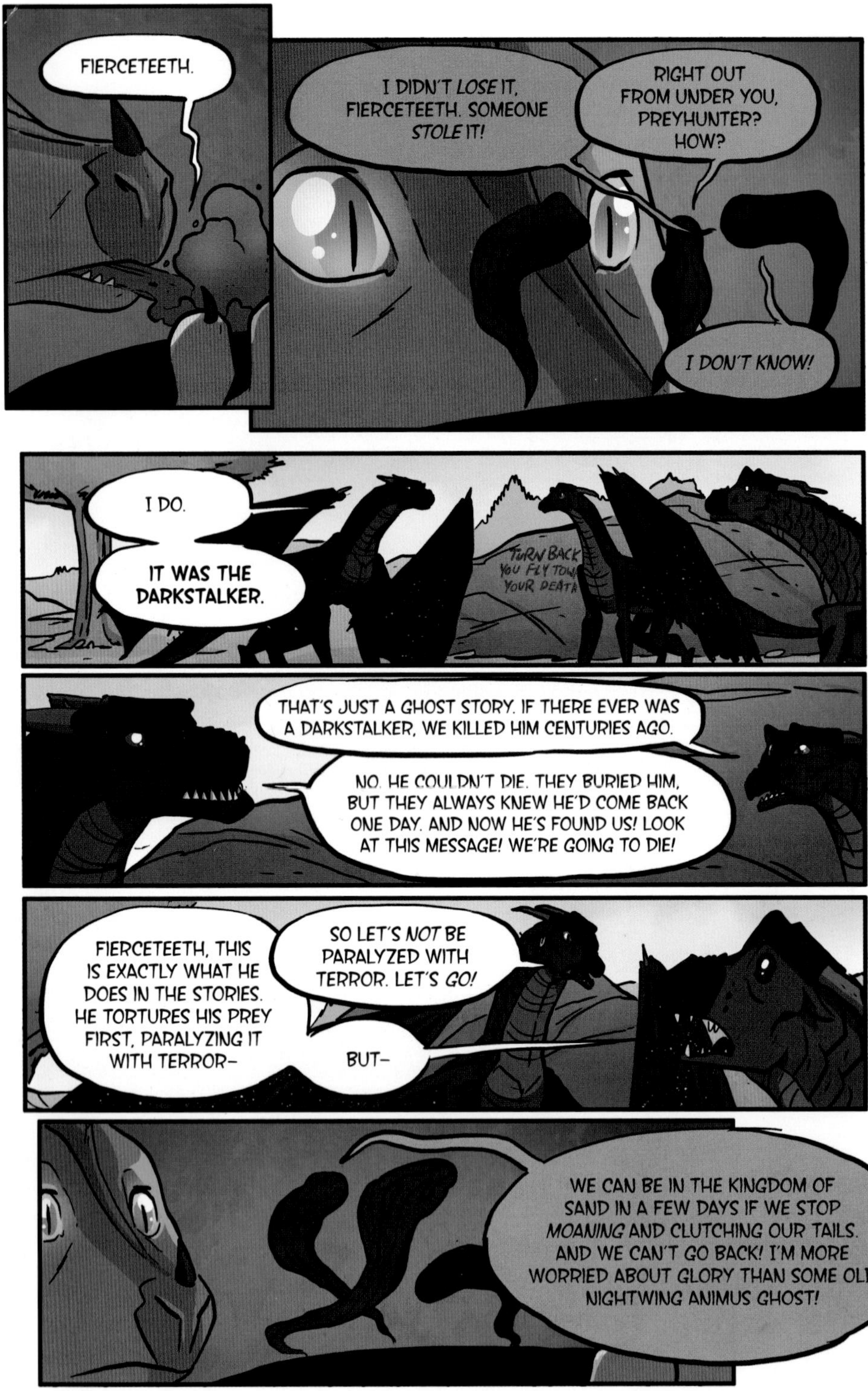
FIERCETEETH.
I DIDN'T *LOSE* IT, FIERCETEETH. SOMEONE *STOLE* IT!
RIGHT OUT FROM UNDER YOU, PREYHUNTER? HOW?
I DON'T KNOW!
I DO.
IT WAS THE DARKSTALKER.
TURN BACK YOU FLY TOW YOUR DEATH
THAT'S JUST A GHOST STORY. IF THERE EVER WAS A DARKSTALKER, WE KILLED HIM CENTURIES AGO.
NO. HE COULDN'T DIE. THEY BURIED HIM, BUT THEY ALWAYS KNEW HE'D COME BACK ONE DAY. AND NOW HE'S FOUND US! LOOK AT THIS MESSAGE! WE'RE GOING TO DIE!
FIERCETEETH, THIS IS EXACTLY WHAT HE DOES IN THE STORIES. HE TORTURES HIS PREY FIRST, PARALYZING IT WITH TERROR–
SO LET'S *NOT* BE PARALYZED WITH TERROR. LET'S *GO!*
BUT–
WE CAN BE IN THE KINGDOM OF SAND IN A FEW DAYS IF WE STOP *MOANING* AND CLUTCHING OUR TAILS. AND WE CAN'T GO BACK! I'M MORE WORRIED ABOUT GLORY THAN SOME OLD NIGHTWING ANIMUS GHOST!

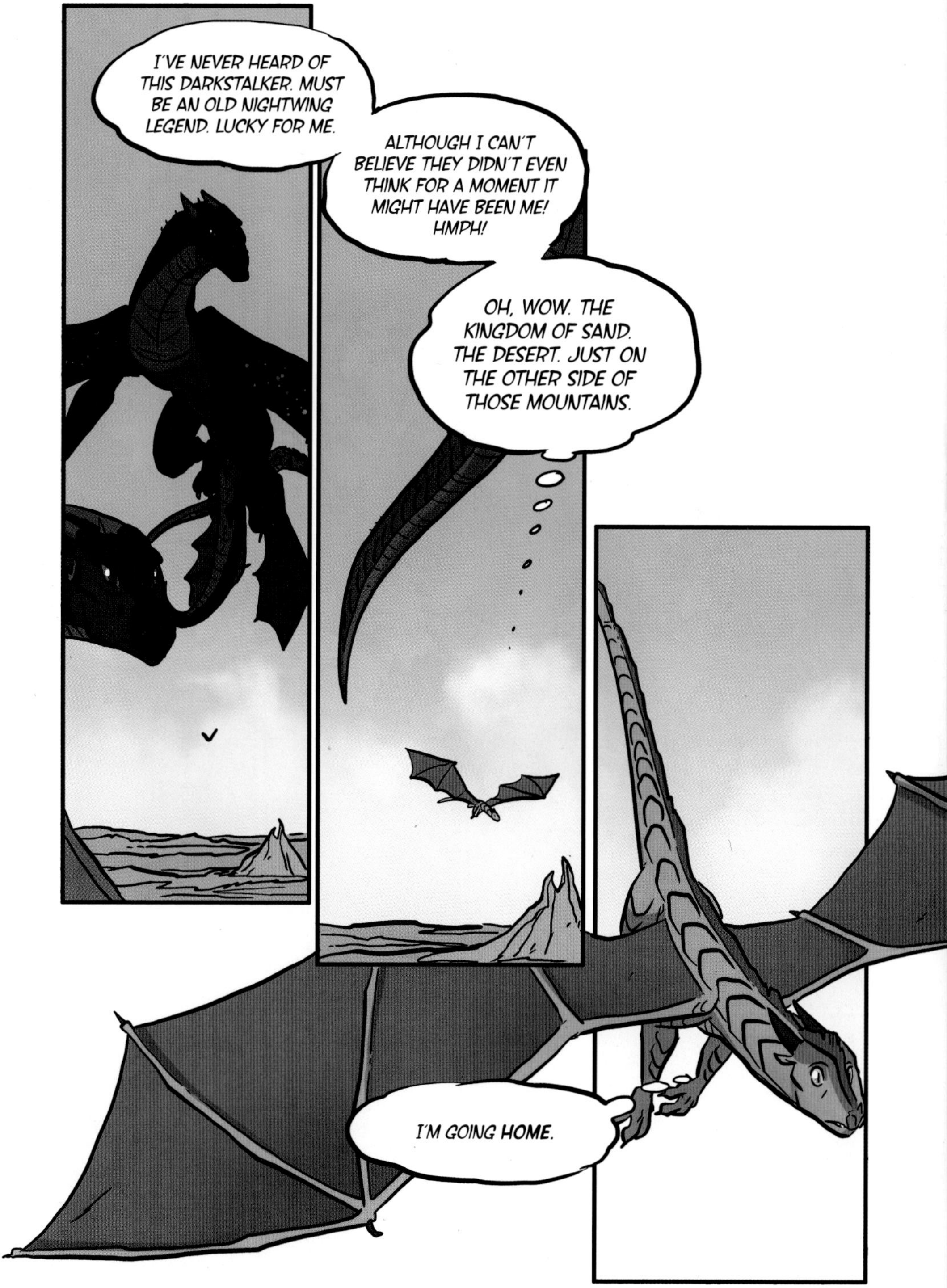
I'VE NEVER HEARD OF THIS DARKSTALKER. MUST BE AN OLD NIGHTWING LEGEND. LUCKY FOR ME.
ALTHOUGH I CAN'T BELIEVE THEY DIDN'T EVEN THINK FOR A MOMENT IT MIGHT HAVE BEEN ME! HMPH!
OH, WOW. THE KINGDOM OF SAND. THE DESERT. JUST ON THE OTHER SIDE OF THOSE MOUNTAINS.
I'M GOING **HOME**.

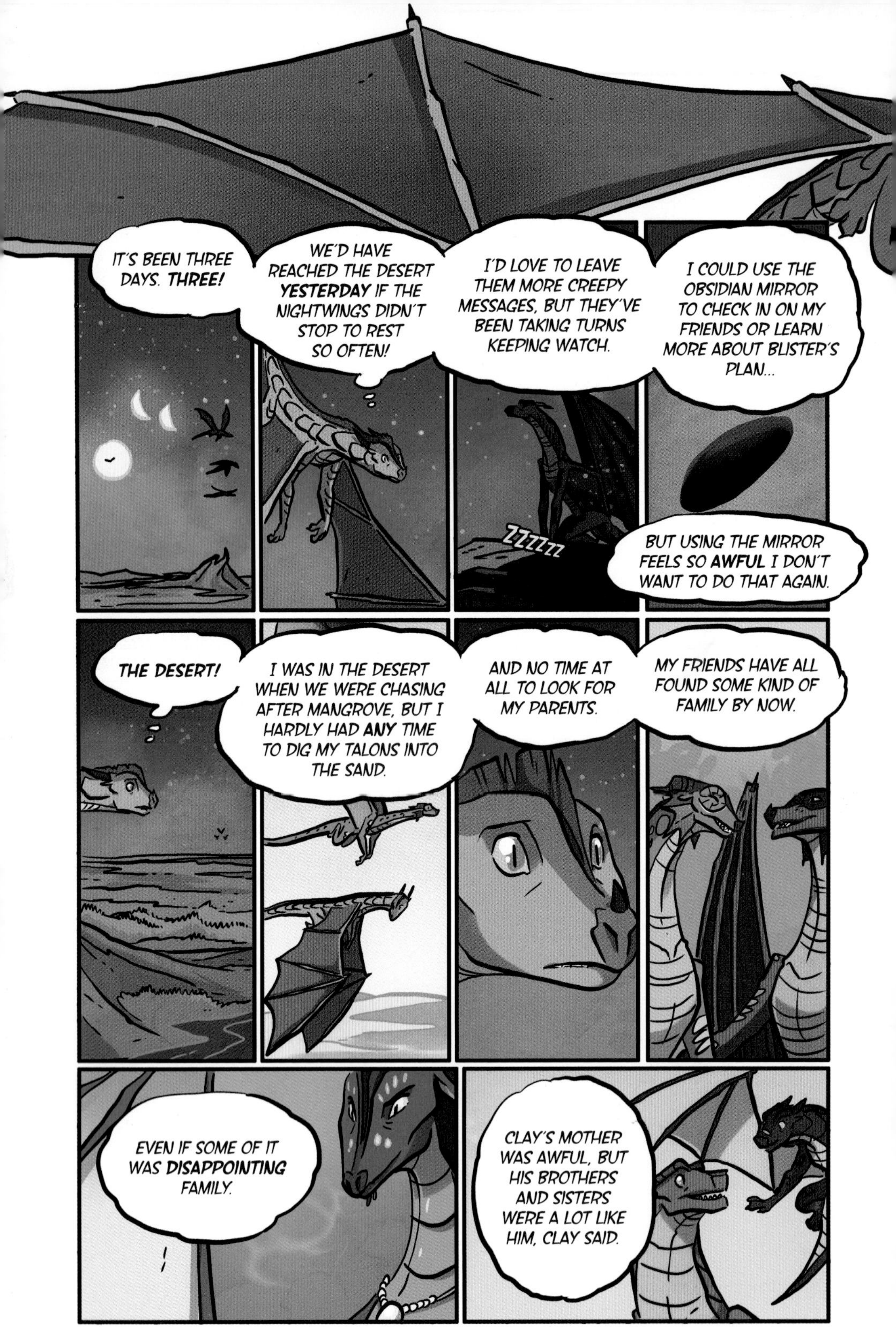
IT'S BEEN THREE DAYS. THREE!
WE'D HAVE REACHED THE DESERT YESTERDAY IF THE NIGHTWINGS DIDN'T STOP TO REST SO OFTEN!
I'D LOVE TO LEAVE THEM MORE CREEPY MESSAGES, BUT THEY'VE BEEN TAKING TURNS KEEPING WATCH.
ZZZZZZ
I COULD USE THE OBSIDIAN MIRROR TO CHECK IN ON MY FRIENDS OR LEARN MORE ABOUT BLISTER'S PLAN...
BUT USING THE MIRROR FEELS SO AWFUL I DON'T WANT TO DO THAT AGAIN.
THE DESERT!
I WAS IN THE DESERT WHEN WE WERE CHASING AFTER MANGROVE, BUT I HARDLY HAD ANY TIME TO DIG MY TALONS INTO THE SAND.
AND NO TIME AT ALL TO LOOK FOR MY PARENTS.
MY FRIENDS HAVE ALL FOUND SOME KIND OF FAMILY BY NOW.
EVEN IF SOME OF IT WAS DISAPPOINTING FAMILY.
CLAY'S MOTHER WAS AWFUL, BUT HIS BROTHERS AND SISTERS WERE A LOT LIKE HIM, CLAY SAID.

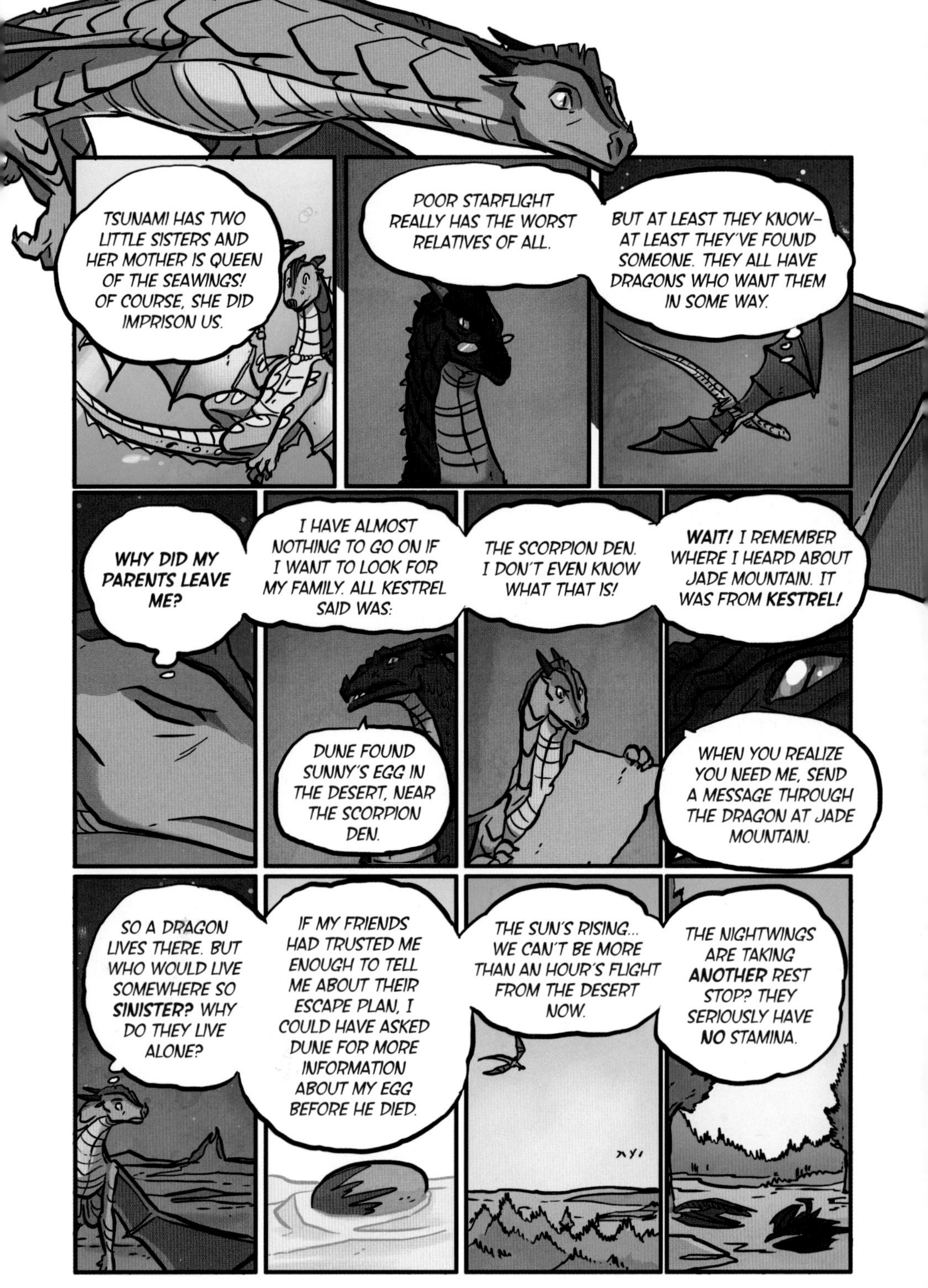

TSUNAMI HAS TWO LITTLE SISTERS AND HER MOTHER IS QUEEN OF THE SEAWINGS! OF COURSE, SHE DID IMPRISON US.
POOR STARFLIGHT REALLY HAS THE WORST RELATIVES OF ALL.
BUT AT LEAST THEY KNOW— AT LEAST THEY'VE FOUND SOMEONE. THEY ALL HAVE DRAGONS WHO WANT THEM IN SOME WAY.
WHY DID MY PARENTS LEAVE ME?
I HAVE ALMOST NOTHING TO GO ON IF I WANT TO LOOK FOR MY FAMILY. ALL KESTREL SAID WAS:
DUNE FOUND SUNNY'S EGG IN THE DESERT, NEAR THE SCORPION DEN.
THE SCORPION DEN. I DON'T EVEN KNOW WHAT THAT IS!
WAIT! I REMEMBER WHERE I HEARD ABOUT JADE MOUNTAIN. IT WAS FROM **KESTREL!**
WHEN YOU REALIZE YOU NEED ME, SEND A MESSAGE THROUGH THE DRAGON AT JADE MOUNTAIN.
SO A DRAGON LIVES THERE. BUT WHO WOULD LIVE SOMEWHERE SO **SINISTER?** WHY DO THEY LIVE ALONE?
IF MY FRIENDS HAD TRUSTED ME ENOUGH TO TELL ME ABOUT THEIR ESCAPE PLAN, I COULD HAVE ASKED DUNE FOR MORE INFORMATION ABOUT MY EGG BEFORE HE DIED.
THE SUN'S RISING... WE CAN'T BE MORE THAN AN HOUR'S FLIGHT FROM THE DESERT NOW.
THE NIGHTWINGS ARE TAKING **ANOTHER** REST STOP? THEY SERIOUSLY HAVE **NO** STAMINA.

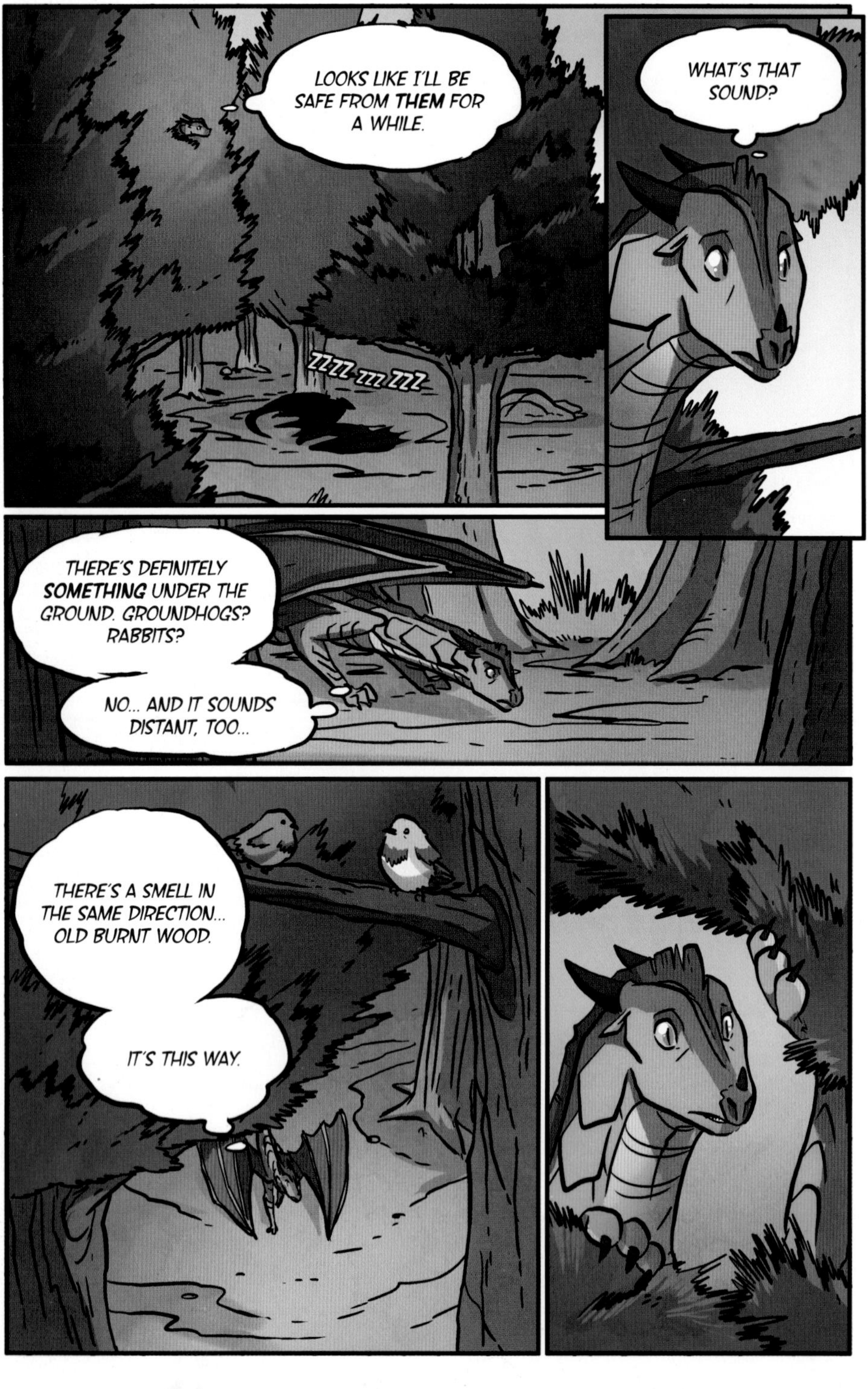
LOOKS LIKE I'LL BE SAFE FROM **THEM** FOR A WHILE.
ZZZZ ZZZ ZZZ
WHAT'S THAT SOUND?
THERE'S DEFINITELY **SOMETHING** UNDER THE GROUND. GROUNDHOGS? RABBITS?
NO... AND IT SOUNDS DISTANT, TOO...
THERE'S A SMELL IN THE SAME DIRECTION... OLD BURNT WOOD.
IT'S THIS WAY.

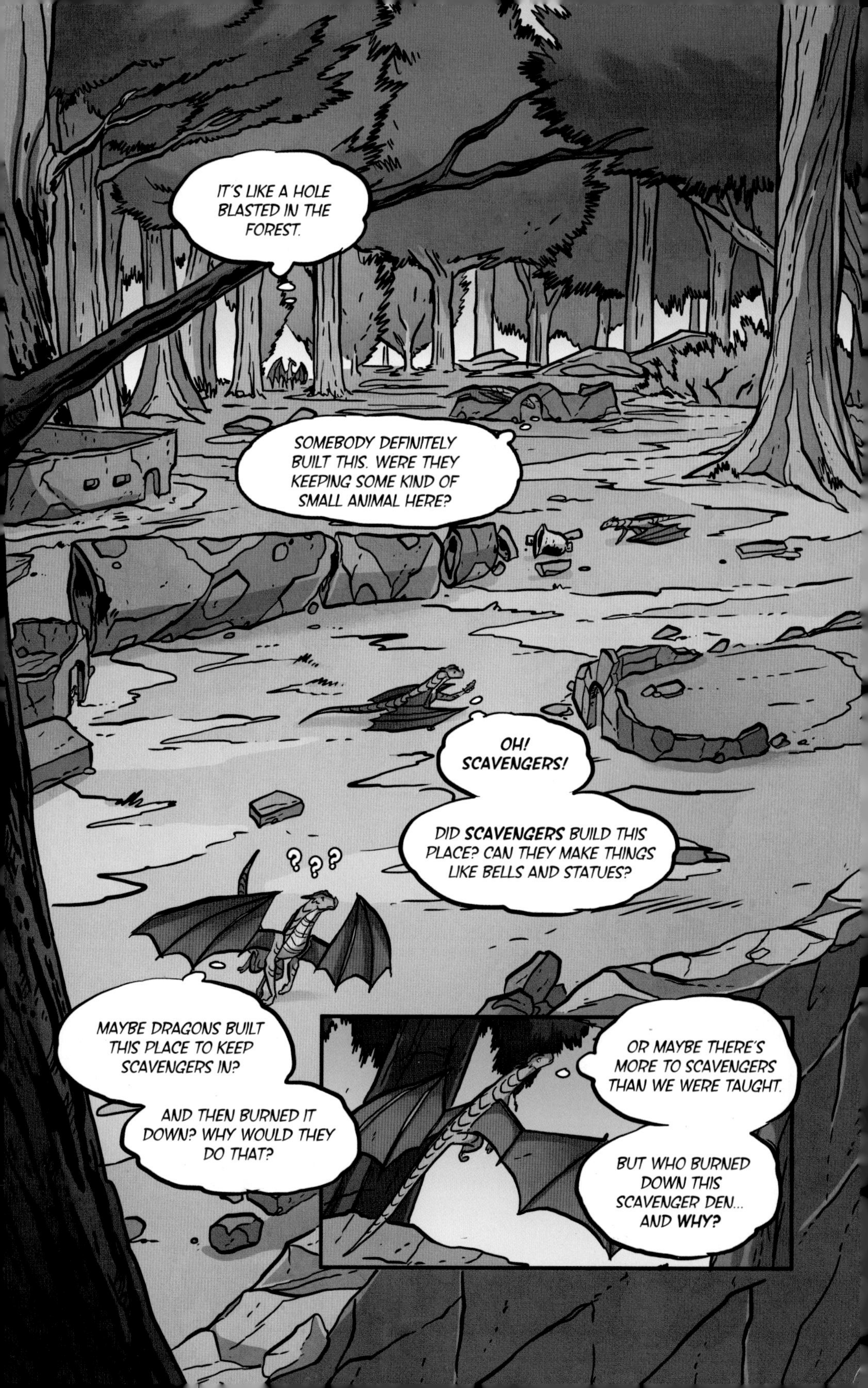

IT'S LIKE A HOLE BLASTED IN THE FOREST.
SOMEBODY DEFINITELY BUILT THIS. WERE THEY KEEPING SOME KIND OF SMALL ANIMAL HERE?
OH! SCAVENGERS!
DID **SCAVENGERS** BUILD THIS PLACE? CAN THEY MAKE THINGS LIKE BELLS AND STATUES?
???
MAYBE DRAGONS BUILT THIS PLACE TO KEEP SCAVENGERS IN?
AND THEN BURNED IT DOWN? WHY WOULD THEY DO THAT?
OR MAYBE THERE'S MORE TO SCAVENGERS THAN WE WERE TAUGHT.
BUT WHO BURNED DOWN THIS SCAVENGER DEN... AND **WHY?**

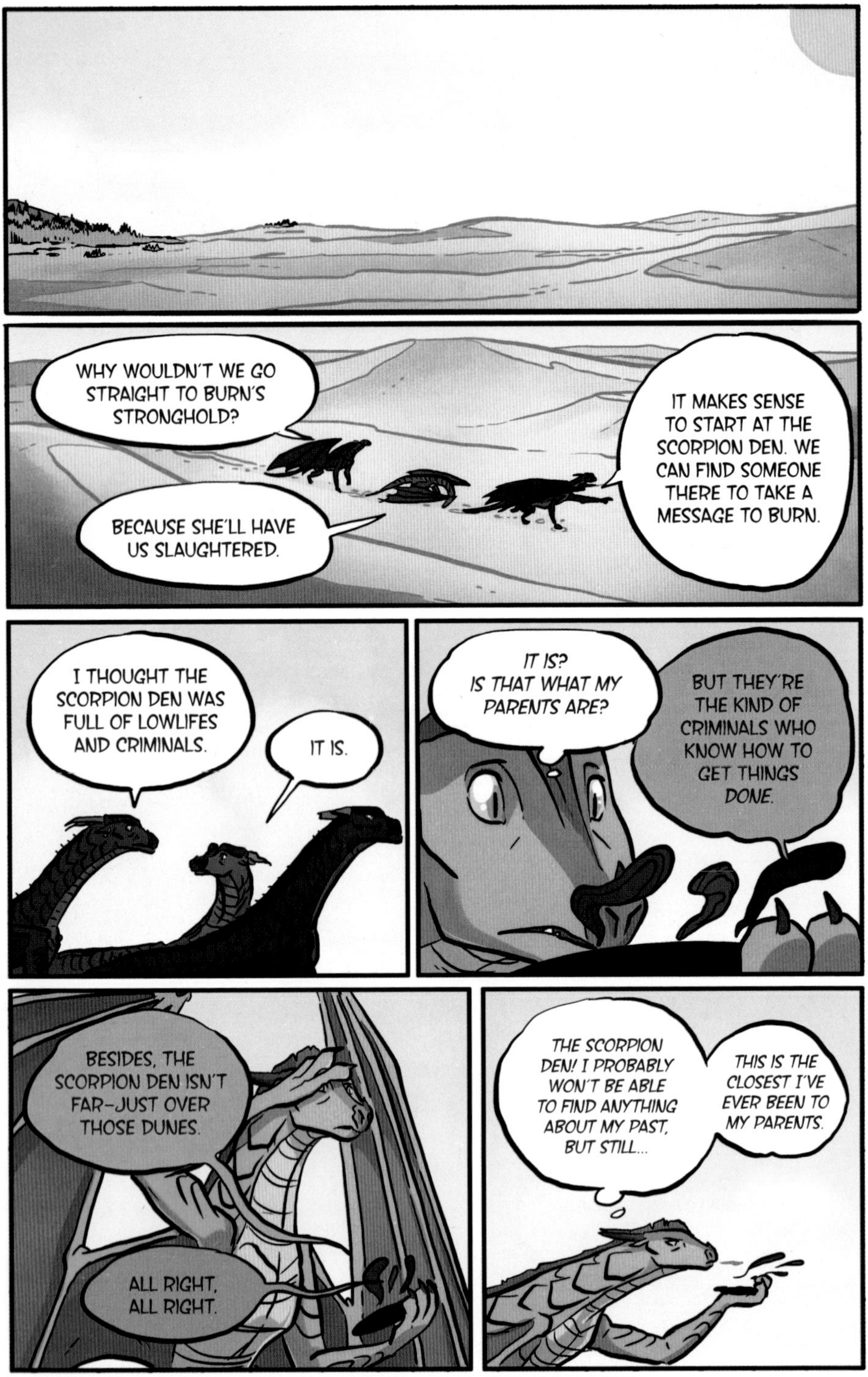
WHY WOULDN'T WE GO STRAIGHT TO BURN'S STRONGHOLD?
BECAUSE SHE'LL HAVE US SLAUGHTERED.
IT MAKES SENSE TO START AT THE SCORPION DEN. WE CAN FIND SOMEONE THERE TO TAKE A MESSAGE TO BURN.
I THOUGHT THE SCORPION DEN WAS FULL OF LOWLIFES AND CRIMINALS.
IT IS.
IT IS? IS THAT WHAT MY PARENTS ARE?
BUT THEY'RE THE KIND OF CRIMINALS WHO KNOW HOW TO GET THINGS DONE.
BESIDES, THE SCORPION DEN ISN'T FAR—JUST OVER THOSE DUNES.
ALL RIGHT, ALL RIGHT.
THE SCORPION DEN! I PROBABLY WON'T BE ABLE TO FIND ANYTHING ABOUT MY PAST, BUT STILL...
THIS IS THE CLOSEST I'VE EVER BEEN TO MY PARENTS.

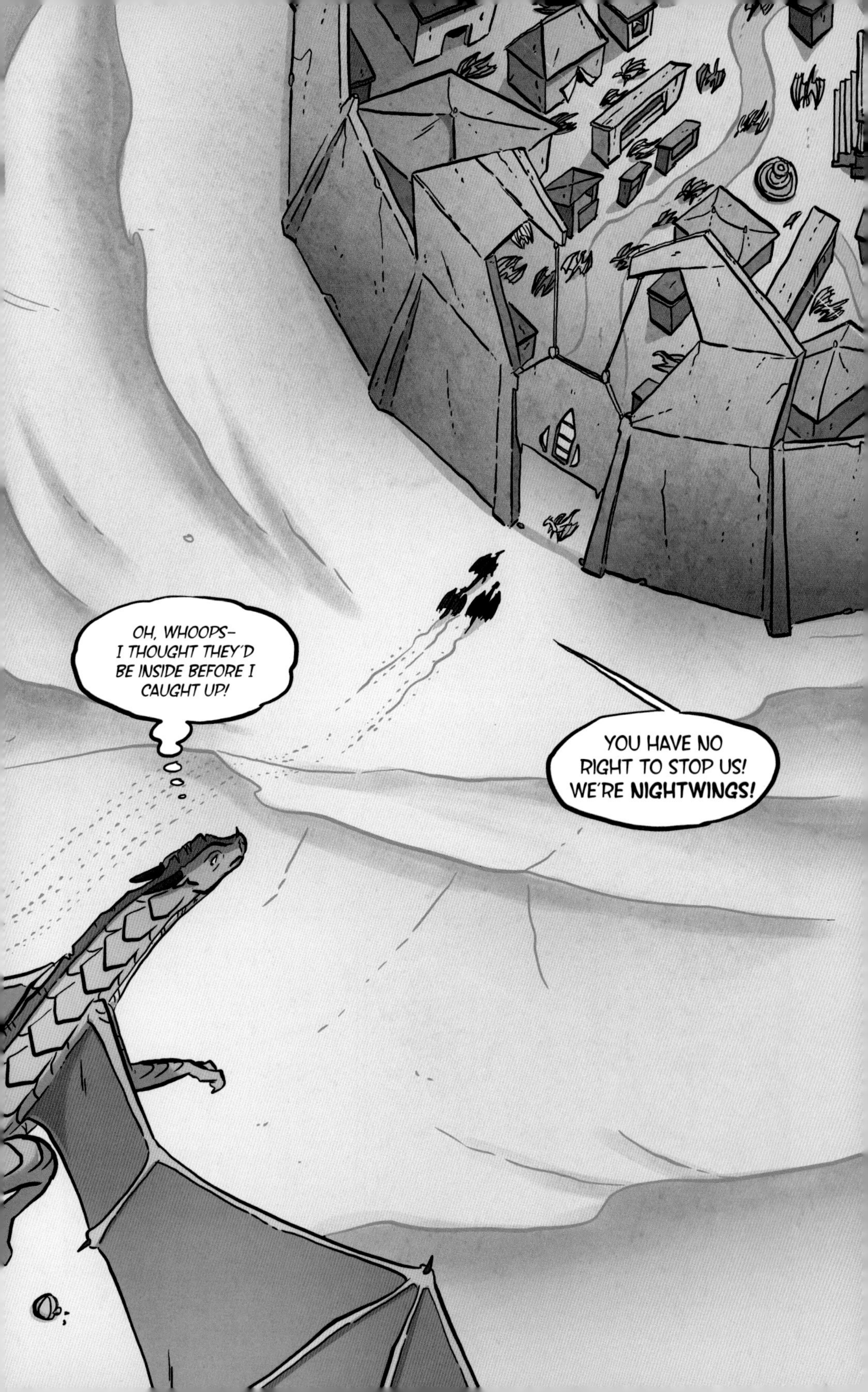
OH, WHOOPS–
I THOUGHT THEY'D
BE INSIDE BEFORE I
CAUGHT UP!
YOU HAVE NO
RIGHT TO STOP US!
WE'RE **NIGHTWINGS!**

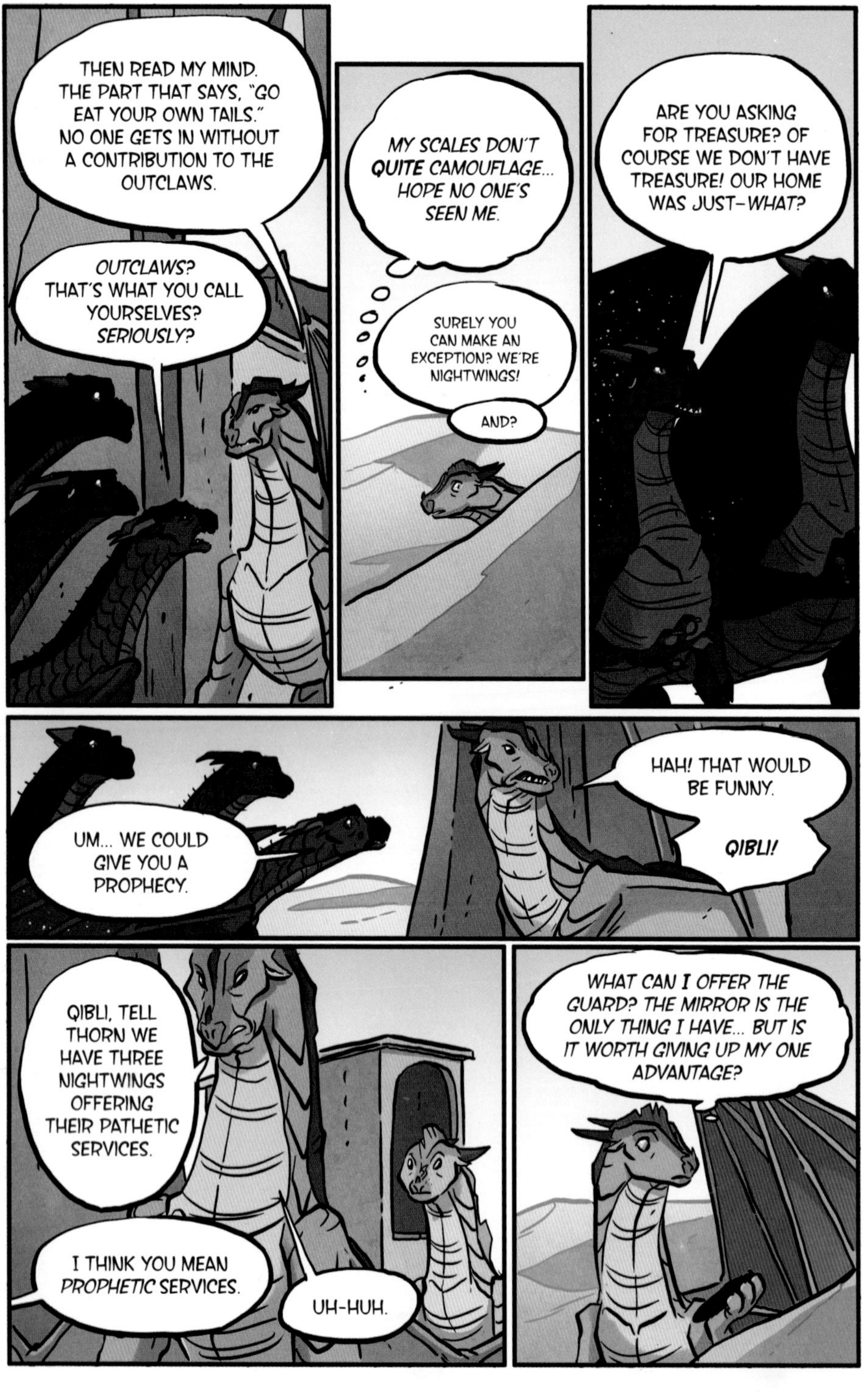
THEN READ MY MIND. THE PART THAT SAYS, "GO EAT YOUR OWN TAILS." NO ONE GETS IN WITHOUT A CONTRIBUTION TO THE OUTCLAWS.
OUTCLAWS? THAT'S WHAT YOU CALL YOURSELVES? *SERIOUSLY?*
MY SCALES DON'T ***QUITE*** *CAMOUFLAGE... HOPE NO ONE'S SEEN ME.*
SURELY YOU CAN MAKE AN EXCEPTION? WE'RE NIGHTWINGS!
AND?
ARE YOU ASKING FOR TREASURE? OF COURSE WE DON'T HAVE TREASURE! OUR HOME WAS JUST—*WHAT?*
UM... WE COULD GIVE YOU A PROPHECY.
HAH! THAT WOULD BE FUNNY.
QIBLI!
QIBLI, TELL THORN WE HAVE THREE NIGHTWINGS OFFERING THEIR PATHETIC SERVICES.
I THINK YOU MEAN *PROPHETIC* SERVICES.
UH-HUH.
WHAT CAN ***I*** *OFFER THE GUARD? THE MIRROR IS THE ONLY THING I HAVE... BUT IS IT WORTH GIVING UP MY ONE ADVANTAGE?*

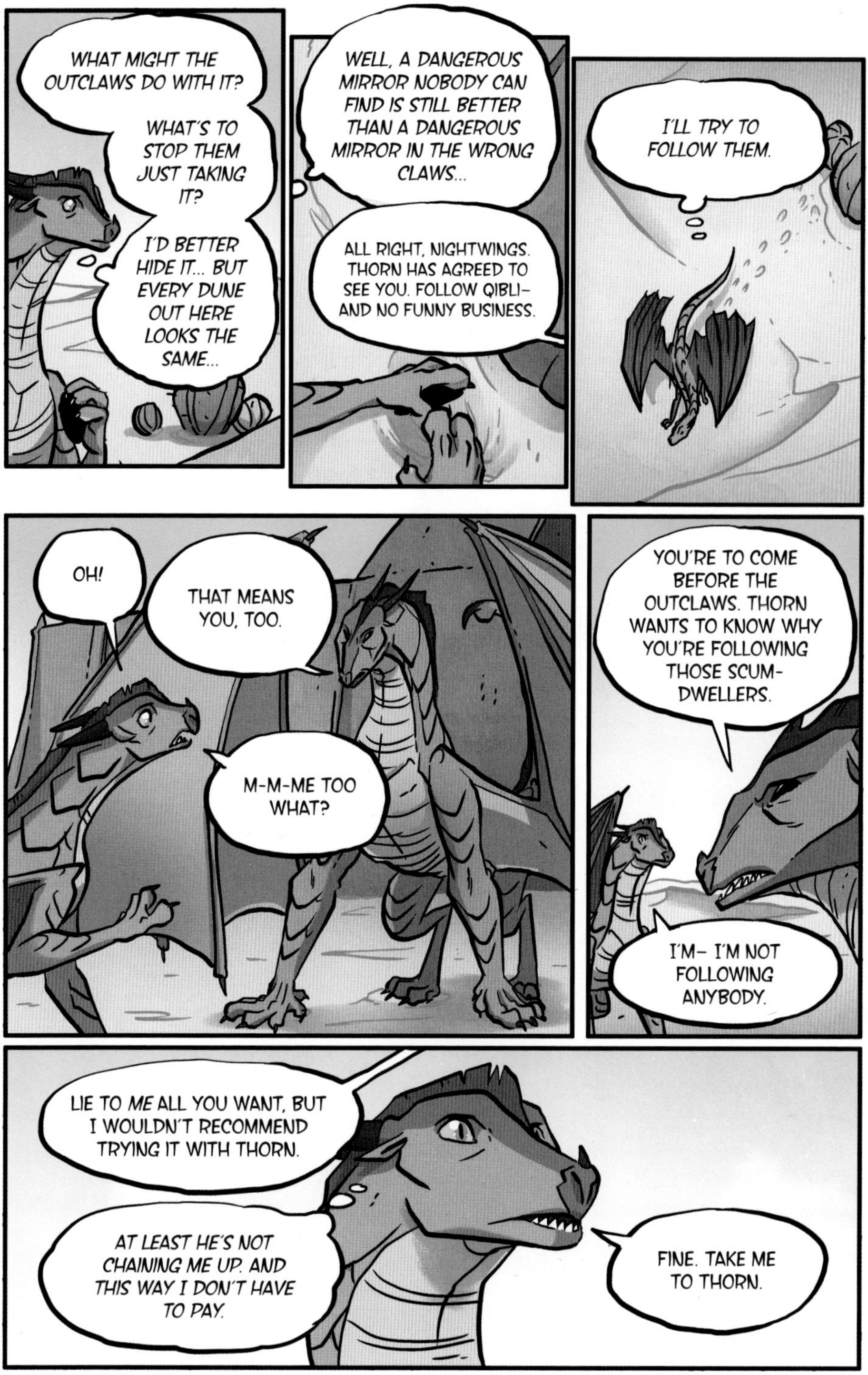
WHAT MIGHT THE OUTCLAWS DO WITH IT?
WHAT'S TO STOP THEM JUST TAKING IT?
I'D BETTER HIDE IT... BUT EVERY DUNE OUT HERE LOOKS THE SAME...
WELL, A DANGEROUS MIRROR NOBODY CAN FIND IS STILL BETTER THAN A DANGEROUS MIRROR IN THE WRONG CLAWS...
ALL RIGHT, NIGHTWINGS. THORN HAS AGREED TO SEE YOU. FOLLOW QIBLI– AND NO FUNNY BUSINESS.
I'LL TRY TO FOLLOW THEM.
OH!
THAT MEANS YOU, TOO.
M-M-ME TOO WHAT?
YOU'RE TO COME BEFORE THE OUTCLAWS. THORN WANTS TO KNOW WHY YOU'RE FOLLOWING THOSE SCUM-DWELLERS.
I'M– I'M NOT FOLLOWING ANYBODY.
LIE TO *ME* ALL YOU WANT, BUT I WOULDN'T RECOMMEND TRYING IT WITH THORN.
AT LEAST HE'S NOT CHAINING ME UP. AND THIS WAY I DON'T HAVE TO PAY.
FINE. TAKE ME TO THORN.

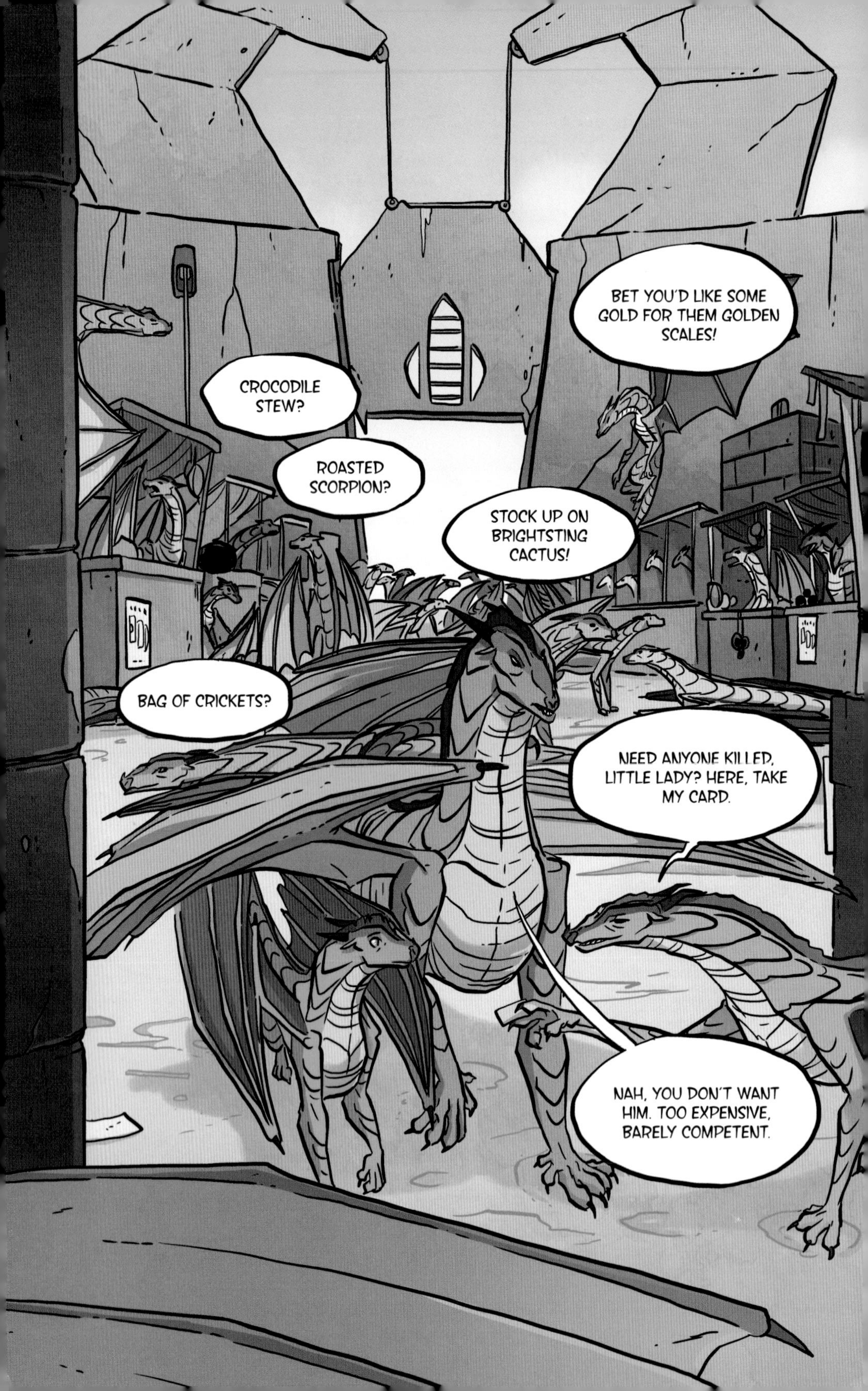
CROCODILE STEW?
ROASTED SCORPION?
BET YOU'D LIKE SOME GOLD FOR THEM GOLDEN SCALES!
STOCK UP ON BRIGHTSTING CACTUS!
BAG OF CRICKETS?
NEED ANYONE KILLED, LITTLE LADY? HERE, TAKE MY CARD.
NAH, YOU DON'T WANT HIM. TOO EXPENSIVE, BARELY COMPETENT.

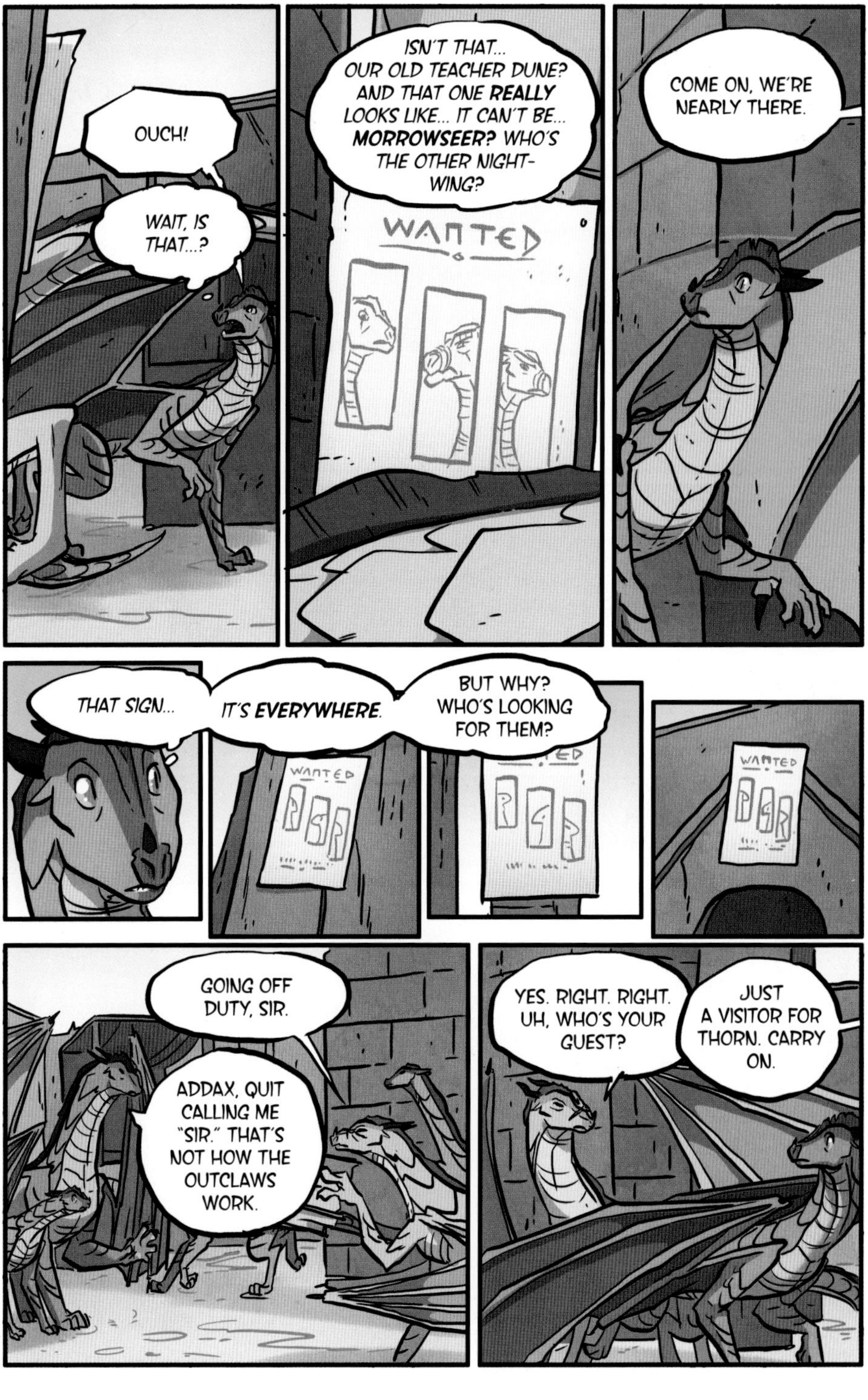

OUCH!
WAIT, IS THAT...?
ISN'T THAT... OUR OLD TEACHER DUNE? AND THAT ONE **REALLY** LOOKS LIKE... IT CAN'T BE... **MORROWSEER?** WHO'S THE OTHER NIGHT-WING?
WANTED
COME ON, WE'RE NEARLY THERE.
THAT SIGN...
IT'S **EVERYWHERE**.
BUT WHY? WHO'S LOOKING FOR THEM?
WANTED
WANTED
WANTED
GOING OFF DUTY, SIR.
ADDAX, QUIT CALLING ME "SIR." THAT'S NOT HOW THE OUTCLAWS WORK.
YES. RIGHT. RIGHT. UH, WHO'S YOUR GUEST?
JUST A VISITOR FOR THORN. CARRY ON.

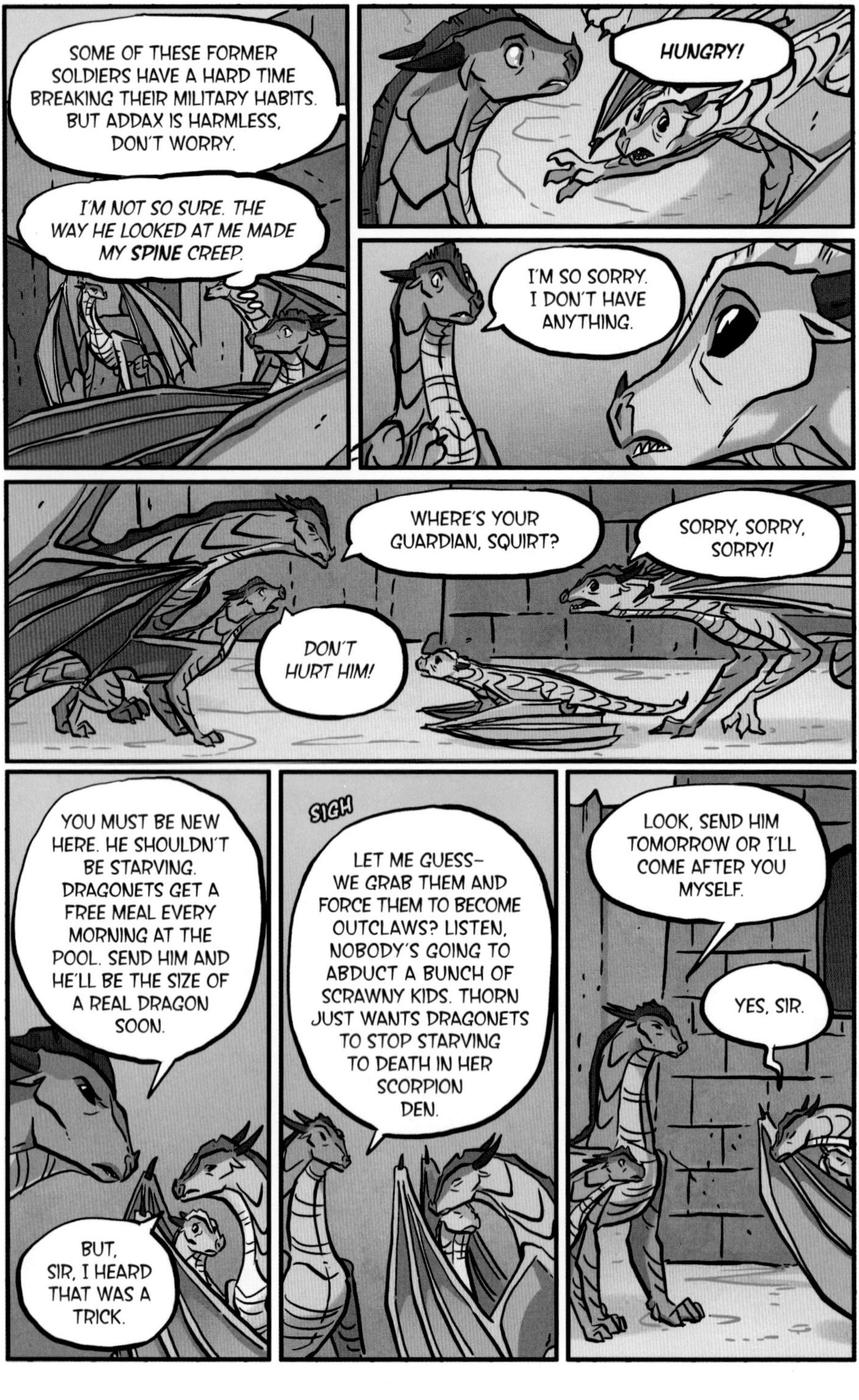
SOME OF THESE FORMER SOLDIERS HAVE A HARD TIME BREAKING THEIR MILITARY HABITS. BUT ADDAX IS HARMLESS, DON'T WORRY.
I'M NOT SO SURE. THE WAY HE LOOKED AT ME MADE MY SPINE CREEP.
HUNGRY!
I'M SO SORRY. I DON'T HAVE ANYTHING.
WHERE'S YOUR GUARDIAN, SQUIRT?
SORRY, SORRY, SORRY!
DON'T HURT HIM!
YOU MUST BE NEW HERE. HE SHOULDN'T BE STARVING. DRAGONETS GET A FREE MEAL EVERY MORNING AT THE POOL. SEND HIM AND HE'LL BE THE SIZE OF A REAL DRAGON SOON.
BUT, SIR, I HEARD THAT WAS A TRICK.
SIGH
LET ME GUESS— WE GRAB THEM AND FORCE THEM TO BECOME OUTCLAWS? LISTEN, NOBODY'S GOING TO ABDUCT A BUNCH OF SCRAWNY KIDS. THORN JUST WANTS DRAGONETS TO STOP STARVING TO DEATH IN HER SCORPION DEN.
LOOK, SEND HIM TOMORROW OR I'LL COME AFTER YOU MYSELF.
YES, SIR.

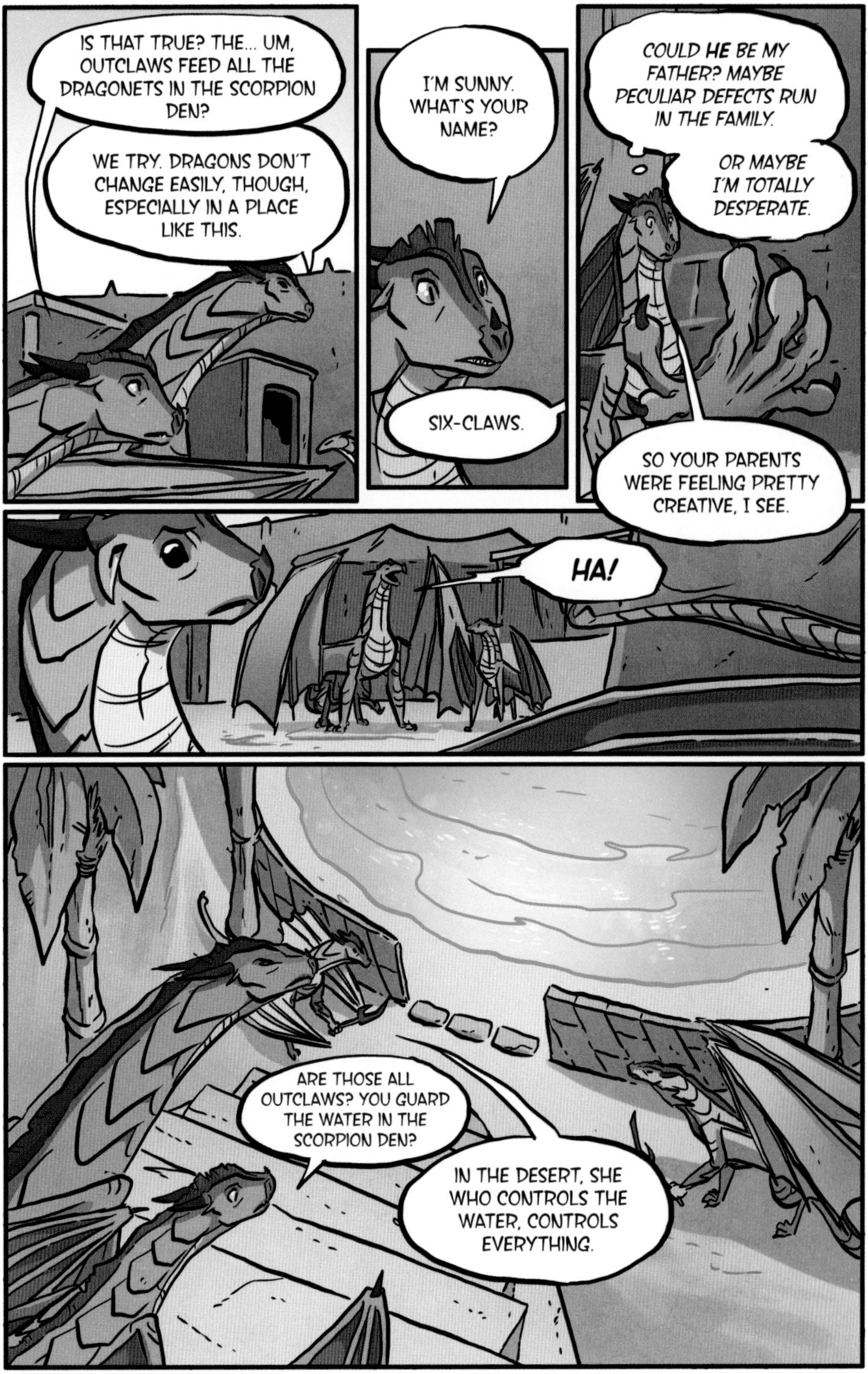
IS THAT TRUE? THE... UM, OUTCLAWS FEED ALL THE DRAGONETS IN THE SCORPION DEN?
WE TRY. DRAGONS DON'T CHANGE EASILY, THOUGH, ESPECIALLY IN A PLACE LIKE THIS.
I'M SUNNY. WHAT'S YOUR NAME?
SIX-CLAWS.
COULD **HE** BE MY FATHER? MAYBE PECULIAR DEFECTS RUN IN THE FAMILY.
OR MAYBE I'M TOTALLY DESPERATE.
SO YOUR PARENTS WERE FEELING PRETTY CREATIVE, I SEE.
HA!
ARE THOSE ALL OUTCLAWS? YOU GUARD THE WATER IN THE SCORPION DEN?
IN THE DESERT, SHE WHO CONTROLS THE WATER, CONTROLS EVERYTHING.

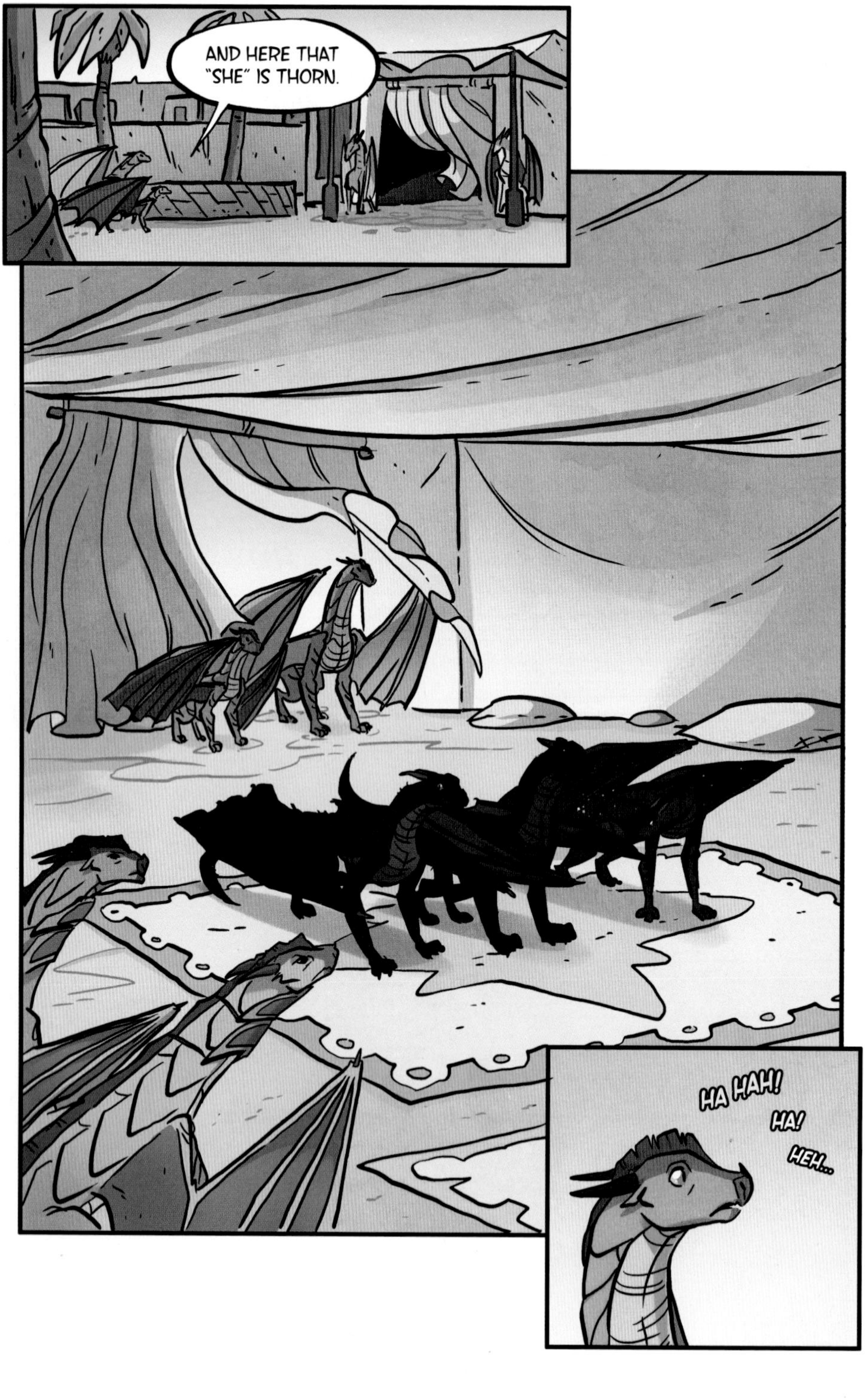
AND HERE THAT "SHE" IS THORN.
HA HAH!
HA!
HEH...

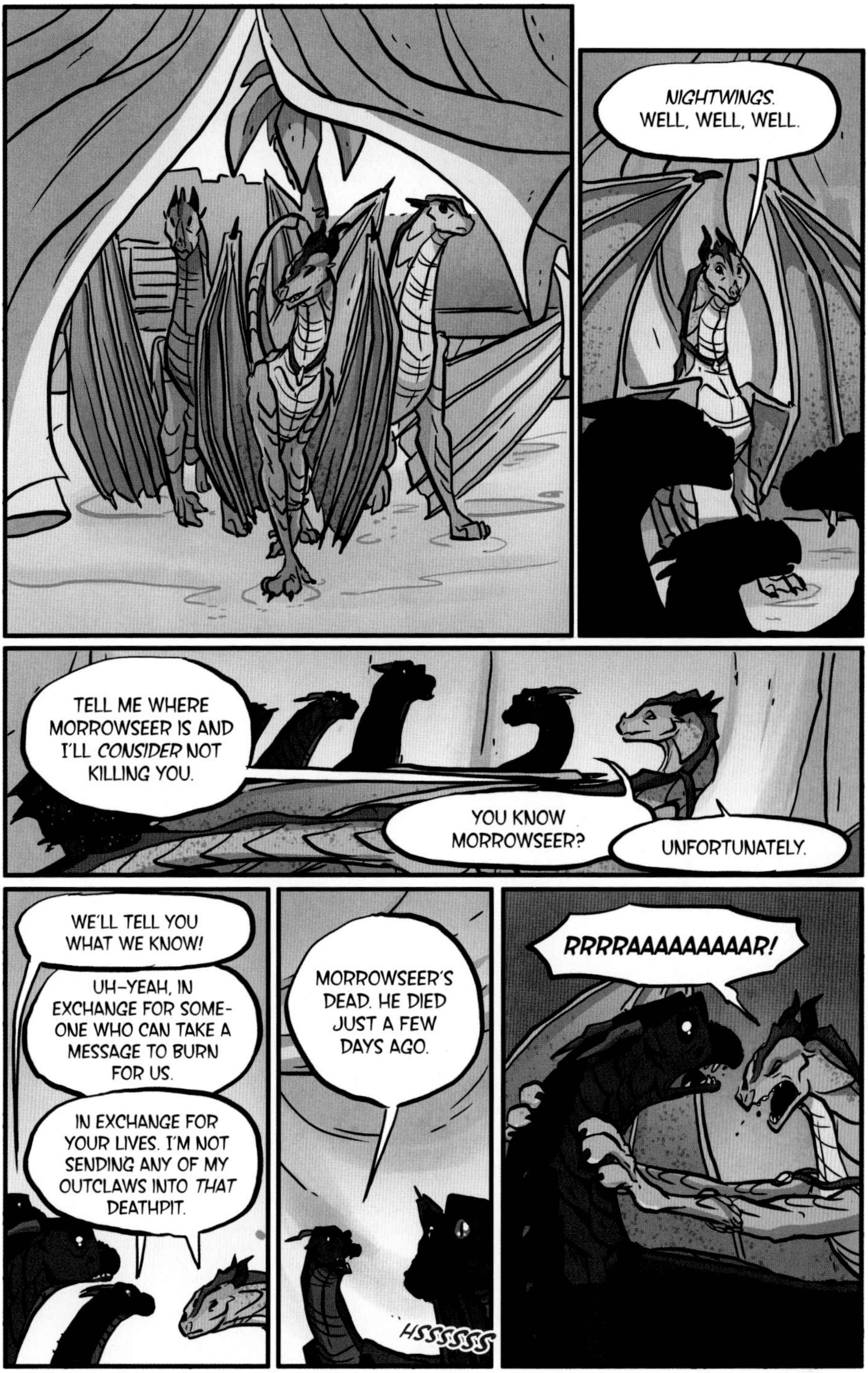
NIGHTWINGS. WELL, WELL, WELL.
TELL ME WHERE MORROWSEER IS AND I'LL CONSIDER NOT KILLING YOU.
YOU KNOW MORROWSEER?
UNFORTUNATELY.
WE'LL TELL YOU WHAT WE KNOW!
UH-YEAH, IN EXCHANGE FOR SOME-ONE WHO CAN TAKE A MESSAGE TO BURN FOR US.
IN EXCHANGE FOR YOUR LIVES. I'M NOT SENDING ANY OF MY OUTCLAWS INTO THAT DEATHPIT.
MORROWSEER'S DEAD. HE DIED JUST A FEW DAYS AGO.
HSSSSSS
RRRRAAAAAAAAAAR!

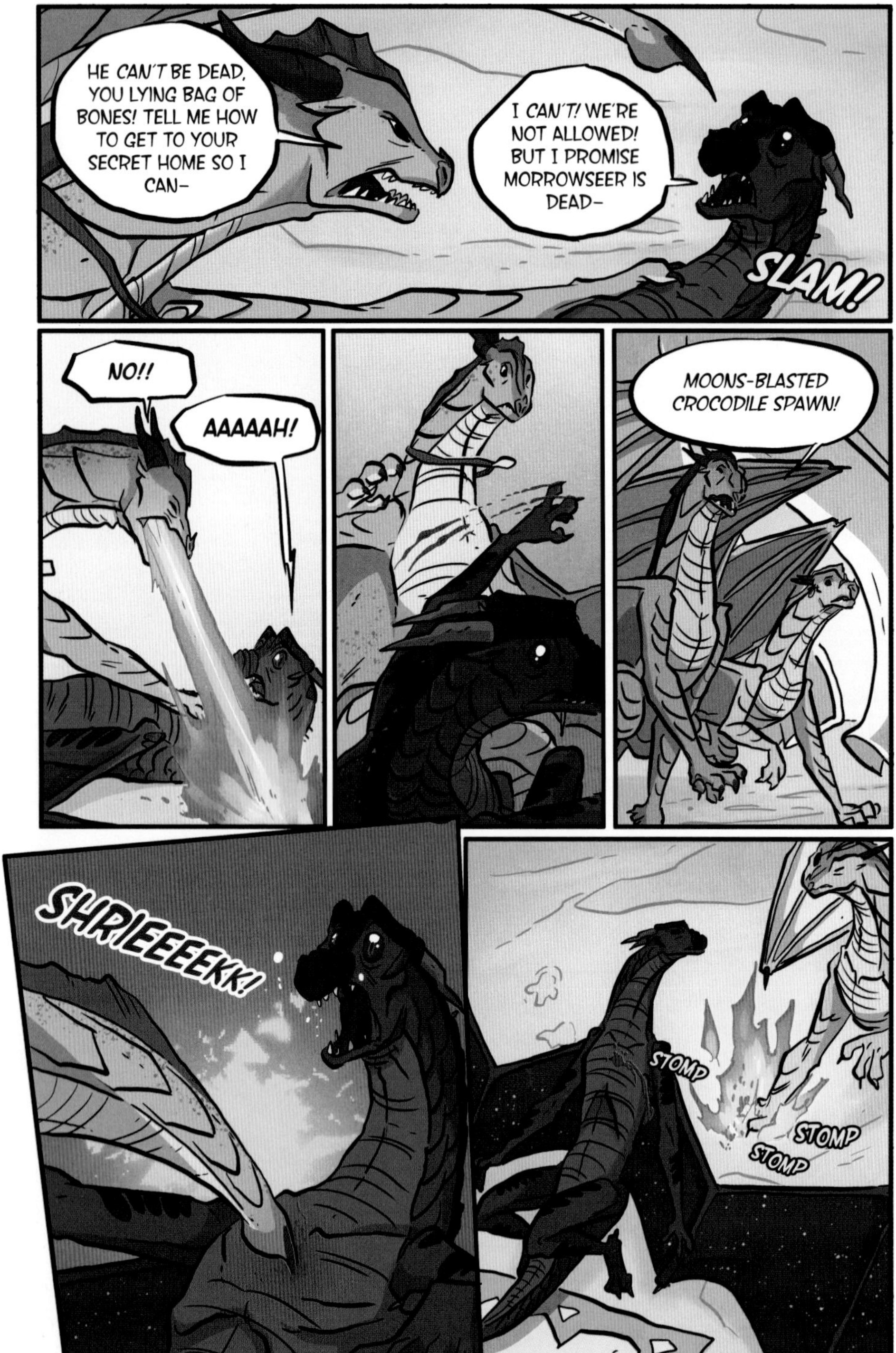
HE CAN'T BE DEAD, YOU LYING BAG OF BONES! TELL ME HOW TO GET TO YOUR SECRET HOME SO I CAN–
I CAN'T! WE'RE NOT ALLOWED! BUT I PROMISE MORROWSEER IS DEAD–
SLAM!
NO!!
AAAAAH!
MOONS-BLASTED CROCODILE SPAWN!
SHRIEEEEEKK!
STOMP
STOMP
STOMP

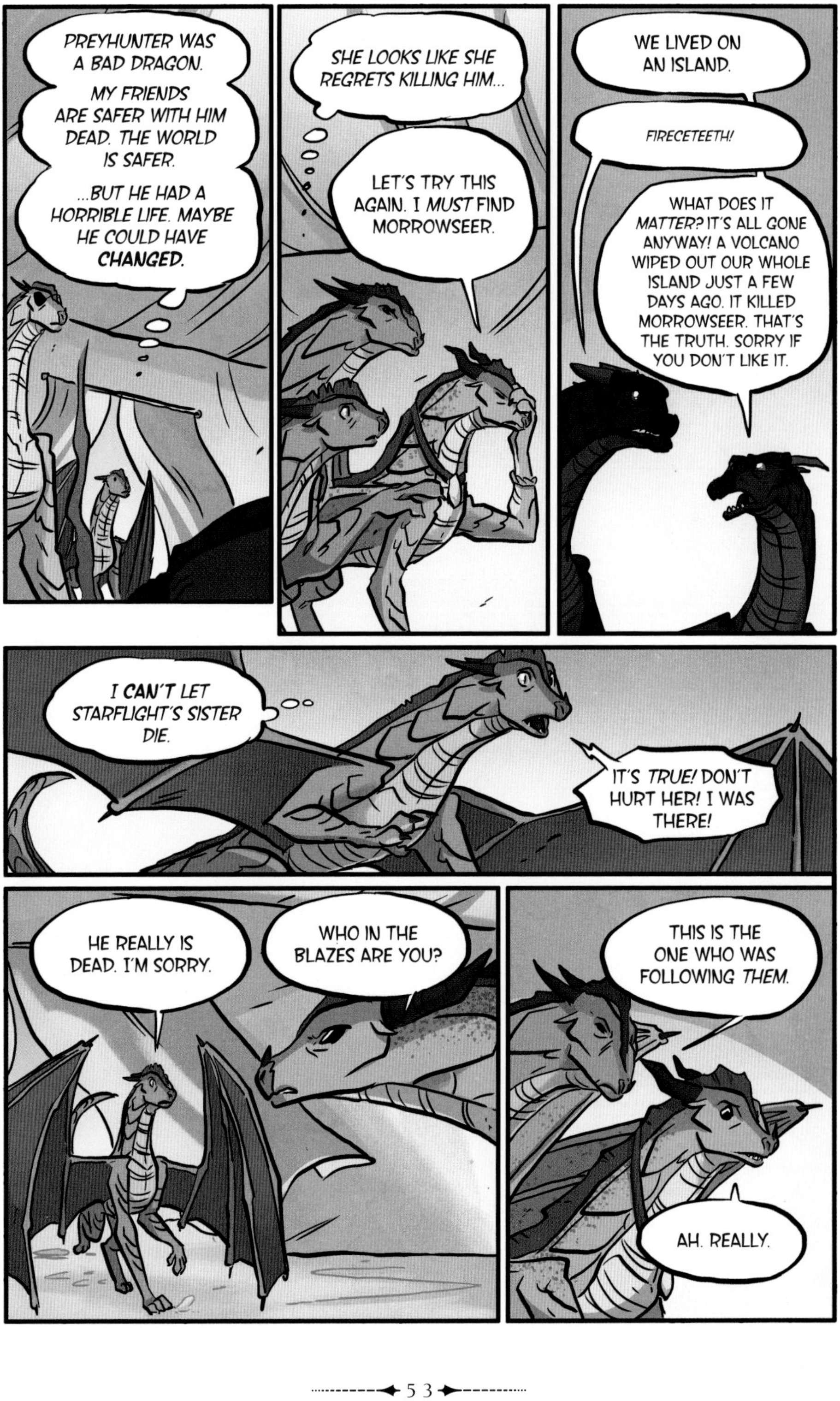
PREYHUNTER WAS A BAD DRAGON.
MY FRIENDS ARE SAFER WITH HIM DEAD. THE WORLD IS SAFER.
...BUT HE HAD A HORRIBLE LIFE. MAYBE HE COULD HAVE **CHANGED.**
SHE LOOKS LIKE SHE REGRETS KILLING HIM...
LET'S TRY THIS AGAIN. I *MUST* FIND MORROWSEER.
WE LIVED ON AN ISLAND.
FIRECETEETH!
WHAT DOES IT *MATTER?* IT'S ALL GONE ANYWAY! A VOLCANO WIPED OUT OUR WHOLE ISLAND JUST A FEW DAYS AGO. IT KILLED MORROWSEER. THAT'S THE TRUTH. SORRY IF YOU DON'T LIKE IT.
I **CAN'T** LET STARFLIGHT'S SISTER DIE.
IT'S *TRUE!* DON'T HURT HER! I WAS THERE!
HE REALLY IS DEAD. I'M SORRY.
WHO IN THE BLAZES ARE YOU?
THIS IS THE ONE WHO WAS FOLLOWING *THEM.*
AH. REALLY.

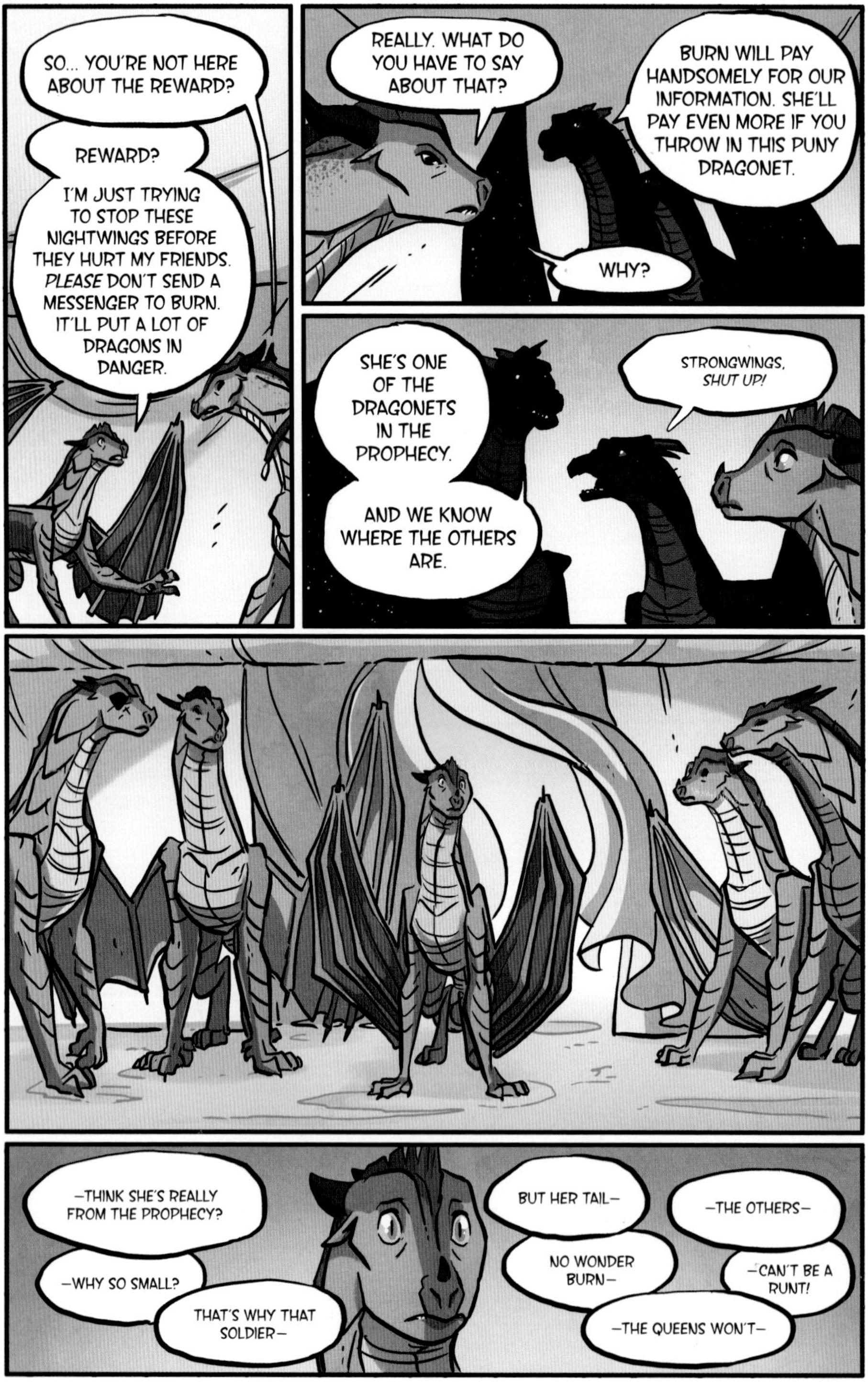
SO... YOU'RE NOT HERE ABOUT THE REWARD?
REWARD?
I'M JUST TRYING TO STOP THESE NIGHTWINGS BEFORE THEY HURT MY FRIENDS. *PLEASE* DON'T SEND A MESSENGER TO BURN. IT'LL PUT A LOT OF DRAGONS IN DANGER.
REALLY. WHAT DO YOU HAVE TO SAY ABOUT THAT?
BURN WILL PAY HANDSOMELY FOR OUR INFORMATION. SHE'LL PAY EVEN MORE IF YOU THROW IN THIS PUNY DRAGONET.
WHY?
SHE'S ONE OF THE DRAGONETS IN THE PROPHECY.
AND WE KNOW WHERE THE OTHERS ARE.
STRONGWINGS, *SHUT UP!*
—THINK SHE'S REALLY FROM THE PROPHECY?
—WHY SO SMALL?
THAT'S WHY THAT SOLDIER—
BUT HER TAIL—
NO WONDER BURN—
—THE OTHERS—
—CAN'T BE A RUNT!
—THE QUEENS WON'T—

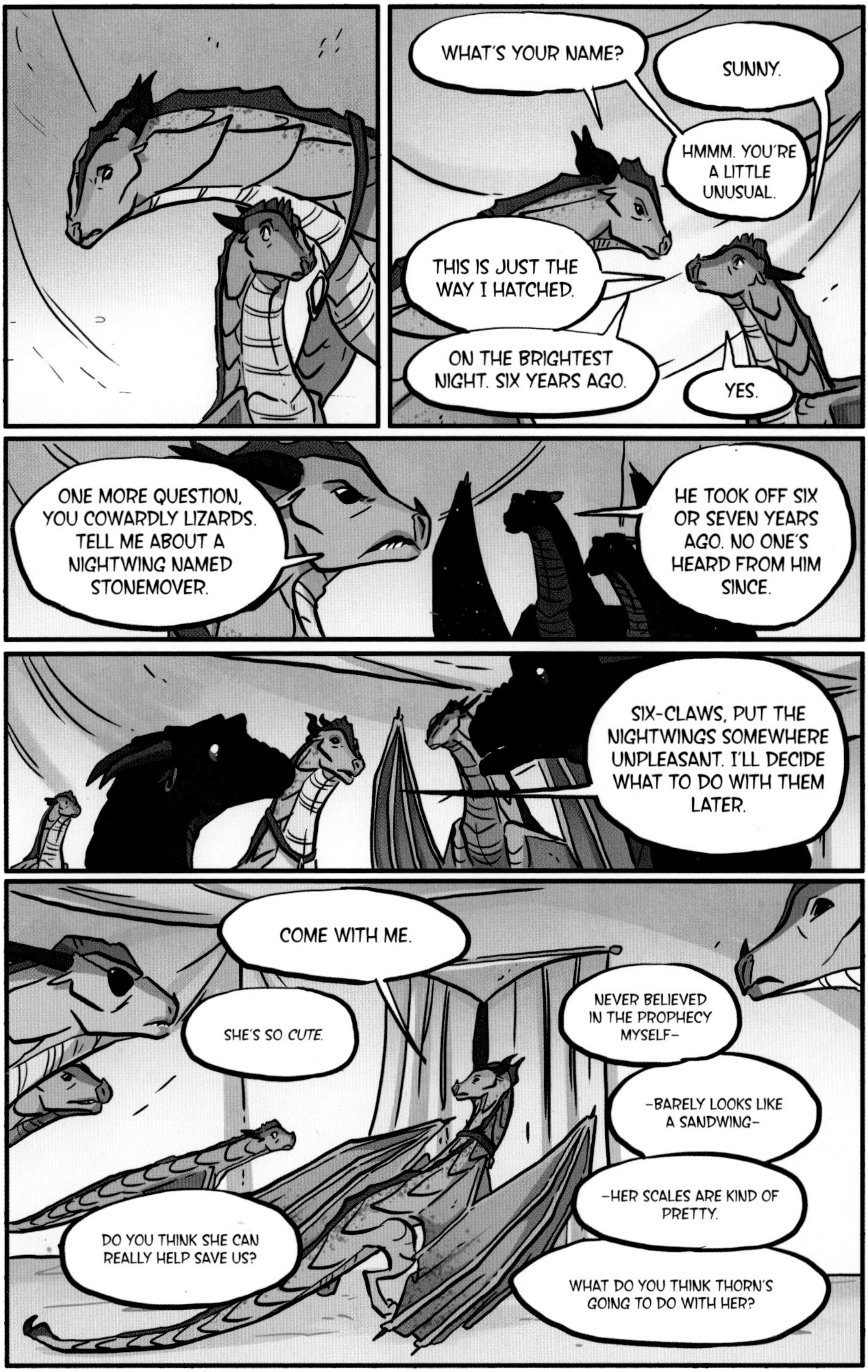

WHAT'S YOUR NAME?
SUNNY.
HMMM. YOU'RE A LITTLE UNUSUAL.
THIS IS JUST THE WAY I HATCHED.
ON THE BRIGHTEST NIGHT. SIX YEARS AGO.
YES.
ONE MORE QUESTION, YOU COWARDLY LIZARDS. TELL ME ABOUT A NIGHTWING NAMED STONEMOVER.
HE TOOK OFF SIX OR SEVEN YEARS AGO. NO ONE'S HEARD FROM HIM SINCE.
SIX-CLAWS, PUT THE NIGHTWINGS SOMEWHERE UNPLEASANT. I'LL DECIDE WHAT TO DO WITH THEM LATER.
COME WITH ME.
SHE'S SO *CUTE*.
NEVER BELIEVED IN THE PROPHECY MYSELF–
–BARELY LOOKS LIKE A SANDWING–
–HER SCALES ARE KIND OF PRETTY.
DO YOU THINK SHE CAN REALLY HELP SAVE US?
WHAT DO YOU THINK THORN'S GOING TO DO WITH HER?

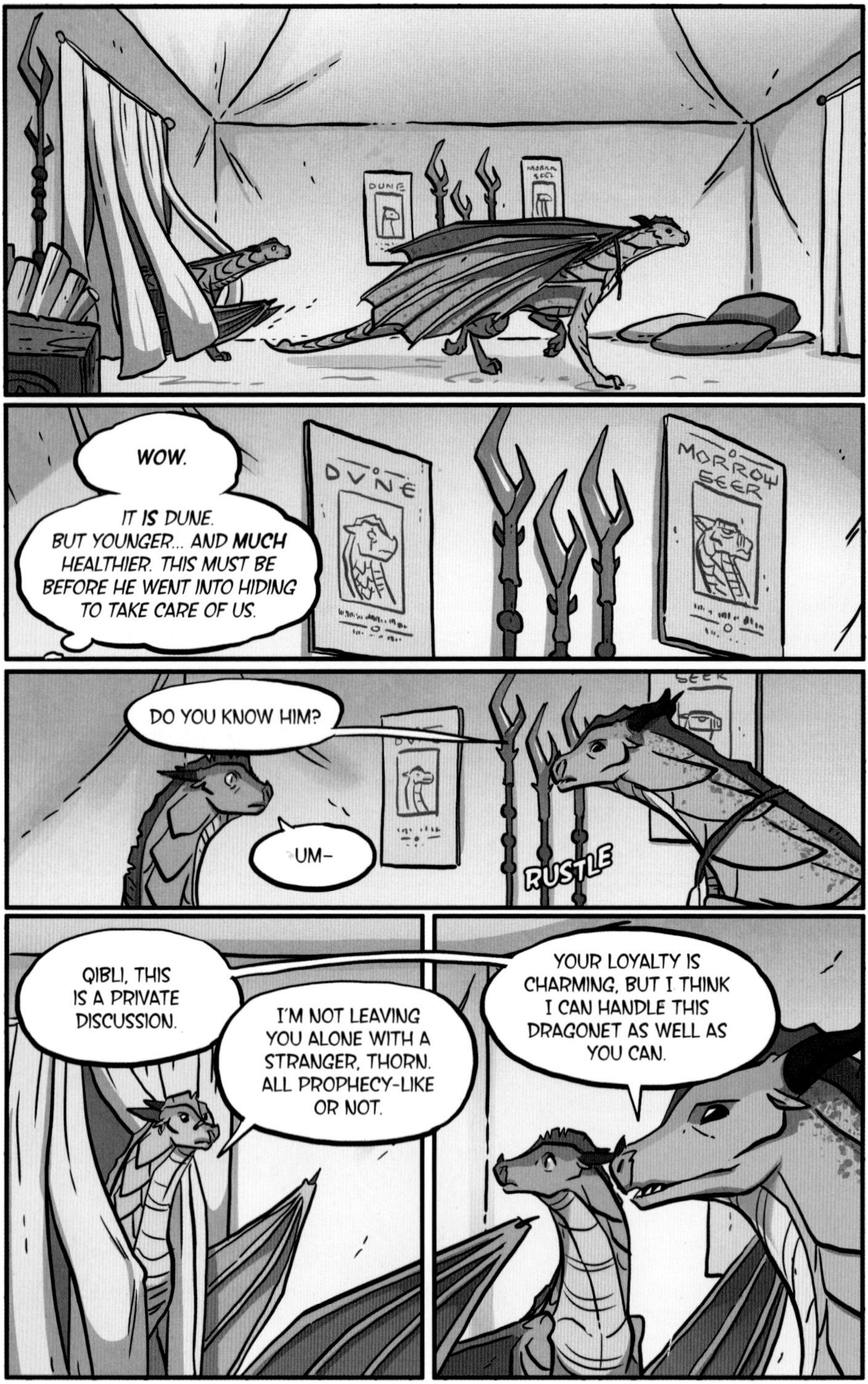
DUNE
MORROWSEER
WOW.
IT IS DUNE. BUT YOUNGER... AND MUCH HEALTHIER. THIS MUST BE BEFORE HE WENT INTO HIDING TO TAKE CARE OF US.
DO YOU KNOW HIM?
UM–
RUSTLE
QIBLI, THIS IS A PRIVATE DISCUSSION.
I'M NOT LEAVING YOU ALONE WITH A STRANGER, THORN. ALL PROPHECY-LIKE OR NOT.
YOUR LOYALTY IS CHARMING, BUT I THINK I CAN HANDLE THIS DRAGONET AS WELL AS YOU CAN.

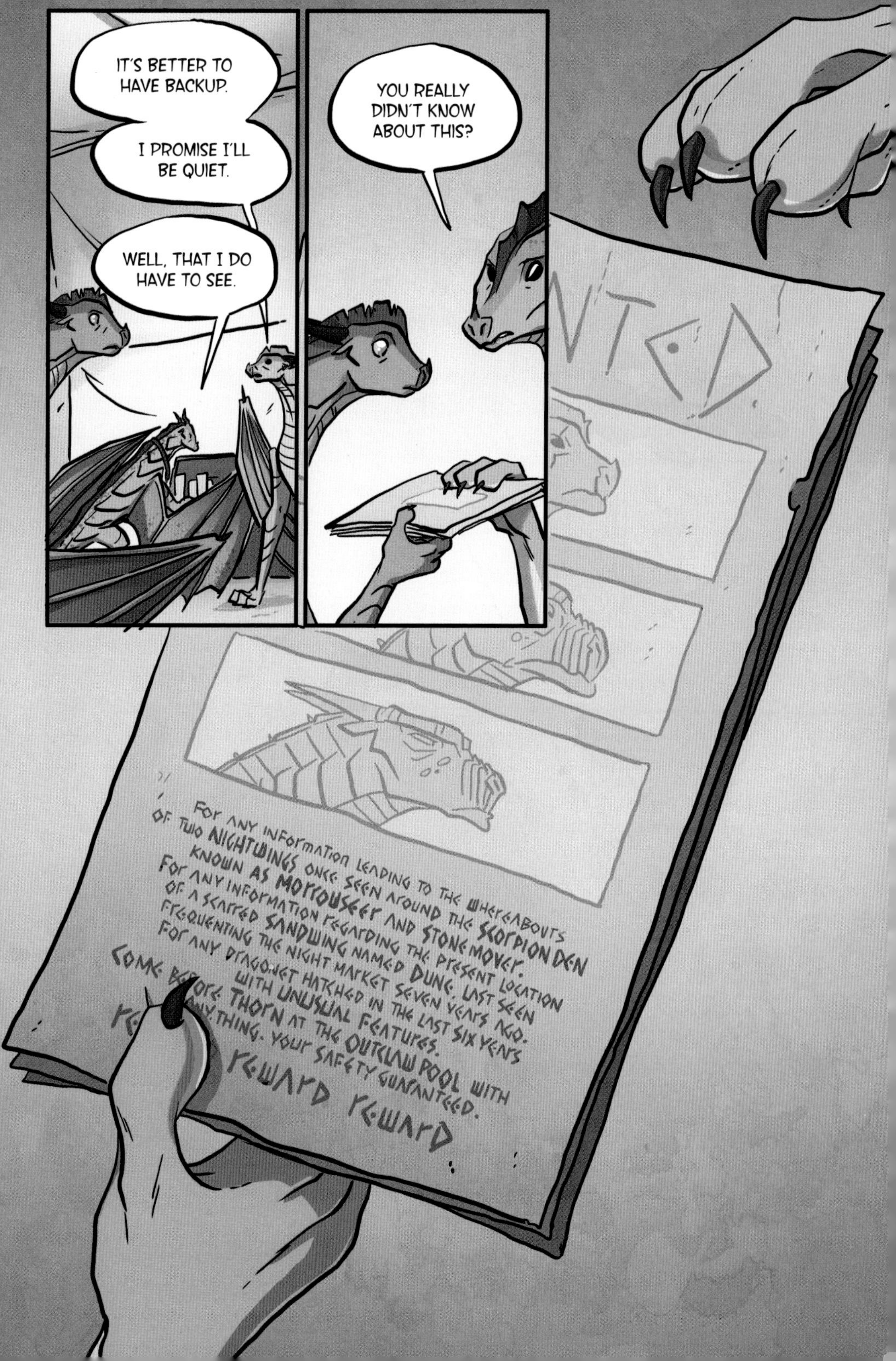
IT'S BETTER TO HAVE BACKUP.
I PROMISE I'LL BE QUIET.
WELL, THAT I DO HAVE TO SEE.
YOU REALLY DIDN'T KNOW ABOUT THIS?
NTED
FOR ANY INFORMATION LEADING TO THE WHEREABOUTS OF TWO NIGHTWINGS ONCE SEEN AROUND THE SCORPION DEN KNOWN AS MORROWSEER AND STONEMOVER.
FOR ANY INFORMATION REGARDING THE PRESENT LOCATION OF A SCARRED SANDWING NAMED DUNE, LAST SEEN FREQUENTING THE NIGHT MARKET SEVEN YEARS AGO.
FOR ANY DRAGONET HATCHED IN THE LAST SIX YEARS WITH UNUSUAL FEATURES.
COME B ORE THORN AT THE OUTCLAW POOL WITH ANYTHING. YOUR SAFETY GUARANTEED.
REWARD REWARD

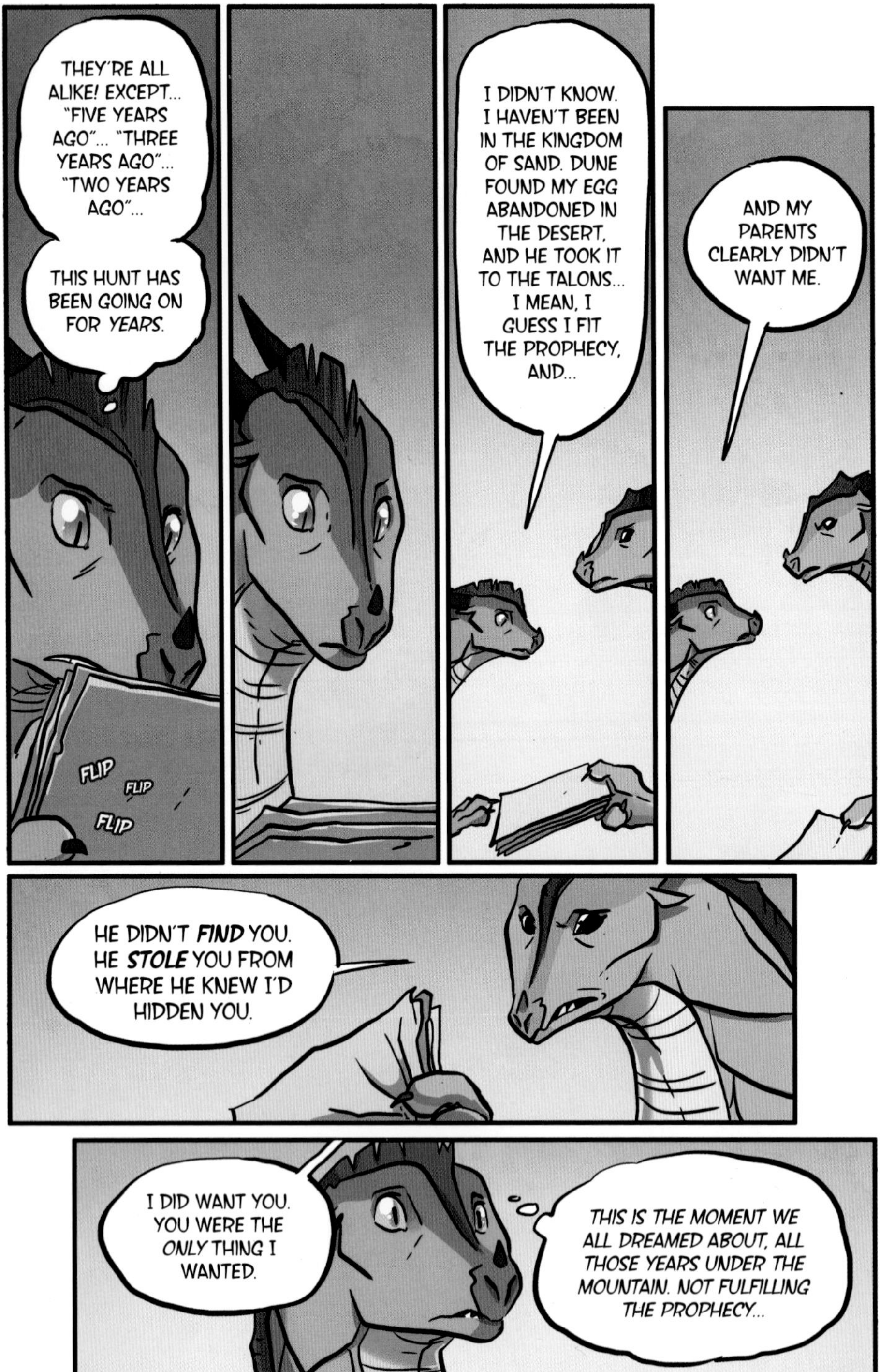
THEY'RE ALL ALIKE! EXCEPT... "FIVE YEARS AGO"... "THREE YEARS AGO"... "TWO YEARS AGO"...
THIS HUNT HAS BEEN GOING ON FOR *YEARS*.
FLIP FLIP FLIP
I DIDN'T KNOW. I HAVEN'T BEEN IN THE KINGDOM OF SAND. DUNE FOUND MY EGG ABANDONED IN THE DESERT, AND HE TOOK IT TO THE TALONS... I MEAN, I GUESS I FIT THE PROPHECY, AND...
AND MY PARENTS CLEARLY DIDN'T WANT ME.
HE DIDN'T ***FIND*** YOU. HE ***STOLE*** YOU FROM WHERE HE KNEW I'D HIDDEN YOU.
I DID WANT YOU. YOU WERE THE *ONLY* THING I WANTED.
THIS IS THE MOMENT WE ALL DREAMED ABOUT, ALL THOSE YEARS UNDER THE MOUNTAIN. NOT FULFILLING THE PROPHECY...

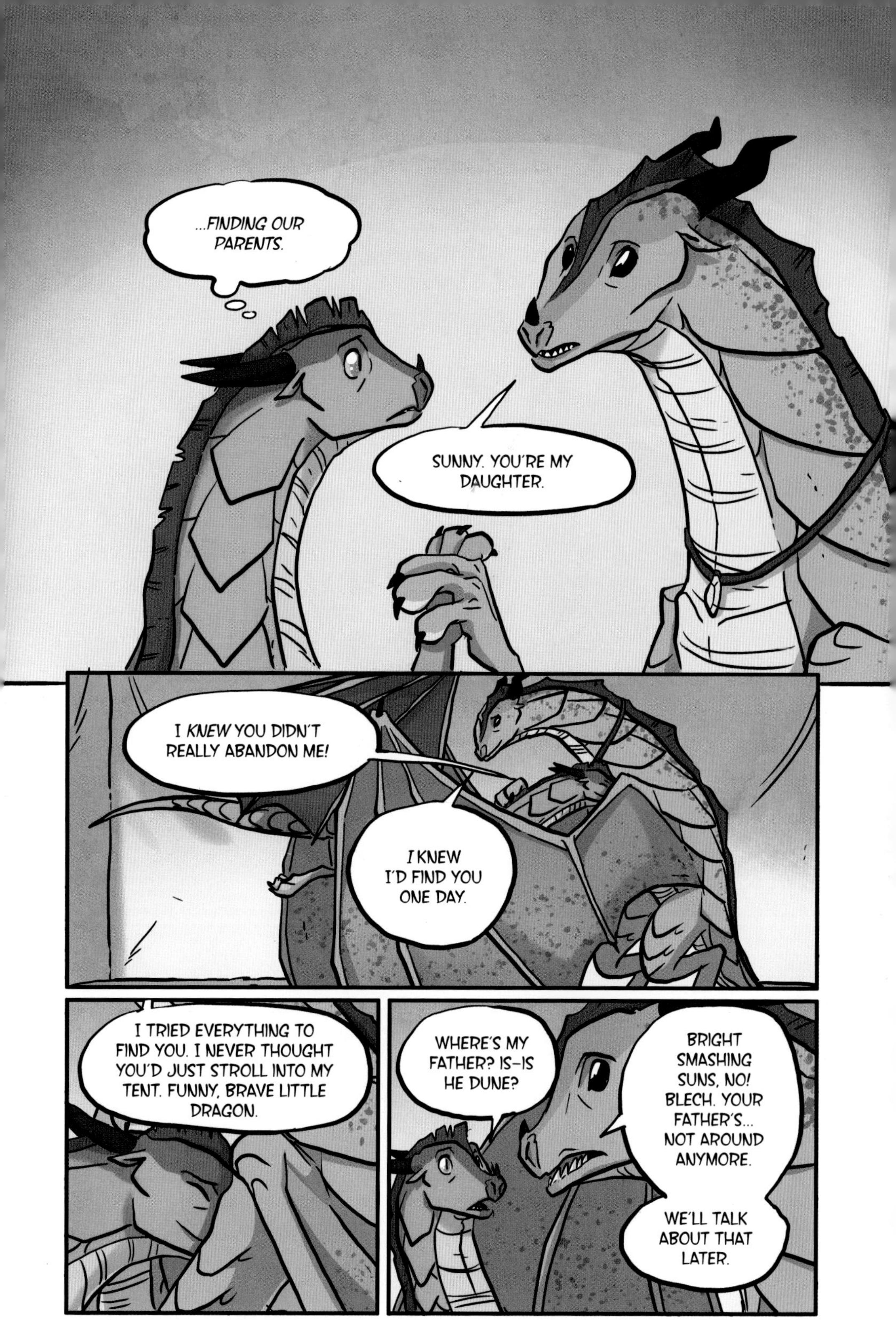
...FINDING OUR PARENTS.
SUNNY. YOU'RE MY DAUGHTER.
I *KNEW* YOU DIDN'T REALLY ABANDON ME!
I KNEW I'D FIND YOU ONE DAY.
I TRIED EVERYTHING TO FIND YOU. I NEVER THOUGHT YOU'D JUST STROLL INTO MY TENT. FUNNY, BRAVE LITTLE DRAGON.
WHERE'S MY FATHER? IS–IS HE DUNE?
BRIGHT SMASHING SUNS, NO! BLECH. YOUR FATHER'S... NOT AROUND ANYMORE.
WE'LL TALK ABOUT THAT LATER.

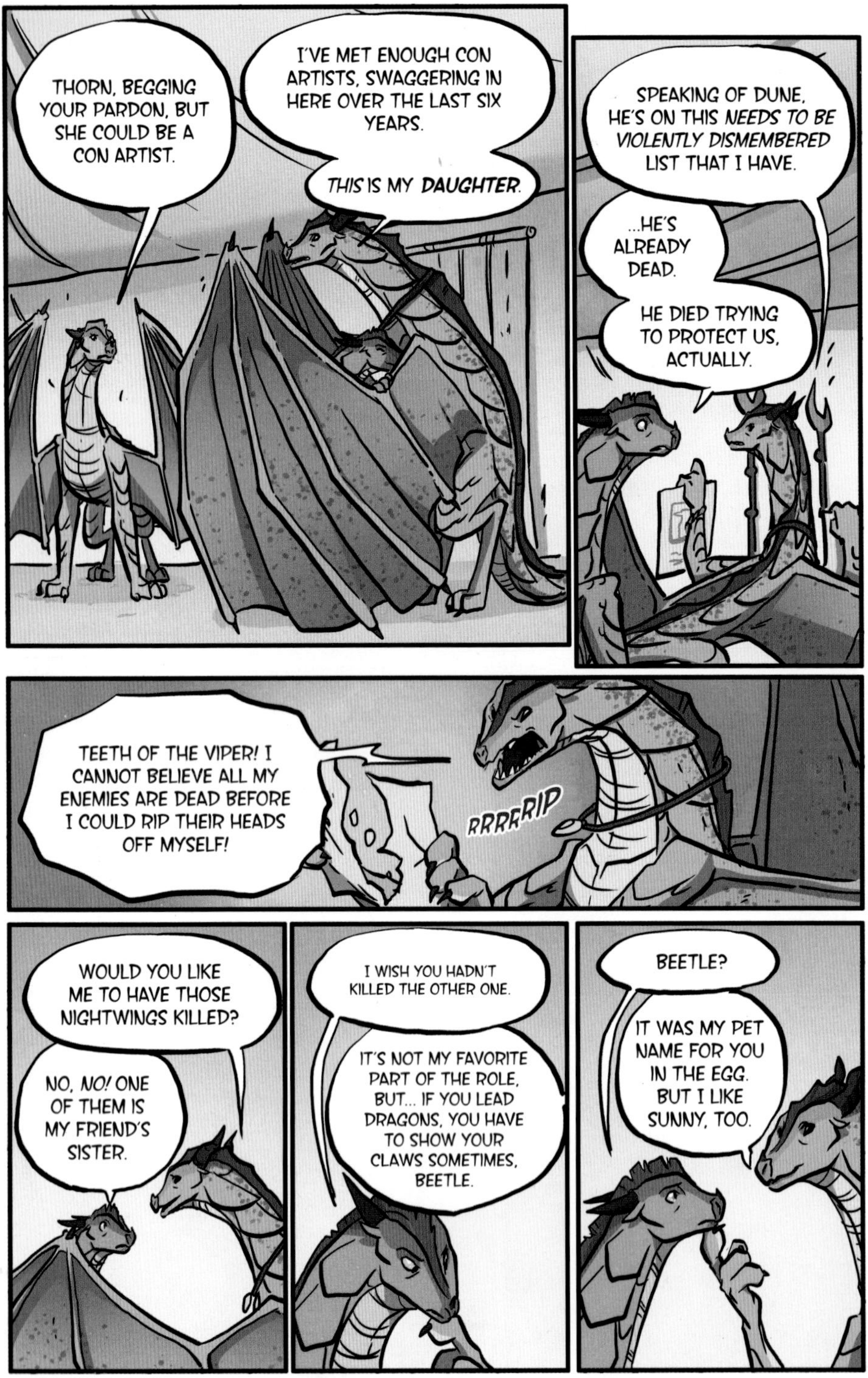
THORN, BEGGING YOUR PARDON, BUT SHE COULD BE A CON ARTIST.
I'VE MET ENOUGH CON ARTISTS, SWAGGERING IN HERE OVER THE LAST SIX YEARS.
THIS IS MY ***DAUGHTER***.
SPEAKING OF DUNE, HE'S ON THIS *NEEDS TO BE VIOLENTLY DISMEMBERED* LIST THAT I HAVE.
...HE'S ALREADY DEAD.
HE DIED TRYING TO PROTECT US, ACTUALLY.
TEETH OF THE VIPER! I CANNOT BELIEVE ALL MY ENEMIES ARE DEAD BEFORE I COULD RIP THEIR HEADS OFF MYSELF!
RRRRRIP
WOULD YOU LIKE ME TO HAVE THOSE NIGHTWINGS KILLED?
NO, *NO!* ONE OF THEM IS MY FRIEND'S SISTER.
I WISH YOU HADN'T KILLED THE OTHER ONE.
IT'S NOT MY FAVORITE PART OF THE ROLE, BUT... IF YOU LEAD DRAGONS, YOU HAVE TO SHOW YOUR CLAWS SOMETIMES, BEETLE.
BEETLE?
IT WAS MY PET NAME FOR YOU IN THE EGG. BUT I LIKE SUNNY, TOO.

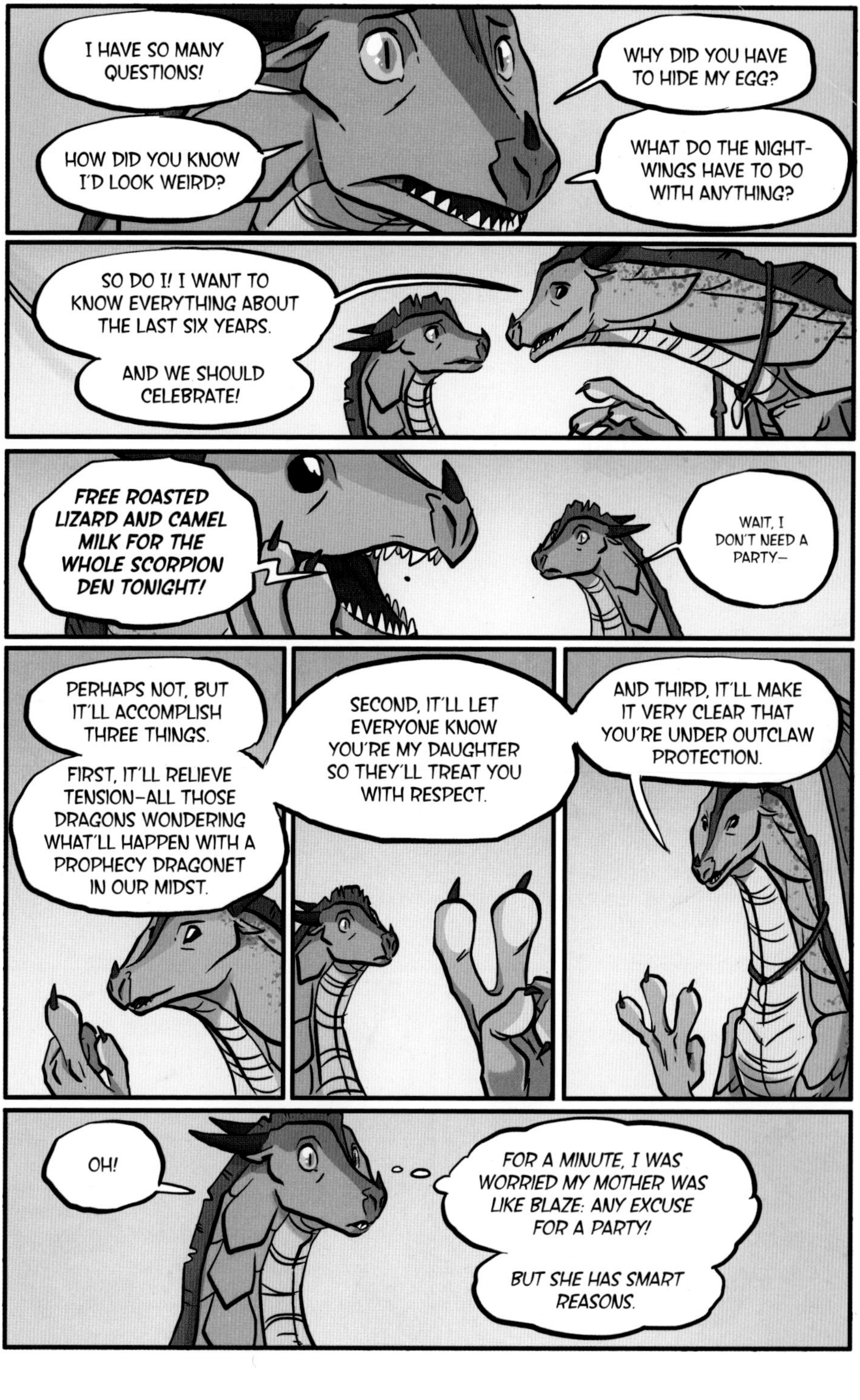
I HAVE SO MANY QUESTIONS!
WHY DID YOU HAVE TO HIDE MY EGG?
HOW DID YOU KNOW I'D LOOK WEIRD?
WHAT DO THE NIGHT-WINGS HAVE TO DO WITH ANYTHING?
SO DO I! I WANT TO KNOW EVERYTHING ABOUT THE LAST SIX YEARS.
AND WE SHOULD CELEBRATE!
FREE ROASTED LIZARD AND CAMEL MILK FOR THE WHOLE SCORPION DEN TONIGHT!
WAIT, I DON'T NEED A PARTY—
PERHAPS NOT, BUT IT'LL ACCOMPLISH THREE THINGS.
FIRST, IT'LL RELIEVE TENSION—ALL THOSE DRAGONS WONDERING WHAT'LL HAPPEN WITH A PROPHECY DRAGONET IN OUR MIDST.
SECOND, IT'LL LET EVERYONE KNOW YOU'RE MY DAUGHTER SO THEY'LL TREAT YOU WITH RESPECT.
AND THIRD, IT'LL MAKE IT VERY CLEAR THAT YOU'RE UNDER OUTCLAW PROTECTION.
OH!
FOR A MINUTE, I WAS WORRIED MY MOTHER WAS LIKE BLAZE: ANY EXCUSE FOR A PARTY!
BUT SHE HAS SMART REASONS.

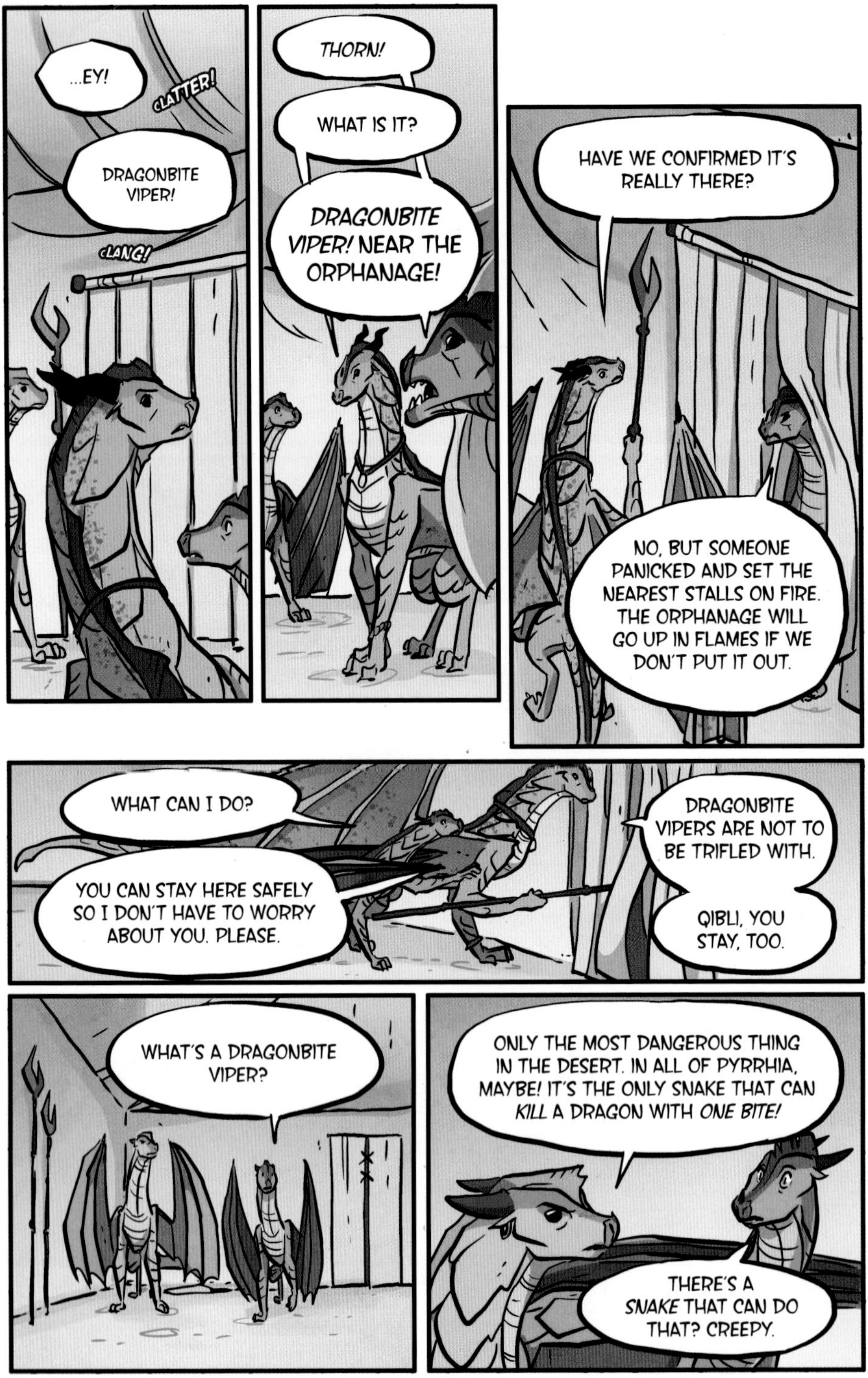
...EY!
CLATTER!
DRAGONBITE VIPER!
CLANG!
THORN!
WHAT IS IT?
DRAGONBITE VIPER! NEAR THE ORPHANAGE!
HAVE WE CONFIRMED IT'S REALLY THERE?
NO, BUT SOMEONE PANICKED AND SET THE NEAREST STALLS ON FIRE. THE ORPHANAGE WILL GO UP IN FLAMES IF WE DON'T PUT IT OUT.
WHAT CAN I DO?
YOU CAN STAY HERE SAFELY SO I DON'T HAVE TO WORRY ABOUT YOU. PLEASE.
DRAGONBITE VIPERS ARE NOT TO BE TRIFLED WITH.
QIBLI, YOU STAY, TOO.
WHAT'S A DRAGONBITE VIPER?
ONLY THE MOST DANGEROUS THING IN THE DESERT. IN ALL OF PYRRHIA, MAYBE! IT'S THE ONLY SNAKE THAT CAN *KILL* A DRAGON WITH *ONE BITE!*
THERE'S A *SNAKE* THAT CAN DO THAT? CREEPY.

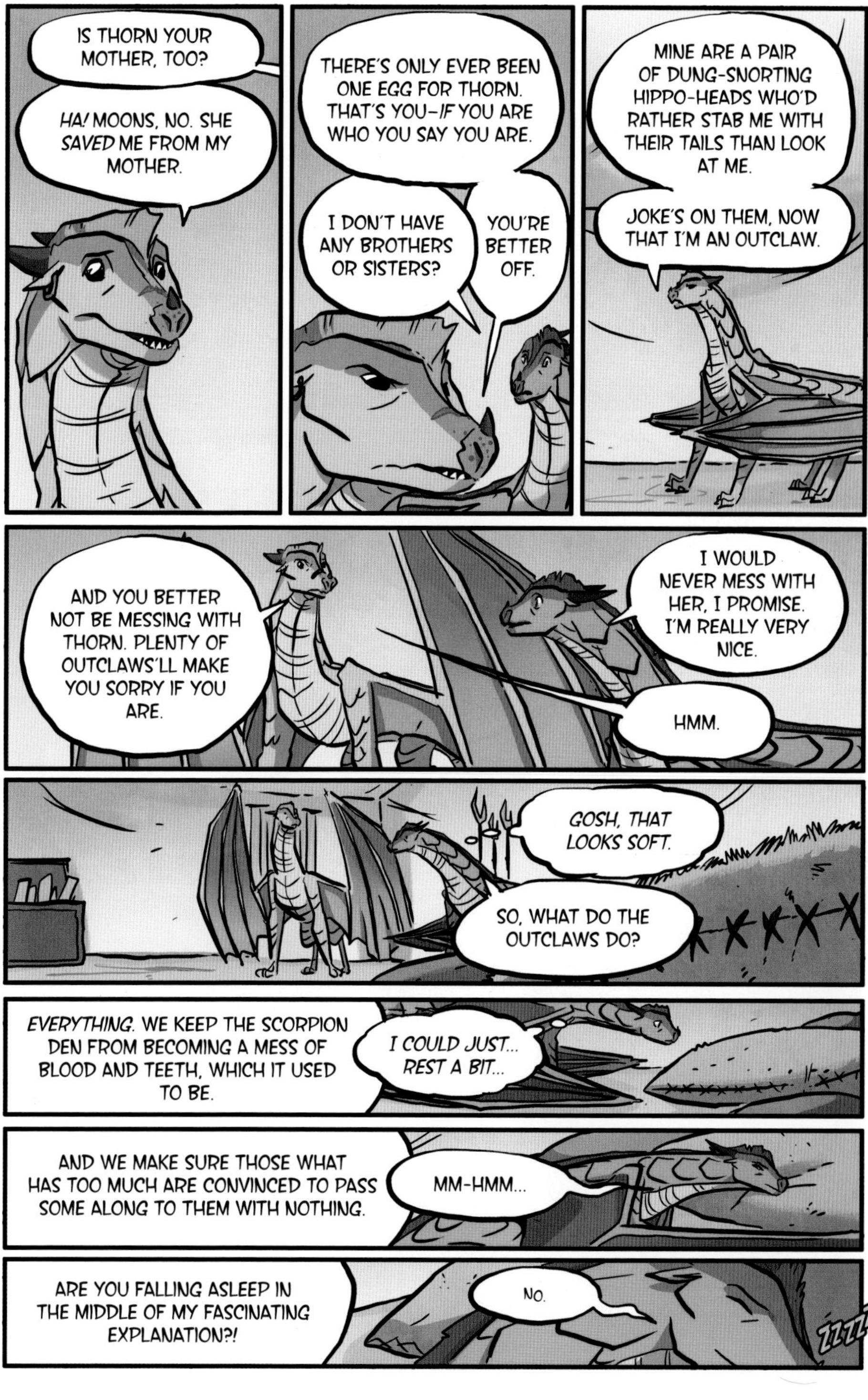
IS THORN YOUR MOTHER, TOO?
HA! MOONS, NO. SHE SAVED ME FROM MY MOTHER.
THERE'S ONLY EVER BEEN ONE EGG FOR THORN. THAT'S YOU–IF YOU ARE WHO YOU SAY YOU ARE.
I DON'T HAVE ANY BROTHERS OR SISTERS?
YOU'RE BETTER OFF.
MINE ARE A PAIR OF DUNG-SNORTING HIPPO-HEADS WHO'D RATHER STAB ME WITH THEIR TAILS THAN LOOK AT ME.
JOKE'S ON THEM, NOW THAT I'M AN OUTCLAW.
AND YOU BETTER NOT BE MESSING WITH THORN. PLENTY OF OUTCLAWS'LL MAKE YOU SORRY IF YOU ARE.
I WOULD NEVER MESS WITH HER, I PROMISE. I'M REALLY VERY NICE.
HMM.
GOSH, THAT LOOKS SOFT.
SO, WHAT DO THE OUTCLAWS DO?
EVERYTHING. WE KEEP THE SCORPION DEN FROM BECOMING A MESS OF BLOOD AND TEETH, WHICH IT USED TO BE.
I COULD JUST... REST A BIT...
AND WE MAKE SURE THOSE WHAT HAS TOO MUCH ARE CONVINCED TO PASS SOME ALONG TO THEM WITH NOTHING.
MM-HMM...
ARE YOU FALLING ASLEEP IN THE MIDDLE OF MY FASCINATING EXPLANATION?!
NO.
ZZZZ

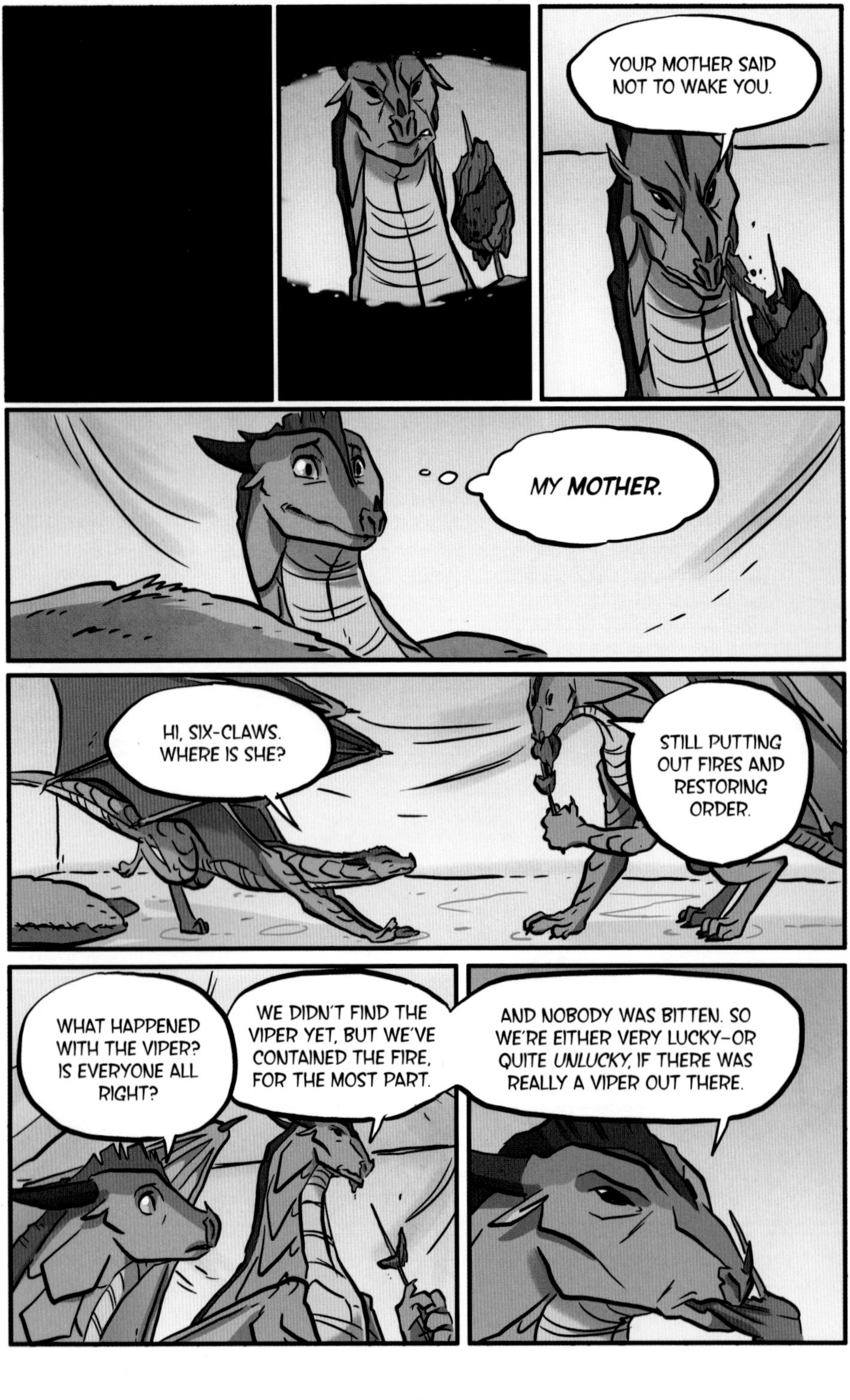

YOUR MOTHER SAID NOT TO WAKE YOU.
MY *MOTHER.*
HI, SIX-CLAWS. WHERE IS SHE?
STILL PUTTING OUT FIRES AND RESTORING ORDER.
WHAT HAPPENED WITH THE VIPER? IS EVERYONE ALL RIGHT?
WE DIDN'T FIND THE VIPER YET, BUT WE'VE CONTAINED THE FIRE, FOR THE MOST PART.
AND NOBODY WAS BITTEN. SO WE'RE EITHER VERY LUCKY–OR QUITE *UNLUCKY,* IF THERE WAS REALLY A VIPER OUT THERE.

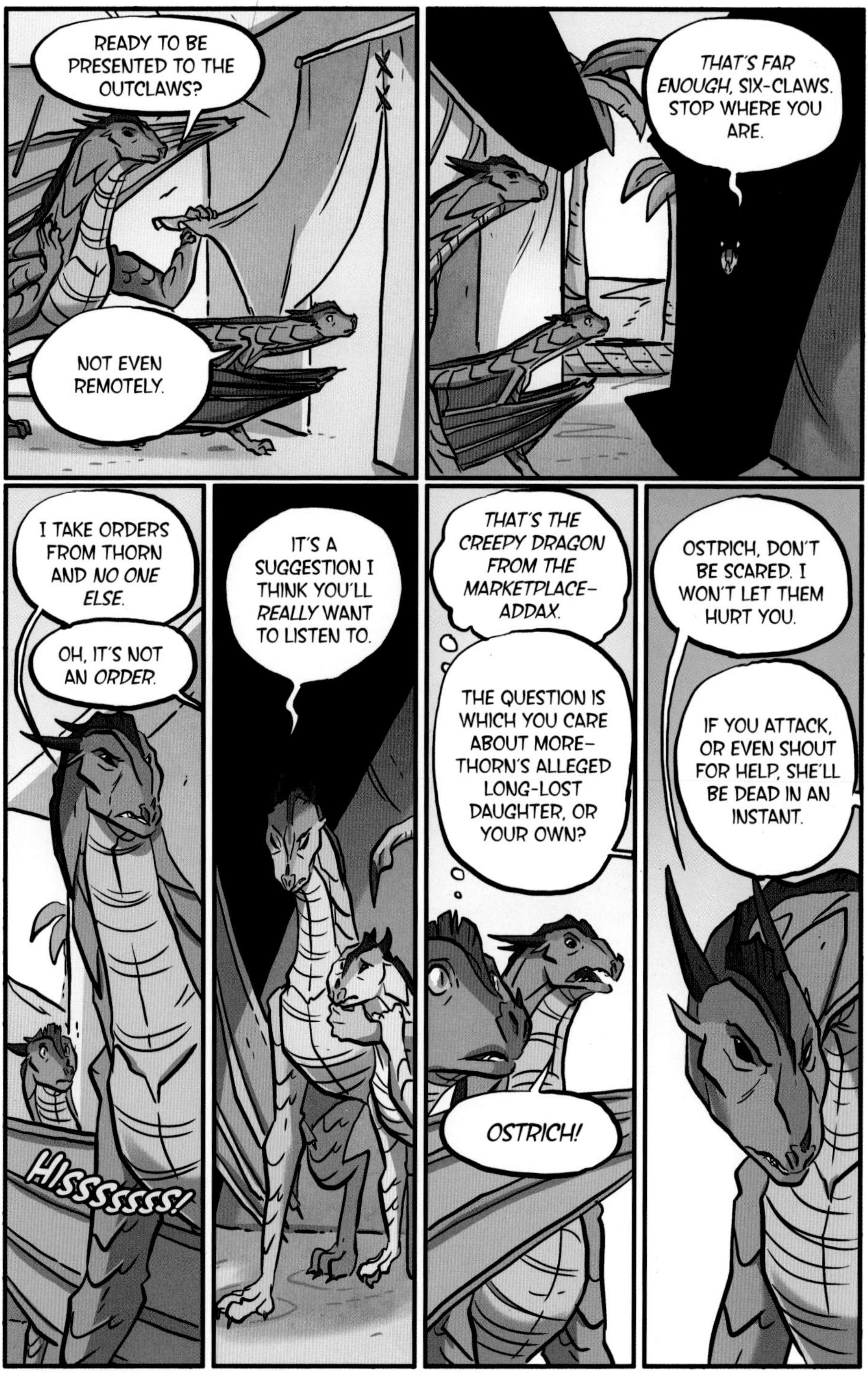
READY TO BE PRESENTED TO THE OUTCLAWS?
NOT EVEN REMOTELY.
THAT'S FAR ENOUGH, SIX-CLAWS. STOP WHERE YOU ARE.
I TAKE ORDERS FROM THORN AND *NO ONE ELSE.*
OH, IT'S NOT AN *ORDER.*
HISSSSSSS!
IT'S A SUGGESTION I THINK YOU'LL *REALLY* WANT TO LISTEN TO.
THAT'S THE CREEPY DRAGON FROM THE MARKETPLACE— ADDAX.
THE QUESTION IS WHICH YOU CARE ABOUT MORE— THORN'S ALLEGED LONG-LOST DAUGHTER, OR YOUR OWN?
OSTRICH!
OSTRICH, DON'T BE SCARED. I WON'T LET THEM HURT YOU.
IF YOU ATTACK, OR EVEN SHOUT FOR HELP, SHE'LL BE DEAD IN AN INSTANT.

PART TWO: BURN'S STRONGHOLD

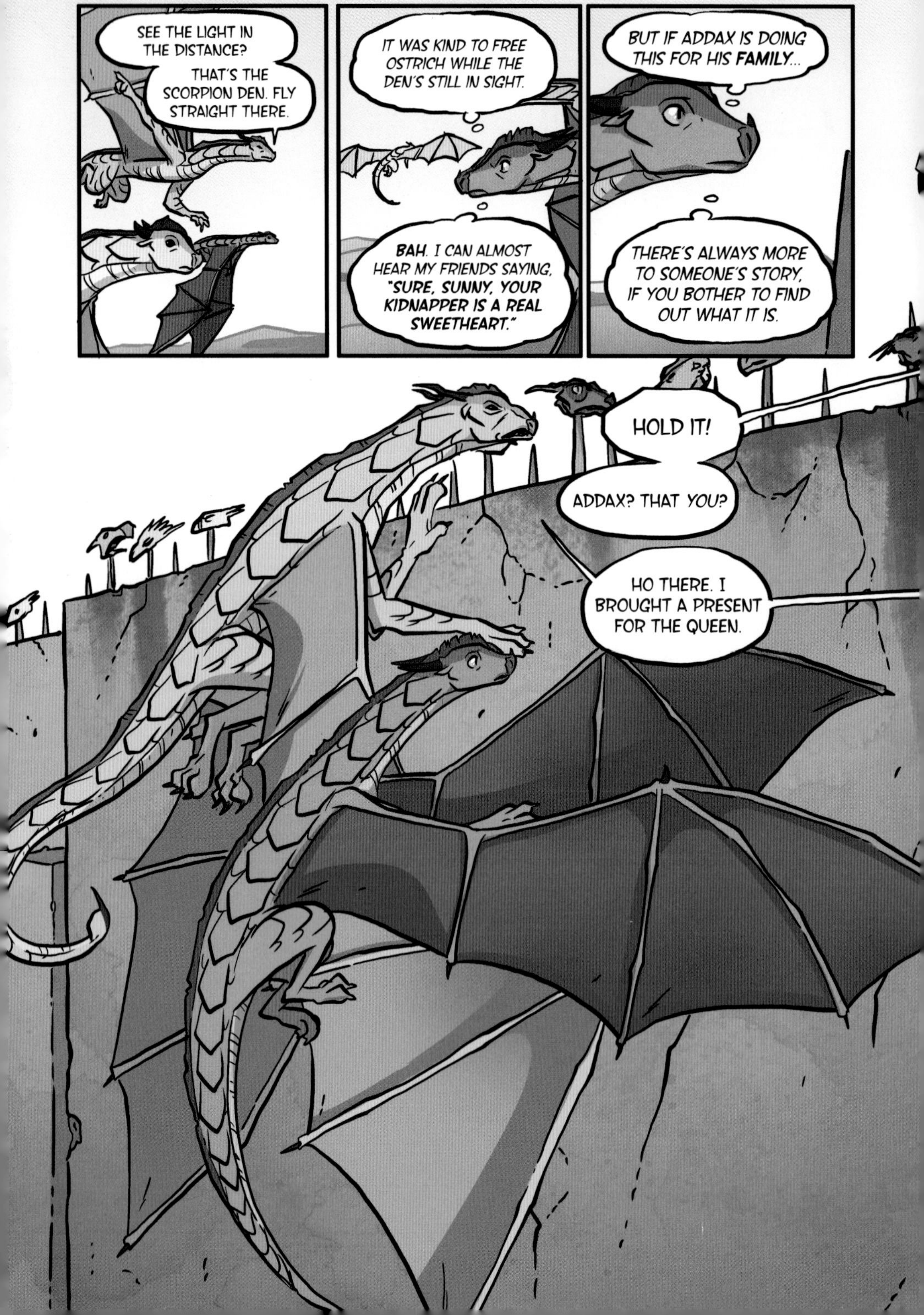
SEE THE LIGHT IN THE DISTANCE?
THAT'S THE SCORPION DEN. FLY STRAIGHT THERE.
IT WAS KIND TO FREE OSTRICH WHILE THE DEN'S STILL IN SIGHT.
BAH. I CAN ALMOST HEAR MY FRIENDS SAYING, **"SURE, SUNNY, YOUR KIDNAPPER IS A REAL SWEETHEART."**
BUT IF ADDAX IS DOING THIS FOR HIS **FAMILY**...
THERE'S ALWAYS MORE TO SOMEONE'S STORY, IF YOU BOTHER TO FIND OUT WHAT IT IS.
HOLD IT!
ADDAX? THAT *YOU*?
HO THERE. I BROUGHT A PRESENT FOR THE QUEEN.

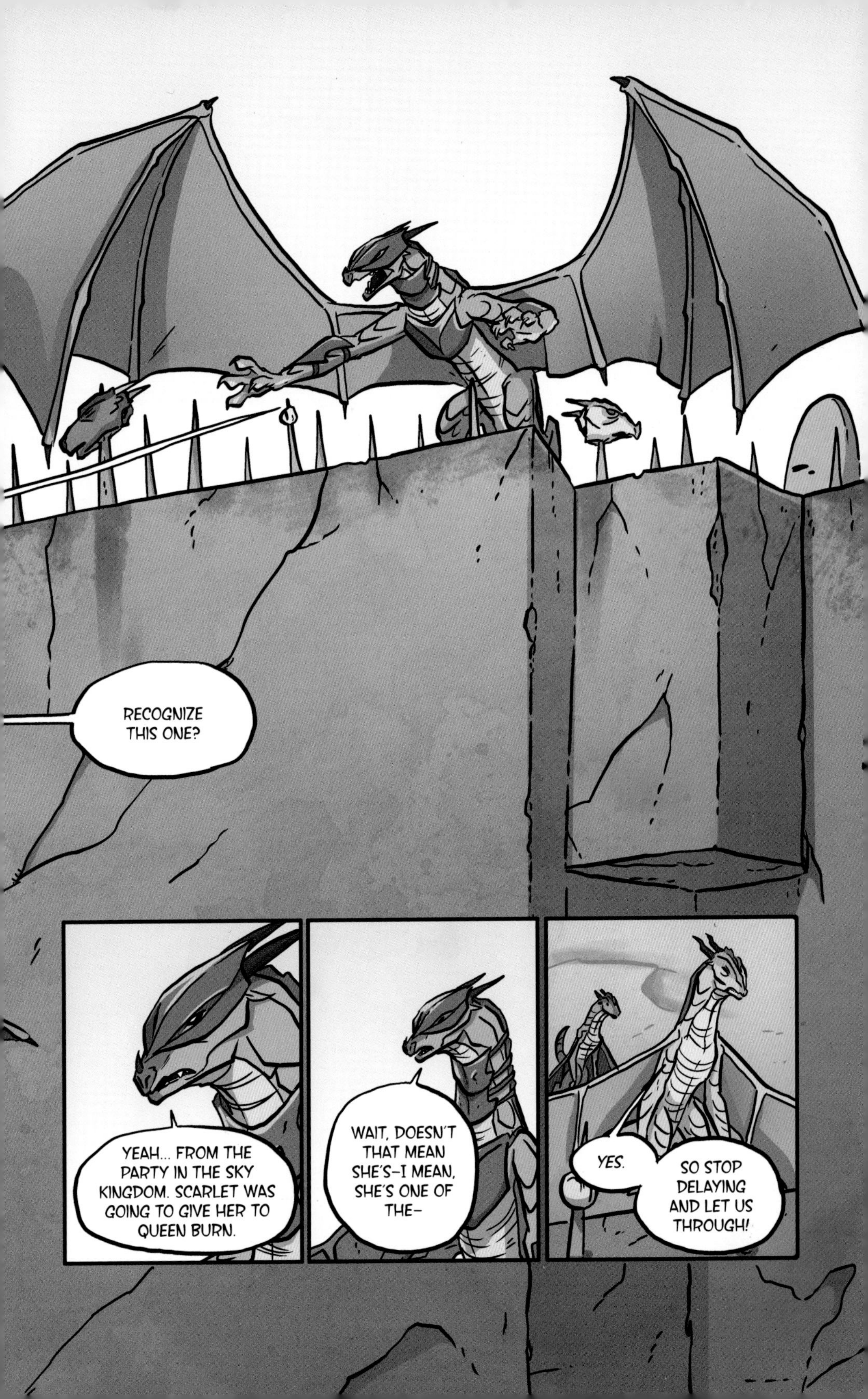
RECOGNIZE THIS ONE?
YEAH... FROM THE PARTY IN THE SKY KINGDOM. SCARLET WAS GOING TO GIVE HER TO QUEEN BURN.
WAIT, DOESN'T THAT MEAN SHE'S–I MEAN, SHE'S ONE OF THE–
YES.
SO STOP DELAYING AND LET US THROUGH!

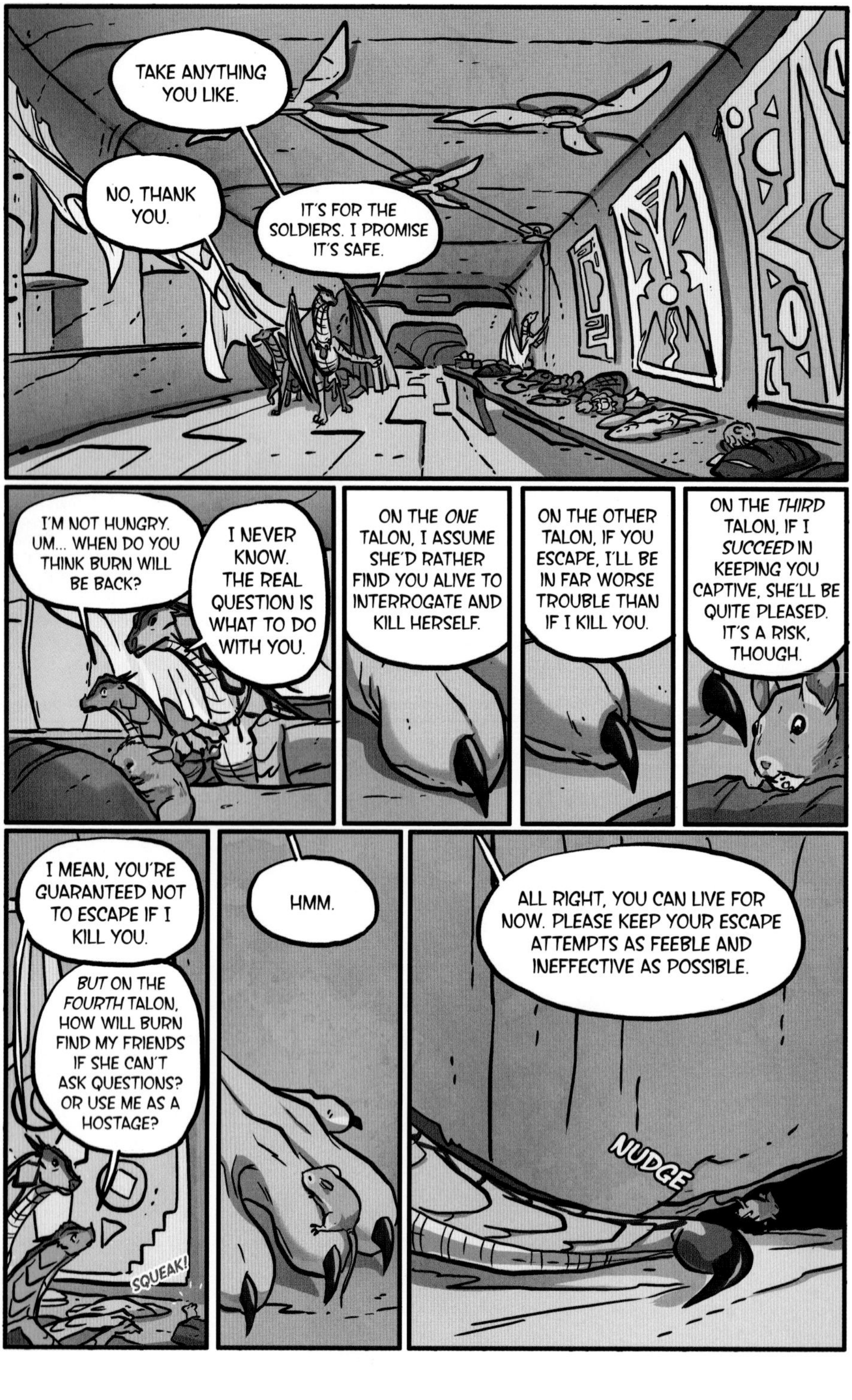
TAKE ANYTHING YOU LIKE.
NO, THANK YOU.
IT'S FOR THE SOLDIERS. I PROMISE IT'S SAFE.
I'M NOT HUNGRY. UM... WHEN DO YOU THINK BURN WILL BE BACK?
I NEVER KNOW. THE REAL QUESTION IS WHAT TO DO WITH YOU.
ON THE *ONE* TALON, I ASSUME SHE'D RATHER FIND YOU ALIVE TO INTERROGATE AND KILL HERSELF.
ON THE OTHER TALON, IF YOU ESCAPE, I'LL BE IN FAR WORSE TROUBLE THAN IF I KILL YOU.
ON THE *THIRD* TALON, IF I *SUCCEED* IN KEEPING YOU CAPTIVE, SHE'LL BE QUITE PLEASED. IT'S A RISK, THOUGH.
I MEAN, YOU'RE GUARANTEED NOT TO ESCAPE IF I KILL YOU.
BUT ON THE *FOURTH* TALON, HOW WILL BURN FIND MY FRIENDS IF SHE CAN'T ASK QUESTIONS? OR USE ME AS A HOSTAGE?
SQUEAK!
HMM.
ALL RIGHT, YOU CAN LIVE FOR NOW. PLEASE KEEP YOUR ESCAPE ATTEMPTS AS FEEBLE AND INEFFECTIVE AS POSSIBLE.
NUDGE

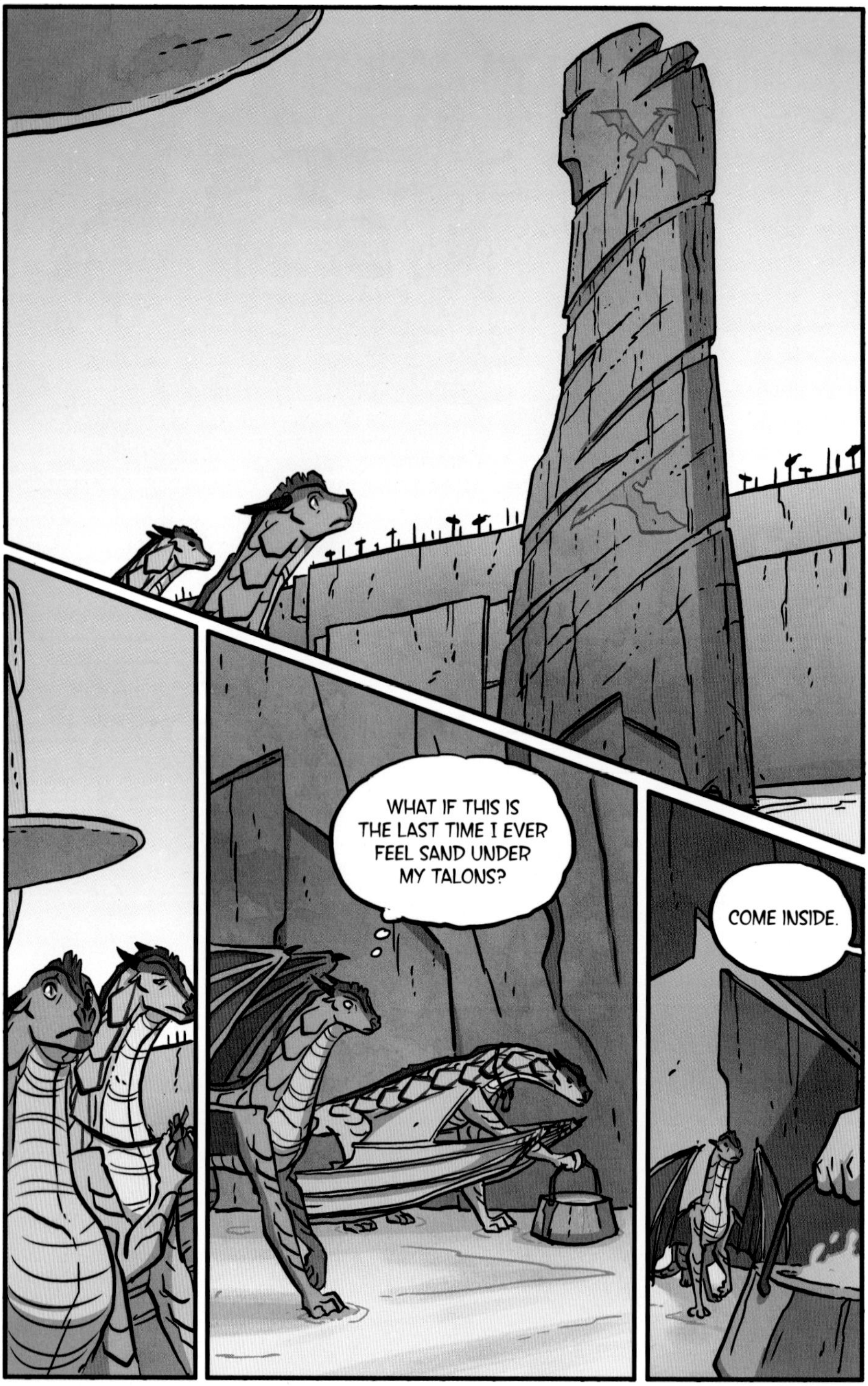
WHAT IF THIS IS THE LAST TIME I EVER FEEL SAND UNDER MY TALONS?
COME INSIDE.

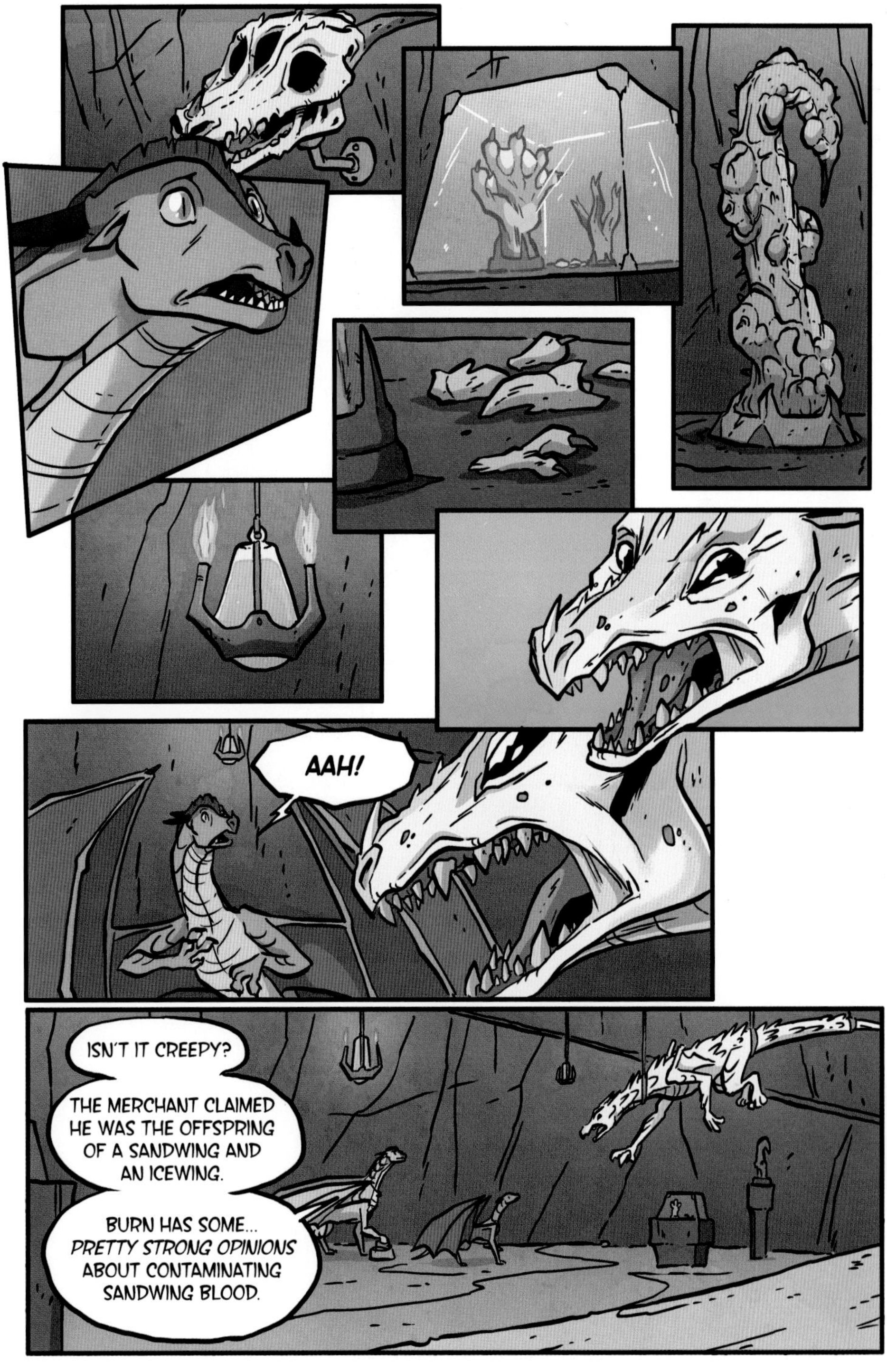
AAH!
ISN'T IT CREEPY?
THE MERCHANT CLAIMED HE WAS THE OFFSPRING OF A SANDWING AND AN ICEWING.
BURN HAS SOME... *PRETTY STRONG OPINIONS* ABOUT CONTAMINATING SANDWING BLOOD.

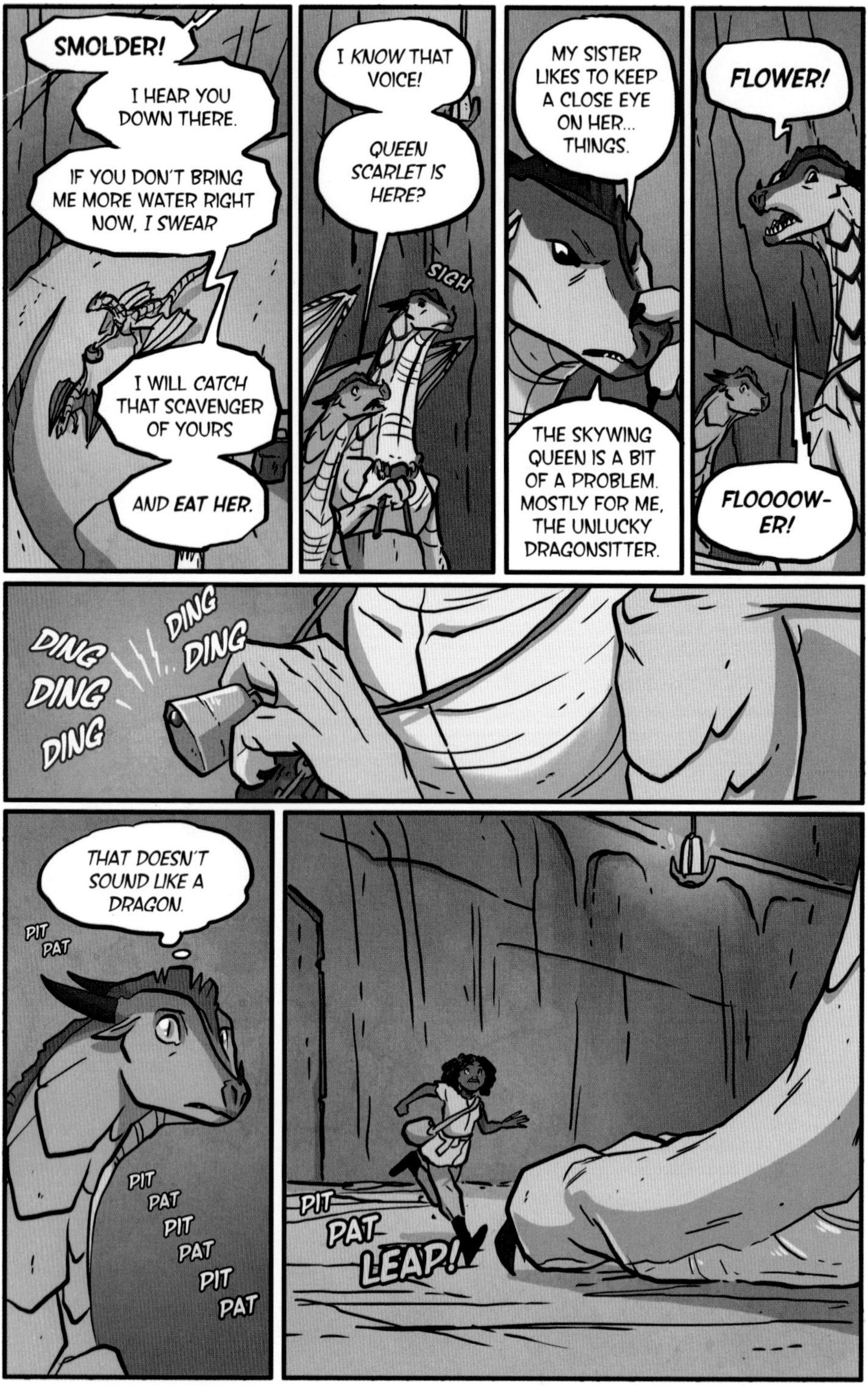
SMOLDER!
I HEAR YOU DOWN THERE.
IF YOU DON'T BRING ME MORE WATER RIGHT NOW, I SWEAR
I WILL CATCH THAT SCAVENGER OF YOURS
AND EAT HER.
I KNOW THAT VOICE!
QUEEN SCARLET IS HERE?
SIGH
MY SISTER LIKES TO KEEP A CLOSE EYE ON HER... THINGS.
THE SKYWING QUEEN IS A BIT OF A PROBLEM. MOSTLY FOR ME, THE UNLUCKY DRAGONSITTER.
FLOWER!
FLOOOOW-ER!
DING
DING
DING
DING
DING
THAT DOESN'T SOUND LIKE A DRAGON.
PIT
PAT
PIT
PAT
PIT
PAT
PIT
PAT
PIT
PAT
LEAP!

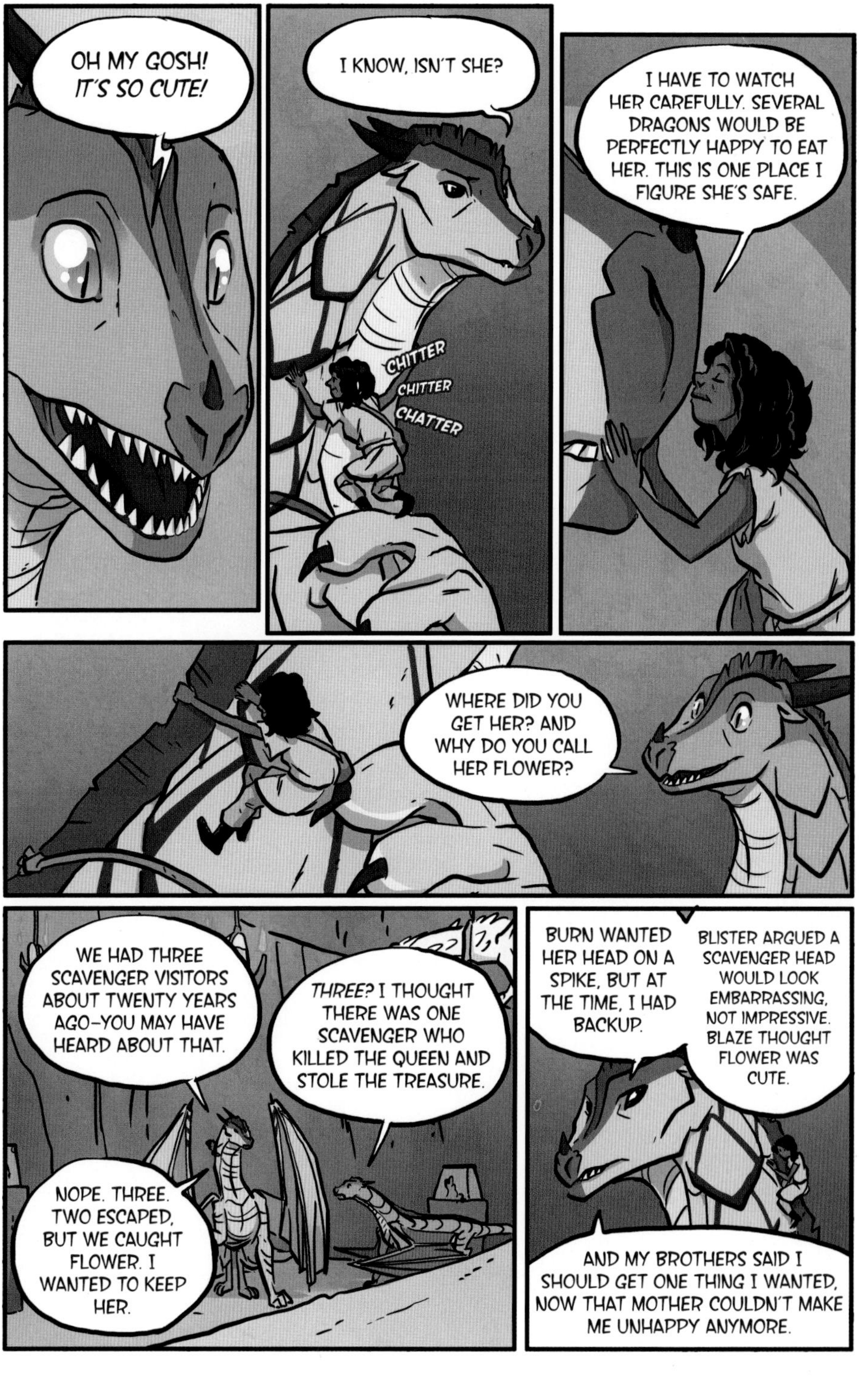
OH MY GOSH! IT'S SO CUTE!
I KNOW, ISN'T SHE?
CHITTER
CHITTER
CHATTER
I HAVE TO WATCH HER CAREFULLY. SEVERAL DRAGONS WOULD BE PERFECTLY HAPPY TO EAT HER. THIS IS ONE PLACE I FIGURE SHE'S SAFE.
WHERE DID YOU GET HER? AND WHY DO YOU CALL HER FLOWER?
WE HAD THREE SCAVENGER VISITORS ABOUT TWENTY YEARS AGO—YOU MAY HAVE HEARD ABOUT THAT.
THREE? I THOUGHT THERE WAS ONE SCAVENGER WHO KILLED THE QUEEN AND STOLE THE TREASURE.
NOPE. THREE. TWO ESCAPED, BUT WE CAUGHT FLOWER. I WANTED TO KEEP HER.
BURN WANTED HER HEAD ON A SPIKE, BUT AT THE TIME, I HAD BACKUP.
BLISTER ARGUED A SCAVENGER HEAD WOULD LOOK EMBARRASSING, NOT IMPRESSIVE. BLAZE THOUGHT FLOWER WAS CUTE.
AND MY BROTHERS SAID I SHOULD GET ONE THING I WANTED, NOW THAT MOTHER COULDN'T MAKE ME UNHAPPY ANYMORE.

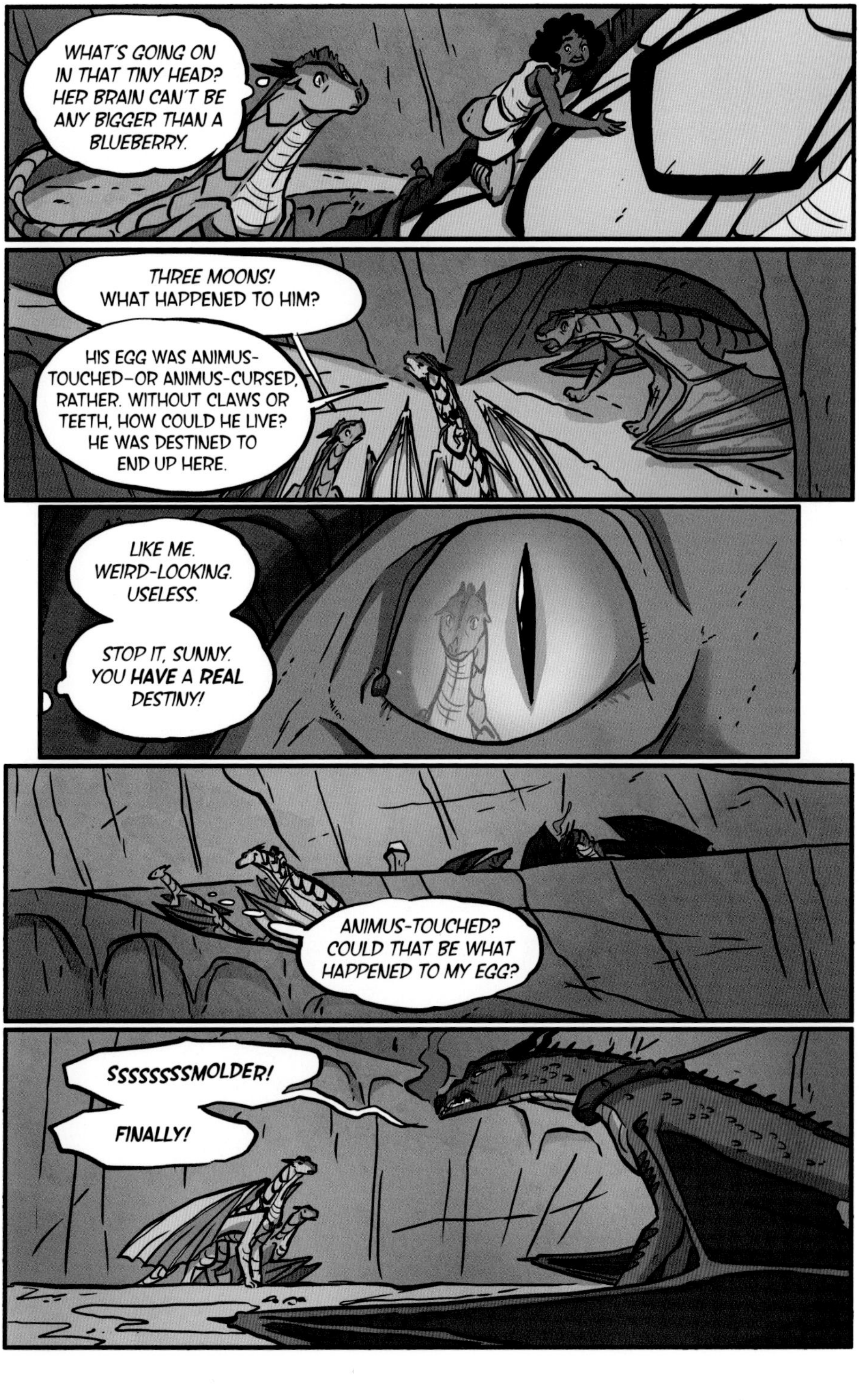
WHAT'S GOING ON IN THAT TINY HEAD? HER BRAIN CAN'T BE ANY BIGGER THAN A BLUEBERRY.
THREE MOONS! WHAT HAPPENED TO HIM?
HIS EGG WAS ANIMUS-TOUCHED—OR ANIMUS-CURSED, RATHER. WITHOUT CLAWS OR TEETH, HOW COULD HE LIVE? HE WAS DESTINED TO END UP HERE.
LIKE ME. WEIRD-LOOKING. USELESS.
STOP IT, SUNNY. YOU **HAVE** A **REAL** DESTINY!
ANIMUS-TOUCHED? COULD THAT BE WHAT HAPPENED TO MY EGG?
SSSSSSSSMOLDER!
FINALLY!

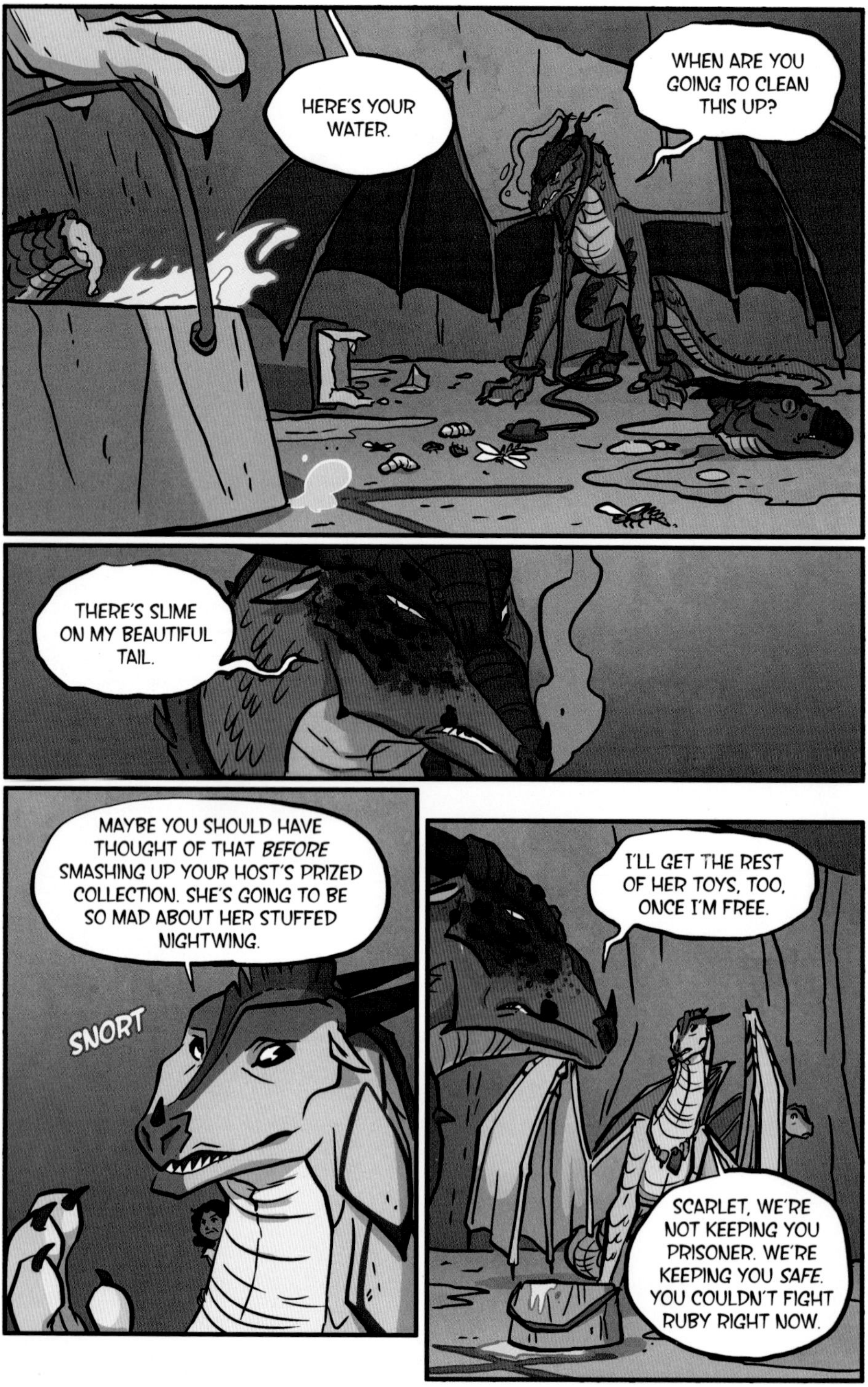
HERE'S YOUR WATER.
WHEN ARE YOU GOING TO CLEAN THIS UP?
THERE'S SLIME ON MY BEAUTIFUL TAIL.
MAYBE YOU SHOULD HAVE THOUGHT OF THAT *BEFORE* SMASHING UP YOUR HOST'S PRIZED COLLECTION. SHE'S GOING TO BE SO MAD ABOUT HER STUFFED NIGHTWING.
SNORT
I'LL GET THE REST OF HER TOYS, TOO, ONCE I'M FREE.
SCARLET, WE'RE NOT KEEPING YOU PRISONER. WE'RE KEEPING YOU *SAFE*. YOU COULDN'T FIGHT RUBY RIGHT NOW.

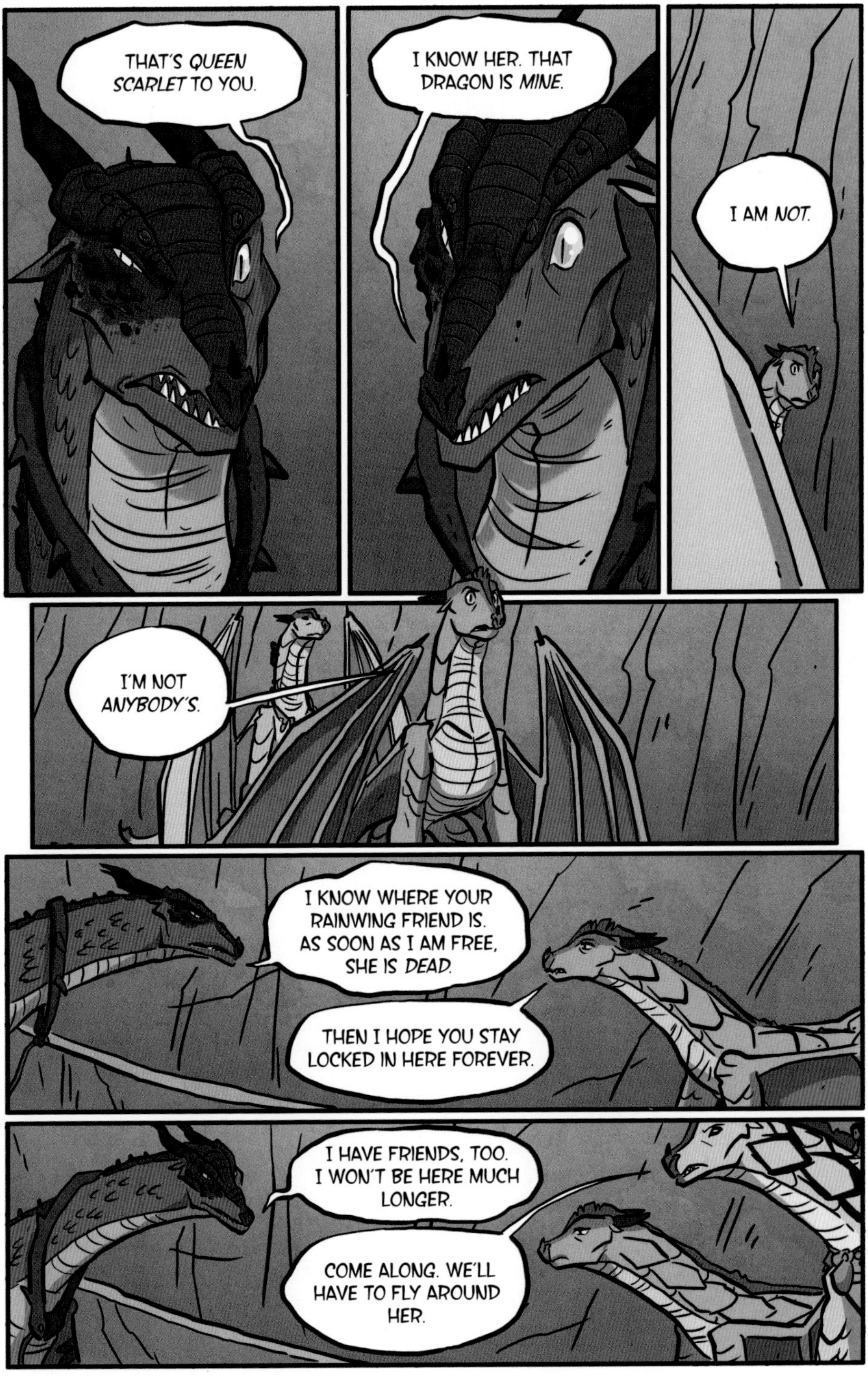
THAT'S *QUEEN SCARLET* TO YOU.
I KNOW HER. THAT DRAGON IS *MINE*.
I AM *NOT*.
I'M NOT *ANYBODY'S*.
I KNOW WHERE YOUR RAINWING FRIEND IS. AS SOON AS I AM FREE, SHE IS *DEAD*.
THEN I HOPE YOU STAY LOCKED IN HERE FOREVER.
I HAVE FRIENDS, TOO. I WON'T BE HERE MUCH LONGER.
COME ALONG. WE'LL HAVE TO FLY AROUND HER.

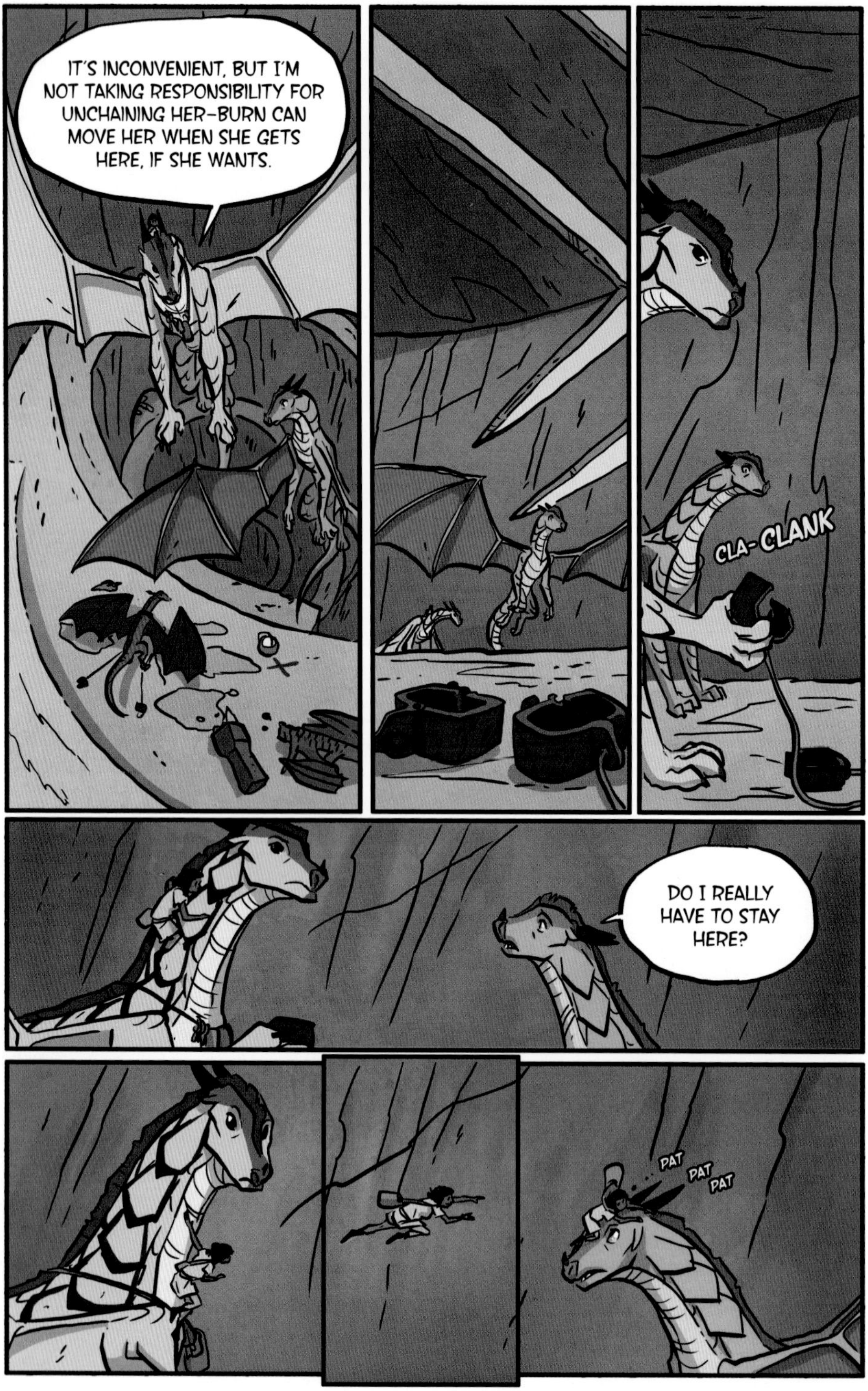
IT'S INCONVENIENT, BUT I'M NOT TAKING RESPONSIBILITY FOR UNCHAINING HER—BURN CAN MOVE HER WHEN SHE GETS HERE, IF SHE WANTS.
CLA-CLANK
DO I REALLY HAVE TO STAY HERE?
PAT PAT PAT

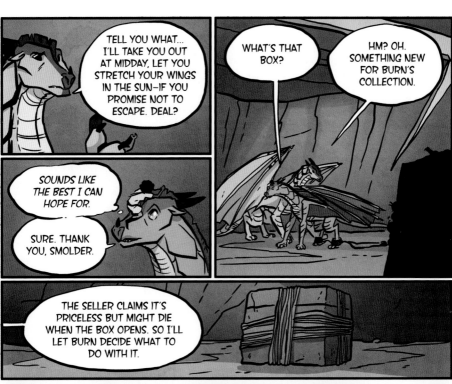

TELL YOU WHAT... I'LL TAKE YOU OUT AT MIDDAY, LET YOU STRETCH YOUR WINGS IN THE SUN—IF YOU PROMISE NOT TO ESCAPE. DEAL?

WHAT'S THAT BOX?

HM? OH. SOMETHING NEW FOR BURN'S COLLECTION.

SOUNDS LIKE THE BEST I CAN HOPE FOR.

SURE. THANK YOU, SMOLDER.

THE SELLER CLAIMS IT'S PRICELESS BUT MIGHT DIE WHEN THE BOX OPENS. SO I'LL LET BURN DECIDE WHAT TO DO WITH IT.

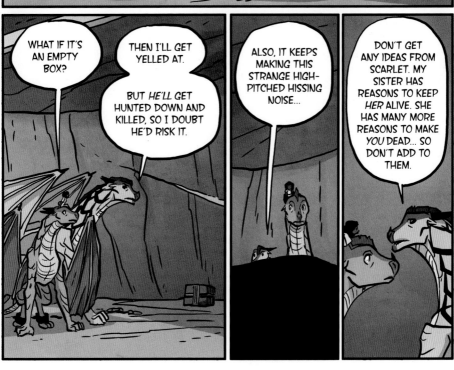

WHAT IF IT'S AN EMPTY BOX?

THEN I'LL GET YELLED AT.

BUT HE'LL GET HUNTED DOWN AND KILLED, SO I DOUBT HE'D RISK IT.

ALSO, IT KEEPS MAKING THIS STRANGE HIGH-PITCHED HISSING NOISE...

DON'T GET ANY IDEAS FROM SCARLET. MY SISTER HAS REASONS TO KEEP HER ALIVE. SHE HAS MANY MORE REASONS TO MAKE YOU DEAD... SO DON'T ADD TO THEM.

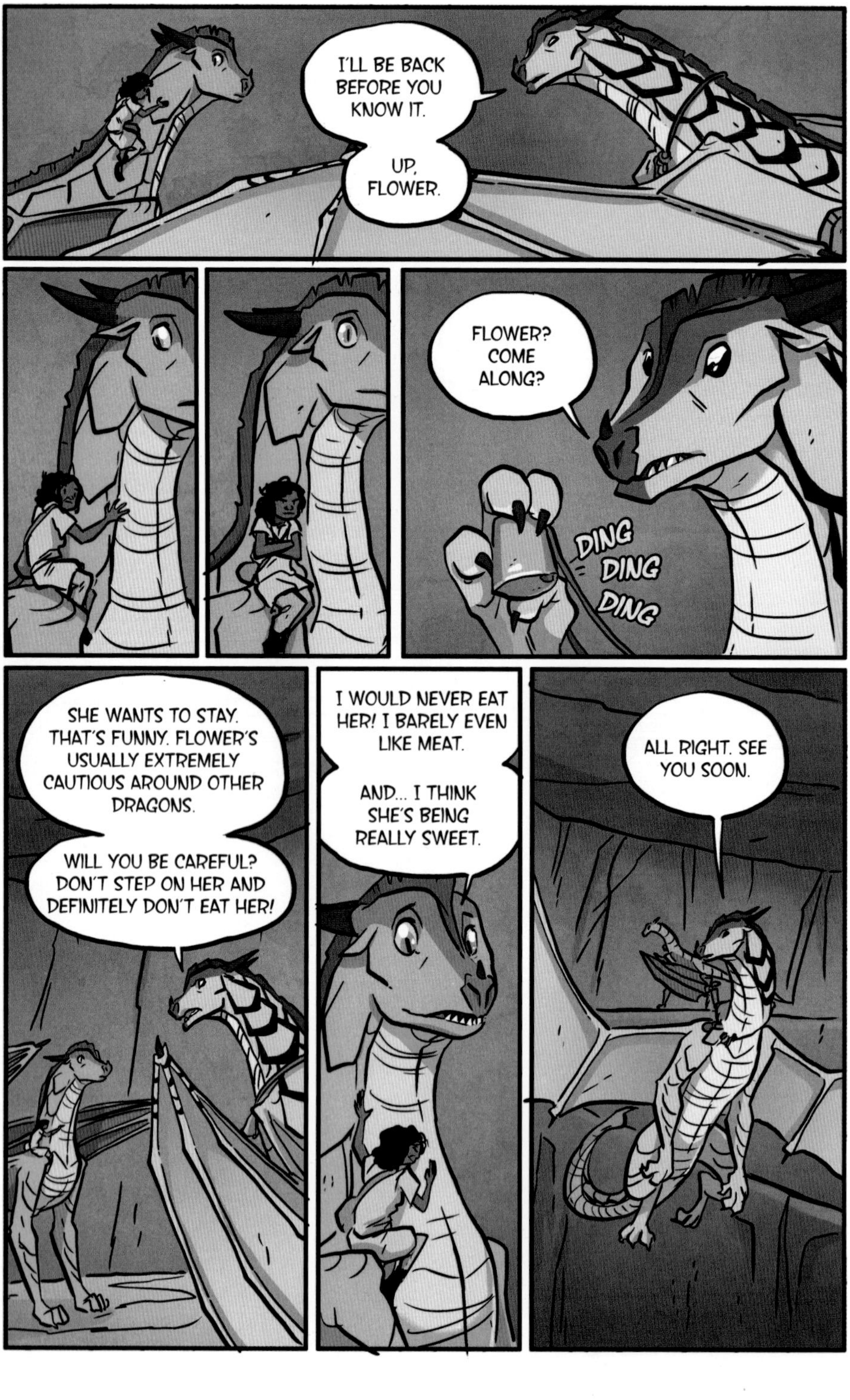
I'LL BE BACK BEFORE YOU KNOW IT.
UP, FLOWER.
FLOWER? COME ALONG?
DING DING DING
SHE WANTS TO STAY. THAT'S FUNNY. FLOWER'S USUALLY EXTREMELY CAUTIOUS AROUND OTHER DRAGONS.
WILL YOU BE CAREFUL? DON'T STEP ON HER AND DEFINITELY DON'T EAT HER!
I WOULD NEVER EAT HER! I BARELY EVEN LIKE MEAT.
AND... I THINK SHE'S BEING REALLY SWEET.
ALL RIGHT. SEE YOU SOON.

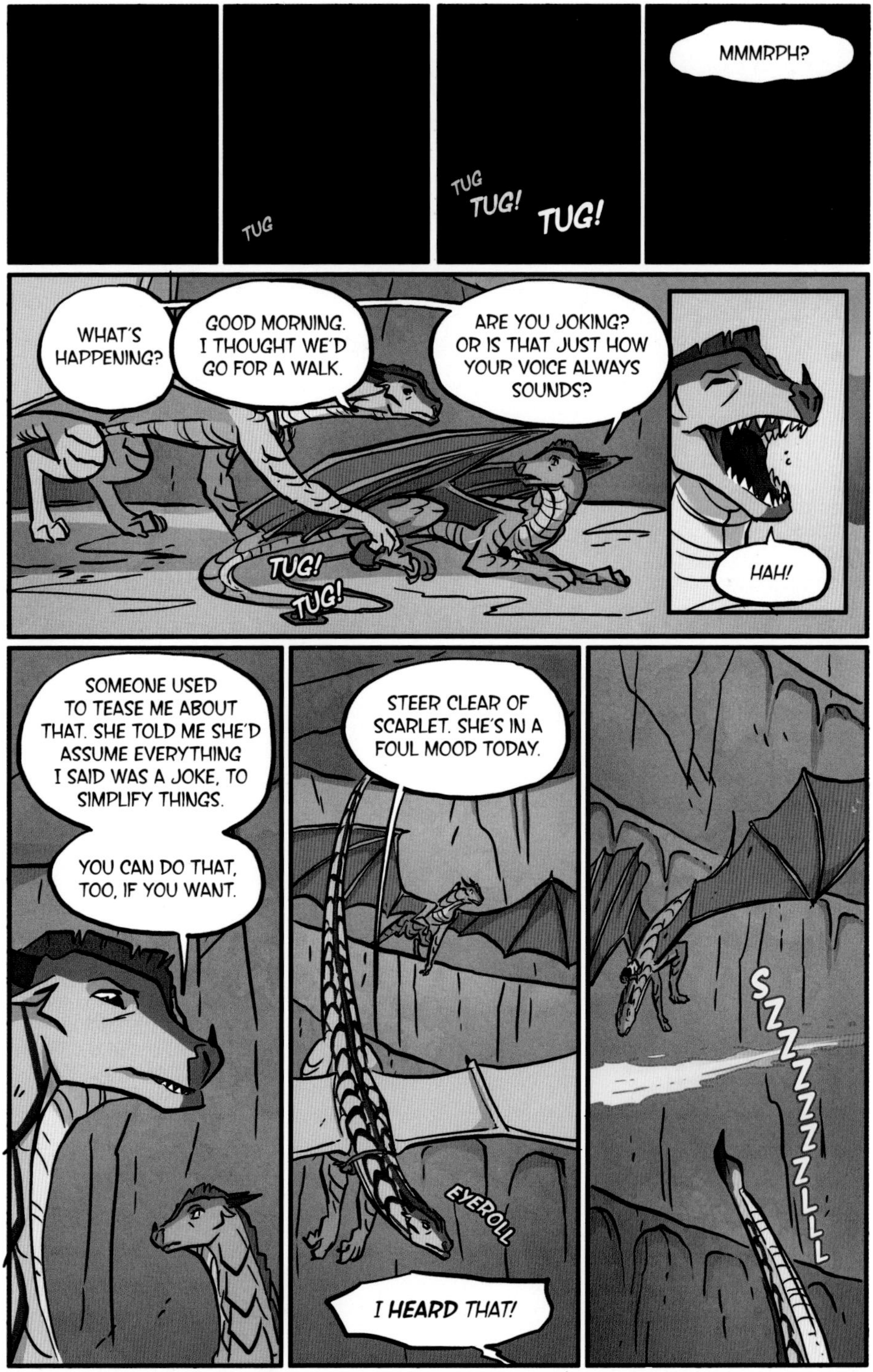
TUG
TUG
TUG!
TUG!
MMMRPH?
WHAT'S HAPPENING?
GOOD MORNING. I THOUGHT WE'D GO FOR A WALK.
ARE YOU JOKING? OR IS THAT JUST HOW YOUR VOICE ALWAYS SOUNDS?
TUG!
TUG!
HAH!
SOMEONE USED TO TEASE ME ABOUT THAT. SHE TOLD ME SHE'D ASSUME EVERYTHING I SAID WAS A JOKE, TO SIMPLIFY THINGS.
YOU CAN DO THAT, TOO, IF YOU WANT.
STEER CLEAR OF SCARLET. SHE'S IN A FOUL MOOD TODAY.
EYEROLL
I HEARD THAT!
SZZZZZZLLL

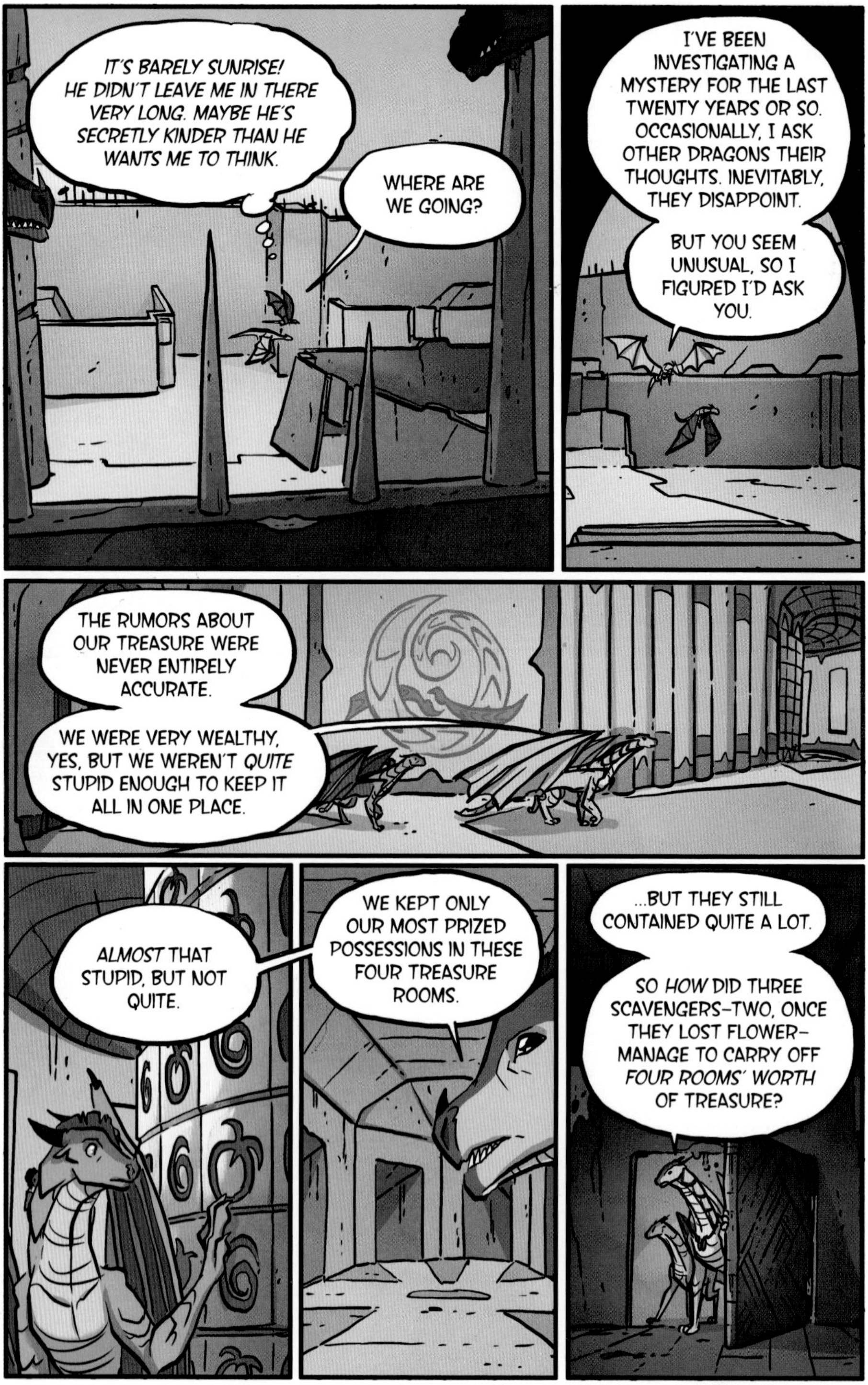
IT'S BARELY SUNRISE! HE DIDN'T LEAVE ME IN THERE VERY LONG. MAYBE HE'S SECRETLY KINDER THAN HE WANTS ME TO THINK.
WHERE ARE WE GOING?
I'VE BEEN INVESTIGATING A MYSTERY FOR THE LAST TWENTY YEARS OR SO. OCCASIONALLY, I ASK OTHER DRAGONS THEIR THOUGHTS. INEVITABLY, THEY DISAPPOINT.
BUT YOU SEEM UNUSUAL, SO I FIGURED I'D ASK YOU.
THE RUMORS ABOUT OUR TREASURE WERE NEVER ENTIRELY ACCURATE.
WE WERE VERY WEALTHY, YES, BUT WE WEREN'T *QUITE* STUPID ENOUGH TO KEEP IT ALL IN ONE PLACE.
ALMOST THAT STUPID, BUT NOT QUITE.
WE KEPT ONLY OUR MOST PRIZED POSSESSIONS IN THESE FOUR TREASURE ROOMS.
...BUT THEY STILL CONTAINED QUITE A LOT.
SO *HOW* DID THREE SCAVENGERS—TWO, ONCE THEY LOST FLOWER—MANAGE TO CARRY OFF *FOUR ROOMS' WORTH* OF TREASURE?

MAYBE A WAGON? THEY'RE GOOD AT MAKING THINGS.

WE ONLY FOUND HOOFPRINTS—THREE HORSES, GALLOPING FLAT OUT.

DID YOU FOLLOW THE PRINTS?

FOLLOW THEM! IF ONLY WE'D THOUGHT OF THAT!

OK, THAT WAS *DEFINITELY* SARCASM.

THERE WAS A LOT OF CONFUSION THE NIGHT THE QUEEN DIED.

WE ALL HEARD HER ROARING IN THE MIDDLE OF THE NIGHT AND FLEW OUT OF THE PALACE.

AND THERE SHE WAS, DEAD. HAD BURN OR BLISTER—OR EVEN BLAZE—KILLED HER? WHY NOT IN A PROPER DUEL? WHO ELSE WOULD DARE? WHO ELSE *COULD*?

THE FIRST CLUE WE FOUND WAS FLOWER, TRYING TO HIDE. SHE WAS INJURED. THE ONLY "TREASURE" SHE HAD WAS A CUTE CLAW-SWORD THING.

THAT'S WHEN WE REALIZED WE WERE DEALING WITH SCAVENGER THIEVES. BURN WAS *FURIOUS*. WE FOLLOWED THEIR HOOFPRINTS—AND BURN DECIDED TO LET THEM LEAD US STRAIGHT TO THEIR DEN.

WE BURNED IT TO THE GROUND.

AND THEN WE SEARCHED THE ASHES. NO SIGN OF TREASURE. SOME SCAVENGER MUST HAVE ESCAPED WITH IT, AND HAS IT EVEN NOW.

YOU BURNED THE *WHOLE* VILLAGE? YIKES.

BURN SAID WE HAD TO STAMP OUT THE VERMIN BEFORE THEY DID IT AGAIN.

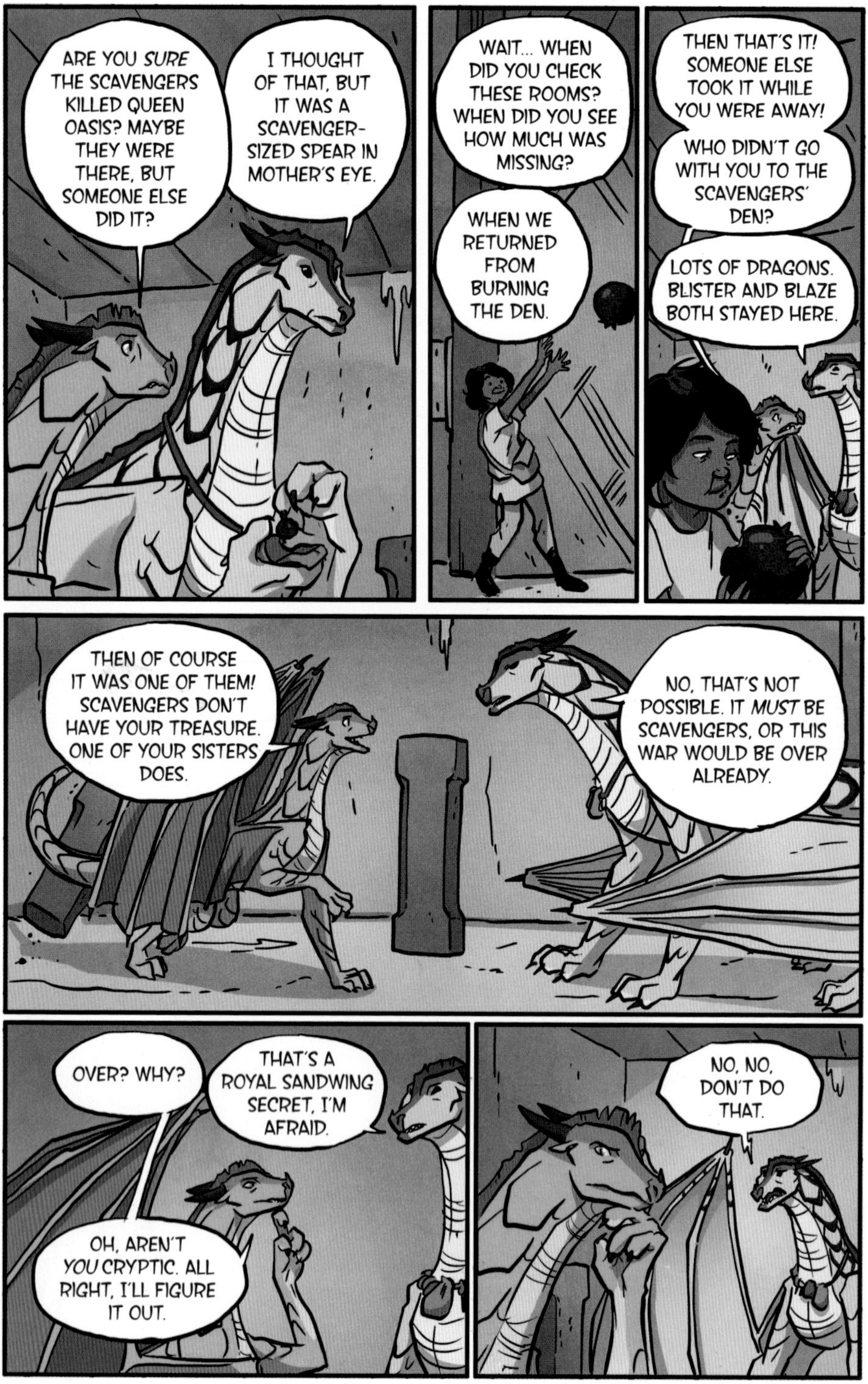
ARE YOU *SURE* THE SCAVENGERS KILLED QUEEN OASIS? MAYBE THEY WERE THERE, BUT SOMEONE ELSE DID IT?
I THOUGHT OF THAT, BUT IT WAS A SCAVENGER-SIZED SPEAR IN MOTHER'S EYE.
WAIT... WHEN DID YOU CHECK THESE ROOMS? WHEN DID YOU SEE HOW MUCH WAS MISSING?
WHEN WE RETURNED FROM BURNING THE DEN.
THEN THAT'S IT! SOMEONE ELSE TOOK IT WHILE YOU WERE AWAY!
WHO DIDN'T GO WITH YOU TO THE SCAVENGERS' DEN?
LOTS OF DRAGONS. BLISTER AND BLAZE BOTH STAYED HERE.
THEN OF COURSE IT WAS ONE OF THEM! SCAVENGERS DON'T HAVE YOUR TREASURE. ONE OF YOUR SISTERS DOES.
NO, THAT'S NOT POSSIBLE. IT *MUST* BE SCAVENGERS, OR THIS WAR WOULD BE OVER ALREADY.
OVER? WHY?
THAT'S A ROYAL SANDWING SECRET, I'M AFRAID.
OH, AREN'T *YOU* CRYPTIC. ALL RIGHT, I'LL FIGURE IT OUT.
NO, NO, DON'T DO THAT.

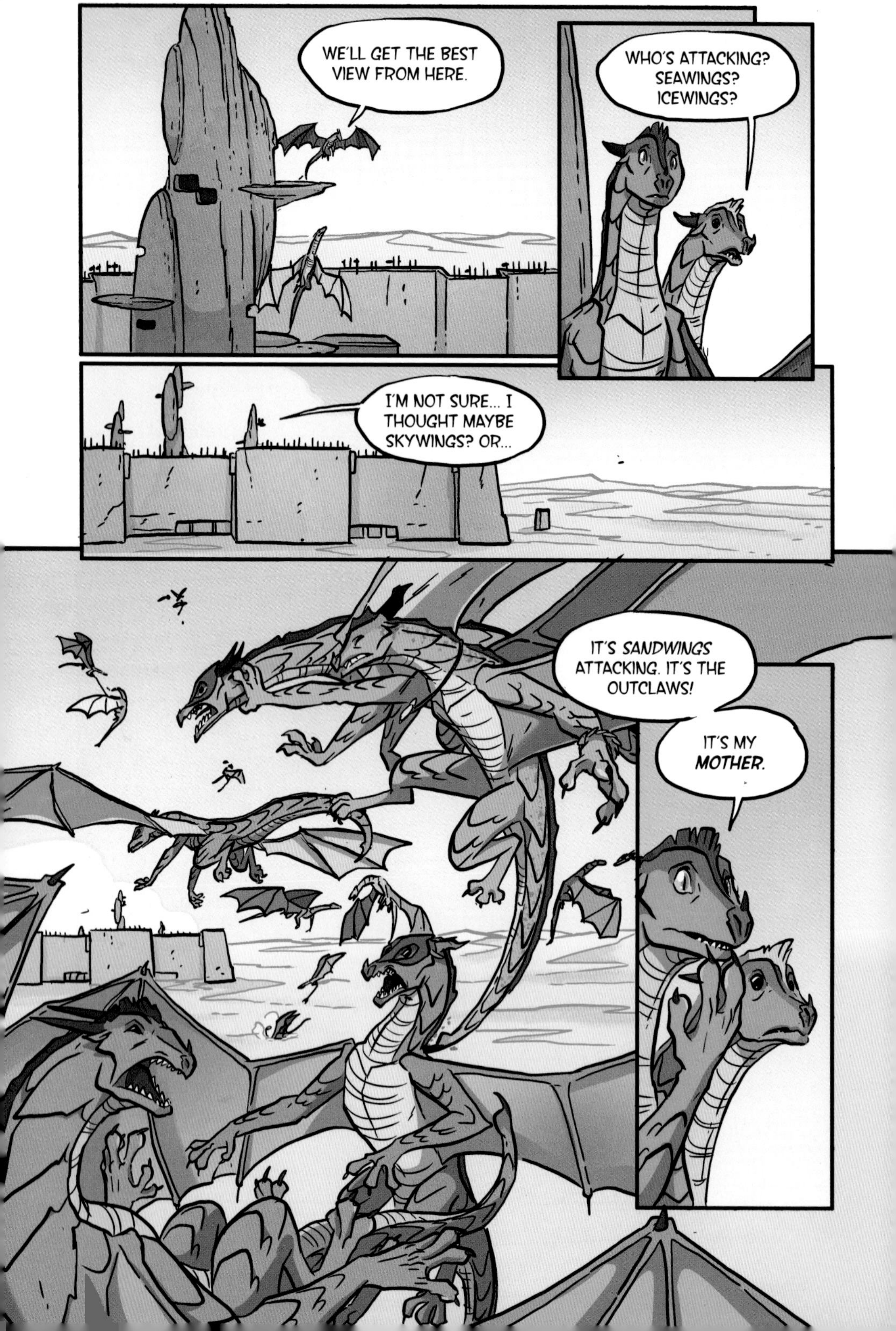
WE'LL GET THE BEST VIEW FROM HERE.
WHO'S ATTACKING? SEAWINGS? ICEWINGS?
I'M NOT SURE... I THOUGHT MAYBE SKYWINGS? OR...
IT'S *SANDWINGS* ATTACKING. IT'S THE OUTCLAWS!
IT'S MY ***MOTHER.***

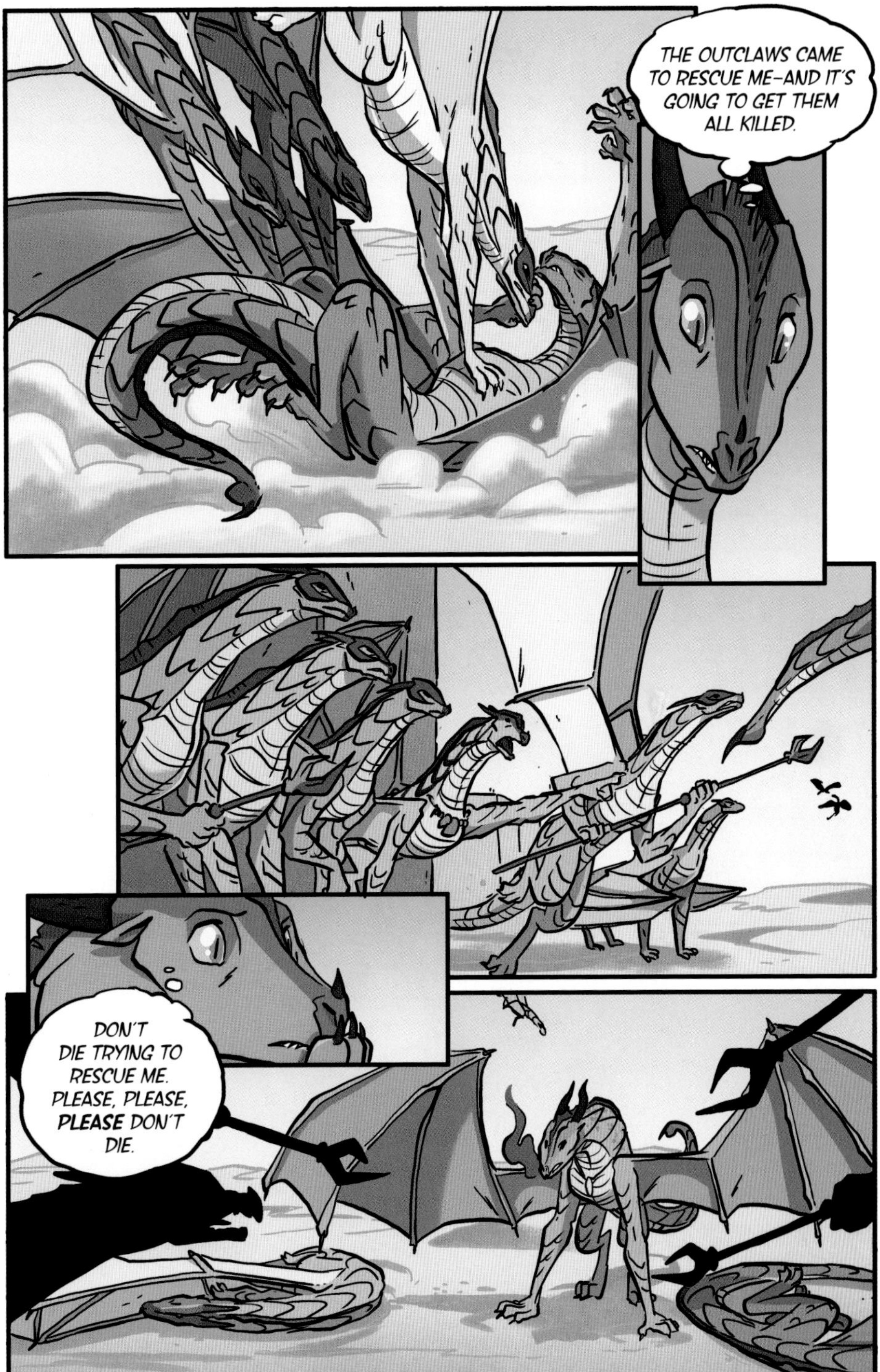
THE OUTCLAWS CAME TO RESCUE ME—AND IT'S GOING TO GET THEM ALL KILLED.
DON'T DIE TRYING TO RESCUE ME. PLEASE, PLEASE, **PLEASE** DON'T DIE.

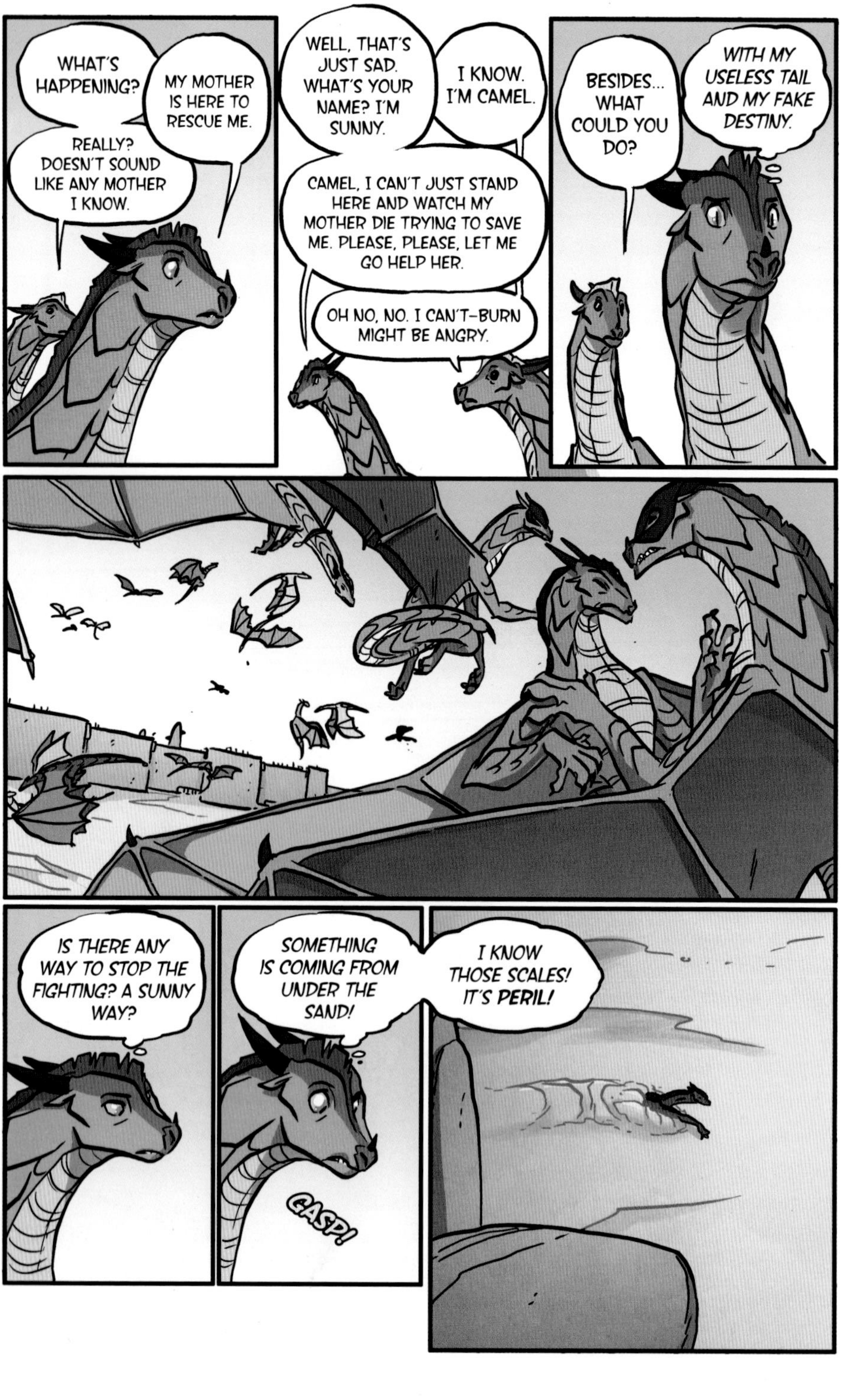
WHAT'S HAPPENING?
MY MOTHER IS HERE TO RESCUE ME.
REALLY? DOESN'T SOUND LIKE ANY MOTHER I KNOW.
WELL, THAT'S JUST SAD. WHAT'S YOUR NAME? I'M SUNNY.
I KNOW. I'M CAMEL.
CAMEL, I CAN'T JUST STAND HERE AND WATCH MY MOTHER DIE TRYING TO SAVE ME. PLEASE, PLEASE, LET ME GO HELP HER.
OH NO, NO. I CAN'T—BURN MIGHT BE ANGRY.
BESIDES... WHAT COULD YOU DO?
WITH MY USELESS TAIL AND MY FAKE DESTINY.
IS THERE ANY WAY TO STOP THE FIGHTING? A SUNNY WAY?
SOMETHING IS COMING FROM UNDER THE SAND!
GASP!
I KNOW THOSE SCALES! IT'S PERIL!

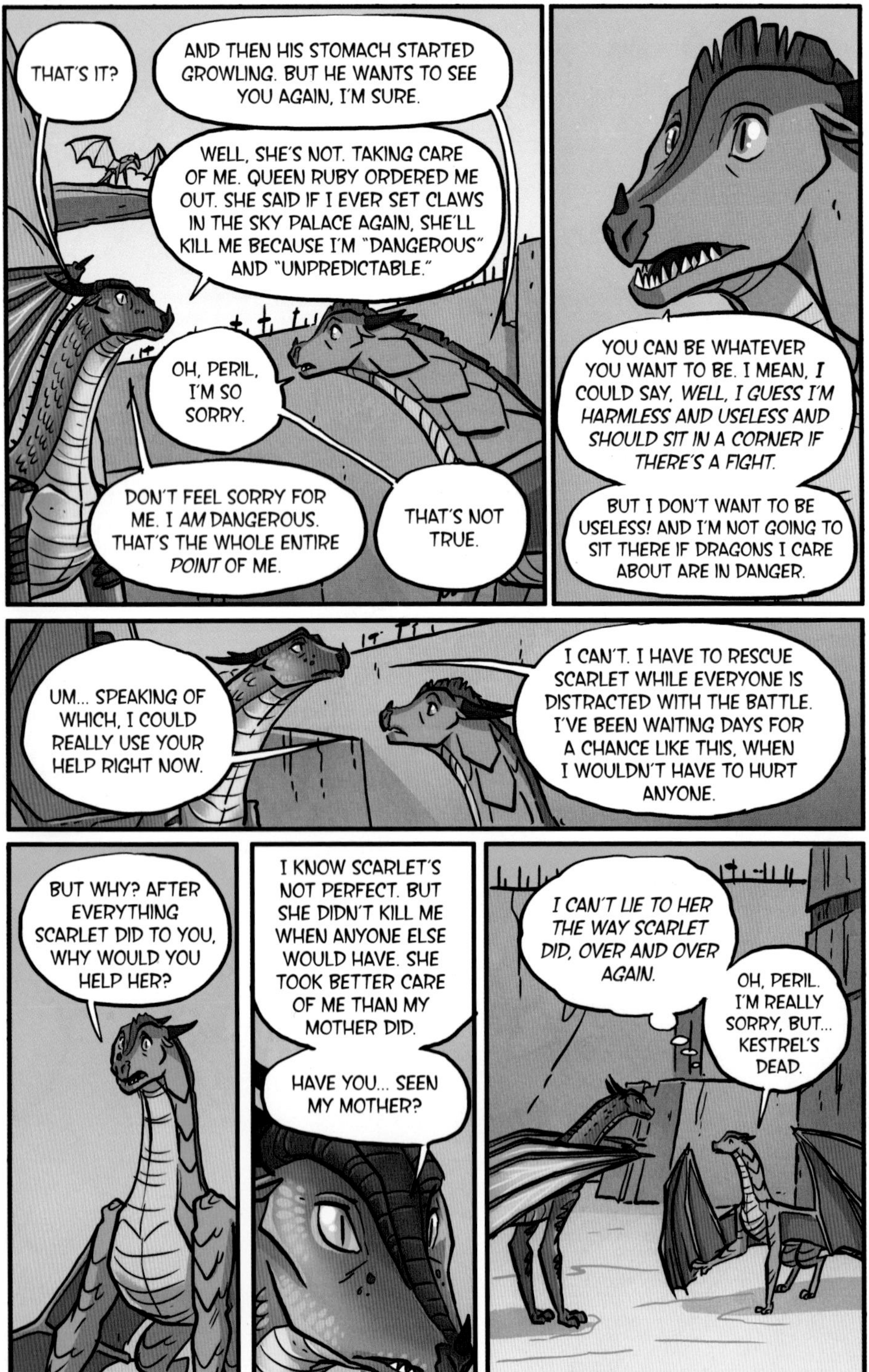

THAT'S IT?
AND THEN HIS STOMACH STARTED GROWLING. BUT HE WANTS TO SEE YOU AGAIN, I'M SURE.
WELL, SHE'S NOT. TAKING CARE OF ME. QUEEN RUBY ORDERED ME OUT. SHE SAID IF I EVER SET CLAWS IN THE SKY PALACE AGAIN, SHE'LL KILL ME BECAUSE I'M "DANGEROUS" AND "UNPREDICTABLE."
OH, PERIL, I'M SO SORRY.
DON'T FEEL SORRY FOR ME. I *AM* DANGEROUS. THAT'S THE WHOLE ENTIRE *POINT* OF ME.
THAT'S NOT TRUE.
YOU CAN BE WHATEVER YOU WANT TO BE. I MEAN, *I* COULD SAY, *WELL, I GUESS I'M HARMLESS AND USELESS AND SHOULD SIT IN A CORNER IF THERE'S A FIGHT.*
BUT I DON'T WANT TO BE USELESS! AND I'M NOT GOING TO SIT THERE IF DRAGONS I CARE ABOUT ARE IN DANGER.
UM... SPEAKING OF WHICH, I COULD REALLY USE YOUR HELP RIGHT NOW.
I CAN'T. I HAVE TO RESCUE SCARLET WHILE EVERYONE IS DISTRACTED WITH THE BATTLE. I'VE BEEN WAITING DAYS FOR A CHANCE LIKE THIS, WHEN I WOULDN'T HAVE TO HURT ANYONE.
BUT WHY? AFTER EVERYTHING SCARLET DID TO YOU, WHY WOULD YOU HELP HER?
I KNOW SCARLET'S NOT PERFECT. BUT SHE DIDN'T KILL ME WHEN ANYONE ELSE WOULD HAVE. SHE TOOK BETTER CARE OF ME THAN MY MOTHER DID.
HAVE YOU... SEEN MY MOTHER?
I CAN'T LIE TO HER THE WAY SCARLET DID, OVER AND OVER AGAIN.
OH, PERIL. I'M REALLY SORRY, BUT... KESTREL'S DEAD.

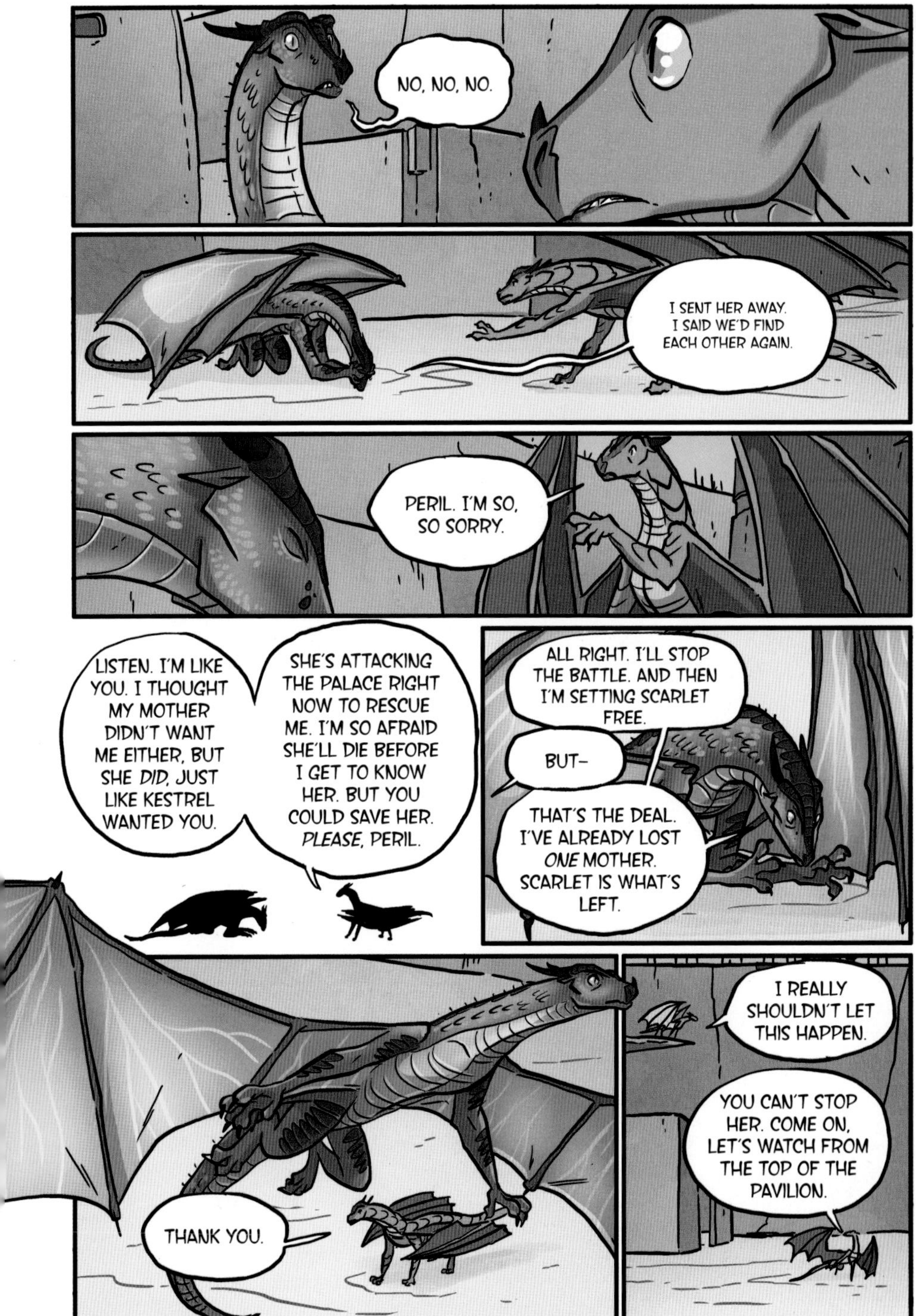
NO, NO, NO.
I SENT HER AWAY. I SAID WE'D FIND EACH OTHER AGAIN.
PERIL. I'M SO, SO SORRY.
LISTEN. I'M LIKE YOU. I THOUGHT MY MOTHER DIDN'T WANT ME EITHER, BUT SHE *DID*, JUST LIKE KESTREL WANTED YOU.
SHE'S ATTACKING THE PALACE RIGHT NOW TO RESCUE ME. I'M SO AFRAID SHE'LL DIE BEFORE I GET TO KNOW HER. BUT YOU COULD SAVE HER. *PLEASE*, PERIL.
ALL RIGHT. I'LL STOP THE BATTLE. AND THEN I'M SETTING SCARLET FREE.
BUT–
THAT'S THE DEAL. I'VE ALREADY LOST *ONE* MOTHER. SCARLET IS WHAT'S LEFT.
THANK YOU.
I REALLY SHOULDN'T LET THIS HAPPEN.
YOU CAN'T STOP HER. COME ON, LET'S WATCH FROM THE TOP OF THE PAVILION.

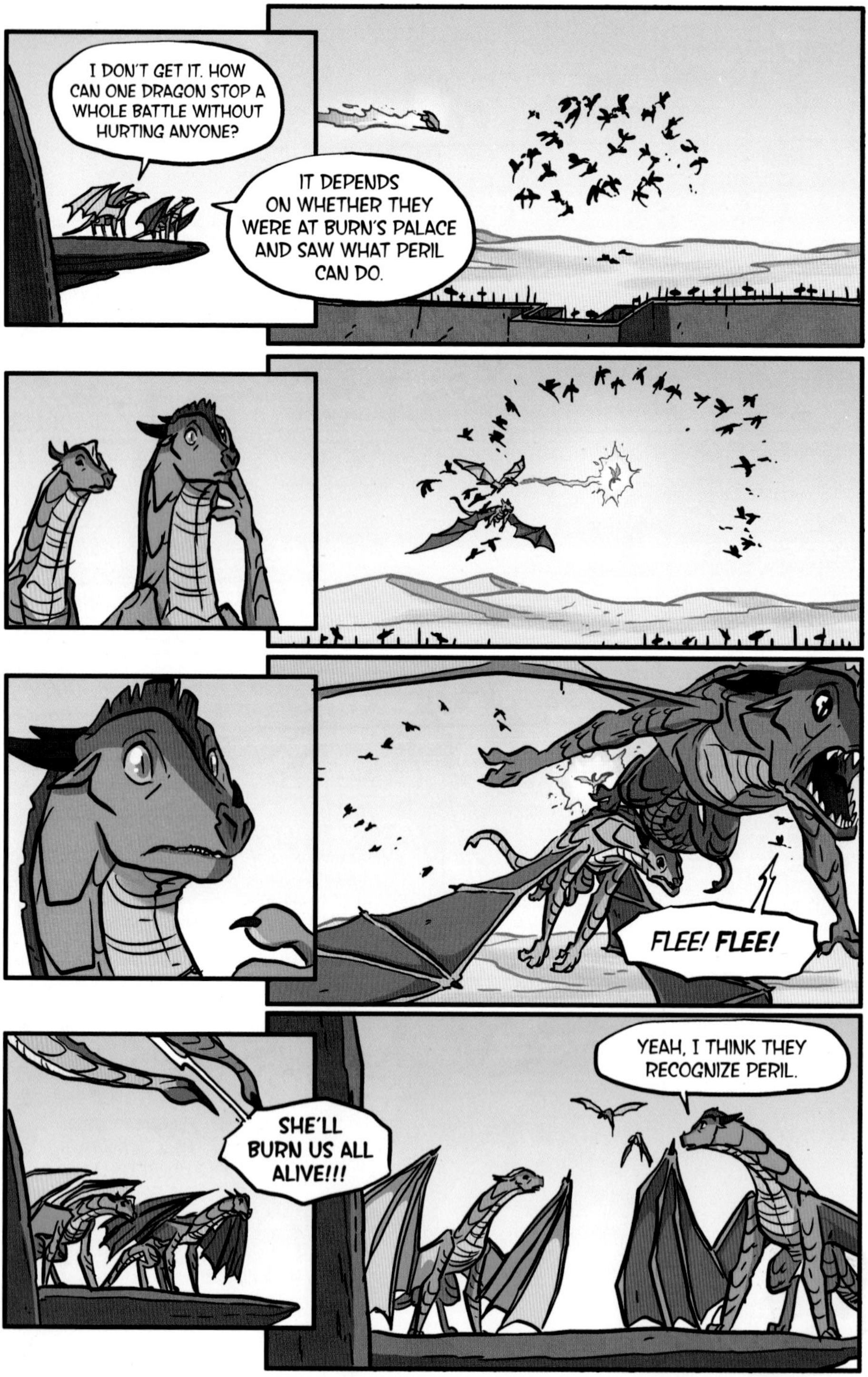
I DON'T GET IT. HOW CAN ONE DRAGON STOP A WHOLE BATTLE WITHOUT HURTING ANYONE?
IT DEPENDS ON WHETHER THEY WERE AT BURN'S PALACE AND SAW WHAT PERIL CAN DO.
FLEE! FLEE!
SHE'LL BURN US ALL ALIVE!!!
YEAH, I THINK THEY RECOGNIZE PERIL.

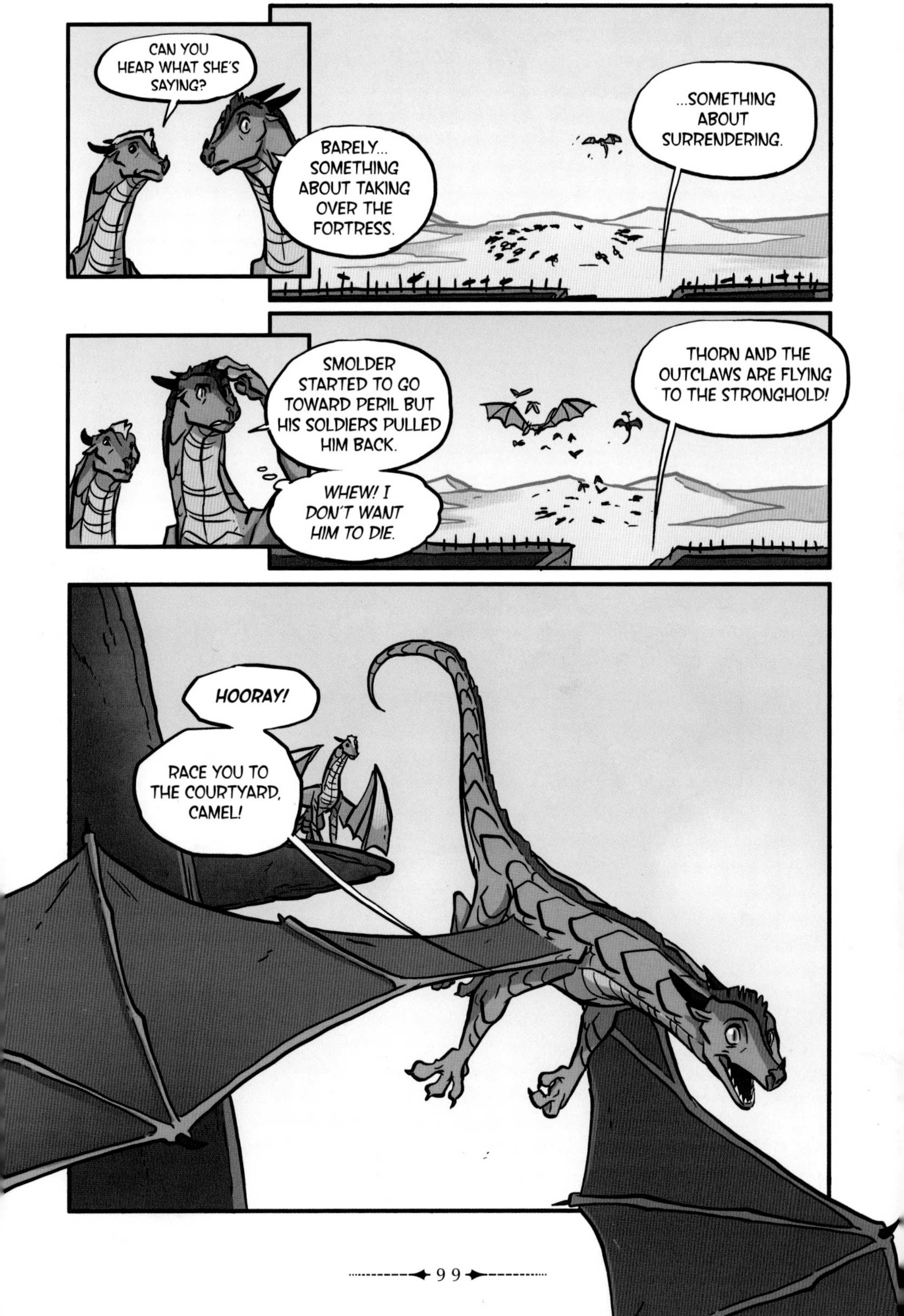
CAN YOU HEAR WHAT SHE'S SAYING?
BARELY... SOMETHING ABOUT TAKING OVER THE FORTRESS.
...SOMETHING ABOUT SURRENDERING.
SMOLDER STARTED TO GO TOWARD PERIL BUT HIS SOLDIERS PULLED HIM BACK.
WHEW! I DON'T WANT HIM TO DIE.
THORN AND THE OUTCLAWS ARE FLYING TO THE STRONGHOLD!
HOORAY!
RACE YOU TO THE COURTYARD, CAMEL!

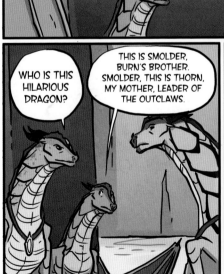

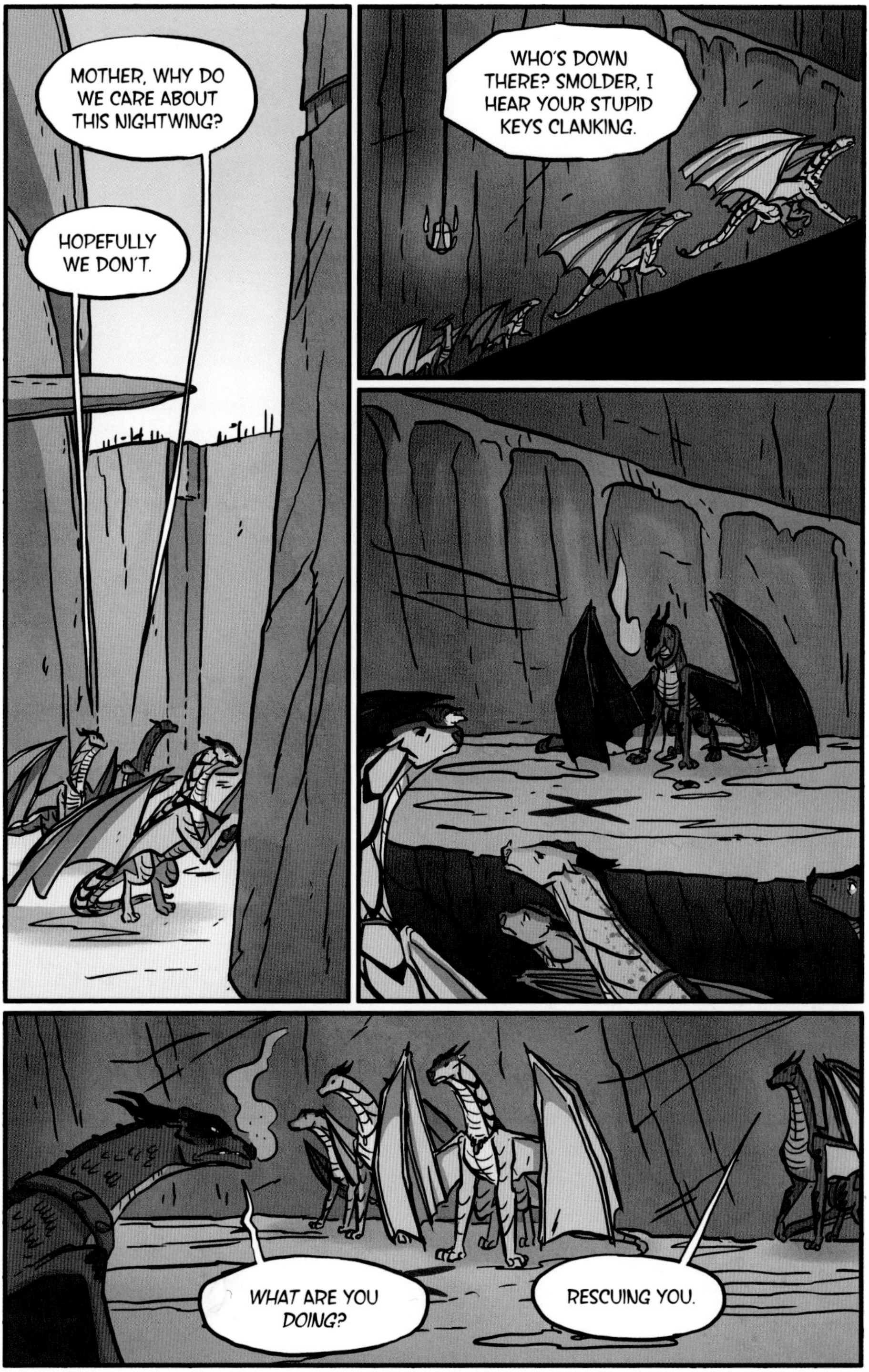
MOTHER, WHY DO WE CARE ABOUT THIS NIGHTWING?
HOPEFULLY WE DON'T.
WHO'S DOWN THERE? SMOLDER, I HEAR YOUR STUPID KEYS CLANKING.
WHAT ARE YOU DOING?
RESCUING YOU.

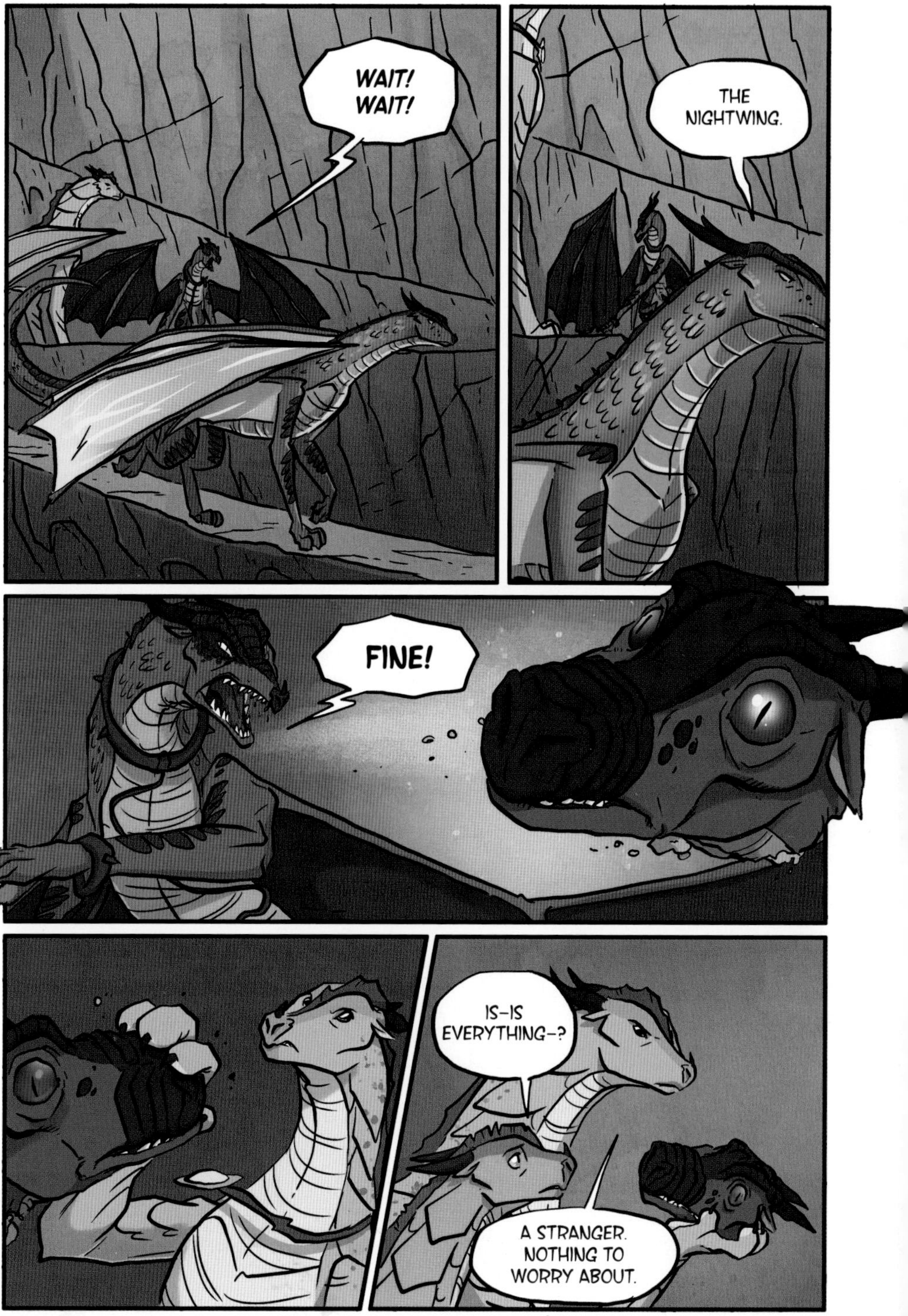
WAIT! WAIT!
THE NIGHTWING.
FINE!
IS—IS EVERYTHING—?
A STRANGER. NOTHING TO WORRY ABOUT.

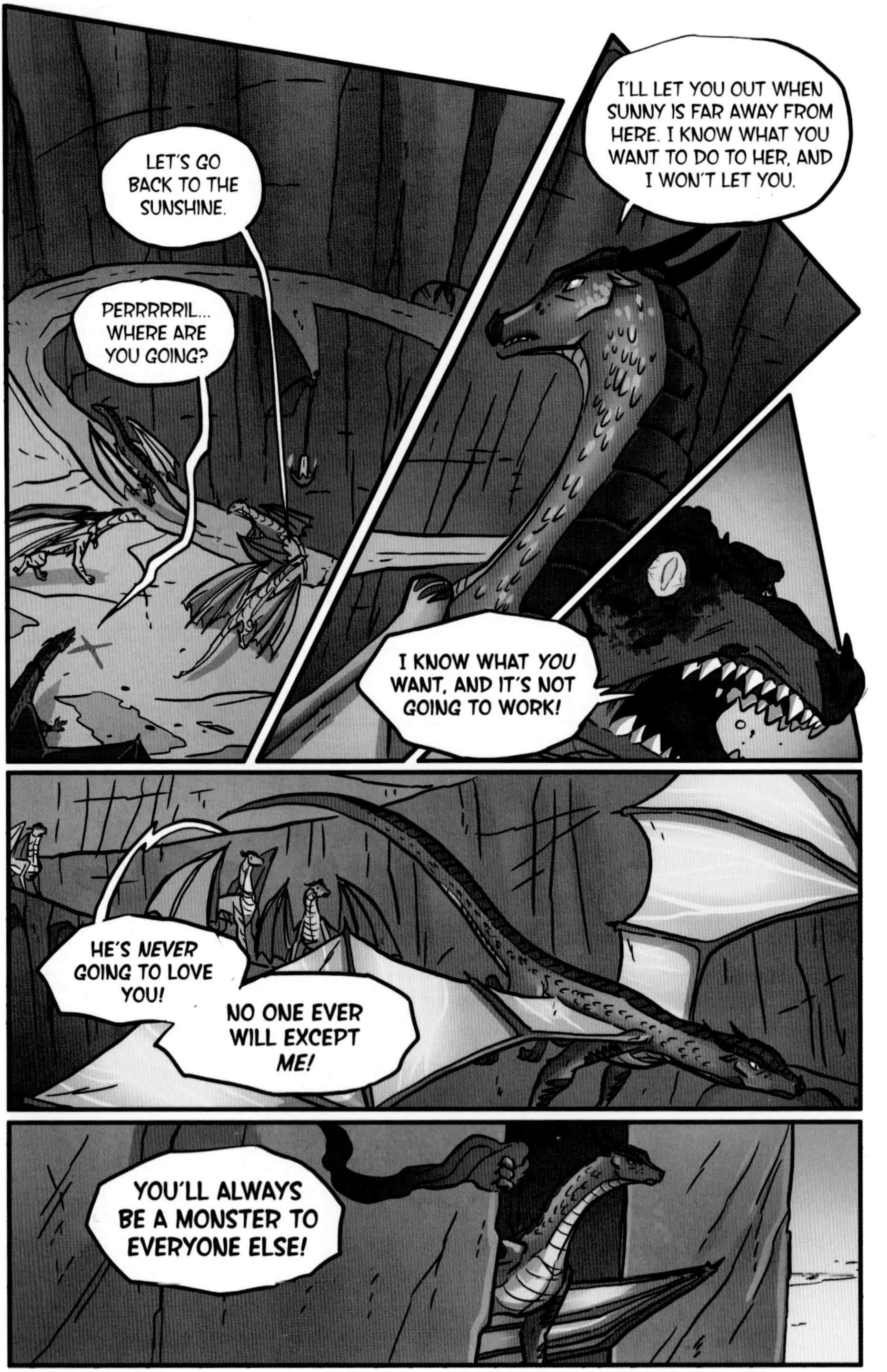
LET'S GO BACK TO THE SUNSHINE.
PERRRRRIL... WHERE ARE YOU GOING?
I'LL LET YOU OUT WHEN SUNNY IS FAR AWAY FROM HERE. I KNOW WHAT YOU WANT TO DO TO HER, AND I WON'T LET YOU.
I KNOW WHAT *YOU* WANT, AND IT'S NOT GOING TO WORK!
HE'S *NEVER* GOING TO LOVE YOU!
NO ONE EVER WILL EXCEPT *ME!*
YOU'LL ALWAYS BE A MONSTER TO EVERYONE ELSE!

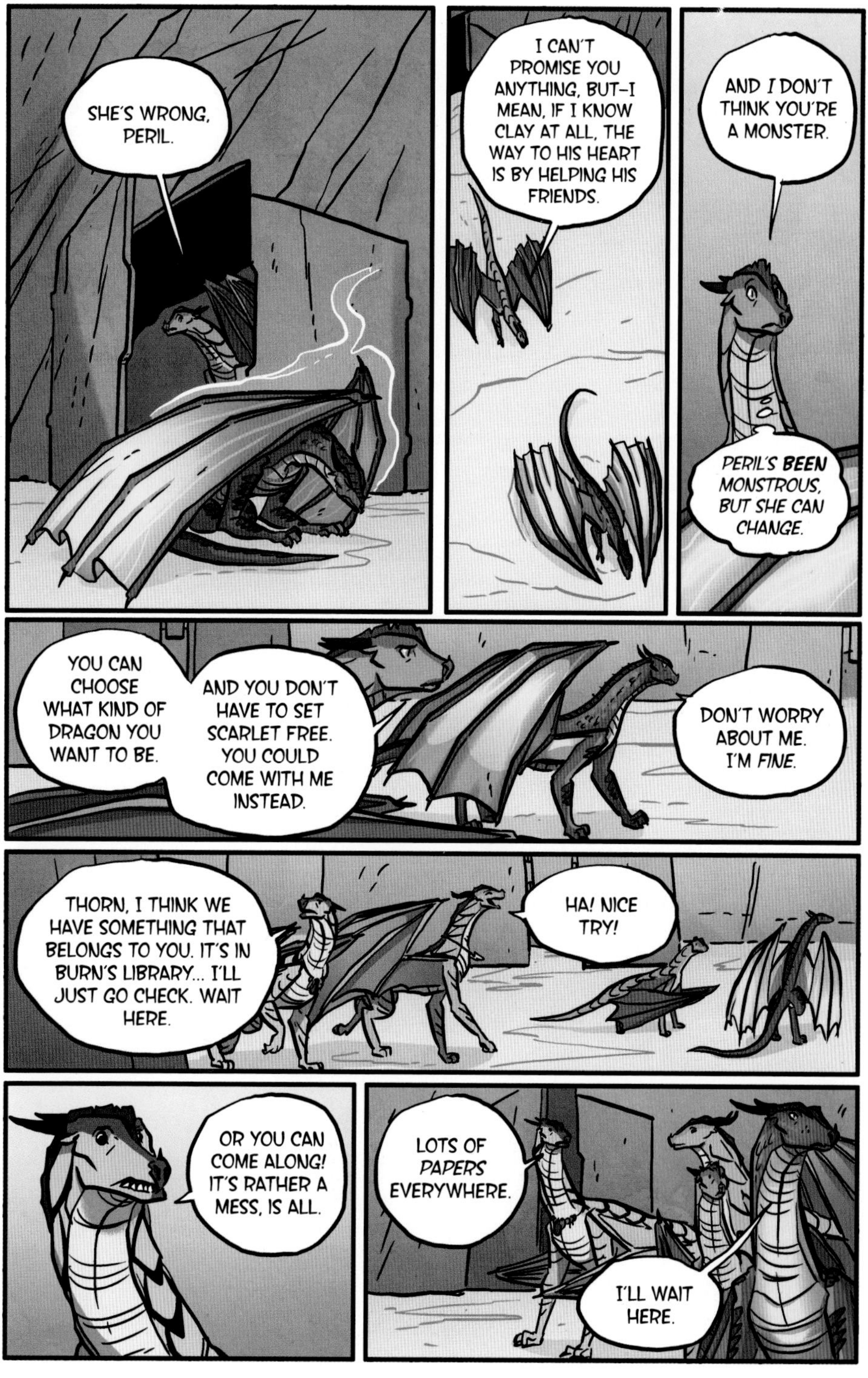
SHE'S WRONG, PERIL.
I CAN'T PROMISE YOU ANYTHING, BUT—I MEAN, IF I KNOW CLAY AT ALL, THE WAY TO HIS HEART IS BY HELPING HIS FRIENDS.
AND *I* DON'T THINK YOU'RE A MONSTER.
PERIL'S ***BEEN*** *MONSTROUS, BUT SHE CAN CHANGE.*
YOU CAN CHOOSE WHAT KIND OF DRAGON YOU WANT TO BE.
AND YOU DON'T HAVE TO SET SCARLET FREE. YOU COULD COME WITH ME INSTEAD.
DON'T WORRY ABOUT ME. I'M *FINE.*
THORN, I THINK WE HAVE SOMETHING THAT BELONGS TO YOU. IT'S IN BURN'S LIBRARY... I'LL JUST GO CHECK. WAIT HERE.
HA! NICE TRY!
OR YOU CAN COME ALONG! IT'S RATHER A MESS, IS ALL.
LOTS OF *PAPERS* EVERYWHERE.
I'LL WAIT HERE.

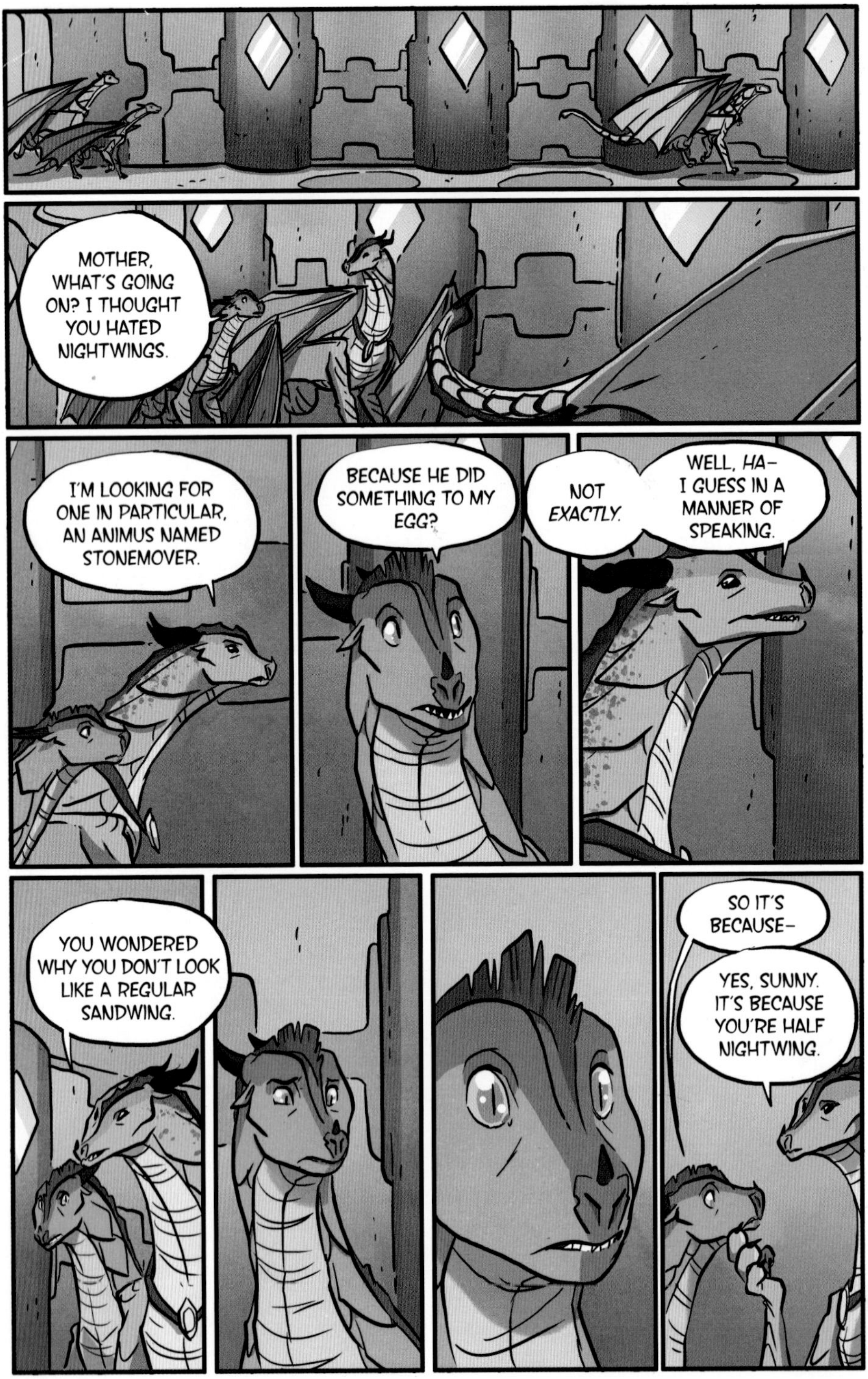
MOTHER, WHAT'S GOING ON? I THOUGHT YOU HATED NIGHTWINGS.
I'M LOOKING FOR ONE IN PARTICULAR, AN ANIMUS NAMED STONEMOVER.
BECAUSE HE DID SOMETHING TO MY EGG?
NOT *EXACTLY.*
WELL, *HA*— I GUESS IN A MANNER OF SPEAKING.
YOU WONDERED WHY YOU DON'T LOOK LIKE A REGULAR SANDWING.
SO IT'S BECAUSE—
YES, SUNNY. IT'S BECAUSE YOU'RE HALF NIGHTWING.

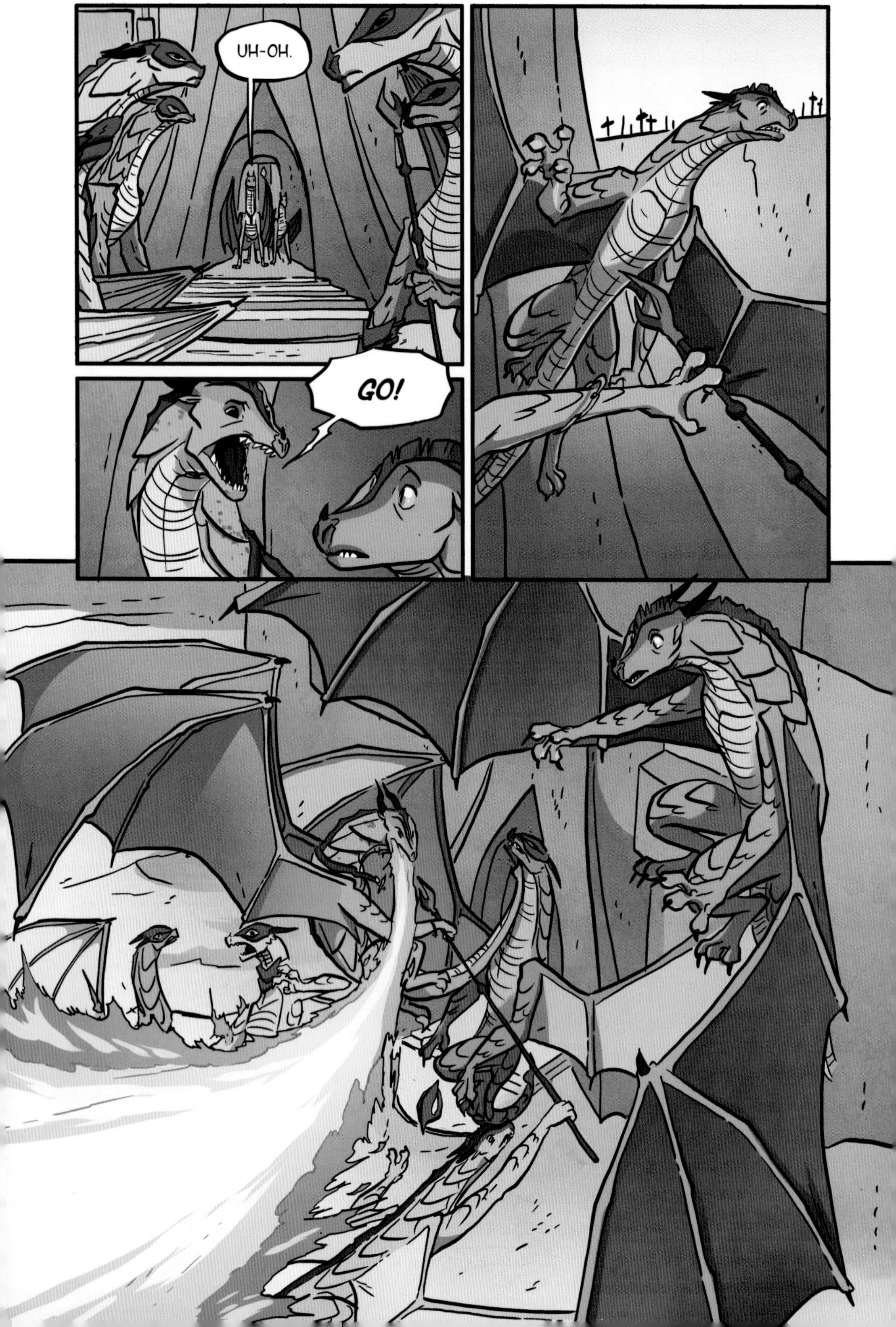
UH-OH.
GO!

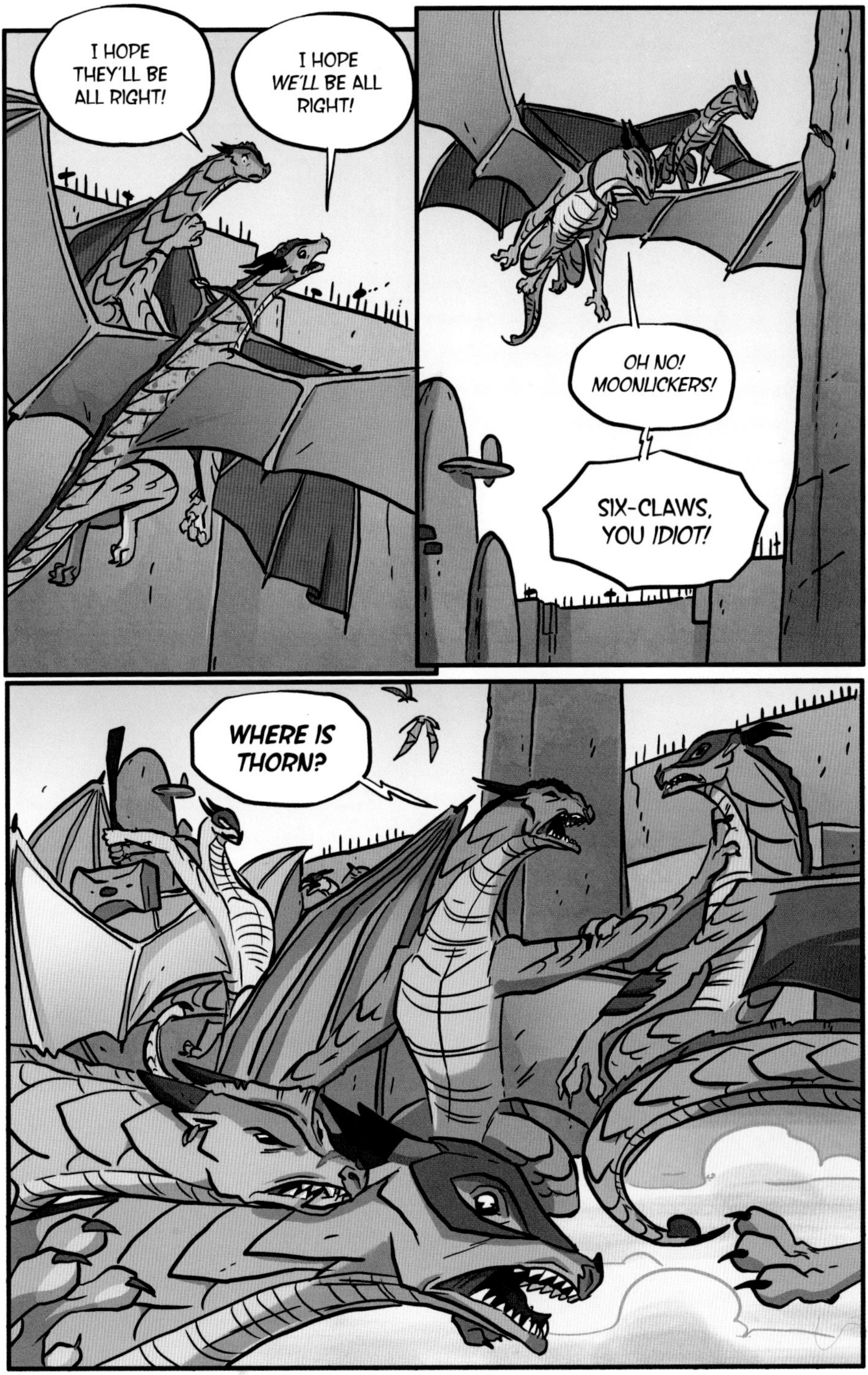
I HOPE THEY'LL BE ALL RIGHT!
I HOPE WE'LL BE ALL RIGHT!
OH NO! MOONLICKERS!
SIX-CLAWS, YOU IDIOT!
WHERE IS THORN?

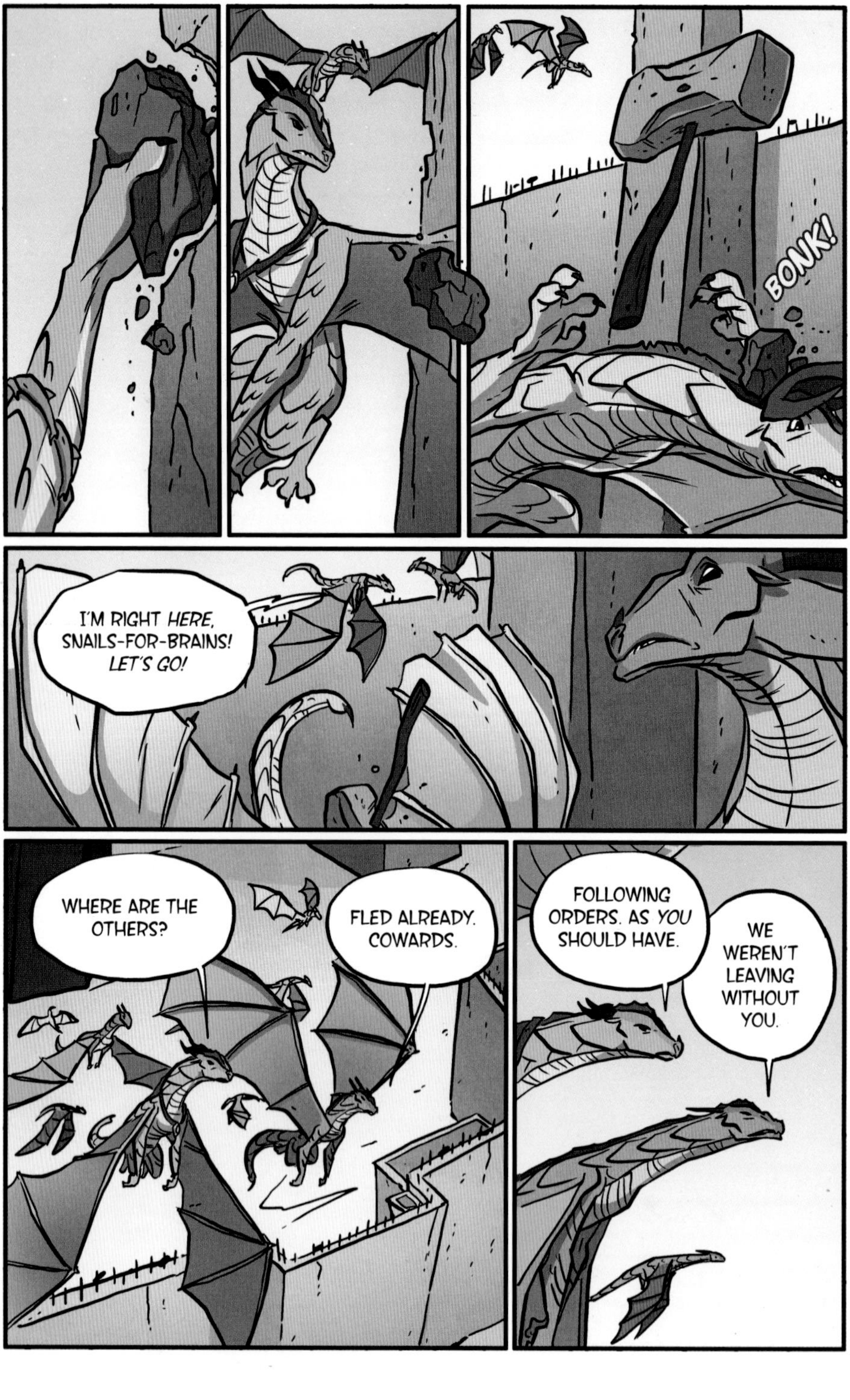
BONK!
I'M RIGHT *HERE*, SNAILS-FOR-BRAINS! *LET'S GO!*
WHERE ARE THE OTHERS?
FLED ALREADY. COWARDS.
FOLLOWING ORDERS. AS *YOU* SHOULD HAVE.
WE WEREN'T LEAVING WITHOUT YOU.

DREAMVISITOR? TREASURE? *WHERE?*

WHOA.

I DIDN'T EXPECT THAT TO ACTUALLY *WORK!*

THANK YOU. WHERE'S THE REST OF THE TREASURE?

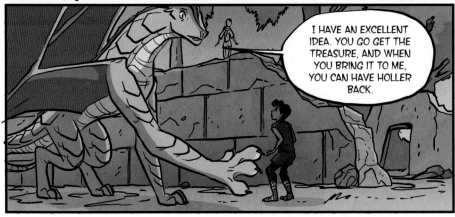

I HAVE AN EXCELLENT IDEA. YOU GO GET THE TREASURE, AND WHEN YOU BRING IT TO ME, YOU CAN HAVE HOLLER BACK.

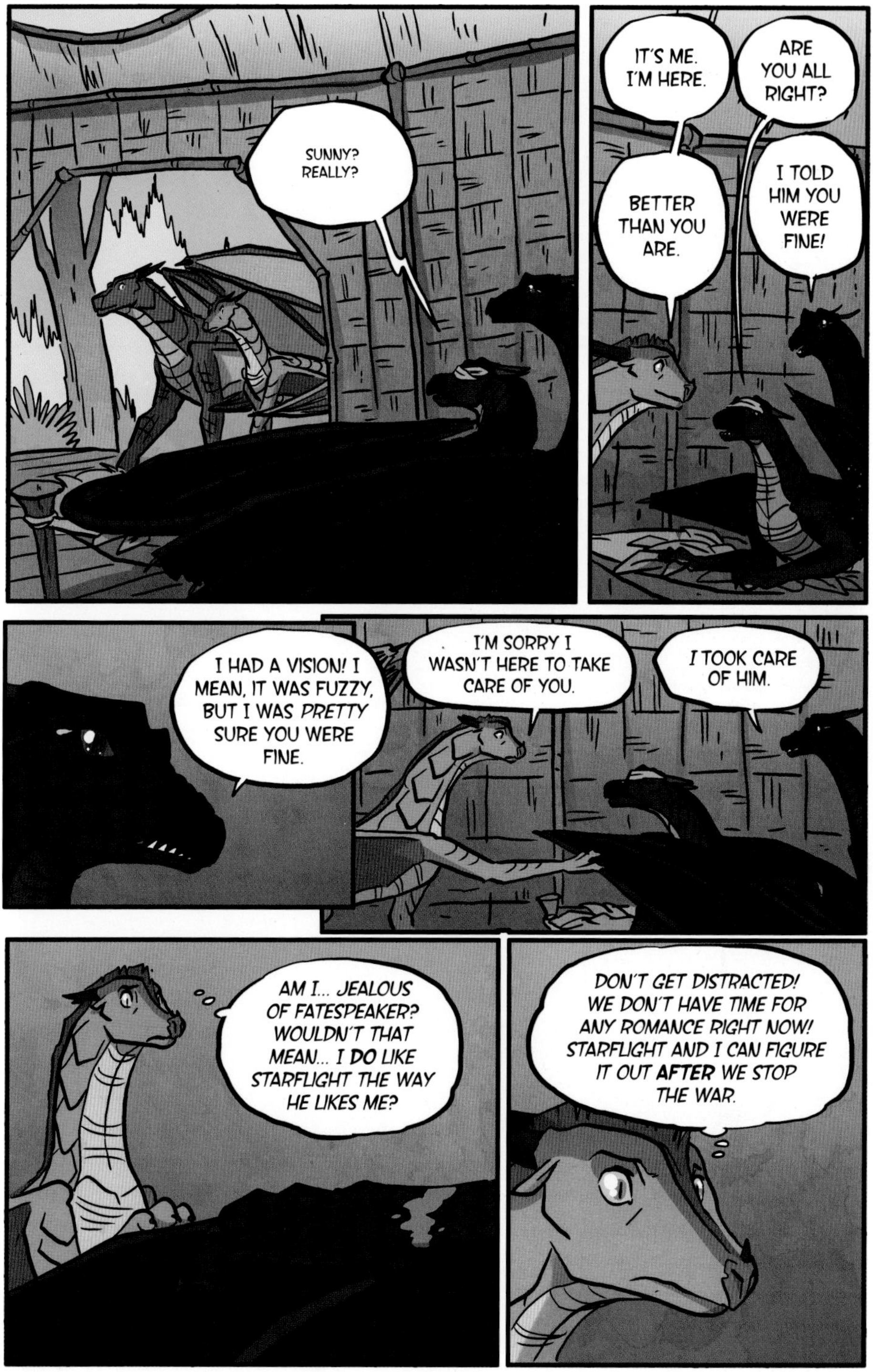
SUNNY? REALLY?
IT'S ME. I'M HERE.
ARE YOU ALL RIGHT?
BETTER THAN YOU ARE.
I TOLD HIM YOU WERE FINE!
I HAD A VISION! I MEAN, IT WAS FUZZY, BUT I WAS PRETTY SURE YOU WERE FINE.
I'M SORRY I WASN'T HERE TO TAKE CARE OF YOU.
I TOOK CARE OF HIM.
AM I... JEALOUS OF FATESPEAKER? WOULDN'T THAT MEAN... I DO LIKE STARFLIGHT THE WAY HE LIKES ME?
DON'T GET DISTRACTED! WE DON'T HAVE TIME FOR ANY ROMANCE RIGHT NOW! STARFLIGHT AND I CAN FIGURE IT OUT AFTER WE STOP THE WAR.

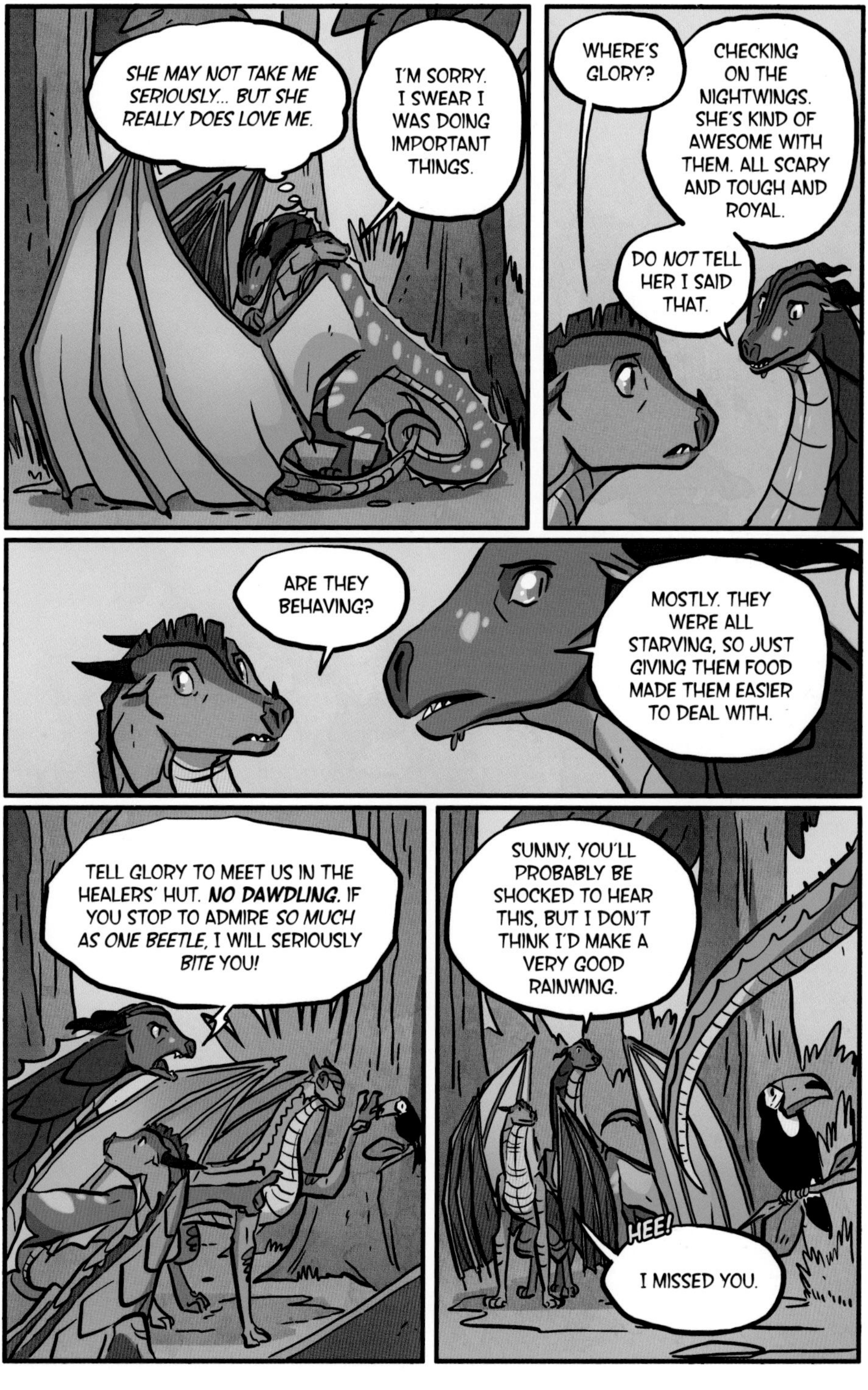
SHE MAY NOT TAKE ME SERIOUSLY... BUT SHE REALLY DOES LOVE ME.
I'M SORRY. I SWEAR I WAS DOING IMPORTANT THINGS.
WHERE'S GLORY?
CHECKING ON THE NIGHTWINGS. SHE'S KIND OF AWESOME WITH THEM. ALL SCARY AND TOUGH AND ROYAL.
DO *NOT* TELL HER I SAID THAT.
ARE THEY BEHAVING?
MOSTLY. THEY WERE ALL STARVING, SO JUST GIVING THEM FOOD MADE THEM EASIER TO DEAL WITH.
TELL GLORY TO MEET US IN THE HEALERS' HUT. ***NO DAWDLING.*** IF YOU STOP TO ADMIRE *SO MUCH AS ONE BEETLE,* I WILL SERIOUSLY *BITE* YOU!
SUNNY, YOU'LL PROBABLY BE SHOCKED TO HEAR THIS, BUT I DON'T THINK I'D MAKE A VERY GOOD RAINWING.
HEE!
I MISSED YOU.

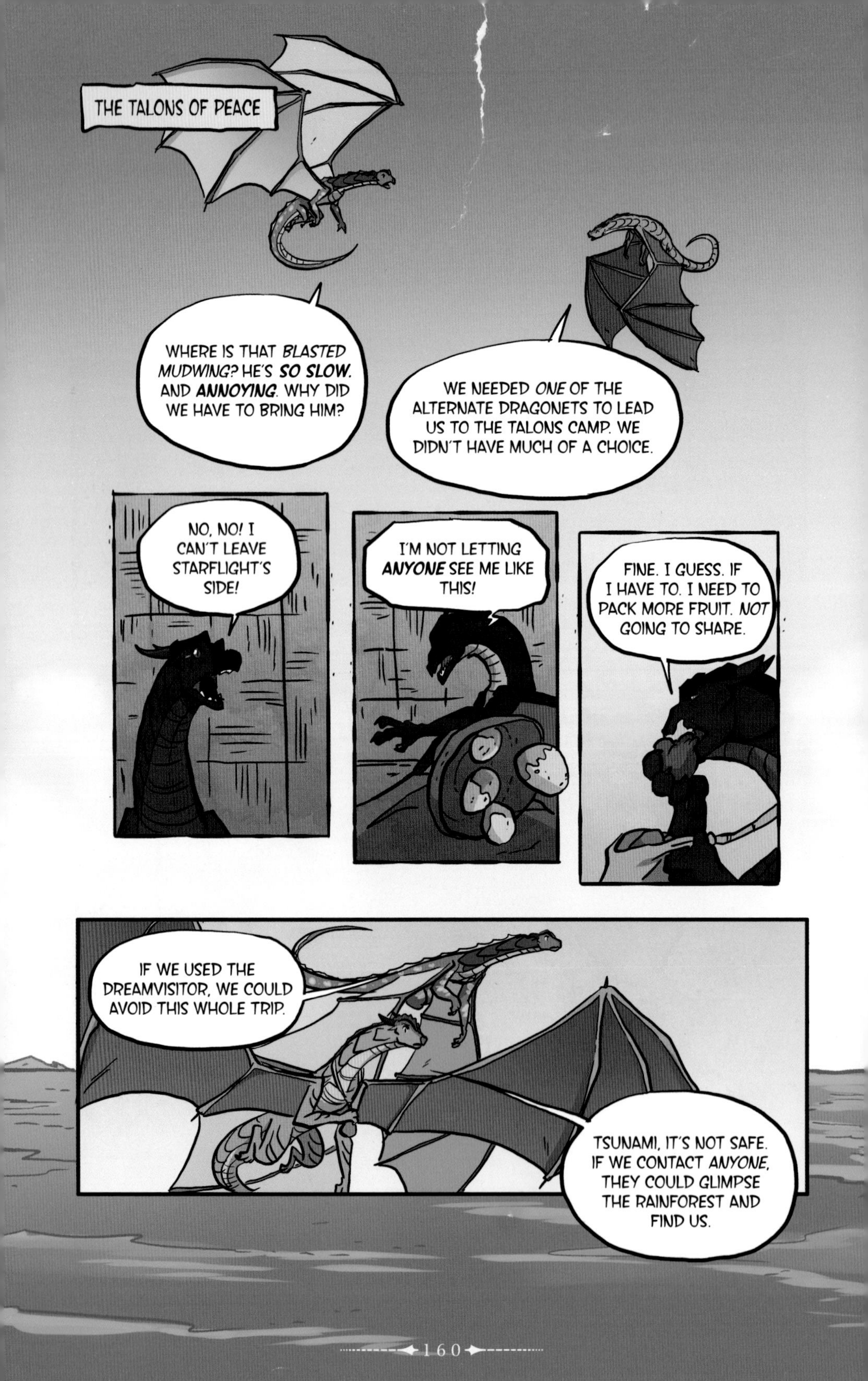
THE TALONS OF PEACE
WHERE IS THAT *BLASTED MUDWING?* HE'S **SO SLOW**. AND **ANNOYING**. WHY DID WE HAVE TO BRING HIM?
WE NEEDED *ONE* OF THE ALTERNATE DRAGONETS TO LEAD US TO THE TALONS CAMP. WE DIDN'T HAVE MUCH OF A CHOICE.
NO, NO! I CAN'T LEAVE STARFLIGHT'S SIDE!
I'M NOT LETTING ***ANYONE*** SEE ME LIKE THIS!
FINE. I *GUESS*. IF I HAVE TO. I NEED TO PACK MORE FRUIT. *NOT* GOING TO SHARE.
IF WE USED THE DREAMVISITOR, WE COULD AVOID THIS WHOLE TRIP.
TSUNAMI, IT'S NOT SAFE. IF WE CONTACT *ANYONE*, THEY COULD GLIMPSE THE RAINFOREST AND FIND US.

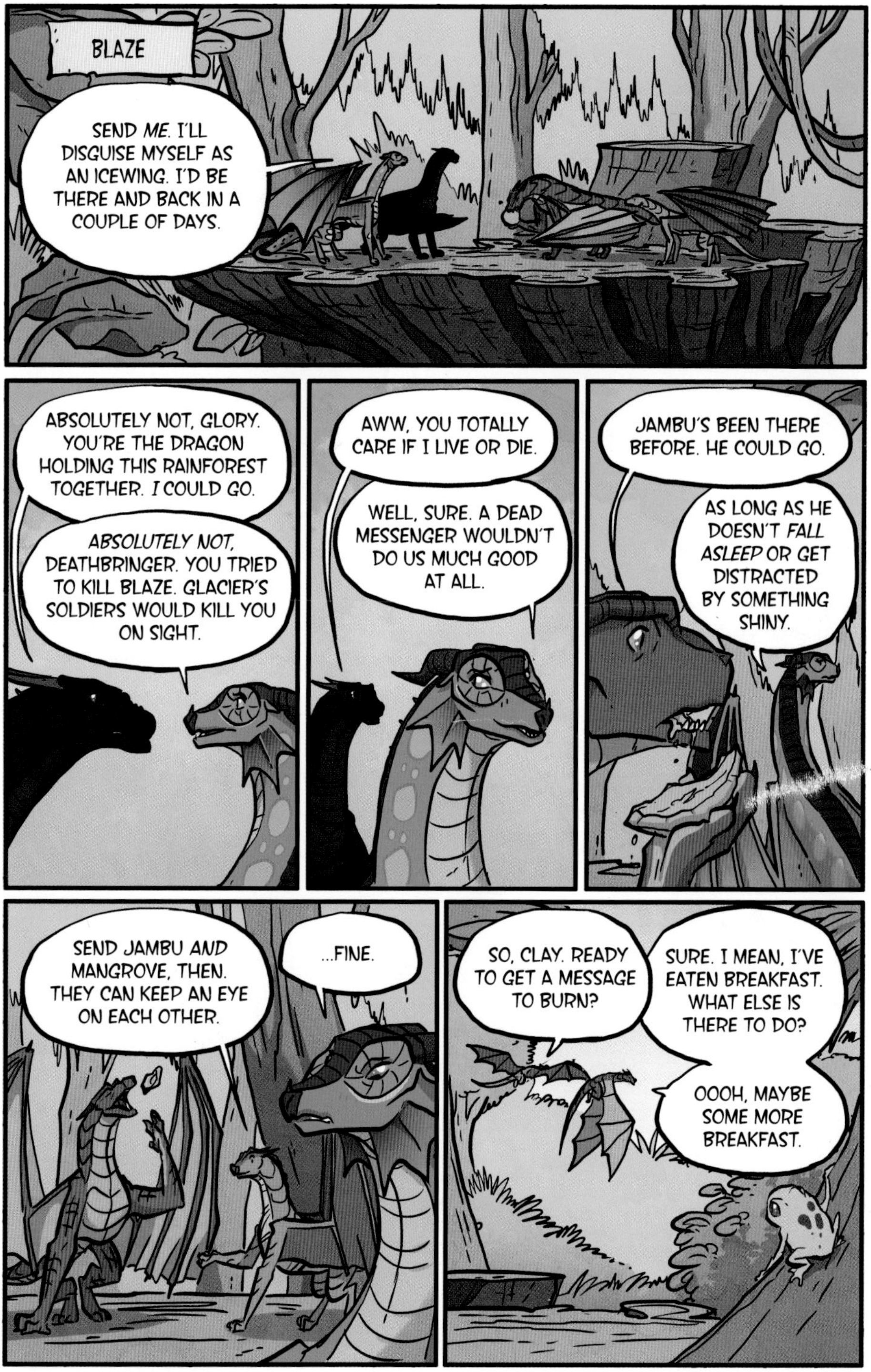
BLAZE
SEND *ME*. I'LL DISGUISE MYSELF AS AN ICEWING. I'D BE THERE AND BACK IN A COUPLE OF DAYS.
ABSOLUTELY NOT, GLORY. YOU'RE THE DRAGON HOLDING THIS RAINFOREST TOGETHER. *I* COULD GO.
ABSOLUTELY NOT, DEATHBRINGER. YOU TRIED TO KILL BLAZE. GLACIER'S SOLDIERS WOULD KILL YOU ON SIGHT.
AWW, YOU TOTALLY CARE IF I LIVE OR DIE.
WELL, SURE. A DEAD MESSENGER WOULDN'T DO US MUCH GOOD AT ALL.
JAMBU'S BEEN THERE BEFORE. HE COULD GO.
AS LONG AS HE DOESN'T *FALL ASLEEP* OR GET DISTRACTED BY SOMETHING SHINY.
SEND JAMBU AND MANGROVE, THEN. THEY CAN KEEP AN EYE ON EACH OTHER.
...FINE.
SO, CLAY. READY TO GET A MESSAGE TO BURN?
SURE. I MEAN, I'VE EATEN BREAKFAST. WHAT ELSE IS THERE TO DO?
OOOH, MAYBE SOME MORE BREAKFAST.

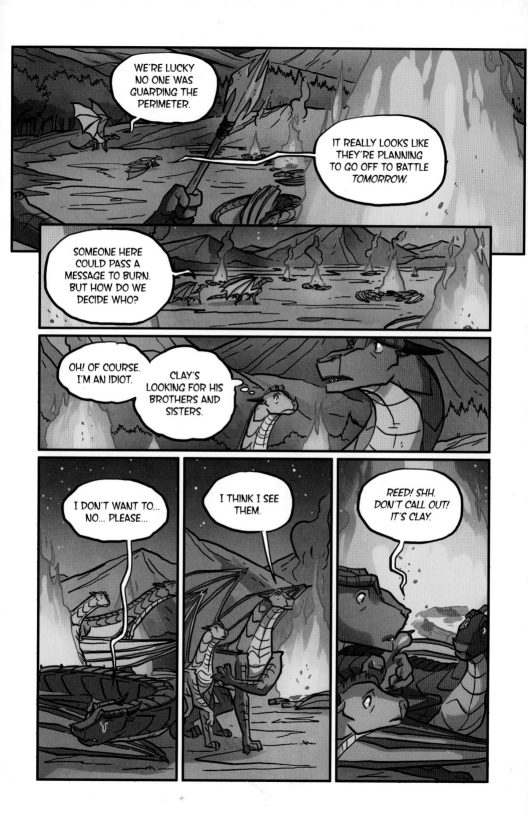

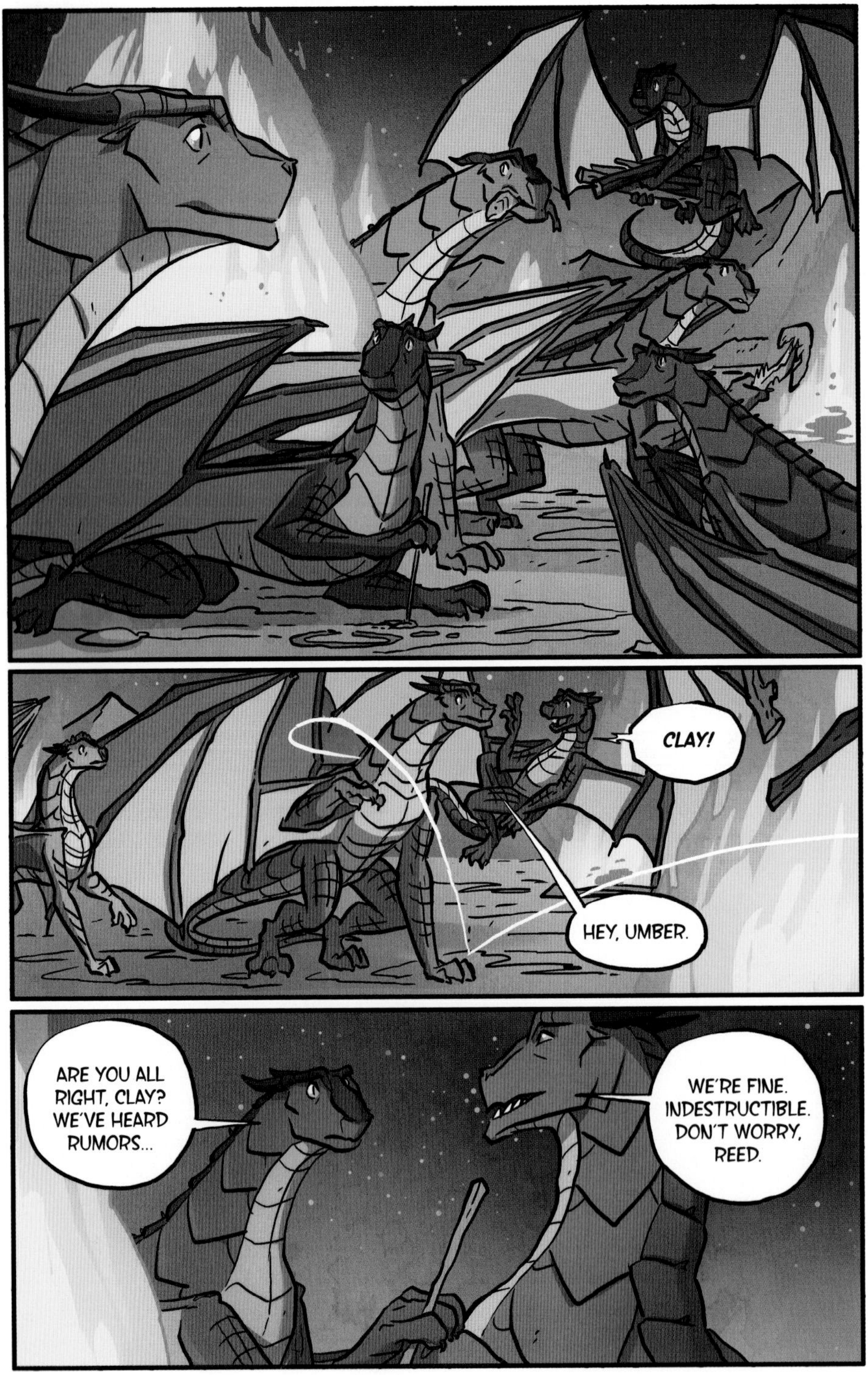
CLAY!
HEY, UMBER.
ARE YOU ALL RIGHT, CLAY? WE'VE HEARD RUMORS...
WE'RE FINE. INDESTRUCTIBLE. DON'T WORRY, REED.

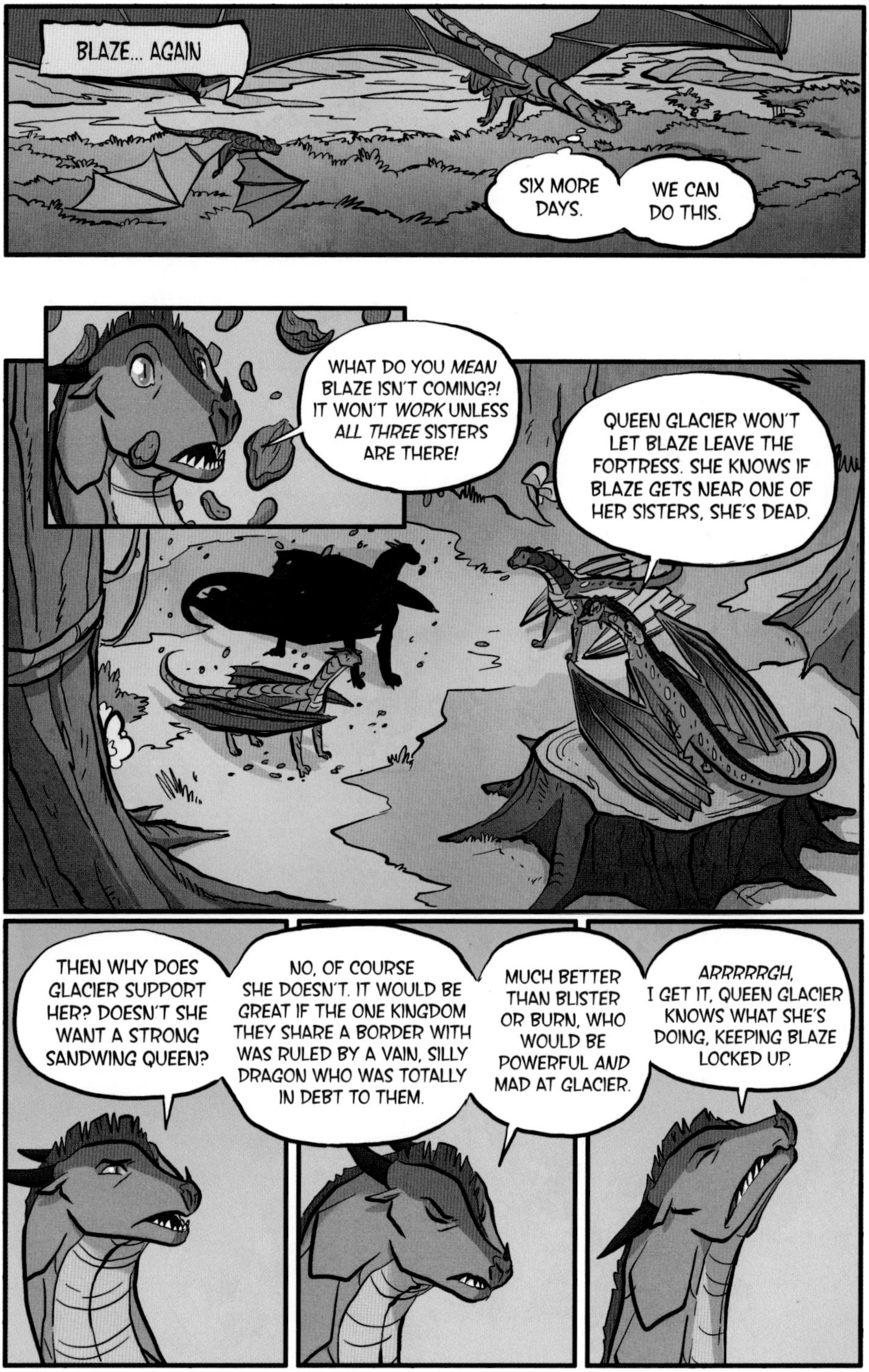
BLAZE... AGAIN
SIX MORE DAYS.
WE CAN DO THIS.
WHAT DO YOU *MEAN* BLAZE ISN'T COMING?! IT WON'T *WORK* UNLESS *ALL THREE* SISTERS ARE THERE!
QUEEN GLACIER WON'T LET BLAZE LEAVE THE FORTRESS. SHE KNOWS IF BLAZE GETS NEAR ONE OF HER SISTERS, SHE'S DEAD.
THEN WHY DOES GLACIER SUPPORT HER? DOESN'T SHE WANT A STRONG SANDWING QUEEN?
NO, OF COURSE SHE DOESN'T. IT WOULD BE GREAT IF THE ONE KINGDOM THEY SHARE A BORDER WITH WAS RULED BY A VAIN, SILLY DRAGON WHO WAS TOTALLY IN DEBT TO THEM.
MUCH BETTER THAN BLISTER OR BURN, WHO WOULD BE POWERFUL AND MAD AT GLACIER.
ARRRRRGH, I GET IT, QUEEN GLACIER KNOWS WHAT SHE'S DOING, KEEPING BLAZE LOCKED UP.

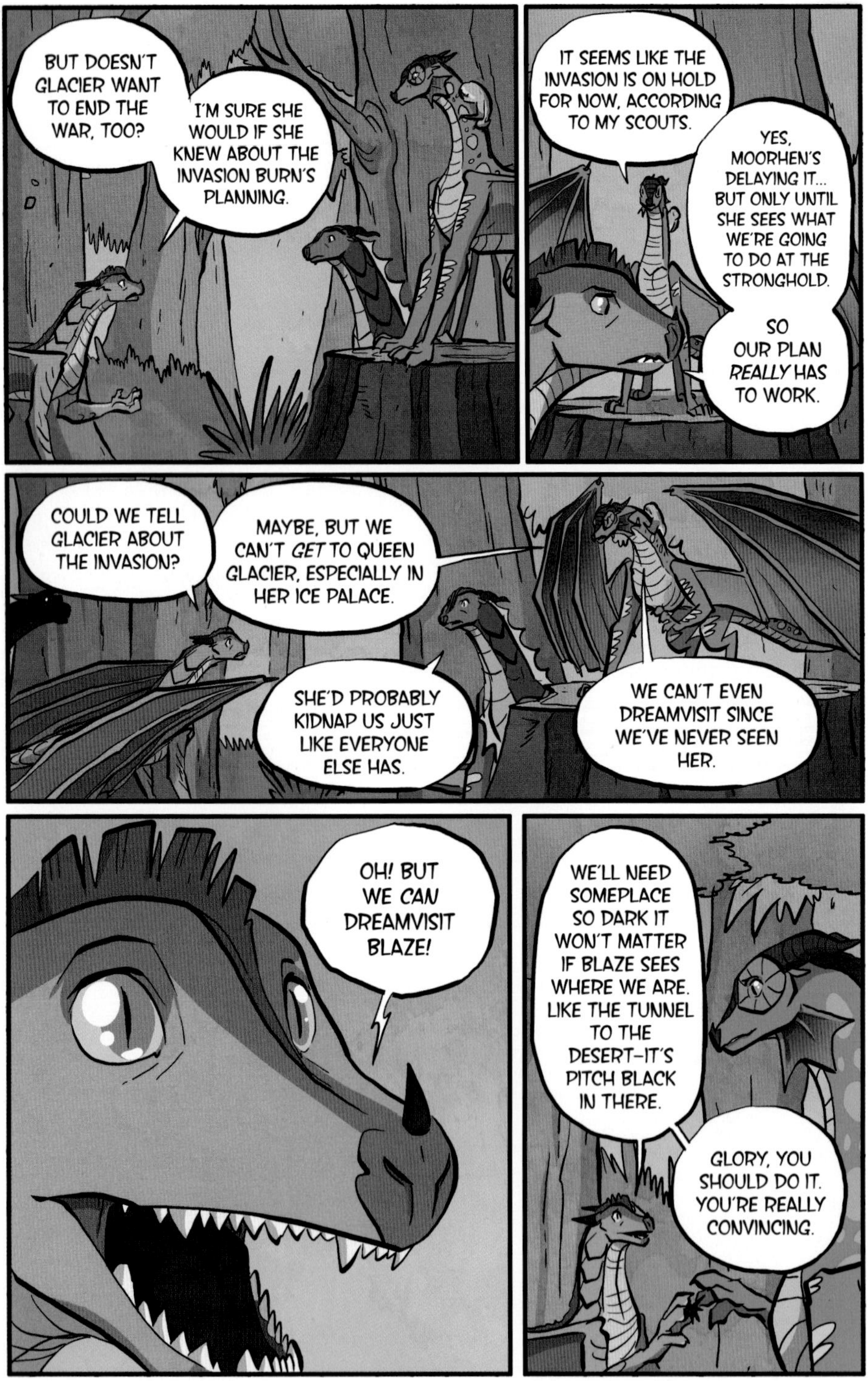
BUT DOESN'T GLACIER WANT TO END THE WAR, TOO?
I'M SURE SHE WOULD IF SHE KNEW ABOUT THE INVASION BURN'S PLANNING.
IT SEEMS LIKE THE INVASION IS ON HOLD FOR NOW, ACCORDING TO MY SCOUTS.
YES, MOORHEN'S DELAYING IT... BUT ONLY UNTIL SHE SEES WHAT WE'RE GOING TO DO AT THE STRONGHOLD.
SO OUR PLAN *REALLY* HAS TO WORK.
COULD WE TELL GLACIER ABOUT THE INVASION?
MAYBE, BUT WE CAN'T *GET* TO QUEEN GLACIER, ESPECIALLY IN HER ICE PALACE.
SHE'D PROBABLY KIDNAP US JUST LIKE EVERYONE ELSE HAS.
WE CAN'T EVEN DREAMVISIT SINCE WE'VE NEVER SEEN HER.
OH! BUT WE *CAN* DREAMVISIT BLAZE!
WE'LL NEED SOMEPLACE SO DARK IT WON'T MATTER IF BLAZE SEES WHERE WE ARE. LIKE THE TUNNEL TO THE DESERT—IT'S PITCH BLACK IN THERE.
GLORY, YOU SHOULD DO IT. YOU'RE REALLY CONVINCING.

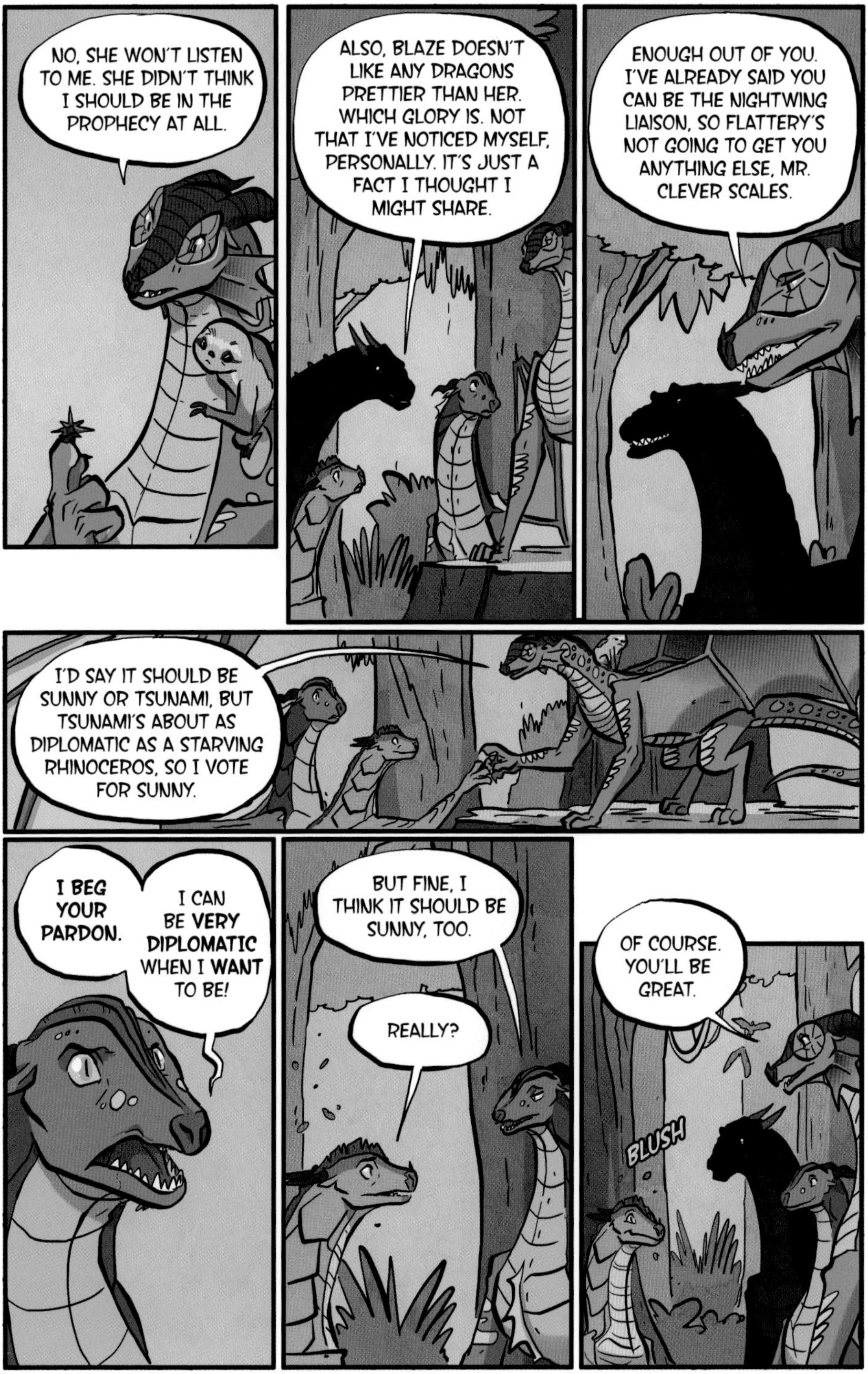
NO, SHE WON'T LISTEN TO ME. SHE DIDN'T THINK I SHOULD BE IN THE PROPHECY AT ALL.
ALSO, BLAZE DOESN'T LIKE ANY DRAGONS PRETTIER THAN HER. WHICH GLORY IS. NOT THAT I'VE NOTICED MYSELF, PERSONALLY. IT'S JUST A FACT I THOUGHT I MIGHT SHARE.
ENOUGH OUT OF YOU. I'VE ALREADY SAID YOU CAN BE THE NIGHTWING LIAISON, SO FLATTERY'S NOT GOING TO GET YOU ANYTHING ELSE, MR. CLEVER SCALES.
I'D SAY IT SHOULD BE SUNNY OR TSUNAMI, BUT TSUNAMI'S ABOUT AS DIPLOMATIC AS A STARVING RHINOCEROS, SO I VOTE FOR SUNNY.
I BEG YOUR PARDON.
I CAN BE VERY DIPLOMATIC WHEN I WANT TO BE!
BUT FINE, I THINK IT SHOULD BE SUNNY, TOO.
REALLY?
OF COURSE. YOU'LL BE GREAT.
BLUSH

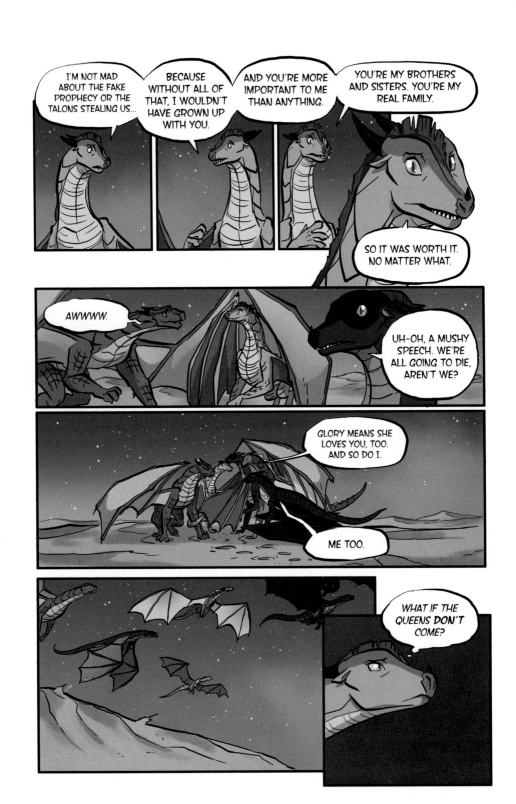

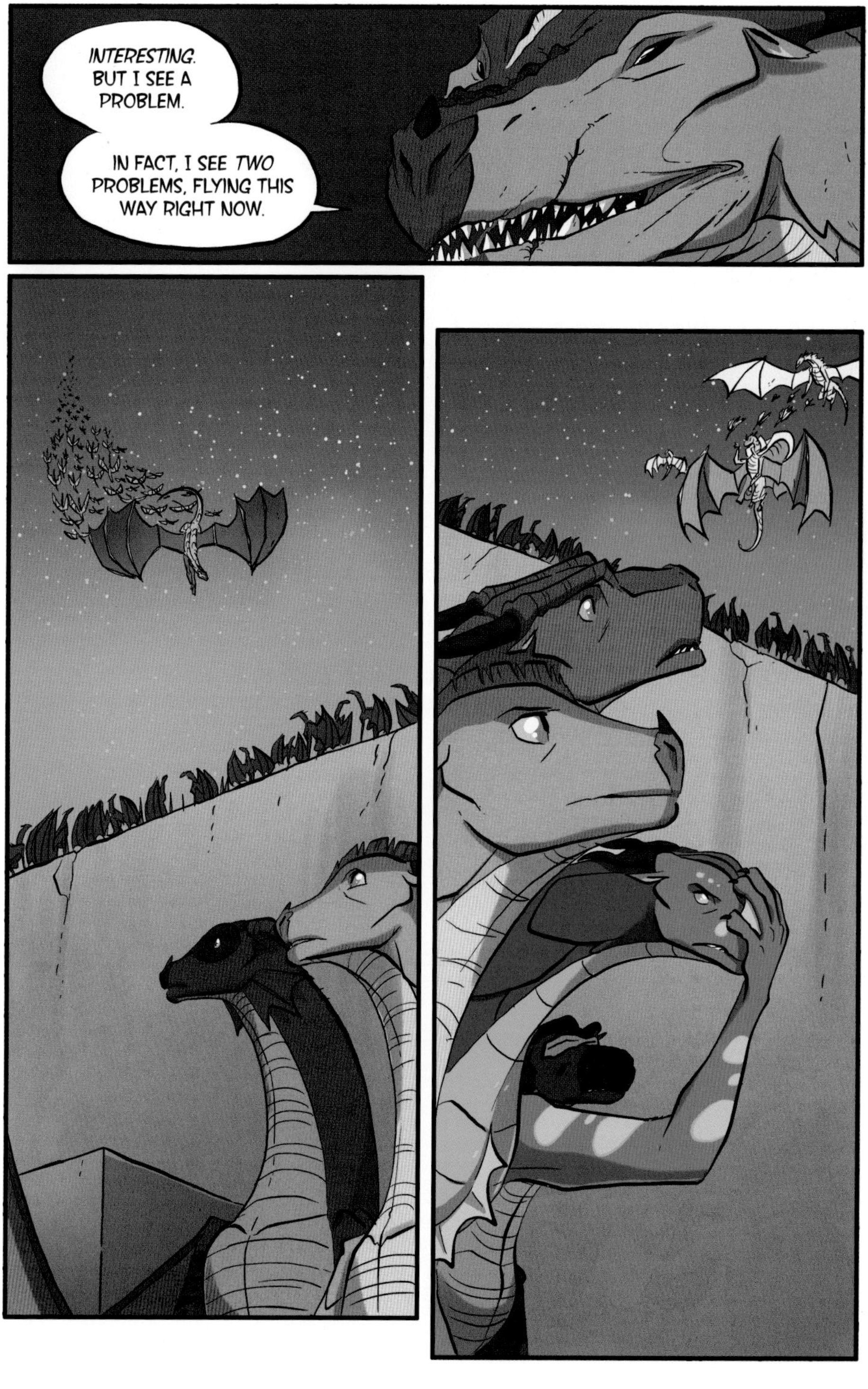
INTERESTING. BUT I SEE A PROBLEM.
IN FACT, I SEE *TWO* PROBLEMS, FLYING THIS WAY RIGHT NOW.

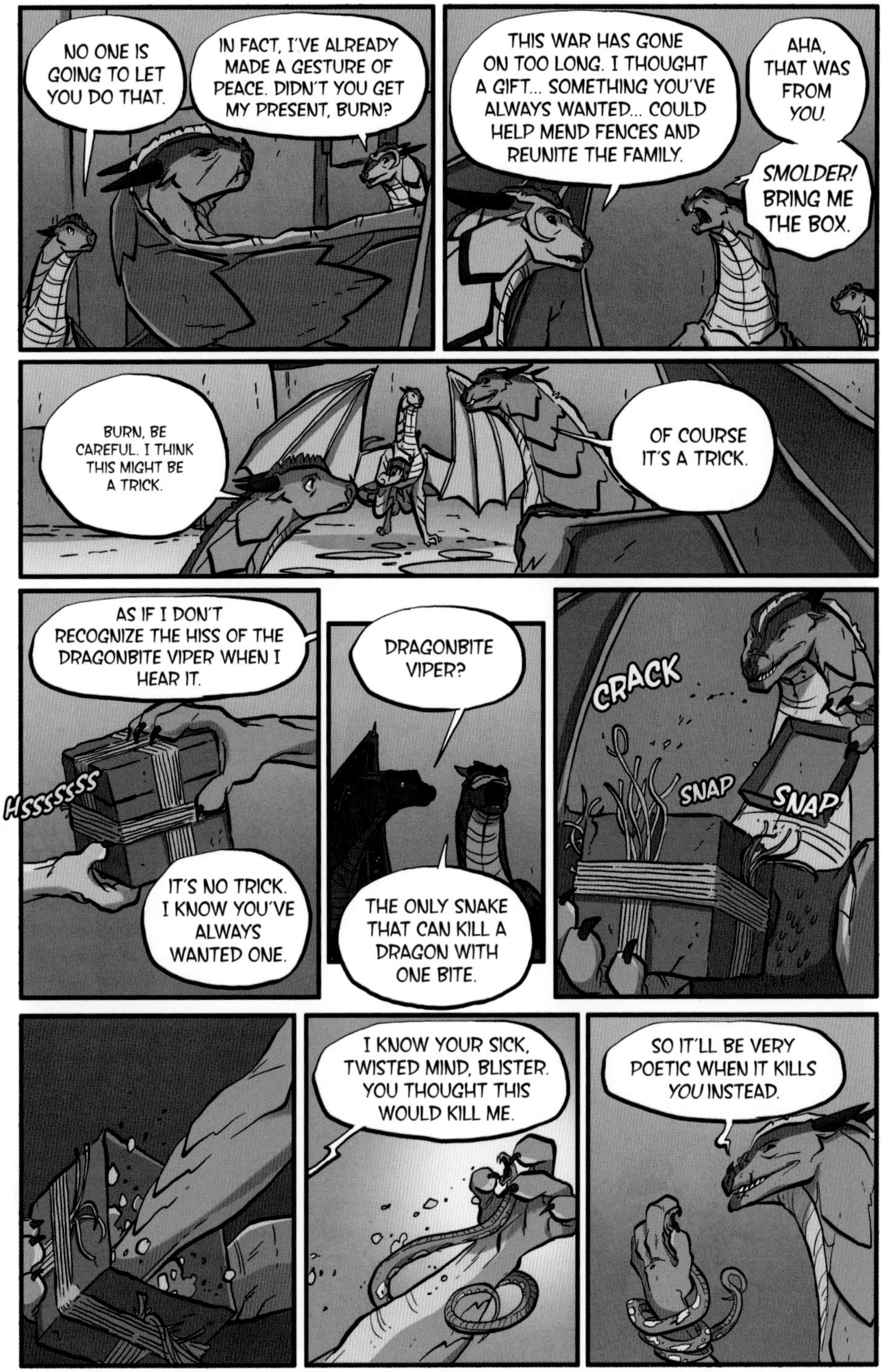
NO ONE IS GOING TO LET YOU DO THAT.
IN FACT, I'VE ALREADY MADE A GESTURE OF PEACE. DIDN'T YOU GET MY PRESENT, BURN?
THIS WAR HAS GONE ON TOO LONG. I THOUGHT A GIFT... SOMETHING YOU'VE ALWAYS WANTED... COULD HELP MEND FENCES AND REUNITE THE FAMILY.
AHA, THAT WAS FROM *YOU*.
SMOLDER! BRING ME THE BOX.
BURN, BE CAREFUL. I THINK THIS MIGHT BE A TRICK.
OF COURSE IT'S A TRICK.
AS IF I DON'T RECOGNIZE THE HISS OF THE DRAGONBITE VIPER WHEN I HEAR IT.
HSSSSSS
IT'S NO TRICK. I KNOW YOU'VE ALWAYS WANTED ONE.
DRAGONBITE VIPER?
THE ONLY SNAKE THAT CAN KILL A DRAGON WITH ONE BITE.
CRACK
SNAP
SNAP
I KNOW YOUR SICK, TWISTED MIND, BLISTER. YOU THOUGHT THIS WOULD KILL ME.
SO IT'LL BE VERY POETIC WHEN IT KILLS *YOU* INSTEAD.

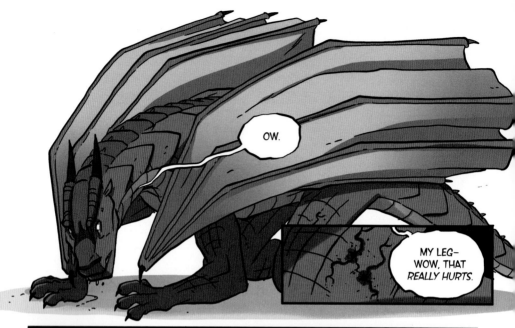

OW.

MY LEG— WOW, THAT *REALLY HURTS.*

CLAY!

SUNNY! *STAY BACK!* THE VIPER'S *STILL ALIVE!*

CLAY, PLEASE DON'T DIE.

I'M— I'M, UH— OPEN TO SUGGESTIONS.

WHERE'S THE SNAKE?

IT'S NOT... SUCH A BAD DESTINY, SUNNY. I'D DIE TO SAVE YOU AND STARFLIGHT OVER AND OVER.

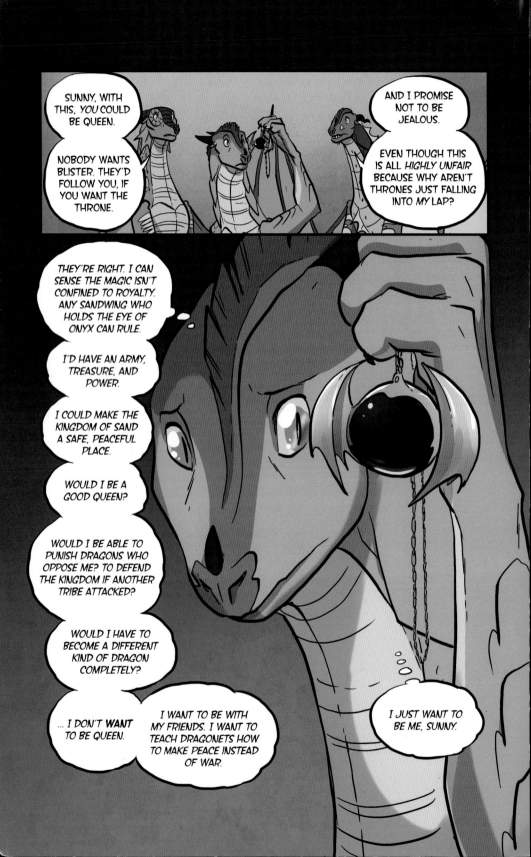

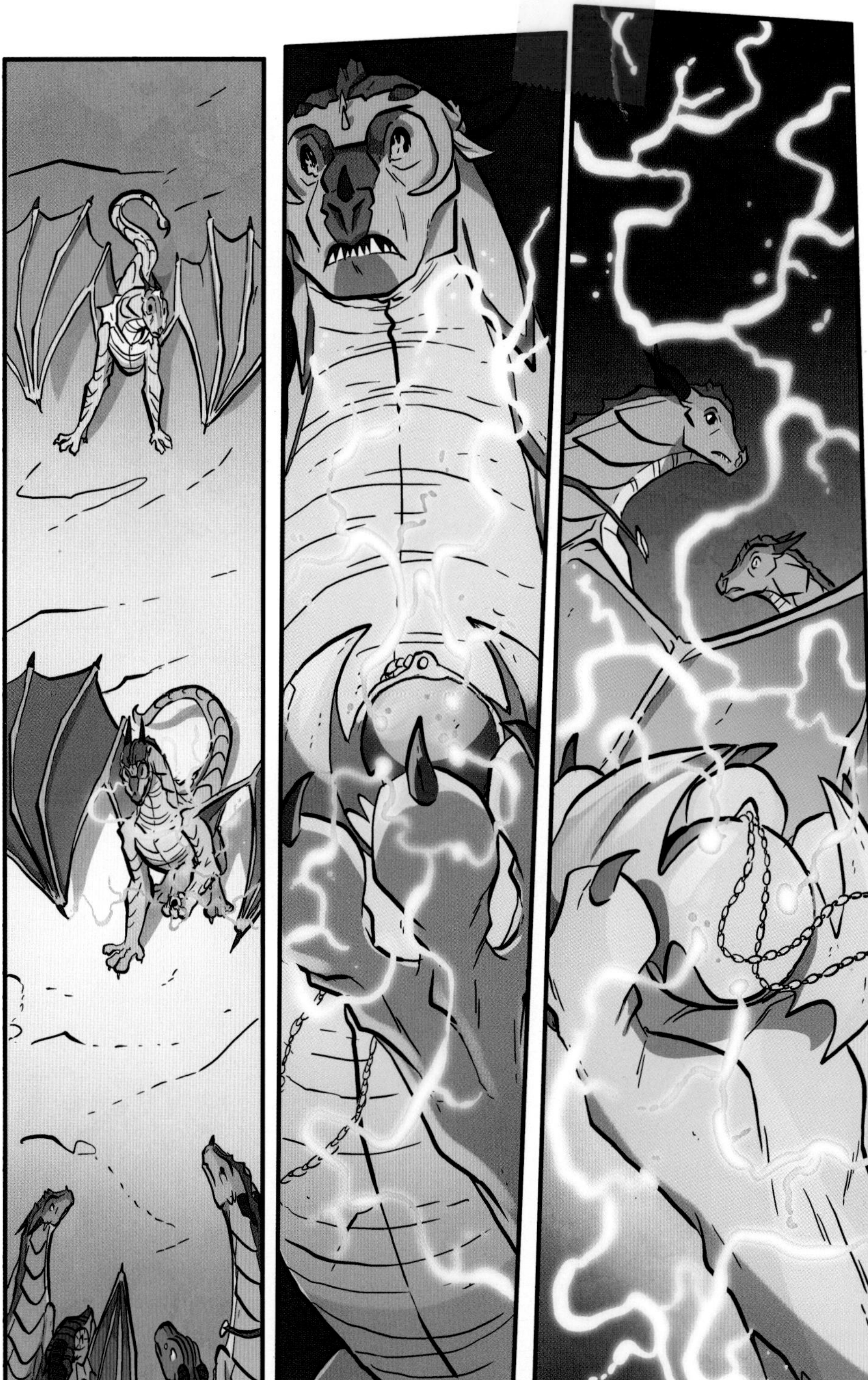

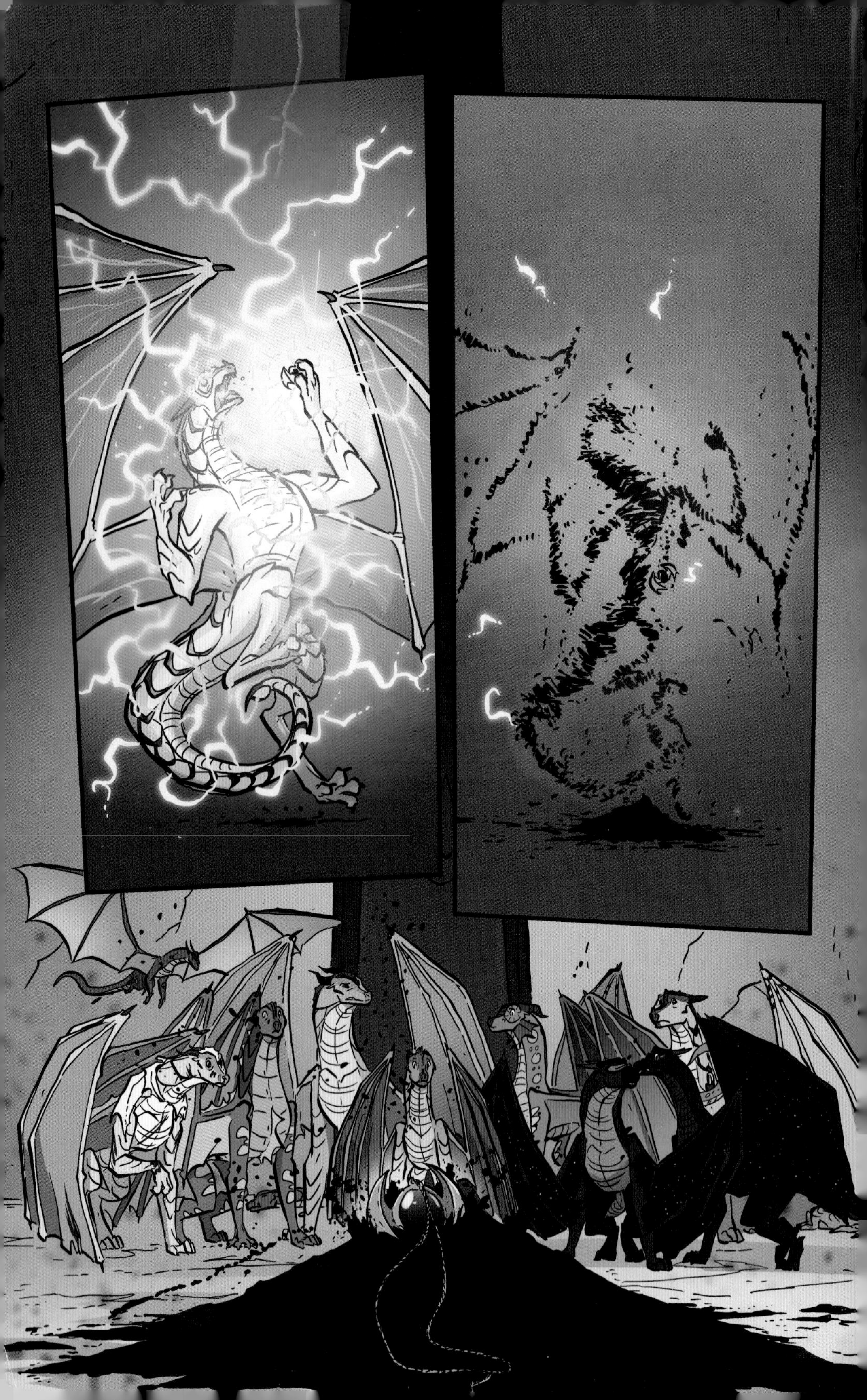

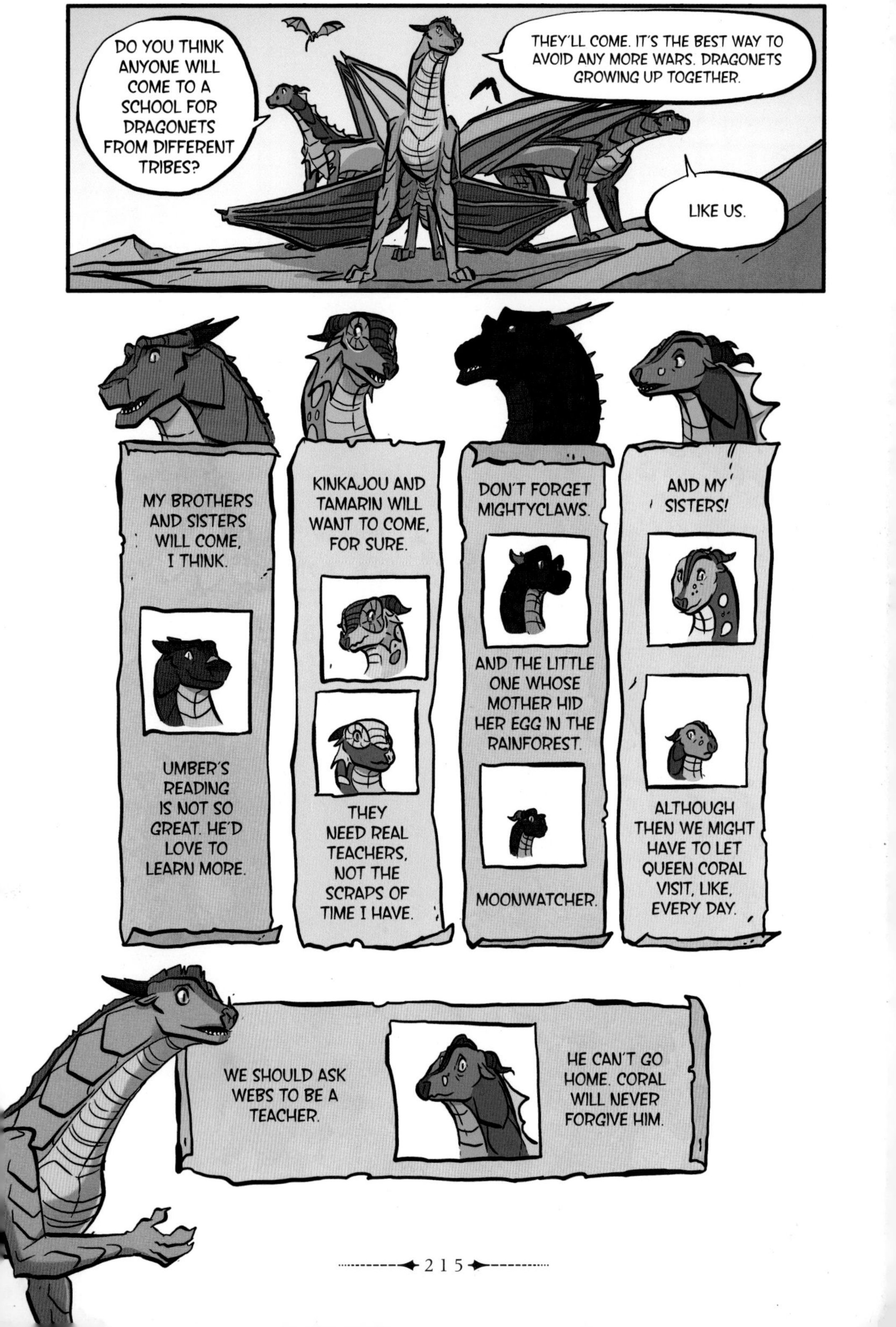
DO YOU THINK ANYONE WILL COME TO A SCHOOL FOR DRAGONETS FROM DIFFERENT TRIBES?
THEY'LL COME. IT'S THE BEST WAY TO AVOID ANY MORE WARS. DRAGONETS GROWING UP TOGETHER.
LIKE US.
MY BROTHERS AND SISTERS WILL COME, I THINK.
UMBER'S READING IS NOT SO GREAT. HE'D LOVE TO LEARN MORE.
KINKAJOU AND TAMARIN WILL WANT TO COME, FOR SURE.
THEY NEED REAL TEACHERS, NOT THE SCRAPS OF TIME I HAVE.
DON'T FORGET MIGHTYCLAWS.
AND THE LITTLE ONE WHOSE MOTHER HID HER EGG IN THE RAINFOREST.
MOONWATCHER.
AND MY SISTERS!
ALTHOUGH THEN WE MIGHT HAVE TO LET QUEEN CORAL VISIT, LIKE, EVERY DAY.
WE SHOULD ASK WEBS TO BE A TEACHER.
HE CAN'T GO HOME. CORAL WILL NEVER FORGIVE HIM.

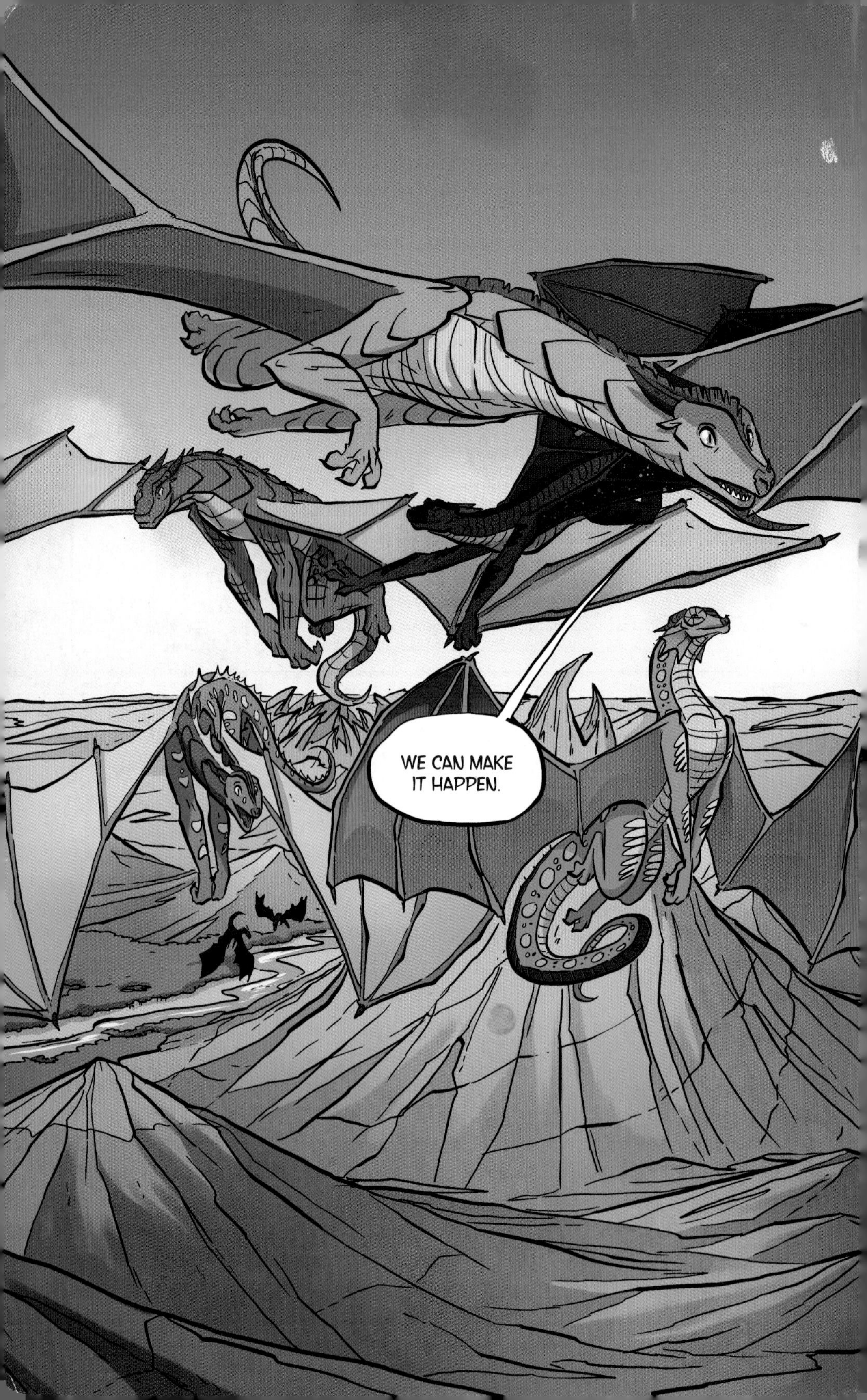
WE CAN MAKE
IT HAPPEN.